LUST IN

Her hair was a rich, glowing auburn, sparkling where the flames from the lamps caught its natural deep copper highlights. She wore it in ringlets, long curls that hung gracefully over the bare ivory white skin of her shoulders. The maroon of the gown complimented her hair, emphasizing the fullness of her firm, high-perched breasts and the deep curves of her hips.

Desire spread through his loins, despite his crouched position. He continued to gaze at her as she stood with one hand resting on the Doric column, staring out wistfully into the night.

GISELLE

Richard Tresillian

SPHERE BOOKS LIMITED

SPHERE BOOKS LTD

Published by the Penguin Group
27 Wrights Lane, London w8 5tz, England
Viking Penguin Inc., 40 West 23rd Street, New York, New York 10010, USA
Penguin Books Australia Ltd, Ringwood, Victoria, Australia
Penguin Books Canada Ltd, 2801 John Street, Markham, Ontario, Canada l3r 1b4
Penguin Books (NZ) Ltd, 182–190 Wairau Road, Auckland 10, New Zealand

Penguin Books Ltd, Registered Offices: Harmondsworth, Middlesex, England

First published in Great Britain by Century Hutchinson Ltd 1988
Published by Sphere Books Ltd 1989

Copyright © 1988 Richard Tresillian

Made and printed in Great Britain by
Richard Clay Ltd, Bungay, Suffolk

For my friend
Pricilla 'Tino' McCoy
in Old Lyme, Ct.

BOOK ONE
Virginia, 1809

CHAPTER ONE

Pat Romain heard someone approaching across the field, treading carefully through the rows of young tobacco plants. He took no notice, concentrating instead on his task of pressing the top of each stalk between his thumb and forefinger until it was severed. With his back bent low, he moved swiftly from one small plant to another, performing the topping operation with the skill of an expert.

Although the sun burned into his back through the coarse linen of his shirt and the rich loam of the Virginia soil was hot under his bare feet, he worked without thought of complaining. He was accustomed to crouching over the plants, not straightening up until he reached the end of one row then paused before starting another. The faster he finished the field, the sooner he could dally on the bank of the Mattaponi River with one of the Allason girls.

'Pat . . .'

His loins stirred at the invitation he heard in the suggestive uttering of his name. He swallowed and raised his head casually. She was standing at the end of the row, waiting for him by the edge of the forest.

Her lips were parted and she was breathing nervously, her bosom rising and falling with exaggeration under the scant covering of her cambric bodice. He glanced around the field as he stood up and the cut plant in his hand dropped to the ground.

'Mary Allason,' he said, a note of caution in his voice. 'Does my mother know you're here?'

'No,' the girl said coyly. 'I came through the wood. She couldn't have seen me.'

A heat began to rise in his chest. He looked around the field a second time, making absolutely sure they were alone.

'I brought you a flask of water,' she said, surprising him. 'In this hot sun . . .' She stepped backwards into the shade of

3

the forest that surrounded the tobacco field, her eyes beckoning him to follow.

'I shouldn't stop.' He gestured at the field, only half completed.

'A few minutes . . .' She held the flask out towards him as she drew further into the trees.

He tossed his head back, the tousled mop of unruly locks falling like a lion's mane over his shoulders. He raised his arms to the sky, extending himself to his full six feet. 'It's good to stretch,' he said, lowering his eyes to meet hers.

She smiled knowingly and eased herself down on her knees in the grass. 'Won't you drink?'

'Aye.' He ambled over to her and took the flask, his innards leaping at the touch of her fingers on his. He raised the flask to his lips and tilted his head to drink, knowing that the hardness he felt in his breeches was level with her eyes.

They were both hidden from view, shaded by the forest glade from the sun that burned down on the tobacco plants only feet away. He flinched when her hands stroked his thigh.

'Mary?' Water spilled from his lips.

She raised one hand and took the flask from him, placing it on the ground beside her. Her other hand was working at the pouch of his breeches.

'This is crazy.'

'I know.' She smiled, her fingers grasping him and drawing him out. She lowered her head so all he could see were the ruffles of her cotton bonnet as her mouth closed over him.

The sensation of her lips enveloping him sent a flood of wanting coursing through his limbs. His knees felt weak and he leaned back against the trunk of a tree, placing his hands on her shoulders as her head moved faster up and down.

Mary Allason, he thought, closing his eyes. *You're as bad as your sister*.

Pat was weak in a woman's hands, and he knew it. He was blessed with the rugged looks of a stalwart country lad, a tanned complexion the colour of dry golden oronoco tobacco and laughing eyes that were a startling emerald green against his bronzed features. With a body that was lean and muscular, honed by a childhood running wild in the Virginia woods and

4

five years of working in Cletus Braxton's tobacco fields, he was never short of female admirers.

Neither of his two brothers shared his roguish good looks and his energy. The eldest, Mort, was studious and as thin as a hoe, the other a sickly bumpkin. Pat was his parents' third child, his elder brother and sister both living away from home. His sister, Jeanette, came after him, with the simpleton Tombo a year behind her.

Pat outshone the others, plaguing his mother with worry about what devilment he would get up to next. She had been relieved when Cletus Braxton took him to work on the plantation. His earliest memory was the view of rows of tobacco plants stretching from the porch of their clapboard house to the horizon. He knew the work by instinct.

He became one of the few hands entrusted to top the young tobacco plants so that instead of growing tall and producing leaves of thin texture, they would be stunted with large leaves of full body. The other hands found the work laborious and irksome. Not Pat. He had the Allason girls, the Sprowle twins and even the shy Carter girl believing they were in love with him. What better life could he want than to be favoured by so many obliging women?

'I love you, Mary . . .!' he said glibly, squeezing her shoulder. He took a deep draught from the flask of water.

She laughed with disbelief. 'That's what you told my sister.'

'How do you know?'

'I heard you tell her so last night.'

'You're lying.' He tweaked her cheek affectionately. 'You never saw us.'

'I did. By the river. I saw everything, in the moonlight.'

He looked down at her, shaking his head with amusement. 'Is that why . . .'

'Yes!' She grinned. 'I can do it just as good as her. Better!' She puckered her lips. 'I'll see you there tonight.'

'I promised your sister . . .' He stopped as her hand caressed his buttocks.

'And I've promised you!'

He held her off, amused by her boldness and more than a little concerned that her touch was beginning to stir him again.

'I must work,' he said with a shrug of his shoulders. 'I want to finish this field so I can bathe in the river before sundown.'

'I'll be there,' she said, her eyes glimmering as she stepped towards the field.

'Wait!' He gripped her wrist and pulled her back into the forest. He could hear the sound of a carriage racing along the track that bordered the far side of the field. 'Someone's coming. Go home through the wood.'

'That'll be Mr Braxton. He's been to Jamestown to collect his daughter. She arrived there from England last week.'

Pat would have liked to ask Mary about Cletus Braxton's daughter. He hadn't seen Deborah since she left for England when he was fourteen. Now there was no time to talk lest Mr Braxton see him skulking in the wood when he should be working.

He waved to Mary and darted out to the field, crouching low so he would not be seen from the cart track. Instinctively his fingers flew from the top of one plant to another, slicing the stems with his thumb nail as he hurried along the row.

The encounter with the Allason girl inspired him and he was almost running when he reached the end of the row and turned, without pausing, into the next row that ran parallel to it. The heat in his body subsided although his shirt, damp with sweat, stuck to his back. By following a rhythm, he made the work easy and his thumb and forefinger were no longer blistered and sore as they were when he began topping the plants two weeks previously.

Although he heard the carriage slowing as it neared the junction where the trail passed through the trees to the Braxton mansion, he kept his head down. Mr Braxton's moods were unpredictable. It was better, Pat had learned, to avoid him.

Cletus Braxton was the largest landowner in Braxton County. Over the years he had bought out his neighbours until he owned an enormous tract of plantation and forest. Each year, more trees were felled and the ground tilled to grow more tobacco. Tobacco only flourished in rich, virgin soil. Cletus Braxton was ruthless in his acquisition of fresh land because his fortune depended on good quality tobacco.

He had used his wealth to buy himself favours. He was well known throughout the State of Virginia and was on the fringes of the group that surrounded James Madison himself. It was four months earlier, in March when the tobacco seeds were being sown, that James Madison had been installed as the fourth president of the United States.

Cletus Braxton's political involvement meant that he was often absent from the plantation. That suited Pat who had a rebellious spark in his affable nature that was liable to flare up suddenly. His mother had warned him to keep out of Mr Braxton's way in case he said anything they would all regret.

Pat smiled to himself as he plucked at the plants. If his mother knew what he was doing with the Allason girls she would have a fit. Mr Braxton, too, would have been surprised to learn what happened at night in the woods around the Mattaponi River.

Pat peeped over the tops of the taller plants and caught a glimpse of two people sitting back to back on a dog cart, not in a carriage as he expected. Mr Braxton had the reins of the horse in his hands; his daughter sat on the transverse seat behind him, her head engulfed in a blinkered bonnet that concealed her features.

So you're Deborah, he thought, observing the proud way the young woman held herself despite the swaying of the light two-wheeled cart. It was typical of her father's thoughtlessness that he was subjecting her to a rough, fast ride, instead of transporting her home more leisurely by coach.

Pat was surprised at feeling sorry for Deborah. After five years learning how to be a lady in England, she was bound to find her father's uncouth way of life a shock. He straightened up to observe her better, now there was no danger that Mr Braxton, concentrating on negotiating the junction, would turn his head and see him.

He was curious about Deborah. She was two years older than him but he could remember little about her. As children they never met. He had seen her when she played with her brother on the piazza in front of the Braxton mansion and he passed by on an errand, or when she drove past their homestead in a carriage with her parents. Mr Braxton had sent her away to be educated to please his wife while his son, Marlon, remained on the plantation.

7

Pat pulled at his ear, wondering what sort of woman had returned. *I'll wager she's a honey!* He stared at the figure gripping the side of the cart to steady herself.

She was swathed in a cloak whose sheen of bright blue was dulled by the red dust thrown up by the cart as it raced along the trail. She held a scarf to her mouth with her free hand. As the cart turned onto the trail to the mansion, he saw her eyes.

She was not looking at him. She seemed to be concentrating on something else, pretending he was not there. Her eyes were narrowed in scorn.

He was stunned by her deliberate attempt to snub him. It made him defiant and angry, the first time he had been challenged by a woman's disdain. He turned away from the cart as it receded rapidly into the distance and glared instead at the thousands of plants that were lined up in rows in front of him.

He snapped the top off one and squeezed it between his fingers, muttering to himself between clenched teeth: *the bitch!* He bent his back low and broke into a run, slashing at the plants with his forefinger and thumb as he passed them, breaking their necks.

He worked with fury for the rest of the afternoon, his resentment at Deborah's glance competing with his desire to possess her. Each plant he topped was her, cut off before she could grow to humiliate him. His rage was fuelled by the knowledge that she lived off the fruit of his labour. It was his skill that nurtured the tender seedlings into the dry oronoco tobacco, sliced and pressed, that brought her father his fortune.

His five years of toil paid for her five years in England. What was his reward? To be regarded as though he didn't exist.

'Surely you didn't expect her to wave at you?'

It was his sister's question. He was lying on the mattress of his bed, stripped to his waist, face down with his head resting on his arms. Jeanette was massaging his back, her firm hands easing away the pain he felt from staying too long with his back stooped parallel to the soil.

8

He had finished the field without noticing the agony, and returned home in a daze. His mother, sensing his discomfort but believing it was physical, had ordered him to lie down for her to pummel feeling into his aching muscles. Jeanette, more sensitive to his mood, offered to do it instead.

'What does she . . . look like?' He gasped out the words as Jeanette's hands manipulated his back.

'Nothing special. I don't know why you're so het up.'

He could feel her concern through her finger tips. Jeanette was the closest to him; they understood each other. She had been working as a servant in Mr Braxton's house for three years, since she was fourteen. She was beautiful with eyes that matched his but a complexion of rose-like purity, not the hard, tanned skin that was his reward for working in Cletus Braxton's tobacco fields.

'I'm not . . . het up.' He wished she'd let him speak.

'Then why did you top those plants like you were crazy?'

'You saw me?'

'Of course I did. When I came from the mansion. You were swooping down the rows like a bat. If Mr Braxton knows you did the field so quickly, he'll give you double the task tomorrow.'

'He won't notice.'

Jeanette slapped his backside, apparently pleased that he was thinking of other things at last. 'Come on,' she said. 'I've massaged you for twenty minutes already. That's enough. I'm tired.'

'I'm sorry, sis.' He rolled over and sat up, swinging his legs over the edge of the bed. Playfully, he pulled her down beside him, tucking his arm around her waist and squeezing. He gave her a peck on her cheek.

She laughed. 'That's better, more like the brother I love.'

'Mary was at the field this afternoon.'

'Oh, Pat!' She looked shocked. 'You didn't!'

'I didn't,' he said with a grin. 'But she did.'

'You're impossible.'

'Why not, sis?' He stood up, reaching for his shirt which she held out to him. 'It's not my fault.'

'You're just playing with her.'

'Of course I am.' He paused, narrowing his eyes. 'One day

I'll stop playing. I'll find the woman who's serious, who doesn't play with me like Mary and her sister, like the Sprowle twins, like . . .'

'Shh!' Jeanette glanced at the open door where their mother was bustling around setting the table for supper. 'Don't let mother hear your list of conquests.'

The feeling that he'd said too much made him grin foolishly. He embraced Jeanette and led her out into the parlour. His father, seated by the open window, sucking on his pipe, stared out over the field where the tobacco plants waved in the evening breeze. His younger brother, Tombo, sat in the doorway, his head lolling forward and a drool of spittle trickling down his chin.

'Supper ain't ready yet!' his mother said before he could ask. She banged down the wares on the crudely made wooden table and hurried out of the room, scowling.

'What's the matter with Ma?' he asked Jeanette as he walked out onto the porch with her.

'She thinks you're in a hurry to go out. The Carter girl was here this afternoon. She asked Ma if you'd be dropping by their place to do some book reading this evening.'

He laughed at the expression on Jeanette's face. 'You're right, sis. That's not the way to my heart, is it? Book reading!' His scorn evaporated as he glanced in the direction of the Braxton mansion. Its chimneys could be seen on the bluff above the pine trees. He was troubled by his sudden thought of Deborah.

'I suppose that's what *she* does.'

Jeanette's eyes followed his gaze. 'I suppose so.'

He noticed the tone of disapproval in her voice. 'Why don't you like her, sis?'

'I don't know her. She arrived breathless from Jamestown and went straight to her chamber. She's brought her own maid, a bossy baggage from London, and trunks of dresses. It took the servants the whole afternoon to unload them from the wagon and carry them upstairs.'

'Breathless?'

'What?'

'You said she arrived breathless.'

'Of course. Mr Braxton drove so fast, she was worn out.'

'Didn't you see her face? If she was breathless, you must have seen her face.'

Jeanette sighed and he thought she was taking pity on him. 'She's got auburn hair which was dishevelled and dusty from the ride, her eyes are cold and unfriendly, and her face is coarse and reddened by the English weather. She wore a dress that was too tight for her, or perhaps she's too fat. Her legs when she climbed the stairs looked quite shapeless.'

Pat laughed. 'She's obviously quite beautiful.'

His sister's retort was interrupted by their mother calling for them to sit down and eat. He followed Jeanette silently into the parlour so his mother wouldn't suspect what they were talking about.

He ate quickly, wolfing down the food because he was hungry, letting his mother's chatter drift unanswered over his head. The meal was heavy, a vegetable stew made from produce his mother grew in the garden at the back of the house.

The garden was all that remained of the acres of land his father had once owned. In a good year, it fed them for several months. The money he, his brother Mort, and his two sisters earned supplied the rest. In a bad year, they went hungry.

As he spooned the mess of grey potatoes and turnips into his mouth, he wondered what they were having for supper at the Braxton mansion. There would be a celebration. Marlon would get drunk as usual and Mr Braxton would sit on the piazza and declaim to his wife how he could solve the country's problems if President Madison would give him a post. What of Deborah? Would she sit demurely with a sampler of embroidery on her lap, or discourse with her father, telling him of her time in England.

He cleared his plate and pushed it from him, aware that his mother's chatter had ceased. There was a silence in the room that distracted him. He looked at his mother and tugged his ear lobe, puzzled at what had been said.

'So you've come back to us, have you?' she asked, banging the metal plates together as she scooped them into a pile in her arms. 'Thinkin' of who to favour with your charms tonight, eh?' She laughed scornfully. 'Ain't no use tellin' you to bed down early tonight? You've got Five Acre Field to top tomorrow.'

'Yes, Ma,' he said meekly, rising to his feet. Jeanette was already on the porch. 'I'm going for a walk.'

'Tom cattin'!' His mother scowled and swept from the room. His father ambled without a word back to his seat at the window while Tombo sat at the table and honked to himself.

'I'll walk you to the mansion, sis,' he said, desperate to get out of the tiny house.

'No need. It won't be dark for ages. I'm sure you've got *other* things to do.'

He grinned at her meaning. 'Those girls can do without me for tonight.' He lifted her in his arms from the porch and she squealed with alarm, begging him to put her down.

'Pat!' she exclaimed, her face colouring when he released her and she stood on the trail beside him. 'You might have hurt me!'

'You're as tough as I am. That's why Mrs Braxton employs you. She couldn't find a harder worker anywhere. Hey, don't sleep there tonight! Let's go to the river. I know where to find a bottle of whiskey. The Allason girls hid one for me.'

'No, Pat.' She sounded sad. 'Mr Braxton says I must sleep in the house every night.'

The odd note in her voice puzzled him but before he could ask her what she meant, she said quickly, too quickly, 'In case Mrs Braxton is taken sick.' She blushed.

His curiosity about seeing Deborah again made him deaf to the anguish behind his sister's remark. Even her blush of guilt went unnoticed as he grasped her hand in his and strode out eagerly towards the mansion.

CHAPTER TWO

'Dammit, woman, the very least you could have done was come back with a wealthy English milord as a husband.'

'I don't *like* the English, father.'

'Like!' Mr Braxton spun around on his heels and looked with scorn across the piazza at his daughter. 'What does "like" have to do with it? What else do you have to show for your years in England apart from this fancy notion that you can do what you *like*?'

Pat, crouched on his haunches behind a magnolia bush, listened with astonishment. He had crept through the garden, shielding himself behind the bushes and taking advantage of nightfall, until he was within a few feet of the piazza edge. His object was to get a good glimpse of Deborah who sat at the back of the piazza, by the door to the drawing room, concealed in the shadows thrown by the frieze of flickering lamps. Mr Braxton, standing opposite her with his hands on his hips like an indignant slave mammy, obscured Pat's view.

Deborah said nothing at her father's outburst. Her silence seemed to anger him more. He raised one hand and pointed at her in a dramatic gesture more suited to a political meeting.

'I tell you this, young lady. You've had too much freedom!' He wagged his finger. 'I'm not letting you become worthless like your brother. You've got to play your part too.'

Marlon, who was standing at the other side of the piazza with a glass of whiskey in his hand, sniggered. 'Why so pompous, papa? Ain't you glad she's home?'

'I aim to start off on the right foot, me lad.' Mr Braxton's anger evaporated to despair when he glanced at Marlon. 'She needs a husband now, one who's going to contribute capital so I can expand the plantation . . .'

'I'm sure Deborah will find a young man we'll all approve of.' Mrs Braxton rose from her chair and walked over to her husband's side. She patted his arm. 'Try to relax, dear. She's been a good girl while she was staying with my sister in London. She had many suitors but, as my sister said in her letter, Lords they may be but they really wouldn't be suitable as Virginia tobacco barons.'

Mr Braxton pulled his arm away from his wife's clutch. 'It was your idea to send her to England.'

'You will see I was right, Cletus. She'll be a credit to you. President Madison himself will be enchanted with her. In a few weeks, when it's known what a flower of sophistication we have in our humble home, you'll be invited to every plantation where there's an eligible bachelor.'

Mr Braxton stared at his wife, his expression of contempt changing to a smile of cunning. She ignored him and continued speaking.

'Class and culture are what Virginia families lack. They're like you. All you and they think of is tobacco, profits, politicking and more tobacco. There's no background, no breeding. Deborah, with all she's learned in England because of my sister's position in London society, has been transformed from a planter's spoilt daughter to a young lady of distinction. She'll be sought after. Just think how popular that will make you!'

'You're right, my dear!' Mr Braxton was too insensitive to notice his wife's mockery. He steered her towards the door into the house. 'I see what you mean. I'll advance in society through her. By jove, she'll be an asset after all, if I can land the right fish with her as the bait. There's no limit to how far I'll climb. It's a shame the President don't have a son in the fishpond too.'

Pat heard him chuckle as he escorted Mrs Braxton inside the house. A silence descended on the piazza, broken by the clink of a bottle against a glass as Marlon poured himself another drink. Pat watched the young man raise the tumbler to his lips, throw his head back and gulp down the contents.

'Night cap,' he said, a slur to his voice. 'Need that when Pa starts politicking.'

Deborah, still seated in the shadows, said nothing.

'Oh, I know what you're thinking.' Marlon lurched towards the door, caught it and steadied himself. He peered at Deborah. 'You're quite right, of course ... drink too much ...

be the death of me.' He swayed, and for a moment it seemed he was going to collapse at Deborah's feet.

'What d'you 'xpect . . . Pa like that . . . running my life . . . *ruining* my life! He'll do the same to you . . .' Marlon's voice trailed off and a bemused expression entered his eyes as he tried to remember what he was saying. He gave up, turned into the doorway and stumbled through.

Pat held his breath, waiting to see what Deborah would do. Night had fallen completely, cloaking the gardens in darkness. The arc of light thrown by the lamps beyond the piazza's edge did not penetrate his hiding place. He felt no guilt at spying on Mr Braxton and his family. The servants and slaves gossiped anyway and whatever happened in the mansion was public knowledge throughout the country the next day.

His interest was Deborah. He thought of calling her name so she would move from her chair at the back of the piazza and step forward where he could see her. Yet he wanted to observe her silently first, before he made himself known. He had a feeling that she was different, not simply because she had been away from home for so long, but in other ways.

''Pon my soul, Miss Deborah, you sit here in this damp night air? You'll catch a chill.'

Pat stared at the woman bustling onto the piazza from inside the house. She was rosy cheeked with a cotton bonnet and a dress that flowed out from her ample hips with an air of authority as she swept across the piazza admonishing Deborah. This was the maid, the 'baggage' that Jeanette had told him accompanied Deborah from England.

'I am used to this climate, Mrs Walsh.'

'You can't stay out here alone.' The maid glanced suspiciously at the darkness of the garden. 'There might be . . . Indians . . . out there.'

'Virginia, Mrs Walsh, may not be fashionable like London but there are no Indians. This is my father's land, his county. I am at home here; quite safe, I assure you.'

'You must come inside. It's time for your beauty sleep.'

'In a minute! Please leave me alone. I want to think.'

The maid recoiled at the determined tone in Deborah's voice and seemed to recognize that she could do nothing about it. 'Very well! If you have fever tomorrow, don't blame me.'

She flounced off the piazza, making it clear by the shake of her broad hips that she was upset by Deborah's behaviour.

Pat smiled to himself, delighted that Deborah was not cowed by the woman's manner. He wondered why she had remained silent when her father was hectoring her. He shifted his position; his thighs were beginning to ache after so long crouched down in the bushes. He had taken up his position after escorting Jeanette to the kitchen door while the family were still at supper. It was his good fortune that they had come out onto the piazza before retiring.

He nearly stood up in his excitement when he heard Deborah move from her chair. It seemed she was going inside before he could take a good look at her. He wanted to shout her name, somehow draw her to the edge of the piazza. Perhaps he should whoop like an Indian.

She reached the door and paused. With a sigh that he heard even where he was hidden, she turned away from the door and crossed the piazza. He watched open mouthed.

Her hair was a rich, glowing auburn, sparkling where the flames from the lamps caught its natural deep copper highlights. She wore it in ringlets, long curls that hung gracefully over the bare ivory white skin of her shoulders. She moved slowly over the piazza tiles, gliding almost soundlessly to its edge, her skirts rustling gently around her ankles. The maroon of the gown complimented her hair, emphasizing the fullness of her firm, high-perched breasts and the deep curves of her hips.

He gasped as he realized she was more beautiful than he dared think. How wrong his sister had been in her description. Beneath the flowing skirts he imagined her thighs were lithe and shapely with agile, slender and ankles of a delicate trimness.

Desire spread through his loins, despite his crouched position. He continued to gaze at her as she stood with one hand resting on the Doric column, staring out wistfully into the night. He saw her in profile. She had a strong, well-moulded face held regally in the kind of stance that brooks no nonsense. Yet her throat looked warm and shapely above her low-cut bodice and her lonely loveliness seemed to beckon him.

Her back was straight; she was tall and long-limbed with a

body that craved activity not the idleness of reading or sewing. She exuded an aura of determination that he sensed even across the yards that separated them. He wanted to see her eyes, to see what they revealed of her inner thoughts.

As though in answer to his wish, she turned away from gazing out at the darkness that obscured the tobacco fields. She glanced about her, curious to see what surrounded the piazza. Then she looked in his direction.

He was certain she could not see him. Only his eyes where he peered between the leaves would have been visible to her even in daylight. Yet she stared straight at him, through him. He gulped, clutching himself lest somehow his hardening penis leap out and reveal his presence to her.

Her eyes shocked him. They were hard and passionless, as unreadable as stone. What thoughts were in her mind were not of romance or of the tranquil beauty of the night. There was a warning in them, an emotion too deep and too awful for him to contemplate.

His ardour withered quickly and he rose to his feet, turning his back on the house and creeping away without looking round.

There was no moon that night. Although he knew the path home he had to tread carefully, peering into the dark ahead of him. Something slapped him across his face and he gasped with fear, almost breaking into a run. Instead, he raised his hand and found a low hanging branch shaking where he had walked into it. He smiled to himself at his foolishness and continued to hurry homeward.

He couldn't get Deborah out of his mind. It was impossible to connect her with the girl who had gone away, or see a resemblance to Cletus Braxton in her. She had a grace and hauteur he lacked and, despite her femininity, gave an impression of obstinacy. She would be a match for her bullying father if she chose to defy him. The drunken Marlon had recognized her superiority immediately.

What will she do here? Pat wondered. There wasn't a man of her class within a hundred miles. The wealthy fops who were the heirs to the great plantations and caroused together or rode hellbent on busts terrorizing the poor farmers of the neighbourhood, would not be able to master her. He knew

17

that from the callous glint in her eye and the toughness he sensed beneath her veneer of sophistication.

His reaction to Deborah changed as he believed he understood her. A few weeks on the plantation and she would be like any other grasping Virginia wench. She would probably seek him out in the fields, finding an excuse to sit with him on the river bank. The arrogance she had learned in London would melt under the Virginia sun that ripened the tobacco crop. He could wait.

With his self-confidence restored, Pat was careless. His mother was too poor to keep a lantern burning in the house all night. As darkness came, she went to bed. Without a light to guide him he had only a vague idea of the whereabouts of the house.

Five Acre Field, where he was supposed to work the next morning, adjoined his house. The field used to belong to his father until Mr Braxton tricked the old man into selling it, naturally well below its market value. There was woodland on one side of the field, bordering the Mattaponi. He listened for the sound of the river's flow to show him he was close to the field so he could take a short cut along the trail through the wood. His eyes searched the tops of the trees for a break in the gloom that would indicate the gap he sought.

Suddenly he tripped. He was wearing boots so his toes weren't damaged but he was unable to stop toppling headlong onto the trail. He cursed loudly as he pulled himself to his feet, feeling with his foot for the cause of his fall. A log lay across the path. He frowned, wondering why he had not seen it there when he passed that way earlier with his sister.

He stood up, slapping his hands to shake off the dirt that stuck on them from the muddy trail, and listened again. The gurgling of the river seemed to have an echo. The hair at the nape of his neck prickled a warning and he bunched his hands into fists, peering warily into the darkness.

'Who's there?' His voice sounded braver than he felt.

He could hear the loud thump of his heart in the silence that greeted him. Even the river seemed to hold its breath. He swung around cautiously in an arc, assessing how close he was to his home. The bushes and trees around him assumed new shapes in the blackness, suggesting foes poised to leap out at him.

He was not a coward. His strength was well known and he had gained a reputation for brawling with the itinerant labourers who thirsted for a fight at the end of the season when the tobacco was being floated down the river to Yorktown. He crouched, waiting, every muscle tense. There could be a pack of runaway slaves on the loose, or a cut-throat robber lurking in the bush.

A rushing noise close to his shoulder made his heart leap. His fist shot out but failed to connect with anyone. He jumped back and listened again. The noise, a stifled wheezing now, erupted into a snort and a giggle.

'Who the devil's there?' He relaxed, his tension replaced by concern. The high-pitched sound carried no threat, only a note of triumph at his own frightened reaction. He bent down and reached towards the sound, touching the soft flesh of a girl's bosom with his fingers.

A hand closed over his wrist. 'Pat, were you really scared?'

'Of course I wasn't,' he said gruffly. 'Damned stupid girlish thing to do. I could have hurt myself on that log.'

'You didn't, did you?' The tone was contrite. 'It's the only way I could think of stopping you.'

He pulled the girl out from the bush beside the path and made her walk into the open of the field where the sky was less obscured by the branches of the trees. He looked at her reprovingly, knowing she couldn't see the pained expression on his face. He didn't want her to guess how much she had startled him.

'What do you want? What are you doing here?'

'I saw you taking Jeanette to the mansion, so I followed.' She broke from his grasp and shook her hair free, its tresses like spun shadows in the gloom.

He scowled, still feeling the blow on his shins where he bumped into the log. The Allason girls knew the woods better than him. 'Why?'

'Mary saw you in the field today. I thought you might be meeting her.'

'Well, I wasn't!' He felt the girl's hand entwine around his waist. He shrugged his shoulders to show her he didn't care but already a tremor was spreading through his limbs at her touch. His body knew instinctively how Sarah Allason could please it.

'Why were you hiding in the garden watching the piazza?'

'That's my business.' He tried to pull away from her but her hand slid down to his buttocks. The tantalizing touch sent a tingling of anticipation through him.

'Let's go to the river,' she said. 'I can find whiskey in the dark.'

'You've got cat's eyes.'

'Cat's claws too.'

He flinched as her fingers dug into his flesh. Snatching her hand away, he pulled her along by it through the trees in the direction of the river bank. He knew where he was now, it was a path he and Sarah and her sister, Mary, had walked often.

'You're in a hurry?'

'I need a drink!'

'I *did* frighten you!' She giggled again.

There was silence between them when they reached the river bank. Sarah freed herself from his grasp and left him by a tree. He sat down, leaning his back against it. He had been brought up in these woods, they were his school. He had hunted here, first beetles and snakes, and then raccoon and opossum. Girls came later. Sarah and Mary and the Sprowle twins were his teachers until the childhood games lost their innocence and grew into a compelling need.

He wondered if the girls had deliberately decided to share him. Theirs were the only houses along this part of the river. Mr Braxton had bought up and evicted all the other settlers. He and his brother were the only single men for miles, unless he included the itinerant labourers camped behind the Braxton mansion. He suspected that occasionally the girls did include them.

Even Tombo had been initiated by Jane Sprowle who had developed a fondness for his addlepated brother. His elder brother, Mort, the serious one, was too dour to be interested in women. He spent most of his time in the village five miles away as clerk in the hardware store. So it was left to Pat to please them all, and he was content. *Or was he?*

Sarah's abrupt return with her flinging herself down in the grass beside him, startled him. She thrust the jug of whiskey, already unstoppered, at him. The sour sweetness of the liquor on her breath wafted into his face. He grimaced and took a swig.

'You're thoughtful tonight,' Sarah said when he didn't speak.

The whiskey seared his throat. Her father made it; it was fiery with an earthy taste and the punch of a prize fighter. She took the jug from him and sipped at it with relish. After moments of silence, he felt her hand on his thigh. He pushed it away.

'What's wrong, Pat?' She leaned closer to him, her warm breath fluttering against his cheek. Her hand found a way inside his loose-fitting shirt and she began to caress his chest.

The whiskey burned inside him, melting him. His limbs seemed to be turning to liquid. He tried to prize her hand from him but instead found she was in his arms. He kissed her, tasting whiskey on her tongue and feeling her hands tugging at the drawstring of his breeches.

'I'm sorry I frightened you,' she giggled, misunderstanding his reluctance to return her embrace.

'You didn't.' He shrugged, aware that his body was responding of its own accord to her attempts to hold him. 'I was thinking.'

'About Mr Braxton's daughter?'

He sat up, wondering how she knew.

'She ain't for you, Pat.' Sarah crooned as she slid her hand inside his breeches. He was ready to burst.

'Don't do that!' He reached for her chin and pulled her face to his. He kissed her with a fury, trying to drive the haunting memory of Deborah's hard, cold eyes from his mind.

'Ah,' she said when they parted. 'Now I know you want me.'

He shook his head vigorously, a gesture lost on her in the dark. She straddled him, her knees squeezing his waist. His hand was drawn downwards by hers until it was resting between her thighs. He probed roughly, the hard skin of his tobacco-topping finger causing her to shudder.

'You're wet!'

'That's waiting for you!' She wriggled, thrusting herself at him, leaning down and grabbing his face in her hands.

He drove into her as he responded to her kiss, gnawing at

her tongue and arching his thighs to meet hers. She groaned, breathing the sound into his mouth.

With a rhythm that began slowly and built up to a crescendo, she writhed against him, her knees gripping his waist, her backside rising and falling rapidly as she rode him like a horse. She broke away from his lips and tossed her head back as she pounded faster and faster against the hardness of his body lodged inside her.

She cried out once, twice, then shrieked his name, shuddering and shaking as she collapsed on top of him.

'Now, now, for God's sake now!'

He remained rigid inside her, feeling the velvet wetness of her body flowing over him. He was straining against her, knowing her need, poised deep within her, yet strangely unmoved.

To please her, he thrust up, driving inside her. It made her keen with agony and the sound of her pain spurred him. He exploded at the peak of a mounting roar of satisfaction as an image of Deborah Braxton's hard, passionless eyes filled his mind.

CHAPTER THREE

He worked hard in Five Acre Field. The knowledge that his mother, standing on the canting porch of their ramshackle house, could see him, added to his determination to finish the field quickly. He was paid by the task. There was an agreed price for the field and the sooner he finished it, the sooner he could spend more time by the Mattaponi River.

It was July, the middle of the tobacco season. After the plants were topped, they would be suckered, then primed and weeded and wormed. In about six weeks, when they reached five feet in height and before the leaves began to spot and discolour, they would be cut off at the base. Drying took another six weeks, then a couple of weeks to sort the leaf and bind it into hands. When the weather changed to dampness and the atmosphere was moist, it could be packed into hogsheads and floated on rafts down the Mattaponi for sale.

Four months. Pat faltered in his progress along the row, flexing his calloused thumb and forefinger in dismay at the thought. Four months to go before the season was over and he would be free of tobacco. The temper of the plantation changed then. Winter work was casual and he had time to help his mother with the house, shoring up the walls, repairing the leaks in the roof and fixing the hinges on the shutters. He was a man then instead of some kind of pack animal working at the behest of Mr Braxton and his overseer.

He bent back to his task and continued to top the young plants. He was surprised at himself for thinking bad about the overseer, Arnie Goodpaster. Despite his shaven head and ugly, ogreish appearance, Arnie was fair if he was treated right. He knew Pat worked better without supervision and left him alone. Arnie was feared by the slaves and respected for his ruthlessness by the labourers. To Pat he was another of the neighbourhood's men who were in thrall to Cletus Braxton.

Pat sighed. That's what he was himself; bonded by his

father's bad luck to serve Mr Braxton for life. *My whole life?* The question had never occurred to him before. He glanced over the tops of the plants to see if his mother was on the porch watching him.

The dilapidated house looked out of place in the orderly rows of green plants, with the wood and the river behind it. It seemed abandoned, waiting to be cleared away in the next cutting of the trees to gain fresh land for planting. Only the presence of Pat's family prevented Mr Braxton from opening up the land down to the river.

When his father was born, his father's father farmed the land where Pat now toiled. They were a proud, free family then and when Pat's father inherited the farmstead he worked it leisurely, marrying Doris and raising his family. Either through his father's negligence or Mr Braxton's trickery, circumstances changed. Cletus Braxton bought their farm, leaving only the house plot and the small tract of land to the river behind it. Their pride and freedom were gone.

Pat shook his head, wondering why he was feeling so disgruntled. Frustration had been eating at him all day. His mother had seen the signs, warning him to control himself and give no lip to Mr Goodpaster and to stay clear of the Braxton mansion.

He could see her standing on the porch, gazing out at him. He was too far away to see her face. It would be wrinkled with age and worry and she would be biting her lower lip, praying to herself that he and Jeanette and Mort would keep out of trouble and not lose their jobs.

He looked up at the sun. He was nearly at the end of a row and the shade of the trees at the field's edge was inviting. Tombo had already brought his lunch and he had eaten it quickly so he could continue his task. He was well ahead of where he needed to be.

His mother, evidently satisfied, had left the lopsided porch and gone back into the house. *One day*, he thought, standing up and straightening his back, *I must cut some posts and fix that porch. In the fall.*

He sauntered into the shade of the coppice, yawning and stretching. He was tired, relieved when the persistent ache in his back eased. *Five minutes' sleep*, he thought, trampling the grass with his bare feet and selecting a spot to lie. Within seconds of putting his head on the ground, he was asleep.

Deborah's hand was in his. He was guiding her through the trees to the river. She was laughing, her eyes sparkling with happiness. She called his name softly and he turned to face her. Her lips parted and she gazed at him with longing. He drew her to him, threaded his arms around her waist, and clasped her against his body.

He brushed her ear with his lips, tracing the curves of her neck to her shoulders. His body throbbed with passion as he unlaced her bodice and slipped his tongue down between the silken divide of her breasts. His lips touched one rose-pink nipple; it was marble hard, straining for his caress.

The pressure boiled inside him and he could wait no longer. He forced her down onto the ground and spread her legs apart. She was fighting him off with her hands but he knew she wanted him. He slammed himself into her, pulsing with desire, ignoring the frantic shrieking of his name.

'Pat! Pat! Wake up!'

A hand shook his shoulder and he opened his eyes. He blinked with confusion. 'Jeanette?'

There was a smile of understanding on her face. 'You were dreaming.'

He closed his eyes again and groaned. The stickiness at his crotch embarrassed him and he tried to roll over on his stomach.

'No,' his sister said, restraining him with her hand.

He opened his eyes, puzzled to see her kneeling beside him. 'What are you doing?'

She placed her finger on his lips, forcing his head back so he was lying face up on the grass of the grove, the sun shielded from his eyes by the branches above him. Her fingers were fumbling to unfasten his breeches.

'No!' He tried to knock her hand away, covering his crotch with his other hand. He was still hard from his dream.

'Don't be silly. You're wet.'

He lay back defenceless as his sister opened his breeches. Despite his attempt to will his penis to lie down, it leapt up as she uncovered it. He saw her moisten her lips with her tongue.

'Don't, Jeanette.'

'Why not?'

'You don't know what you're doing.'

'Of course I do. I often have to do this to Tombo. And remember I'm like a nurse to Mrs Braxton when she's confined to bed.'

He closed his eyes, not sure whether to feel ashamed or excited. He tensed, waiting for her touch. Its roughness almost made him cry out. He raised his head in surprise.

She wiped his genitals with her handkerchief, the brisk strokes making it an act of hygiene, not passion. She poured water from the flask she carried onto the handkerchief and wiped again, cleaning him thoroughly.

'Now stand up,' she said. 'Your breeches are wet but they will dry on you in the sun.'

He dressed himself quickly, his penis already calmed to its normal size. He didn't know where to look.

'Tombo often leaks like that when he's sleeping,' Jeanette said conversationally, rinsing the handkerchief and wringing it dry. 'I didn't know you do too.'

'You caught me at the wrong moment.' He grimaced an apology.

'It doesn't worry me.' Her eyes looked wistful. 'It's straight, not ugly and bent like –' She put her hand to her mouth and stared at him in dismay.

'Like what?'

She shook her head. 'I'm talking nonsense. Ma was worried. She sent me with the water to see why you've stopped working.'

'Don't change the subject.' He paused at the edge of the field and stared at her. 'Who's been doing it to you, Jeanette? Who's ugly and bent?'

She shook her head again, lowering her eyes away from his gaze. 'Don't ask me. It's none of your business.'

'Yes, it is!' He felt a rage welling in him.

'I don't ask you about your women.' She looked at him again, defiance bright in her piercing green eyes, mirroring his own.

'That's different.'

'Because you're a man?'

26

'Yes.'

'I'm free too!'

'Free?' He chuckled cynically. 'None of us are free. Look at that.' He waved at the tobacco field. 'We're bound to tobacco.'

'I'm not going to be here all my life!'

Her retort made him pause and her words bored into his mind. He had his dreams too. 'You're right,' he said, guessing her plan. 'Who can you marry to get you away from here?'

'You'll see!' The defiance returned to her eyes.

'You'd sacrifice yourself, marry someone you don't like, who's ugly and bent, just to get away from Braxton County?'

'Wouldn't you?'

He thought for a moment. 'Perhaps . . . perhaps not. No! I couldn't. Anyway, there's not much choice for someone to marry me. I'm a field hand with no chance of improving myself. You're beautiful . . . your background doesn't matter. With your looks and quick mind you could go to Jamestown or Richmond and find a wealthy husband, one who's not bent and ugly.'

'You must forget I said that. It reminded me of something that happened . . . a long time ago.'

Pat understood, at least he had the sense not to pry further. His sister was tough, she could look after herself. 'I must get back to work.' He sighed, hating tobacco, his pride at his skill no longer seeming important.

'So must I. Mr Braxton's out riding but he'll be returning soon. I promised the mistress I'd return before he does.'

'How is . . .' He pretended he'd forgotten her name. 'You know, the daughter.'

'She's a sulky piece of work. Always quarrelling with Mrs Walsh. I don't know why she brought that woman from England if she doesn't like her.'

'It must be hard for her to settle down after being in London so long. There's no life here, and the heat . . .'

'She's no good, Pat. Why do you speak up for her?'

He shrugged, disguising his interest in Deborah. 'I'm just being fair. Who does she have to talk to? Marlon's a drunkard and her father's too full of himself to care one jot for her.'

'And you do?'

'I don't! It troubles me to hear that an attractive young woman is unhappy, that's all.'

'You'll be unhappy if Ma has to come out here. See, she's waving at you to get on.'

He sighed with resignation. 'She's worse than Arnie Goodpaster.'

Jeanette laughed but the sound seemed forced as she turned and left him. It gave him an idea. *Arnie Goodpaster?* The thought was like a slap in his face. *Is he the one she's loving?* He attacked the plants, squeezing off their tops with satisfaction, destroying in his mind anyone who would upset his sister.

He was so engrossed in his thoughts that he didn't bother to raise his head at the drumming of hooves on the trail. When the sound reached close to the row he was culling and stopped, he still did not look up. He remembered his mother's words to keep a civil tongue in his head. She was sure to be watching from the porch.

He worked on, almost forgetting the rider was there in the silence that hung over the field. It was late afternoon, the sun had lost its intensity and the kites were circling high in the dusty sky. He was shirtless now, wearing only his breeches, glad for the cooler air on his body.

'Do you always work hard, or only when someone's watching you?'

The voice was velvet-edged and strong, wonderfully low, soft and clear. His fingers poised over the top of a plant and he hesitated, hardly daring to raise his eyes.

'It's getting late,' she said, a faint note of humour in her voice. 'Surely you don't have to finish this entire field before night fall?'

'No, miss.' He straightened quickly, not wanting her to see how his back was numb with being bent for hours. 'I can finish when I want.'

Her grey eyes considered him, prolonging the silence. The stare was probing, and she showed no sign of hesitation as he gazed up at her.

'You're a very independent boy.' A hard gleam of accusation made him lower his own eyes from her face. 'But since you're a good worker, I shall ignore your insubordination.'

Thank you, miss. The words of obedience stuck in his throat.

He glanced beyond Deborah sitting smugly on her horse to where his mother was standing with her hands gripping the balustrade of their rickety porch. He sensed her prayers that he behave himself without having to hear the words she was surely muttering under her breath.

'I'm Pat Romain, Miss Deborah,' he said, wiping his hands on his thighs. 'I live in that tumbledown shack behind you. That lady over there, watching us, is my mother.'

Deborah's finely drawn eyebrows rose a fraction and her hard eyes glinted with surprise. She didn't turn to look where he pointed. 'You have a pert tongue in your head, *Mister* Romain.'

He ignored her sarcasm, marvelling instead at the regal way she held her head, the graceful curve of her neck and the soft dimples of her throat where the collar of her high-button riding outfit caressed her skin. He swelled, broadening his chest as he stood up straight in front of her.

'What are you watching, boy?' Her voice snapped like a whip.

He noticed the colour stealing into her cheeks. She pulled the horse's rein so it shifted ground, putting her beyond the directness of his gaze. He shrugged his shoulders.

'Nothing, Miss Deborah,' he said lightly, pretending to be puzzled by her question and waiting politely for her next one.

She seemed mollified by his reply and glanced at him again. He sensed her interest but kept his expression innocent. His patience was rewarded when she leaned down from the saddle and looked with curiosity at the tobacco plants.

'What are you doing to them?' she asked, her clear voice crisp.

He reached out for a plant and sliced off its top. 'Pruning them. If they grow tall their leaves have no body.'

'You did that so quickly, I didn't see.' She slid off the saddle and strode across to him. She carried herself with an air of brusqueness, brushing aside the plants with her riding crop. There was no mistaking her business-like intention.

'Do it again,' she said as she reached him.

Pat pretended he was unimpressed by her nearness. He saw her soft, milky white complexion and the coppery sheen of her hair vivid in the sun's dying rays. She was a few inches shorter than him with a stature that was both feminine and commanding.

Despite the weakness in his limbs affecting him when she stood at his side, he leaned forward, almost touching her bodice with his cheek, and pinched off the top of the tobacco plant nearest to her.

'Where is your knife?' she demanded, the amazement bright in her eyes as she thought she was being tricked.

He held up his right hand, showing the abnormal thickness of his thumbnail and the discoloration from the sap of the plants. 'Feel it,' he said, extending his hand towards her.

She looked at him askance and he realized he was no more than a slave to her.

'The nail is sharp. That's my knife.'

She touched his thumb gingerly. 'So it is.'

Her eyes remained impassive and he wondered how he was so moved by the contact between them yet it meant nothing to her. The sight of her slender white hands against the hard, tanned skin of his own, showed how great was the difference between them.

'Do you want to try to do it?' he asked witlessly.

Her eyes flickered with contempt and she drew away, her voice thick with sarcasm at his crass suggestion. 'Certainly not. I've soiled my hands enough already.'

He looked in dismay at his own hands, seeing the stained calluses for the first time as something to be ashamed of. It was a brand mark. He opened his mouth to apologize but before he could speak a shout from the trail saved him from acknowledging his feeling of inferiority with some trite remark.

'Deborah!'

She ignored the angry call and looked straight into Pat's eyes with a matter-of-fact expression emphasized by the calmness of her voice. 'My father is coming. You must get on with your work.'

Mr Braxton galloped up on his horse, reined it in and swung down from the saddle, all in the same hurried movement. He carried a whip in his hand and held it ready as he stormed through the plants, shouting at his daughter before he reached her: 'What's this, what's this?'

He gave her no chance to reply. Grabbing her by her elbow, he swung her around to face him. 'I'll not have you talking to the hands. In Virginia, a lady does not do that, nor does she ride off by herself.'

Deborah coolly removed her elbow from his grasp and withdrew from his side. Her eyes were level with his. Pat sensed she was shaken by her father's boorish behaviour and was trying to ignore it. She was staring at him without speaking.

'What are you doing here?'

'This boy,' Deborah said with an icy coolness, 'is showing me how hard he works for you.'

'Eh?' For the first time, Mr Braxton looked directly at Pat. His anger flared again and his grip tightened on the stock of his whip. 'You!' he exclaimed.

Pat bowed his head, wondering what his poor worried mother must be thinking at the sight of Mr Braxton waving his whip at him. He bit his lip to keep his own temper in check.

'This boy,' said Mr Braxton, jabbing him in his ribs with the whip stock, 'is a notorious troublemaker. He runs wild like a wolf in the woods, seducing –' He stopped in deference to his daughter's sensitivity. 'He is one of the hired hands, Deborah. You are not to speak to him. If you want to know about tobacco, ask Goodpaster or me.'

Pat hoped Deborah would speak up, showing that she was not going to be intimidated by her father. He was disappointed when she said nothing and turned to follow him meekly back to where the horses were waiting. He watched her silently, his eyes on the rise and fall of her hips as she negotiated the tiny mounds of earth supporting the plants.

Mr Braxton seized her arm again brutally, hissing in her ear so Pat could hear. 'These people are trash. You make yourself no better than them if you treat them as equals.'

Pat dug his thumbnail into the palm of his hand, drawing blood. He concentrated on the pain, his eyes watering with the effort. He bit into his lower lip, feeling it go numb as the blood oozed into his mouth. Through the glimmering sheen in his eyes, he saw Mr Braxton push his daughter up onto her horse with a firm hand on her buttocks. She sat facing Pat across the rows of plants, but she gave no sign of seeing him.

Pat contained his anger out of respect for her. He guessed if he was insolent to Mr Braxton, Deborah would suffer. She gave the appearance of being strong-willed and self-assured yet in the presence of her father she was reduced to silence.

He was sorry for her. As they rode off and the danger passed of him cursing Cletus Braxton to his face, he relaxed. He was surprised by the sight of blood on his palm and at the bitter-sweet taste of blood in his mouth. Somehow, he vowed as he gazed after her riding so nobly towards the mansion behind her father, he would find a way to help her.

Given time, she would see he was more than a boy . . . a hired hand . . . poor white trash.

CHAPTER FOUR

'I tell you, Sarah, I ain't coming to the river tonight.'

'I got whiskey.'

He shook his head. He was standing at the side of the house, a hammer in his hand. He tapped the last nail again. It was already firmly in place but he needed something to do so he didn't have to look at Sarah's crestfallen face which might make him change his mind.

'You saw Mary again today.' There was hurt in her voice.

'No, I didn't.' His mouth tightened with annoyance. 'We need new boards along this whole side,' he said, tapping the hammer handle against the rotting wood of the house. 'Don't know where that's coming from.'

'That doesn't stop you coming to the river with me tonight. Pat, it's been a week.'

'Oh yes?' He sighed, immediately regretting the casual answer in case he upset her. 'Look, Sarah, I'm tired. All day Mr Braxton has been chivvying me, like he's expecting me to do something wrong. I came home and Ma starts moaning about this and that needs doing.'

Her eyes were on him. He didn't care if she believed him or not. 'I ain't coming.'

'You want to, even though you say you ain't.'

'Sure.' He brightened at seeing a way out of his predicament. 'Sure, Sarah, I always want to, with you. You *know* that. Maybe tomorrow?'

'You said that last night.'

'I did? Well, I bet you waited by the wood to see if I really stayed at home like I said I would.'

'You sat out on the porch until near midnight.'

'Sure, it was cool out here.'

Sarah frowned. 'What were you watching, peering up at the mansion in the dark? You couldn't see anything.'

He swung the hammer in front of him. 'I don't know. I

was relaxing. It's a relief to sit by myself when everyone's in bed. After Mr Braxton's been goading me all day.'

She grabbed the hammer, stopping him from swinging it. Her touch made him look at her. She wasn't a bad looking girl. She had the wildness of a backwoodsman's daughter, her hair cropped short by her mother and her cheeks glowing with health from her days spent in her father's still.

'I'll be waiting for you,' she said. 'You're wanting, Pat. You're wanting *bad*.'

'I ain't!' He pulled the hammer from her grasp. 'You'd better go before Ma sees you. Anne Carter's already been here twice this week asking for me to go'n read with her. I reckon Ma would like that.'

'Anne Carter!' Sarah hooted with scorn. 'That mouse.'

'She's a nice girl.' He was glad to find a way to divert her. He liked Sarah and her sister, yet somehow he felt different towards them both now.

'Sure.' Sarah laughed again, slapping the side of the house to show what a good joke she thought it was. 'She's as nice as a bowl of hominy grits. Yuck.'

He smiled, poking her playfully under her breast with the hammer handle to make her feel better. 'I'm really going to bed early tonight. Ma wants me up at dawn to pound coffee beans before I go to the field.'

Sarah stopped laughing and looked at him, her wild eyes serious. 'I don't understand you, Pat, boy.'

'You help your parents, don't you?'

'I don't mean that. You ain't never said no before.'

'Maybe there's a time to say no and a time to say yes.' He fidgetted, unhappy with the turn in the conversation. 'I gotta go.'

'So have I. Maybe I'll ask Marlon to sip whiskey with me if you won't.' She paused, taunting him. 'Maybe he'll want to taste more'n that.'

If she had said that a few days before, Pat would have been angry. Now it didn't matter. Yet he was considerate enough of her feelings to keep his reaction from her. 'You wouldn't want me to smash in Marlon's teeth, would you, Sarah? That boy's pecker is pickled in rye. He's no good for you.'

'Maybe you're right.' She sighed. 'You'd better come tomorrow 'case you forget how to do it!'

'Pat!'

He rolled his eyes at his mother's call. 'Yes, ma,' he answered quickly, waving to Sarah as she slipped behind the house to make her way home through the trees. His mother leaned carefully over the balustrade at the end of the porch and looked at him.

'This rail needs fixin' too,' she said, her eyes glinting suspiciously. 'Who you been talkin' to out here?'

Pat loved his mother. He saw, as he grew older, how she struggled to keep the homestead together after his father lost interest. If it weren't for her resistance to Cletus Braxton they would have been driven off what remained of their land long ago. She convinced his father not to sell all the land and her wisdom had saved them from destitution.

'Sarah was here, Ma,' he said, knowing he couldn't deceive her. 'I told her to go away.' He gave the board a final tap with the hammer and walked along the side of the house to the porch, his mother's voice scornful in his ears.

'You ain't got the guts to tell Sarah or any girl to go away, Pat Romain. You may be big and strong but the promise of a woman's lovin' makes you softer'n puddin'.'

Harder'n a bean pole, more like, he thought with a smirk.

'There, you see, ain't I right!' His mother was triumphant at what she thought was the reason for his grin. 'Those girls sure know how to twist you around their fingers.'

'So do you, Ma.' He scrambled up under the railing and stood on the porch beside her. 'Where do you want me to fix this rail?'

'You got time?' Her eyes narrowed in her weary face.

'Sure. I ain't going nowhere tonight.'

'Lord, I got another crazy one in my home.' She looked at him, suspecting a joke.

'Why speak of Tombo and Pa like that? They're not really crazy.'

'So what are you? It ain't like you to stay home nights. Not three nights in a row.'

'Well, I am, Ma.' He kneeled down and lined up the rail, seeing where it needed securing to the house wall. 'We

35

need a new post. I'll cut one tomorrow, if I have time.'

'You're very concerned about fixin' the house so sudden. I ain't fathomed the change in you yet.'

'Ma,' he said, hammering at a nail and using the activity to conceal his own puzzlement at his mood. 'People do change, don't they? You never feel ashamed of yourself?'

'Lord, boy!' She clutched his shoulder. 'What you done now? If one of them backwoods wenches is pregnant you go'n have to marry her 'fore her pa comes for you with a shotgun. I warn you, I –'

'No, Ma!' He stood up and stared at her, amazed by her reaction. 'You worry too much about things that ain't even going to happen. I'm not ashamed of something I've *done*. It's what I am.' He gestured helplessly around the porch, at his father staring dementedly into space, at Tombo gurgling like a child on the floor as he played with a broken bucket.

'Don't you ever feel, well, kind of discontented with life?'

'Oh Lord, it's that Anne Carter.' His mother seemed relieved. 'She's been at you with her books.'

'It's a question, Ma. How do you keep your courage with all this? Don't you ever want to change your life?'

'I'll change yours with a rollin' pin on your backside. What's wrong with my life? I ain't done nothin' I'm 'shamed of.' She paused, seeing the despair in his eyes. 'And don't you do so either, Pat. We're righteous people, hard workin' an' honest. We from good stock, despite your father losin' his mind when he lost his land to Mr Braxton. Tombo's my cross an' I'm humbled by him an' I love him. We're good folks, Pat. You can be proud of what we are, and of what little we have.'

'Thanks, Ma.' He hugged her but she broke away from his embrace and turned before he could see her tears.

'Finish that job an' come for your supper.'

He checked the posts on the porch. If he were to make a proper job of it, he needed to shore up the end where it was rotten. *It ain't fair*, he thought. The old shack could fit into any of the rooms at the mansion. Cletus Braxton never had to worry about shoring up an old wall or finding timber for new posts.

Angrily he slammed the hammer down on the rail. It snapped in two. 'Damn!' he muttered, leaving the broken railing and hurrying into supper.

Although he had told his mother, and Sarah, that he wouldn't go out, he needed to do something. The atmosphere was strained in the parlour. He sat in the spare chair with his legs stretched in front of him, blocking the way of anyone who wanted to pass.

His father watched him balefully as though he was an unwelcome stranger. Tombo crawled around the floor, drooling to himself, happy in a world of his own. His mother washed up in the kitchen.

He felt uncomfortable in the parlour. When he was a child with his brothers and sister, the house was fun, full of activity. Now he was older and accustomed to spending his evenings by the river, he felt like an outsider in his ma's house. There was only Tombo there now. Mort boarded out in the village and Janice, his elder sister, was nanny to the children of a preacher and his wife fifteen miles away, and seldom visited. Jeanette spent most of her time in the mansion with Mrs Braxton because she was often ailing.

He wondered if he should sit on the porch. Sarah would see him there. He could go to bed but he knew he wouldn't sleep. It was a week since Deborah had spoken to him. He wanted to see her again, even if only for a minute, to have a picture of her in his mind to sleep with. He stood up and paced the floor restlessly, causing the dresser to shake and Tombo to regard him with alarm.

'Pat Romain,' his mother demanded from the doorway to the kitchen, 'what's the matter with you?'

He wondered what to tell her.

'Go on with you,' she said. 'Get out. Take a stroll in the woods. The moon's high, that's what's troublin' you. It's the sap.'

'No, Ma.' He clenched his jaw firmly. 'I ain't going to the woods.'

She gave him an old-fashioned look but he was not worried by her doubt. He paced the small area around the table, bumped into a chair and then stopped face to face with his mother. She thrust a bundle of clothes at him.

'That's Jeanette's,' she said. 'Guess she didn't have time to come home for it today. A clean dress for her to wear at work tomorrow.'

37

He waited, not understanding.

'Well, you great lummox, take it to her at the mansion.'

'You mean that?'

'Of course I do. If you stay here you'll shake this old house to pieces.'

He grabbed the bundle from her hand. 'Yes, Ma!' he said happily. An excuse to go to the mansion was exactly what he wanted.

'Don't let Mr Braxton see you!' His mother sounded stern. 'You'll upset him too much with your freshness.'

He didn't stay to argue. With the laundry under his arm he hurried out of the kitchen door, passing around the back of the house, keeping to the shadows of the overhanging eaves so Sarah wouldn't see him go if she was watching. He moved speedily from one dark shadow to another, heading in the opposite direction to the mansion. When he judged he was far enough away to be undetected by Sarah, he doubled back through the trees.

Although he was alert the whole time, he was distracted by his thoughts of Deborah. Would he see her at the mansion? Would she be wearing the maroon dress with its low-cut bodice or another one? Would her shoulders be covered or bare? Perhaps she would be wearing her hair in a bun, exposing the tantalizing curves of her throat and the beautiful symmetry of her lips. His blood ran warm with anticipation.

Deliberately, he refrained from passing through the front garden of the mansion. He was saving the pleasure of gazing on Deborah on the piazza until later. He approached the kitchen from the rear of the house, calling out his presence so as not to alarm any of the servants as he emerged from the darkness.

'Goodnight!' he called, knocking on the jamb of the open kitchen door. The bulky figure of Mrs Walsh appeared in the doorway.

''Pon my soul!' she exclaimed, throwing up her hands in disgust. 'Who are you?'

He was glad he wore a clean shirt and had slicked back the long locks of his hair. 'I've brought something for my sister, Jeanette,' he said, indicating the bundle in his hand.

'She's busy with the Mistress,' Mrs Walsh said pompously. 'Give it here.'

He was about to do so when his natural cheekiness made him ask, 'Who are you?'

'Who am I?' Mrs Walsh drew herself up to her full height, her starched bonnet only reaching to his chin, and put her arms on her hips in outrage as she stared up at him.

'I'll box your ears for your sauciness!' She raised her fists, undaunted by his size.

'I'm sorry, mistress,' he said, grinning pleasantly. 'I thought you might be Miss Deborah's maid but now I see you at close quarters, I know I'm mistaken.'

Mrs Walsh tilted her head to one side and watched him owlishly. 'Mistaken?'

'Yes. You are too young to be Deborah's maid. Perhaps you're Mrs Walsh's daughter?'

The woman's fists flew into the air and slapped Pat on both sides of his head before he could step out of range. A ringing noise resounded in his ears. He thrust the bundle of clothes at her, gaping in amazement. Gradually the laughter of the cook and the slaves in the kitchen penetrated his brain.

'Keep your flattery to your kind, boy.' Mrs Walsh shooed him away and turned her back.

He stepped away from the house, ruefully rubbing his sore head, and almost collided with Marlon.

'By the devil!' Marlon sniggered. 'What are you doing here?'

'I brought clothes for my sister.'

Marlon nodded and walked to the side of the house. Supporting himself with one hand, he leaned against the wall and opened his breeches with the other. He urinated, splashing his feet, then peered drunkenly at Pat.

'Want to come inside for a drink . . .?'

Pat shook his head, suspicious of Marlon's condition. He was not usually so friendly.

'Another time,' he said, moving into the darkness out of Marlon's way. He waited until Marlon had stumbled back into the house and then he slipped through the trees until he reached the shadows at the edge of the piazza.

Deborah was sitting primly in an upright chair, her back straight and her hands clasped in her lap. Her head was raised, the light from the lamp falling on her face, showing its strong

39

bone structure and the firmness of her jaw. Her nose was straight and fine, as though sculpted from alabaster and her hair, in ringlets, framed her face, making a picture, an image he could treasure in his mind.

He did not gaze at her for long. Marlon lurched into the room and Pat was afraid he would mention having seen him in the garden to Cletus Braxton. Deborah was listening politely as Mr Braxton expounded on his hopes for office now that James Madison was President.

Her display of respect for her self-opinionated father deepened Pat's admiration for Deborah. He was sure it was an act to disguise how she was suffering. Her real personality was being stifled by the atmosphere at the Braxton mansion.

He was not content with that night's visit. To placate Sarah, and to get out of his mother's way, he joined her in the woods the next evening. The night after, however, he was back in the mansion garden, observing Deborah and how she carried herself so demurely in the company of her overbearing family.

His visits to the mansion became frequent. He used Jeanette as his excuse, telling Sarah he had to escort her to work, or offering to carry messages from his mother to her when his sister had no chance to come home. Mrs Walsh saw him on several occasions and he always bid her a polite 'Good Evening' while taking care to remain far from her fists. Her greeting for him was the same: a scowl of disapproval.

One evening, about three weeks after Deborah's arrival at the mansion, Pat met Marlon again outside the house, urinating as before. Since Marlon showed no sign of surprise at his presence, Pat took no notice of him. When he settled down in his hiding place in the magnolia tree he saw that Deborah had company. There were two young men sitting with her.

Marlon returned from the garden and poured more whiskeys for them all, handing them around. Deborah and Mrs Braxton declined. Mr Braxton, enjoying the company of the young men as a new audience, was in full voice. But when he paused for a drink, Marlon interrupted him sulkily.

'Pa! Blake and Pons have heard enough. They came here to see me, not you.'

Mrs Braxton twittered. 'I thought Deborah was the attraction, Marlon. We've all heard enough of *you*.'

Pat leaned forward to catch Deborah's reply. He was relieved that she was showing no interest in the two strangers.

Marlon banged his empty glass down on the table by Deborah's chair, preventing her from speaking. 'Blake and Pons are men of action. They came here looking for a bust. They don't want to listen to small talk, or Pa's politicking.'

To Pat's delight, Marlon drew the two men away from Deborah's side. Now he could see her better. She was wearing a dress he had not seen before; it was dark green, its vividness softening the strength of her face. A velvet choker with a diamond brooch was fastened around her neck. Pat stroked himself idly as he feasted his eyes on her.

Cletus Braxton rose to his feet and joined Marlon and the two visitors at the drinks trolley. After a buzz of conversation, Marlon went inside the house and returned with Mrs Walsh. Mr Braxton snapped some questions at her, looked around the piazza and then glared at Deborah.

What's she done? Pat wondered, concerned that her father might attempt to strike her. Deborah lowered her head and rose from her chair accompanying Mrs Walsh into the house. Marlon and his two friends followed.

Pat sighed. He was too lazy to move. It was comfortable sitting in the fork of two branches in the magnolia tree. He toyed with himself, a pleasant warmth pulsing in his limbs. He knew every gesture Deborah made, every nuance of her severe smile. Now he needed only to know her touch . . . He closed his eyes as a flood of ecstasy spread through him.

A hand seized his ankle and suddenly he was falling. He tried to save himself as he was dragged from the tree but he hit the ground with a thump that stunned him. As he struggled to rise, a blow behind his ear felled him again and pain filled his eyes with a flash of yellow. He dimly heard hoots of laughter while his attackers struck him with their fists and feet.

'Twist his bollocks!' said one.

'I'll crack his head open,' said another gleefully.

He lashed out blindly with his feet, feeling his boot contact with the soft flesh of a man's crotch. There was a grunt of pain and the man bent double.

'Don't let him stand up! He'll get away.' Pat recognized Marlon's voice through the haze of agony that engulfed him.

He dived in Marlon's direction, grabbing his legs and locking his hands around his ankles. He managed to hoist him up off the ground, pulling himself to his feet as he did so. Marlon toppled backwards with a shriek. He butted him in the softness of his underbelly and pulled away. A third man was charging him, swinging a club above his head.

Pat feinted to the right, his left foot stuck out in the man's path. As the man tripped over it, Pat caught at the club, wresting it from his grasp. He swung it in an arc, deterring the three of them on the ground from rising up to beat him again.

A guffaw of laughter broke out in the darkness and he turned to see who was next.

Mr Braxton stood on the edge of the piazza, a pistol in his hand. He leered at Pat, pointed the pistol at him, and fired.

CHAPTER FIVE

The hands were gentle. Fingertips traced the gash on his forehead, tingling the soreness of the broken skin. They pressed his temples, searching for pain and then touched his cheek bones, raw from the punches of the men's fists. They squeezed his nose, probing for damage, then seized his jaw, rasping against his unshaven chin.

His eyes were puffy and he was afraid to open them. His limbs ached and were stiff with bruises. He tried to speak but his voice emerged as an indistinct croak. 'Deb . . . or . . . ah?'

'Thank the Lord you're awake!'

His mother's harsh voice chased the haze from his mind. He kept his eyes closed, relishing the balm of the flannel soaked in water that she laid on his brow. He flexed his fingers at his side, bunching them into fists. He raised one leg off the pallet, then the other, testing them for pain. He felt his mother was leaning over him, waiting for an explanation.

When the shot was fired, he had already dropped to the ground. Cletus Braxton's aim was wide and would have missed him even if he hadn't ducked when he pulled the trigger. The whiskey that made the planter murderous also spoiled the shot.

As Mr Braxton had shouted, 'I winged the bugger,' Pat pushed himself to his feet. Despite his throbbing head and the pain when he moved his legs, he kept himself low, beyond the range of the lantern, and crawled through the trees for cover.

No one followed him. The curses and laughter of Marlon and his friends, Blake and Pons, echoing across the darkness of the garden to where he lay in a ditch, showed they had had enough fun for the night. It was a bust, a spree, for them and he was a willing victim thanks to his stupidness. He had found his way home by instinct, his shock at the attack changing briefly to anger and then to an acceptance that, for once, he was wrong.

'I'm sorry, Ma,' he said, opening his eyes and grinning at her ruefully. 'Sun up?'

'Soon.' Her voice was hard to hide her concern.

'I must go to the field.'

'Aye.' She rose to her feet from being on her knees at the side of his pallet and watched him suspiciously.

He grimaced at the spreading ache in his limbs when he tried to stand up. 'I'm all right,' he said, touching the gash in his forehead. 'Walked into a tree in the dark.' He glanced at his mother to see if she believed him.

'It was my fault, Ma. Don't say anything.' He held up his hand, wincing at the pain. 'I know I was wrong.'

'You were at the mansion?'

'Marlon and his drunken friends set on me for sport.'

'I'll go'n see Mr Braxton at sun up.' She turned her back on him and walked out of the room. Tombo was still asleep on the other pallet that took up the rest of the floor space in his tiny room. He followed her out.

'They were right, Ma. They mistook me for an intruder. I was resting in the garden, up a tree, and they found me.' He faced her, shaking his head apologetically. 'I'm all right. Give me my coffee and I'll go to work.'

He heard her mutter under her breath but she said nothing because she didn't want to wake Tombo. She poured him coffee and handed it to him. While he sipped, she took his shirt from behind the door.

'You could stay home today,' she said grudgingly, shaking it.

'No, Ma.' He placed the empty coffee bowl on the table and took the shirt. 'I want Mr Braxton to see me. If he thinks I'm scared of him, he'll try to break me. When he sees me in the fields working, what can he say?' He opened the door and stared out at the sky, lightening with the pink streaks of approaching dawn.

'I could sue him,' he said to bluff her. 'I had a right to be there, seeing my sister, when his son attacked me.'

His mother pursed her lips and shook her head. 'There's a pail of water 'round the back. Sluice yourself well. An' thank the Lord those boys weren't Mr Braxton's regular thugs. They would have strung you up and shot your balls off for a bust.

You can't sue a man from the grave!' She shut the door on him.

The hot coffee and the pail of cold water he tipped over his head before he went to the field partially revived him. Once he picked up the rhythm of the topping routine, only a head-ache and a feeling of remorse remained from the night before. He did not have to wait long for his first visitor.

'Odd,' said Arnie Goodpaster, surprising him by creeping up on him from behind. 'Word had it that you wouldn't be in the fields today, son.'

He kept silent, squeezing the plants and letting the tops flutter to the ground.

'That a cut over your eye, son?'

Pat was worried by the patronising tone of Mr Goodpaster's voice. 'I fell out of a tree,' he said without pausing in his work.

'Did that once myself,' the overseer said. 'Climbed too high on the wrong branch. Hurt me for days afterwards. Didn't tell anyone. Better that way.'

'I suppose it was.' He glanced up curiously, wondering what Arnie was trying to say.

'Didn't want to cause no trouble, see. Mr Braxton's word is law in this county, and beyond it too. If he judges someone is a troublemaker, for instance, that person might as well leave the State. He's a target for anyone who wants to please Mr Braxton.' .

Pat stood up, wincing at the pain in his back, and stared at Arnie Goodpaster. 'I ain't leaving home!'

'That's good, son. You got your ma and poor old pa to take care of. Don't want to go climbin' no trees no more.'

'I'll do what I damn well please –'

The crack of Goodpaster's whip echoed through the field in the early morning air. 'I didn't hear what you said, son.' Mr Goodpaster's bald pate was furrowed with concern. He flicked the whip again, testing it.

Pat scowled, flexing his muscles as he stood in front of the overseer and wondered whether to knock him down with a right hander to his head. His eyes met Arnie's and he saw their customary meanness was clouded with sympathy. He relaxed his fists and lowered his head.

'I'll do what I damn well can ... I said ... to finish this field today. Five Acre Field needs worming before them hornworms eat all the leaves.'

Arnie coiled up the whip. 'I'll tell Mr Braxton that. Hadn't noticed it myself. He'll appreciate your advice.'

Pat grinned and turned back to the plants. He had expected worse. Cletus Braxton was probably relieved he had escaped alive. In the sobering light of day he would have realized that shooting one of his workers would not help his reputation. A scandal would certainly destroy his chances of a post in the President's administration.

What are my chances? Pat asked himself as he trod the rows ignoring the ache from his injuries. What would Deborah think of him now? The pain in his heart matched the one in his back. It was too bitter to contemplate, yet he couldn't go to the mansion for a while.

A whistle made him glance up. Mary was standing by the wood, beckoning him urgently. He waved at her to go away and continued topping the tobacco, working his way along the row towards her. He had forgotten her presence by the time he reached the wood.

'I've brought your breakfast.'

He raised his head in surprise. 'Where's Tombo?'

'I told him I'd bring it for you. Your ma doesn't know.'

'Tombo will tell her.'

Mary giggled and sat down on the grass, patting a place beside her for him to sit. He lowered himself gingerly, trying to keep the pain out of his eyes. He reached for the pancakes and began to feed them into his mouth as he realized how hungry he was.

'I heard what happened last night.'

'I fell out of a tree.'

'Monkeys climb trees.'

'Snakes and cougars do too.'

'So do fools. Which are you?'

He looked at her sharply. 'What have you heard?'

'Mrs Walsh said she'd seen you lurking at the mansion. So did Marlon. They didn't like it.'

'Cletus Braxton didn't like it.'

'Does Deborah?'

He choked, spilling bits of pancake from his mouth. 'How do I know?' He put the remainder of the pancakes back in the basket and laid out on the grass, relishing the relief in his aching limbs.

'Let me rest,' he said, linking his fingers behind his head, making a cradle as a support for his neck. The slanting shafts of sun struck his face and he felt better.

She rubbed her hand across his chest, smoothing out his shirt. 'Where does it hurt?'

He made no answer, half wishing she'd leave him alone.

Her hand slid lower, rubbing in a circular motion over the flat muscles of his abdomen. He flinched when she touched the tenderness of where Marlon's boot had struck him.

The hand slipped under the drawstring of his breeches. He tried to tell her to remove it but a comforting feeling dulled his wits. It seemed to purge his remorse for his foolishness. He lay back as she breathed life into him again.

The rest of the day dragged on slowly. He worked mechanically in the sun, longing for the bliss of rest when the day would be finished and he could soak his tired body in the river.

He saw Cletus Braxton leave the mansion in a closed carriage and wondered if Deborah was with him. The man's face was at the carriage window when it passed close to the field but Pat kept his eyes on the ground, conscious of his malevolent stare.

Mr Braxton didn't return the next day, nor the day after. Pat's mother thanked the Lord and said it saved him from the planter's anger. He bore his mother's criticism and his sister's admonishment without comment. He pleasured Sarah by the river bank and gave the impression of returning to his normal, carefree way of life.

From Jeanette he learned that Deborah had remained at home, watched over zealously by Mrs Walsh. She read, she crocheted doilies, she walked in the garden, accompanied by Mrs Walsh, and she played the harpsichord and sang. She did everything a well behaved young lady of quality was supposed to do.

Pat was tempted, with Cletus Braxton away, to visit the mansion once more. Jeanette begged him not to go. 'There are men in the garden at night now,' she said, 'to keep out prowlers. Besides, Deborah doesn't sit on the piazza any more.'

'All that because of me?' He laughed. They were sitting by the river together. It was afternoon and his sister had an hour before she was due back at the mansion.

'He's protecting his asset. By pretending to be a Peeping Tom, you gave him the idea that someone serious might try to abduct her.'

'I am serious, Jeanette,' he said, taking her hand in his.

Disbelief faltered in her eyes until she looked at him closely. 'Why? The only person she cares for is herself. I know her . . . and her father.'

He noticed her bitterness and assumed it was because of him. 'You haven't given her a chance. I bet I could make her enjoy herself. Surely she doesn't like reading and sewing and –'

'That's what adult women do, Pat, not hang about in the woods all day and all night like the Allason girls.'

'You sound envious of her.'

A tear came to her eyes. 'I don't know what I am, Pat.' She looked like she wanted to tell him something. He reacted too fast and pulled her to his chest, patting her shoulder.

'Have I made you cry?'

She pulled away and wiped her eyes. 'Of course not. I'm tired, that's all. Don't tell Ma. I don't want her to worry.'

'Worry about what?' He picked up a stone and skimmed it across the sluggish surface of the river, only half listening to what she was saying. He had an idea.

'That I'm not feeling myself. It will pass.' Almost under her breath she added wistfully, 'I hope.'

'Sure it will.' He slapped his fist into the palm of his other hand. 'I have an idea. If the garden's guarded at night, then I'll have to see Deborah in the day. You can help me.'

She looked at him scornfully. 'She's not interested in you. She doesn't even know you exist.'

'That's why you must help me so that I can make sure she does know. Don't you think I'd appeal to her, sis? She's not happy at present and you know it. At least I could make her laugh. Away from that English duenna and Mr Braxton's domination, she'll be a different woman.'

Jeanette shook her head wearily. 'I don't think so. She's too set in her ways.'

'She's keeping herself bottled up. Help me to see her, sis. If she rejects me, then I promise I won't ask you to help me again. Give me, and her, one chance.'

'What do you want me to do?'

He swelled with triumph. It didn't occur to him that his sister's agreeing with him was due to her despair and not because of his persuasive charm.

'Do you speak with her often?'

'Only to pass the time of day when she visits Mrs Braxton in her parlour.'

'Befriend her, draw her out. Tell her what nice rides there are by the Mattaponi river. Remind her how the weather and the scenery are beautiful. Say what a shame her father isn't here to go riding with her.'

'What good will that do?'

'You'll see.' He smiled as though he had a secret. It was a gamble and if Deborah was the sort of woman he thought she was, then he wouldn't have to wait long to see if his hunch was right.

As Mr Braxton's absence stretched into a week, Pat began to tell Arnie which field needed suckering or worming. He always chose the ones that were within sight of the mansion lawns so that he could observe the comings and goings of everyone. After five days, his patience was rewarded. The lone rider he glimpsed emerging through the gates was undoubtedly Deborah.

He wondered what battle she had had with Mrs Walsh to get permission to ride alone. Perhaps she had defied her, asserting her right to do what she wanted. Obviously, the seed of the idea that Jeanette had planted in her mind had taken root. His problem now was how to attract her attention so she would stop and talk to him.

He assumed she was only pretending to ride and would be looking for him among the men working in the fields. Since she knew where he lived he expected her to ride along the trail close to his house. He gave up the soulless task of picking hornworms off the leaves and sauntered casually along the edge of the field so his path would cross hers as she rode past.

49

He reached the path and ambled along it, not looking back, pretending to be unaware of her riding up behind him. His pulse raced as the beating of hooves on the dry mud of the trail grew closer. The horse was cantering at a great speed, he could hear it panting as it bore down on him.

The smack of her whip against the horse's rump and the snorting of the animal close to his ear warned him just in time that she wasn't going to stop. He dived off the track into the tobacco plants, feeling the rush of wind from the horse's hooves as they missed him by inches.

He stared after her in amazement, choking on the cloud of dust that rolled after the animal's galloping feet. The shrill sound of her laughter made the accident seem unreal. He was incredulous: *did she mean to ride me down?*

He stood up and shook himself as the dust settled. She was riding with the skill of a practised horsewoman, something he hadn't expected. She must have thought he would jump out of the way in time and she was having a game with him.

His spirit soared at the thought. She *had* noticed him; she *did* have some feeling for him. He felt the hair of his crotch prickle in the challenge.

He followed the billowing dust with his eyes. She was riding so fast in the hot sun, she would soon want to rest and give the horse some water. When he saw her turn off to the left at the junction, he was happy. The track led to the woods by the Mattaponi and then curved along the river bank, emerging half a mile from his home. He cut through the fields, heedless of the plants he was smashing down in his hurry to reach the trail before she did.

This time he surprised her, stepping out into the path before she was aware of his presence. She swerved then brought the horse to a halt. He stood with his hands on his hips watching her, hoping his eyes showed he meant her no harm.

'Good afternoon, Miss Deborah,' he said, reaching out to pat the horse's neck to calm it.

'Leave him alone!' she snapped, tightening the reins so the horse reared up in front of him. He dodged out of the way as its swinging hooves were about to plunge on his chest.

'You ride very well, Miss Deborah.' He smiled as though

nothing unusual had happened. 'I didn't mean to frighten you, or the horse.'

'Get out of my way!'

'I thought you might be interested,' he said, ignoring her command, 'in seeing how the tobacco has grown since I pruned it.' He held up his topping thumb. 'Remember?'

Her mouth was a tight lipped line and her eyes smouldered with fire. Her anger made her fiercely attractive.

He swallowed, trying to keep his approach light and bright, hoping the gleam in his eye and his charm would persuade her to listen to him.

'See,' he said, tearing off a leaf of tobacco and offering it to her. 'There is a texture to it now that gives it body for smoking. Oronoco sells for a lot of money these days. There's a fortune growing as far as you can see.'

She made no move to take the leaf from him so he waved it in an arc encompassing the fields on both sides of the trail. He smiled openly, hoping she'd understand he represented no threat while she was high above him on the back of her horse.

She said nothing. The fire in her glance changed so that her eyes became stony with anger.

'I'm sure you saw people smoking Virginia tobacco in England,' he said, desperate to melt her coolness. 'Maybe it came from these very fields.'

'Boy!' she said, 'stand aside!'

'Of course, Miss Deborah.' He bowed mockingly. 'My name is Pat Romain, in case you've forgotten. I'm not your *boy*.'

'I have not forgotten, neither has my father. I shall tell him you have accosted me when he returns. He has gone for a meeting with the President of the United States.'

Pat was unimpressed. 'I know Mr Madison,' he said blithely. 'Although his father was a planter, he's not interested in plantation hands like me. Yet *underneath*, I'm no different from you . . .'

He was rewarded by seeing a spread of blood burst in her cheeks in an angry blush.

'Perhaps I let myself have more *fun* . . .' He smiled, his eyes deepening to show his true meaning.

'I'm not interested in your bestial ways!' She raised her whip and waved it in his face. 'Stand aside!'

He did so immediately, enraptured by her fury and at the same time unable to believe she was serious.

'You're a miserable specimen of a man,' she said, sounding like a school ma'am. 'You are despicable.'

He raised his eyebrows, spreading his hands wide in mock astonishment. His eyes glimmered with an invitation.

'You think you're irresistible to women. I've news for you, you're not! Only a bitch in heat could see anything in you, *boy!*'

He was unabashed. 'Your father's turned you against me, hasn't he? I could be your friend. You need me. You –'

The leather of her riding crop sliced into his cheek. He blinked in surprise and raised his hands instinctively to defend himself. The whip cut down again and he grabbed it, tugging it from her hand.

Angrily, he smacked it down on the horse's rump, making the animal prance in panic. Deborah screamed and grasped the reins to stop herself falling as the horse cantered off.

'You're the bitch!' he said bitterly, staring after her as rage and frustration pricked his eyes.

CHAPTER SIX

He was sullen for days. His mother, who knew his moods and saw in them a sign that he was maturing, was patient. She gave him no sympathy and left him alone, letting him mope his depression out of his system. Cletus Braxton returned to the mansion and Pat waited for the result of his wrath. He was puzzled that Arnie Goodpaster relayed no comment and the routine of the tobacco season rolled along without disruption.

One afternoon Jeanette came home and asked him to sit with her in the shade of the sycamore tree. He wanted to find out what Deborah had said about her ride. Jeanette wanted to talk and put her hand up to delay his questions.

'How do I look to you, Pat?' She stood in front of him where he sat under the tree and slowly turned around in a complete circle.

'Fine.'

'Look at me, Pat! Tell me the truth.'

He raised his eyes and studied his sister, wondering what this performance was about. She looked all right to him. Perhaps her face was a little drawn. That would be because she had to stay up many nights to tend Mrs Braxton.

'The truth is, sis,' he said, stretching his legs out in front of him, 'you are beautiful. Your hair doesn't sparkle like Deborah's, it's darker. But your eyes could bewitch a man, your smile –'

'What about my figure?' She touched her bosom and smoothed her dress down over her hips.

'It drives men to distraction.'

'I don't look . . . fatter?'

He pursed his lips in concentration, shading his eyes for a better view. 'No.' He put out his hand and pulled her down beside him.

'Are you sure?' She wriggled until she was comfortable.

He nodded his head and she seemed relieved. She opened her mouth to speak but he interrupted her. 'Have there been any rows at the mansion, between Deborah and her father?'

A shadow of annoyance crossed her face. 'You said you wouldn't ask my help again. You got what you deserved.'

'Her riding crop! I thought she'd tell her father and he'd set his thugs on me.'

'If she told him that, he'd know she was riding on the plantation without his permission. Mrs Walsh was in the village, you see. Not even she knows Deborah went out.'

'Why didn't you tell me before?'

She shrugged her shoulders.

He was exuberant. 'I *do* mean something to her. I'm her secret.'

Jeanette's mouth formed a moue of scorn. He lapsed into silence, considering what this news meant, unaware of his sister's own need for reassurance. When she put her hand on his knee, he leaned his head back against the trunk of the tree automatically.

She removed it hastily and stared at him. 'I thought you could help me,' she said in a voice low with despair.

'Of course I will.' He mistook the reason for her husky tone and watched her with curiosity.

'Stop thinking of yourself . . . and Deborah.'

'Whatever you want, sis.' He reached out and squeezed her hand, holding his eyes steady with hers. The sadness in them helped him recognize her distress. He pulled her to her feet and stood in front of her.

'You know you can depend on me, Jeanette, whatever's wrong.'

'Good.' Her voice assumed its normal tone of brisk confidence.

'Won't you tell me?'

'You'll find out in good time.'

'It's not about me?'

She laughed in his face. 'You're not the only one with problems.'

He shrugged and took her arm in his. They walked over to where their mother was watching them from the kitchen door. She turned inside at their approach, hiding her frown of concern.

'Are you walking Jeanette back to the mansion?' she asked suspiciously when they entered the house.

'No, Ma.' He grinned. 'What else would you like to worry about?'

'Pat!' Jeanette held her finger to her lips and he lowered his eyes, ashamed at mocking her.

'Sorry, Ma,' he said contritely. 'I'll stroll down to the Carters' house and see Anne. You'd like me to do that, wouldn't you?'

He heard his mother sigh as he moved away. His father watched him from the porch without a word. Tombo, splashing water over himself from the rain butt in the garden, regarded him warily.

Pat's gloom deepened. *Where do I fit in?* he asked himself silently as he lobbed a stone into the trees. Tombo's antics and his father's blank stare depressed him. He was a problem to his mother and too full of himself when his sister wanted to confide in him.

He was ambitious, but what chance did he have to improve himself? Deborah was right without knowing it. Sarah and Mary and the Sprowle twins gave him no sense of achievement or satisfaction. They weren't a challenge like she was. Yet she wouldn't even listen to him because her father had labelled him *poor white trash*.

His thoughts were interrupted by the sight of Anne Carter waving to him from her porch. He cheered up. She was a shy girl who had avoided him until recently. Then he spent a couple of evenings in her company, sitting on her stoop, talking to her while her parents were inside. She made it clear that she liked him, and he found he liked her very much indeed. He waved back.

'I'm pleased you came by,' she said, her pale cheeks brightened by a blush. She raised her hand to touch his arm when he climbed onto the porch but dropped it swiftly back to her side with embarrassment.

He chuckled, his eyes brimming with tenderness. 'Don't be shy,' he said, grasping her hand. 'Give me a kiss of welcome.'

She opened her mouth to protest and he leaned down and kissed her on the lips. She tore away and stared up at him in speechless dismay.

'Won't you ask me inside? I know your parents aren't here. I saw them go down the trail in the buggy.'

'Is . . . is that why you came?'

His crotch tingled with desire. 'Yes.'

'They'll be back soon,' she uttered in alarm, following him through the swing door into the house. 'Before nightfall.'

'That gives us enough time.'

'Oh dear!' Her hands flew to her face.

'You're pretty when you blush like that. It gives you colour.' He sat in a wooden rocking chair and gently swayed backwards and forwards.

'I'm not pretty.' She glanced at him coquettishly. 'Not like the Allason girls.'

'Why mention them?' He crossed his legs to hide the stirring in his breeches. Despite the knowing glitter in her eye, her face had a disturbing innocence. 'You're not like them, are you?'

Her blush deepened and she lowered her eyes, her fair hair falling in front of her face. She was standing at his side. He reached up and touched her brow, smoothing aside the strands of hair and forcing her to look at him.

'Are you?' he repeated gently.

'No,' she said, withdrawing from his reach. Her lips were trembling.

He rose from the rocking chair and stood opposite her, one hand held in front of him so she wouldn't see how she had roused him.

'You don't have to be *scared* of me,' he said. 'I respect you.'

Relief flooded into her eyes. 'I've never . . .'

'Don't say anything.' He put his hand out to touch her shoulder. For a moment she quivered like a humming bird just beyond his reach, then she came to him. She put her hands on his hips lightly and looked up into his eyes, her lips parted.

He hesitated, his flesh throbbing as he leaned her body against his. He wanted her.

'Kiss me,' she breathed when he did nothing.

'No!' He thrust her away and flung himself down again into the rocking chair. It pitched forward and he put his head in his hands.

Anne knelt at his feet and steadied the chair. 'What have I done wrong?'

He shook his head. 'Nothing, nothing at all. And you shouldn't. You're all right, Anne. Stay that way.'

'I thought you wanted me.'

'I do, God, I do!' He covered his crotch. 'But not this way. You don't *want* to be like the Allason girls, do you?'

'I've such a heat burning inside me,' she said, blushing again as she put her hand on her breast. 'I get wet at night dreaming of you.'

'What's your age?'

'Fifteen.'

He swallowed and clenched his fists to calm himself.

'I'm *not* too young, Pat. The other girls do . . .' She smiled hopefully. 'Your ma likes me.'

He sighed. 'She's a wise old lady, Anne. What does *your* ma think of me?'

She turned away, avoiding the question. He nodded his head in amusement. 'I can guess. She says I'm no good and you should keep away from me. Don't you think she might be right?'

'Oh, no!' She stared at him. 'You can't possibly be as bad as she says.'

'Why not?' He was curious about what Mrs Carter thought of him.

'She says you're the bane of your ma's life, a seducer of women and an agitator among the field hands and Mr Braxton will see you're hung before you're twenty . . .' Breathless now, she regarded him with wide-eyed awe.

'That gives me two months left.'

'Share them with me!' She grasped him around his shins and laid her head on his knees. 'I thought love was supposed to be happy.'

'It's not love that's troubling you,' he said, easing her head away from his thighs. 'Even if you think it is. It's your body stirring, waking up to womanhood. The Allason girls know that. I'm sport for them.'

'Then be sport for me too.'

He stood up, his feelings under control, and laughed. 'I'll always be your friend, Anne. You'll find a man soon enough and then you'll fall in love. That will be the happiness you crave.'

'Don't go!' She hurried to stand in his way by the door. 'I'm feeling so foolish.'

'Why?' He hugged her warmly, but pulled away as soon as she began to respond. 'You should be proud. You're a very pretty young woman, Anne, and I think you've just made a man out of me.'

He left hastily before she asked him what he meant.

Suckering keeps the strength of a tobacco plant in its leaves. It's an operation involving the removal of the small shoots that spring from the junction of each leaf with the stalk. Pat used to like the work; it required little thought or effort beyond inspecting every plant and pressing off the shoots with his thumb and forefinger. Now he found the work irksome.

'Why do I have to do this?' he asked the overseer irritably one morning. 'Mr Braxton's got slaves who could do it.'

'Aye.' Arnie Goodpaster inspected a plant carefully while Pat watched him. 'They could.'

'Why don't you tell him? It'd be a relief for me.' He placed his hands in the small of his back and groaned. 'I reckon this work is for nigras, not men like you and me.'

'Nigras cut when tobacco's ripe,' Arnie said slowly. 'Let nigra loose in this crop now,' he waved his hand around the field, 'and plants'll die, for sure.'

'You may have to do that.' Pat folded his arms. 'If I tell the men to stop work.'

Arnie turned his attention from the plant and eyed him warily. From his glance, Pat knew he had the overseer perplexed, even worried. Pat was popular among the labourers; he was more skilled in tobacco than Arnie and was the one who set the pace for them.

'You'd tell the men to stop work?'

'Well . . .' He tilted his head on one side as though thinking, but he had already worked out his plan during sleepless nights on his pallet wondering how to improve his lot.

'This is back-breaking work, Arnie. I've talked to the men. They agree with me. If Mr Braxton halves the daily task, or doubles our pay, we'll put up with the backache. If not, he'll have to let the nigras do it.'

He snapped a plant off at its stem and held it up in front of the overseer before opening his hand and letting it fall to the ground. 'Be a shame to let such a good crop be destroyed.'

'So that's what you've been up to?' Goodpaster's frown relaxed and he wiped his head with his hand, smoothing back the flesh. 'I wondered why you've been hanging around the work camp instead of the woods at night.'

'What do you think then, Arnie? You know we're all exploited by Mr Braxton. You too.'

'He'll finish you for this.'

'He don't want a strike. Think about it. He's too ambitious.' He paused, adding under his breath, '*So am I.*'

'Your terms are too much, Pat.' Arnie Goodpaster chewed thoughtfully on his fleshy lips. 'If you and the men only do half what you do now, the crop will be choked by suckers and holed by hornworm. Need double the men for all these acres.'

Pat grinned as he realized Arnie was sympathetic. 'Will you tell Mr Braxton to double our pay?'

'Half again for you, Pat. You're one of us. Ten per cent increase for the men.'

'You bastard!' He spat at his feet. 'You've arranged it with Mr Braxton already.'

'Had to protect myself.'

'How much extra is he going to give you?'

'Buy you a bottle of whiskey tonight, Pat, and tell you.' Goodpaster got down on his knees in the soil and ran his hand up the stem of a plant. 'Tobacco really looking good this year. Credit to you.'

'Yes, Arnie.' Pat sighed, resuming his suckering of the plants, not knowing whether to be pleased he'd improved his own pay or annoyed at the way Mr Braxton, through Arnie, had avoided confrontation.

His mother was worried when he told her. 'Why should Mr Braxton raise your pay by half?' she demanded.

'Because Arnie Goodpaster asked him to. He heard about what I was planning.'

'What was you plannin'?'

'A strike.'

His mother sat down abruptly. 'Oh my Lord!' She raised her hands to her temples. 'What's going to become of you?'

'I don't know, Ma. I had to do it, don't you see. Even the nigras are better off than we are. They get their victuals every day. Cletus Braxton is getting rich on my work and knowledge. I bet he could have doubled, even tripled my pay and not noticed it.'

'He sure as hell notices it, Pat. You're troublin' the man too much.'

'I have to do something to improve myself, ma.' He paused before sharing his secret with her. 'I want a plantation of my own one day.'

'You won't live long enough for that.'

'If I can't get it here, Ma, then I'll leave the State.' He was aware of his mother's eyes on him but something drove him on to speak. 'I'm wasting my time here. You know that.'

'You used to say you'd never leave home.'

'That was before . . .'

'Before what?'

He sensed her suspicion again. 'Before I got to thinking.' He didn't want to tell her his sole motive was to be equal with Deborah.

'All I can hope to achieve if I stay in Braxton County is an overseer's post and I'm that already but for the name. How can I profit from that? I want to look after you, Ma. To change all this.' He waved his hand at Tombo grovelling on the floor and his father staring at him.

He realized there was a glint of encouragement in the old man's eye. He looked at him in surprise. 'Pa! You understand! You're on my side.'

His father gawped at him, his eyes clouding over again.

'We're all on your side, Pat,' his mother said sorrowfully. 'That's what's goin' to make it harder for us to bear when Mr Braxton deals with you. After the tobacco's harvested, when you've served your purpose, that's the time. He'll destroy you, Pat, for challenging him.'

She squeezed her husband's hand lovingly, her eyes brimming with tears. 'He'll destroy you the same as he did your pa.'

Pat strode out of the cabin, angry with frustration. The

rickety porch, which he still hadn't fixed, swayed as he
jumped down the two steps to the garden. It was dusk. He
had hurried home from the field when his task was finished to
tell his mother about the raise and the conversation with Arnie.
He thought she'd be pleased. Her anxiety deflated him.

He tore off his shirt, hanging it around his shoulders, and
walked straight through the garden to the wood. He was sticky
and dusty from his day in the fields. He yearned to swim in
the river so it could cleanse more than dirt and sweat from his
body. He was sick of the petty fears and prejudices which
hampered every move he tried to make.

His anger subsided when he reached the river. It was wide
and deep with an undercurrent in its centre despite its sluggish
appearance by the bank. He knew the river's moods better
than his own.

In two months it would be busy with flatboats floating the
tobacco hogsheads down to Yorktown. Now, as the twilight
closed in, it meandered through the overhanging trees.

He tossed his shirt into the grass and rolled down his
breeches. He pulled them off and flung them on top of his
shirt. The cool of the evening air wafted around his naked
body and he relished the sense of freedom the woods, away
from Cletus Braxton's fields, inspired in him. He dived off
the bank, slicing deeply into the Mattaponi's dark, swirling
waters.

The splash disturbed the river birds and they called loudly
to each other as he surfaced and, with powerful strokes, struck
out for the opposite bank. He cut through the water swiftly,
his long arms carrying him into the treacherous flow of the
mid-river current. It tugged at him and he strengthened his
strokes to pull clear.

The river was as cold as death and eager to claim him. If he
relaxed his strokes it would bear him relentlessly in its race,
submerging him in the white water eddies and drowning him
in its embrace until his lifeless body was washed into the
shallows a few miles downstream. He gasped for breath,
knowing the Mattaponi's power and determined to survive it.

He kicked his legs strongly until he was beyond the current's
clutches. He turned over onto his back and splashed leisurely
through the calmer waters to the opposite bank. When he

reached it, he pulled himself out of the water and sat on the grass, panting, humbled by the river's deceptive calm appearance.

He heard the snapping of a twig in the wood behind him. He didn't move or look around. His nose took in the homely, biscuit scent of the woman emerging from the bushes where she was hidden, waiting for him. He clasped his hands around his knees, shaking his head so that water showered from his locks as she approached.

'Pat!' she said in mock rebuke. 'You're splashin' me.'

He stopped the shaking and waited while she hunkered down beside him and put her arms around his shoulders. He turned, trying to guess who she was. The Sprowle twins were so alike in appearance, it was only when they dressed differently that he could tell them apart.

His body soared to life as her fingers traced a line down his spine.

'We thought you weren't coming,' she said. 'My sister's gone home.'

'Good.' He beamed and put his hand out to touch her, cupping her breast in his palm. He squeezed until she whimpered and tried to pull away.

'You're in a mean mood tonight.' Her squeal changed to a giggle as he turned to her and rolled her off her haunches to the ground. She lay back and watched him without protest.

He reached down and tugged at her loose cotton skirt, drawing it up over her hips, revealing her thighs and a thick mat of ginger hair.

'You're Sharon,' he smiled as he identified her. Drops of water fell from his glistening body onto her thighs.

She put her hand on his chest and stroked the crucifix of hair, running her fingers down its length to his navel. Lowering her hand, she grasped him, sending a warm spasm of need shooting through his limbs.

'Sharon,' he murmured again, his long, hard fingers opening her.

She pushed against him, rubbing her bosom against his chest, smearing herself with the wetness of the river from his body. She guided him into her, clinging to him with her arms around his shoulders and her legs encircling his waist.

He made love to her with a rage, trying to resolve his frustrations. She writhed beneath him unaware of the cause of his passion, but inspired by it. The pleasure of release swept away his doubts, at least temporarily, when he lay contented by her side.

His swim homeward across the Mattaponi River took longer, the current dragging him beyond the glade where he'd left his clothes. He had to turn and swim upstream in the shadows when at last he escaped the river's demanding embrace.

The darkness was total by the time he emerged from the river and stood, dripping and shivering, on its bank. He paused to get his bearings, trying to see the lightness of his shirt and breeches against the gloom of the grass.

Suddenly he sensed he was not alone. He stared hard into the darkness, crouching into a fighter's stance and clenching his fists.

The darkness moved towards him. A chill knot of tension tightened in his guts. He poised, ready to leap at his attacker or to dive back into the river if he was outnumbered.

A cold hand brushed against his chest. He caught the wrist and bent it downward, reaching out with his other hand for the person standing in front of him.

'Pat . . .?' The hesitant voice released the tension and he stared stupidly into the blackness, relaxing his panicked grip on his sister's arm.

'What are you doing here, Jeanette?' He forgot his nakedness.

'I thought you'd been . . . drowned. You were such a long time.'

'I didn't expect you to be waiting for me.' He slipped his hand around hers, aware of the tears in her strained voice. 'Are you crying because you thought I'd drowned?'

He heard her choke back her sobs, then she spoke grimly. 'If the Mattaponi had taken you, Pat, I'd jump in too.'

'What's wrong, sis?' He pulled her to him but she froze at his side.

'Your clothes . . .' She handed him his breeches and shirt.

He grinned his thanks and eased the breeches over his wet legs. He dabbed his body dry with his shirt and draped it across his shoulder.

'It's all right now.' He caught her arm and drew her close. It was over a week since she'd been home.

'Have you been home to see Ma?' he asked as he guided her along the trail away from the river. He could see its outline in the moonlight. 'She doesn't know you're here, does she?'

'No, Pat. I can't see Ma. That's why I came here to look for you. I'm scared.'

'Ain't nothing to be afraid of in these woods.' He remembered his own apprehension that it might have been Cletus Braxton's thugs waiting for him by the river bank.

'Please listen to me, Pat. I *must* tell someone.' Her voice quavered. 'I don't know what to do. Ma will kill me.'

Gradually her need for comfort dawned on him. He squeezed her elbow. 'What is it, sis?'

The words rushed out, helped by the darkness that hid her distress. 'I'm going to have a baby.'

Her hand searched for his, her fingers fighting to wrap in his own. He held her tightly, not knowing what to say.

'A *baby*, Pat!' Her voice rose with despair.

'Ma won't kill you for that. She might even be pleased. Who's the father?'

His sister's silence was worse than her tears. A foreboding chilled his heart. 'Who is it, sis?' he demanded again.

'Cletus Braxton.'

He sighed. Amidst the shrill night chorus of the wood he heard Jeanette's soft sobs. He hugged her to him. 'Don't worry, sis,' he said calmly. 'I'll make him pay.'

CHAPTER SEVEN

As soon as he saw Deborah, the yearning returned, not like a river's gentle ripple but with a great wave of excitement that stunned him. He stood at the back door of the mansion and gaped into the parlour where she sat, unaware of his presence, reading a book. The way she held her head, her shoulders bare revealing the apricot and milky colour of her skin and the swelling of her breasts from her low-cut bodice, captivated him.

He wanted to call her name, to see her cast down her book and rise up from her chair and run to his arms and let him hold her. He would crush her to him, making her feel the desire his words couldn't express.

Jeanette moved to close the door in his face. 'Thank you for escorting me,' she said softly. 'I want to go to the mistress now, to see she's all right.'

He stared over her head at Deborah, wondering why she hadn't looked up to see who was at the door. He was lucky to see her at all. Mrs Walsh was obviously elsewhere in the mansion. He had insisted on walking Jeanette back to the house, listening to her account of Cletus Braxton's repeated assault on her over the previous two years.

Every word he heard hardened his resolve to see his sister avenged, and Mr Braxton humiliated for abusing her. He had approached the house determined to fight anyone who challenged him. To his surprise, Jake, the man who was supposed to guard the mansion against intruders, waved him through. Since Jeanette slept in Mrs Braxton's quarters, he was able to walk with her right to the mansion's back door.

Jeanette kissed him lightly on his cheek. 'I feel better now.' She glanced at Deborah and lowered her voice to a whisper. 'I was frightened it showed, that everyone would know.'

'They *will* know,' he said bitterly.

'I'll lose my job!' There was panic in her eyes. 'You mustn't do anything rash.'

The light from the lamp in the parlour lit up the anguish in his sister's face. He felt he was seeing a stranger. The carefree innocence, her radiant smile and sparkling eyes, was blighted. Her eyes, red-rimmed with tears, were puffy from lack of sleep; her shining hair was dull and her smile strained. Now he looked for it, he saw the fullness in her figure.

'It will hurt, Jeanette,' he said softly, not wanting his words to carry to Deborah. 'You must be brave. Trust me. You must tell ma, and Mrs Braxton, everyone, before they find out themselves.'

'I can't do that! The shame . . .'

'Be proud,' he said. 'Like her over there.' He nodded at Deborah who was still reading, apparently undisturbed by their whispered conversation. 'Let people know you're going to have a baby. You won't feel ashamed any more.'

'But . . .' She stared at him in dismay, unable to explain how she was feeling.

'But don't tell anyone who the father is!' He hissed at her, his eyes stern. 'No one must know that. His name is your secret, your weapon.'

'I don't understand.'

'You will.' He kissed her cheek and added, in a voice deliberately raised so Deborah would hear, 'Goodnight, Jeanette!' He was rewarded with a pout of annoyance in Deborah's austere visage.

He held the door and swung it closed, his eyes indicating to Jeanette that she should not worry at what he was about to do. Alarm flashed in her own eyes but it was too late. The door separated them. He kept his foot in the gap so that it was ajar, yet Deborah would think it was closed.

The first sound he heard was the slap of her book landing on the floor and then the scrape of her chair as she stood up. He put his eyes to the gap and watched. Deborah was staring at Jeanette with an odd mixture of annoyance and curiosity in her hard, grey eyes.

'You disturbed me!'

Jeanette stooped to pick up the book. 'I'm sorry, Miss Deborah, I didn't expect you to be here.'

'Where else can I read in peace? Papa's in the drawing room discussing politics with his cronies, Marlon's in the dining room with his whiskey, and Mrs Walsh is fussing in my boudoir. Even here I'm interrupted by your whispering with that *boy*.'

'He's my brother.'

'I know that.' She sniffed suspiciously. 'What did he want?'

'To walk me here because of the dark.'

'How thoughtful of him.' Her voice was deep with sarcasm. 'What was all that whispering about? It was more disturbing than if you'd spoken normally.'

Jeanette hesitated. 'A private matter . . .'

Pat pushed open the door and stepped into the parlour at that moment. Deborah stared at him coldly while Jeanette clutched her bosom, pleading with him with her eyes to go away.

'My sister,' he said slowly so the words would have their full effect, 'is pregnant.'

Jeanette's cry of horror cut into his heart. He didn't want to hurt her and was appalled by the shame that gripped her. She looked about the parlour in panic.

'She'll know soon anyway, sis,' he said, turning back to Deborah. 'She's a woman too, she'll understand, won't you?'

Deborah's face was a mask of pious self-righteousness. It was the reaction he expected. He taunted her some more. 'She could be your friend.'

'Get out of this house,' she said, pointing at the door, her voice husky with menace. 'I'll call my father.'

He grinned, hoping she would. Only Jeanette's distress prevented him enjoying the chance to provoke Deborah.

'I'm going,' he said. 'I don't *want* to stay here. Look after Jeanette for me, won't you? She ought not to work hard in her condition. Nor be bullied.'

'The condition of my father's servants is no concern of mine.'

Through the thin material of Deborah's bodice, he could see the rise and fall of her heart thumping. Her colour had deepened and her hands were twitching.

The signs excited him. He longed for her, and for the time when they would stop sparring and be able to share love. Suddenly he realized how he was dressed, in damp breeches and shirt, with his hair tousled and his feet bare. No wonder she was watching him with disdain.

'I'll come and see you tomorrow, sis,' he said, ignoring Deborah but letting her know his intention. She started to speak.

He pulled the door shut so he didn't hear her angry retort. He was pleased with himself for having upset her.

He whistled cheerfully as he walked home. Although he felt bad about his sister, the chance meeting with Deborah had filled him with hope. He had a plan and the seeds for it were already planted. With Jeanette's unwitting cooperation he would help her, and himself too.

He waited two weeks. This gave his mother time to recover from the shock of Jeanette's news and to grow used to her condition. Jeanette refused to tell her who was the father and Pat stood up for her against their ma's attempt to find out.

During the two weeks, Pat glimpsed Deborah twice when he escorted Jeanette to the mansion. She was watching him from behind the curtain of her boudoir window, and disappeared from view when she saw he had noticed her.

'How is Deborah treating you?' he asked as he approached the mansion again. This time he was dressed in his Sunday best, with a clean shirt open to his chest without a stock, and breeches with boots which he had polished for an hour to bring a shine to their dull, neglected leather.

Jeanette sighed. 'She was never my friend.'

'I know.' He frowned. 'She's taking longer to thaw than I thought.'

'You'll never have her, Pat.'

He didn't answer. He was scanning the mansion windows hoping she could see him as they walked around to the back door. There was no one standing at Deborah's window. Perhaps he had dressed up in vain.

'I was right to tell her you're pregnant. She can't be so hard on you now.'

'She is. She picks on me whenever she can.'

'Perhaps she's jealous.'

'Why?'

'Who does she think the father is?'

'I've no idea.'

'She's only ever seen you with one man.'

'You?' She pulled away from him, a startled cry on her lips. 'Isn't that what everyone thinks, even Ma?'

'They can't . . .'

'They probably think that's why you won't say who the father is. What does Mr Braxton say?'

'I haven't told him.'

'He's stopped trying to rape you in the parlour when his wife's sick?'

'He's been away. I haven't had the chance to talk to him.'

'He could guess for himself now. I want you to tell him to his face. Tonight. Ask him what he's going to do about it.'

'I can't. He's got guests, important politicians. Mrs Braxton told me to stay out of sight upstairs.'

'Ah!' His eyes gleamed. 'Then he does know.'

'What difference does it make? He's sure to dismiss me soon. It's only because Mrs Braxton is sick and she likes me that I'm still employed. It's funny,' she said after a pause. 'She seemed pleased when I told her I'm having a baby. She thinks it's Marlon's.'

'Marlon?' He paused thoughtfully. 'Has he ever –'

'No!' Her blush of anger told him she spoke the truth. 'Mr Braxton was the first, Pat . . . and the last.'

'Tell him tonight, while he's got his important guests. Let *them* see you.'

'Why?'

'He'll be rattled. He'll tell you to get out of his way. It'll make a scene. He knows you're carrying his child. Now you've got to tell him to his face. It's important to my plan.' He encouraged her with his eyes.

She nodded although her face showed the misgiving in her heart.

The next day Pat was on edge as he worked in the field, eager for dusk so he could go to the mansion and meet Jeanette. Mr Braxton had toured the fields with Arnie Goodpaster, inspecting the tobacco. The leaves had begun to spot, to thicken and to discolour, all the signs that it was ready to be harvested.

The plants would be cut off at the base by a special tobacco knife and left in the fields to wilt. After a few days they would be carried to the curing houses to be suspended on rails so that the air could circulate to dry them. Oronoco took six weeks to dry properly.

Usually Pat was put in charge of a team of negroes who had been trained to cut the tobacco stems cleanly. They worked well with him and he never had to resort to the whip like the other drivers. His gang was cheerful and he won their respect through working with them instead of driving them from behind like a slave master.

Pat stood up as the overseer approached him after Mr Braxton had ridden off. 'Well, Arnie,' he said, squeezing a grub and wiping his hands clean on his breeches. 'When do we start? Tobacco's ready.'

'You ain't.'

Pat laughed scornfully. 'If we don't cut these plants this week, they'll spoil. Grubs are having a feast.'

'Cuttin starts tomorrow, Pat, but you don't. Mr Braxton told me to pay you off. Don't want you in the fields again.'

Pat kept his eyes steady, not letting his utter dejection show. The plantation was his life. Despite his brave talk about seeking his future elsewhere, he could not envisage a day without having to work in Cletus Braxton's tobacco fields. The warning of his mother filled his head: at harvest time, Braxton would destroy him.

'Did he say why?' With difficulty he kept the dismay from his voice.

'Said he don't need you no more. I'm sorry, Pat. Maybe he'll change his mind by spring.'

'Maybe he will . . .'

'Now, son, don't do anything rash. He's a powerful man in these parts.'

Pat stroked a leaf of tobacco. He wondered how much was Arnie's doing. The overseer was not to be trusted, his only interest was saving his own job. 'Make sure you pay me my increase,' said Pat, snapping off the leaf. 'I earned it.'

'Where are you going?'

'Home.'

'Keep away from the mansion. He's told the guards not to let you near.'

'Perhaps I should ask him for permission to be alive!'

He skirted around the edge of Five Acre Field towards his home. He looked into the woods, hoping Mary or Sarah would be there. He would have liked to forget his problems with a few minutes of pleasuring. There was no sign of them. He thought of going to see Anne Carter until he remembered she had been sent to stay with an aunt out of his way.

He was pleased to see Jeanette sitting on the porch when he neared home. He called her cheerfully so she wouldn't sense his despair. She raised her head and dabbed at her eyes with a handkerchief. He was shocked to see the accusation in her eyes before she lowered her head and began to sob.

'You too?' he said, stepping on the porch beside her and patting her shoulder. 'Cletus Braxton's thrown you out of the mansion?'

She stared at him through her tears. 'How did you know?'

'I expected it.'

'I did as you suggested. It was your fault. He was so angry when I tried to speak to him in front of his guests. He shouted at me and made Mrs Walsh take me from the parlour. I didn't have a chance to tell him anything. This morning Mrs Walsh told me to take my things and go. She said I must never come back.' She cried into her handkerchief.

'I never even said goodbye to Mrs Braxton. She'll be very upset.'

'Let me dry your eyes, sis.' He took her handkerchief from her hand and wiped it roughly around her face.

She pushed him away. 'You're no comfort. I'm not worried about me. It's Ma.'

He looked up at the scrawny figure of their mother standing, arms akimbo, in the doorway of the house. Her grey hair hung in dank wisps over her brow and her face was pinched and careworn.

'Go back to work, Pat,' she said crossly. 'There're enough people idle in this house.'

'I ain't going.' He stood up. 'At least, not to the fields. I'm going to see Mr Braxton.'

'That's for me to do.'

'No, ma. You have to leave this to me.'

Jeanette tried to restrain him. 'His men will set the dogs on you.'

'I'll take that chance. I *have* to see him.'

'Are you sure it's not his daughter you want to see?'

'Ma, Braxton's fired me too. If I don't get my job back you'll have two extras without wages to keep.' He looked at his sister and smiled. 'By Christmas, it'll be three.'

He didn't wait to hear his mother's wail of protest at the troubles the Lord had wrought on them. He marched up the trail to the mansion, determined to speak to Cletus Braxton. By the time he reached the gates, he had harnessed his anger to a scheme he hoped would succeed.

'You can't come in here!'

Jake was standing in the middle of the trail, a shotgun cradled in his arms. Two other men Pat had never seen before waited at the side of the road behind him. Straining at leashes held not very tightly in their hands were three black hounds, the ones used for hunting runaway slaves. The dogs growled menacingly, their bared fangs white against their sleek, black coats.

'I see that, Jake,' he said, halting and brushing back his hair nervously. 'Are you going to tell those men to set their dogs on me?'

'Mr Braxton's orders.'

'Did he tell you that himself?'

'Yep.'

'Are you supposed to set the dogs on my sister too, if she comes here?'

'Yep.' The man fidgeted with his shotgun. 'Go away Pat, I don't want to have to do anything. You're a pal.'

'You're a pal too, Jake. Thanks for your help.'

'Help?' The man looked puzzled.

'Sure. You can prove what's rotten about Braxton. He's not the kind of man President Madison ought to give a post to, is he? Ordering dogs to be set on a pregnant woman.'

He turned away and walked hurriedly from the gates, ready to run for his life if the two strangers let the dogs loose. He wondered how long it would take for his remark to reach Mr Braxton's ears. It would only help his plan.

Instead of going home, he made his way through the wood to the river. Sarah was outside the cabin which housed her father's still. She was washing bottles in the river and didn't stop when he squatted down at her side.

'Fine day,' he said, gesturing at the sun. The shadows from the trees dappled her face. Her dress was rucked up to her thighs as she sat on her haunches, with a row of bottles in front of her. He copied what she was doing and filled one at the river, shaking it clean and letting the water drip out again.

'Ain't seen you for a while.'

'I've been here,' she answered without looking at him.

'I've time to spare now. I quit work.'

'Braxton fired you.'

He shrugged his shoulders and filled another bottle.

'I can't understand what you see in her.'

'Who?' His mind ranged over the possibilities: Anne Carter, Sharon Sprowle or her own sister, Mary. Sarah was a wood's sprite who loved to spy on him in the dark. She could have seen him with any of them. 'Is that why you're vexed with me? You're jealous?'

'Of her?' Sarah's laugh gusted raucously in his face as she turned to him. 'Deborah Braxton's no competition. She's a stuffed doll without a heart. What do you see in her?'

He sighed and decided to tell her. 'She's educated and attractive; she's exciting with eyes that are so cold, she needs my kind of fire to melt her.'

'You ain't the one to do it, Pat. She's cost you your job.'

'You know a lot about it.'

She nodded, shaking a bottle clean. 'The only thing I don't know . . .' She put the bottle down and reached for another. 'Is who made your sister pregnant?' She eyed him shrewdly.

He put his hand on her thigh and rubbed his thumb up under her skirt. 'Why ask me?' He pinched her playfully.

'Pat, don't do that! Your thumb's sharp.'

'That's all I have to show for five years of my life.' He snorted with disgust, withdrawing his thumb and staring at its nail, sharp and rough-edged from cutting tobacco plants and crushing hornworms.

'That's not all you've learned,' she said, putting her hand on his crotch. Her tongue moistened her lips and she bent her head. 'You always were a good pupil.'

CHAPTER EIGHT

'What about Jeanette Romain?'

The question, shouted at him from someone standing in the shadows at the fringe of the crowd, made Cletus Braxton momentarily falter in his prepared speech. He glanced over the heads of the people surrounding the flat wagon he was using as a platform and tried to see who had spoken.

The crowd murmured impatiently, wondering why he had stopped. Another voice, closer to the wagon, demanded in the silence, 'Who's Jeanette Romain?'

There was a guffaw of laughter from the crowd and Braxton raised his hand to quieten the people gathered around him. 'As I was saying, folks . . .' he began, trying to pick up the lost thread of his speech.

'Ain't she Mad Romain's girl, lives by the 'Poni?'

The interruption made him hesitate again. 'My topic tonight, folks,' he shouted, 'is –'

'Jeanette Romain! What about her?'

It was yet another voice interrupting, this time right by his feet. He glanced down and saw that one of his own supporters had taken up the question so he could have an opportunity to answer it. He scowled.

'Not now, Max,' he hissed at the man. 'Let me tell you, folks, the President's proposals are good for this town, not only for the Nation.' He resumed his speech but his eyes showed his heart wasn't in it.

Pat, who had shouted the question at first, was now sitting on the stoop of the hardware store where his brother worked. He had slipped away from the crowd in the darkness in case Braxton or one of his mob of tough henchmen identified him at the meeting. His interruption achieved more than he had hoped.

'You see,' he said to Mort. 'He's rattled.'

'Why should your shouting our sister's name worry a man like Cletus Braxton?'

74

'That's exactly it, Mort. Why? That's what the crowd wants to know. Wait until I've asked the question often enough and he'll be really worried.'

'I don't understand.' Mort scratched his head and looked at him pityingly. 'You're asking for trouble if you try to hinder Mr Braxton's campaign. He's determined to ride to high office on the President's coat tails.'

'Isn't it strange,' said Pat, changing the subject, 'how a shrimp of a man like Madison is the President of the United States. He don't look big and powerful.'

'He's a good man,' Mort said seriously. 'Ma's brother used to work for his family in Orange County where he started his political career. It's because he was sickly as a child that he don't look much now. And the strain of all his book learning.' Mort sounded envious. 'You don't have to be a giant like you, Pat, to be great.'

'He still lives there?'

Mort frowned at the question, trying to decipher it. 'Ma's brother? Sure he does. He's an old man now with children and grandchildren. He still keeps in touch with Mr Madison's family.'

'Orange County ain't far from here, to the north.'

'North east,' said Mort, correcting him gently. 'You haven't explained what this is about.'

Pat smiled and deliberately ignored the request. Some of the men surrounding Mr Braxton, fired by liquor and sensing his nervousness, were heckling him. He stumbled in mid-sentence and gaped at them, incredulous at being interrupted again.

'If you ain't going to listen,' he shouted at them angrily, 'I ain't gonna speak.'

'Aw, go home!' someone shouted.

'Yeah, we don't want you here.'

The shouts of the crowd grew louder while Braxton tried to quieten them.

'Those fellows have been drinking all evening,' said Mort sadly. 'Mr Braxton paid for the whiskey himself. It don't help him none. They're spoiling for a fight now.'

Braxton's henchmen pushed a way through the crowd so the wagon could leave. He was still trying to speak, standing on its back gripping the rail and shouting over the jeering voices as it rolled down the main street.

'I must be going,' said Pat, watching the wagon drive off into the night. 'I have a long walk home.'

'Won't you stay here?' Mort sounded worried, just like their ma. 'I could ask my boss to let you help around the yard.'

Pat shook his head, still smiling.

'I know it ain't much, but –'

'Thanks, Mort. I appreciate it. I can't stay. I have some matters to settle.'

'Don't waste your life, Pat.'

'I won't.' He shook his brother's hand, aware of Mort's eyes on him. *He probably thinks he'll never see me again*, he thought, releasing his grip and strolling away. *Braxton has all my family scared.*

He chuckled to himself at the effect his question had had on Braxton. He had proved he could be a danger to the politician, if not to the planter. The problem now was how to meet him face to face. He had tried to climb into the mansion grounds at night but the dogs were chained in the yard and barked as soon as they took his scent.

He hoped Deborah would be his ally but she was as hard to approach as her father. Sometimes she did go out riding. It was then that Pat saw her as she really was. She rode hard and skilfully, relishing the open trails. Her face was flushed when she returned to the mansion and there was the gleam of a challenge faced and overcome in her eyes. He had observed from the woods, unable to get near enough to attract her attention.

Her very independence fascinated him, yet she succumbed so dutifully to her father's commands. He reasoned that a woman with her zest for life and fiery temper would not remain submissive for ever. Gossip from the mansion showed she defied her father at least where a husband was concerned. Several eligible bachelors had been presented to her and she had emphatically rejected them all.

He wondered as he walked through the night if he could hire a carriage, borrow some fashionable clothes, trim his hair, and present himself at the mansion door. She would recognize him, of course, but his appearance would give him a better chance than the way she usually saw him, as an out of work, ragtag field labourer.

He strode along the darkened track, deep in thought. There was enough moon for him to follow it without a lantern and he was confident none of Braxton's henchmen had seen him at the village.

The harvesting of tobacco had begun. He had kept away from the plantation and made no attempt to disrupt work by asking the labourers to strike over his dismissal. He was confident he could resolve matters another way, especially after what Mort had said about their relative who had worked for the President's family. All he needed was an opportunity to present his deal to Braxton.

It was nearly dawn when he reached home and he didn't want to disturb his ma to let him in. He dozed on the porch, an image of Deborah drifting in and out of his mind. If only she would give him a chance, she would see he was ideal for her. He wasn't the uncouth troublemaker she imagined.

A kick in his side made him open his eyes and half leap to his feet. 'Ma!' he said with relief when he realized it was she who had kicked him awake and not one of Braxton's thugs. There was a mug of steaming coffee in her hand.

'You frightened me.' He sank back to the board floor of the porch, and it shook under his weight.

'Why are you sleeping outside like a dog?' She put the coffee on the floor beside him.

'I was late last night.'

'I s'pose you were in the woods again, drinkin' whiskey and doin' Lord knows what with them Allason girls.'

'I went to see Mort.'

'Did he send money for us?' The hope in her voice died when he shook his head.

'I'll have money soon, Ma.' He sipped the coffee, feeling strength seep into his limbs.

'All you've ever brought me is disgrace. Your own sister . . .'

'Shut up, Ma!' he said irritably, not liking her to think he was the baby's father. He rose to his feet and leaned over the shaky porch rail. Across the Five Acre Field he could see the chimneys of the mansion above the coppice of tall trees surrounding it. He wondered if Deborah ever gazed out of her window at their ramshackle cabin.

'I'll fix the porch tomorrow, Ma,' he said, hoping to soothe her. 'At least we'll have the house looking good even if we don't have food to eat.'

'There's potatoes to dig,' she said, 'and –'

He swung off the porch and began to run through the field. He could see Mr Braxton's carriage speeding down the drive. If he could intercept it, this would be a chance to speak to him.

He was panting when he reached the track only seconds before the carriage rounded the bend from the mansion. He crouched down in the grass at the side of the trail and leaped up as the carriage passed him. He flung himself at the door, gripped the carriage roof and hung on, trying to get a foothold so he could support himself while the carriage careered down the track.

The startled face of Cletus Braxton stared at him from inside the vehicle.

'Let me in!' Pat shouted. 'I want to talk to you.' His feet found the footboard and he spreadeagled himself against the carriage's side, clutching at the roof with his fingers.

Braxton pitched his might against the door and it swung open, slamming into Pat's groin. He swung it out again, delivering another blow to his body. Pat's feet were swept off the footboard and he clung to the carriage roof in desperation. The carriage sped onward, the trail rushing past his feet.

Braxton slammed the door into him again, shouting in his ears. 'I'll kill you for this!'

They were the last words Pat heard as he fell to the ground, the back wheel of the coach passing an inch from his head before he rolled off the track. He lay for a long time, letting the dust settle on him. He was measuring his bruises, letting the pain score into his mind the stupidity of what he'd just done.

He had lost the advantage. Braxton would destroy him now before he could play his trump card.

All day he lay by the Mattaponi, listening to its gentle flow while he nursed his hurt pride as well as his battered body. He chose a glade in the woods upstream from Sarah's still, and a long way from where the Sprowle twins lived on the opposite bank. He needed to be alone while he planned what action to take before it was too late.

As soon as Braxton returned, he was certain to instruct his men to come for him. He had a reason now, Pat had tried to attack him. He wondered what the men would do.

If they followed the coward's way, they would strike at night. He wouldn't be safe in his home. The door would burst open while they were sleeping and he would be seized from his pallet and dragged out into the field. His family would never see him alive again. Mort had been right.

He had to strike fast, before Braxton gave the order to find him. He knew what to do.

As dusk rolled over the Mattaponi, he settled down in a camouflaged hide he constructed at the corner of Five Acre Field. He was waiting. It was not long before he saw in the darkness the outline of Braxton's carriage returning to the mansion. Four strangers rode with him, the hooves of their horses thundering close to where he lay concealed. The men rode alertly in their saddles with the mean purpose of hired ruffians.

Pat was concerned lest the men seek him at home immediately. They would smash up the house in their anger at not finding him there. He watched the darkness carefully in case they rode back along the trail.

He had three bottles of whiskey with him he had persuaded Sarah to give him that afternoon. He waited an hour and when no one came riding from the mansion, he uncorked the first bottle. He took a hearty swig from it then sprinkled the rest of the contents over a heap of dried leaves and sticks he had piled up in the field.

The fire, when he put a spark to it, flared up quickly, the smell of alcohol pungent to his nose. He ran from it to another heap of leaves and twigs, emptying the second bottle of whiskey on it. It caught fire easily. He set a third heap alight the same way.

To aid the blaze, he threw on bundles of the tobacco plants that had been cut and left to dry. The summer had been kind and the leaves were crisp like paper. They were soon burning in a merry blaze that lit up the entire field. Then he heard shouts of alarm from the guards at the mansion.

He crouched low, level with the path, and ran along it to the mansion gates. There was pandemonium in the grounds as men rushed about, bumping into each other and shouting. The flames in the field in the distance made the fire look much worse than it really was.

'Rouse Goodpaster!' he heard Braxton shout from the piazza. 'He must save the crop.'

Unnoticed in the confusion, he ran through the garden until he was close to the mansion. He was nearly diverted from his purpose by the sight of Deborah rushing onto the piazza.

She wore a cloak over her nightdress; he could see the pink of the diaphanous material underneath it. She clasped the cloak to her throat with her hands, her body unfettered from the stays of the smart gown she usually wore.

To him, she was gorgeous. Her coppery ringlets flowed about her shoulders in glorious disarray; there was the colour of alarm in her cheeks and her eyes sparkled with excitement.

'What is it, father?' she asked, her strong voice carrying across the garden to where he was hidden.

'One of the fields is afire.' Braxton sat down and pulled on his boots. 'I could lose the crop if it spreads. I'll have to go myself. The new men don't know their way around.'

'I'll come with you.'

'No.' His boots on, he leapt to his feet and picked up his coat. 'Stay here. Comfort your mother.'

She pouted with disappointment as she turned from the edge of the piazza. Her cloak gaped open and Pat caught a glimpse of her nipples under the muslin, dark roses abloom in pale full breasts. He came close to abandoning his plan for her father and stepping out of the darkness to seize her.

'That damn Romain boy's done this,' Braxton growled, strapping on his belt. He picked up his pistol and walked to the piazza's edge. 'That boy's a trouble maker, a firebrand, sure enough.'

Reluctantly, Pat drew his eyes away from Deborah as she fastened her cloak. He followed Braxton when he stepped into the garden and hurried through the bushes towards the workers' camp. The garden was strangely quiet now the men who were guarding the house had run off to fight the blaze.

Braxton's laboured breathing revealed his whereabouts in the darkness. Pat waited until he was far enough away from the mansion not to be seen. He sprinted ahead of him and then crouched beside the path. He had a stick in his hand and held it horizontal at ankle level above the ground, as the planter approached.

Braxton tripped over the stick, sprawling heavily on the path. Pat flung himself across his back, landing astride him with a jolt that knocked the air out of him. He clapped one hand over his mouth to stop him shouting for help, and deftly plucked his pistol from his belt with the other. He held the muzzle steady behind the planter's ear.

'If you move, I fire,' he said softly, his voice deadly with menace.

Braxton's body went limp with fear.

'Do you understand? You're a dead man if you call out.'

Braxton murmured his agreement and Pat slowly removed his hand from his mouth, pressing the pistol against his head.

'We're going to have a little talk,' he said, pulling the planter by his collar until he was in a sitting position. He jabbed the pistol into his ribs and brought his face close to his.

Braxton whimpered with rage when he recognized him. 'The pistol . . .' he bleated.

'Yes,' said Pat casually. 'I hope it doesn't go off. What a big hole it would blow in your fat belly.'

'What . . . what do you . . . want?'

'To shoot your balls off for what you did to my sister.' He saw Braxton's eyes widen with fear. 'Yes, what about Jeanette Romain,' he crowed mockingly.

Blaxton flinched, showing he realized it was Pat who had helped cause his political meeting to end in chaos. 'You're crazy like your father,' he blurted out.

The insult didn't goad Pat. He had prepared himself for every trick Braxton would make. The planter was trying to make him lose his temper so he would be careless. He pushed the muzzle harder against his flabby body.

'Pa wasn't crazy until you swindled him out of Five Acre Field. You took away his livelihood and his sanity.'

'He owed me money so I took the land. It was a business deal, witnessed by the bank.'

'He owed you because you crooked him with usurious rates of interest. He trusted you. Yes, he's mad now but not as mad as he was then.' Pat stopped, realizing he was talking too much.

He pushed his face closer to Braxton's. 'You ruined my pa but you ain't ruining my sister.'

'I've done nothing to her!'

'She's carrying your bastard.'

'You can't prove that.'

'I don't have to prove it.' He chuckled grimly, tightening his grip on the pistol. 'You and I know it's true.'

'It could be anyone's bastard. I hear it's yours. She's supposed to be an easy lay.'

Pat grit his teeth until his jaw hurt, telling himself that Braxton was deliberately trying to rile him. 'She was a virgin until you raped her,' he said calmly, his anger under control.

'What are you going to do about it?'

'You're prepared to talk?'

'Anything, so long as you put that pistol down. We'll go to the house. I'll give you money if that's what you want.'

He ground the pistol into Braxton's flesh until he was gibbering with fear. 'I'm not as stupid as you think, Cletus. Of course you'll agree to whatever I suggest so you can go free. Then tomorrow my body will be found in the Mattaponi River.'

Braxton's eyes bulged seeing his hopes dashed.

'Listen to me carefully. Jeanette hasn't named you as the father to anyone, not even to our ma. Do you know why?'

He let the question sink into the planter's mind while he watched him cautiously, knowing he was crafty enough to pretend to be scared so he could try to escape.

'Her secret's her shield. If anything happens to her, or to me, President Madison will receive a letter from someone close to him in Orange County. Your chances of a place in his administration will be finished when Mr Madison learns you are a murderer as well as a rapist.'

'It's not true . . . I wouldn't . . .'

'Do you guarantee nothing will happen to me or to her? You'll send your thugs back where they came from?'

'You have my word.'

'I have better than that. I have my assurance lodged with Mr Madison's family in Orange County.'

'His family?' Braxton shuddered with the pistol still stuck against his ribs. 'What more do you want?' he asked nervously.

'A settlement. Jeanette will say nothing. Your reputation will be unharmed. In return, you must make sure hers is protected too.'

'How much?' Beads of perspiration oozed out on his brow. There was a foul stench of fear from his breeches. 'Stop waggling that pistol, man, for God's sake.'

'Man?' Pat raised his eyebrow, savouring the promotion from 'boy' to 'man'. He liked it.

'As much as you care to spend on her wedding. To give her child a father.'

Braxton grinned weakly.

'Ah, yes. You see the advantages of the idea. Her silence, and mine, will be secured if she is married. They'll be no proof that you're the child's father when she's married. She won't be a threat to your political career, as long as you remember the truth is with someone in Orange County.'

'I agree.' He nodded his head, clawing at the air for Pat to remove the pistol.

'I'll give you a week. In that time you must arrange for Marlon to marry her. She will live in the mansion as your daughter-in-law.' He cocked the pistol.

Braxton deflated at the sound, shrinking back into Pat's arms. 'Marlon? My son?'

'He'll be lucky at getting a wife as understanding as my sister. Mrs Braxton likes her so she'll not object. She thinks Marlon's the father anyway. You've got off lightly.'

Braxton tried to speak. 'Please take away the pistol,' he squawked.

'Sure, in a minute.' He twisted it into his ribs again. 'Just one more matter. You will deed Five Acre Field to me for my trouble. No hassling me or my parents, ever. Agreed?'

Braxton sighed angrily. 'All right, all right!'

'Good.' He pulled the planter to his feet by his collar and turned him to face the fields. The fire was dying down. 'You can go home now. Don't forget the letter . . .' He booted him in the seat of his breeches.

'Remember, Cletus,' he called after him. 'I may be a firebrand but I'm the uncle of your child. I'm your equal now, Cletus, not poor white trash any more.'

CHAPTER NINE

The wedding was a quiet affair, conducted in the parlour of the Braxton mansion. Mrs Braxton left her sick bed, determined to witness her son's marriage. She was vaguely disapproving, not of Jeanette, but of Marlon for seducing her. She admired him, though, for taking the honourable course and marrying her; especially as she would be gaining a daughter-in-law who had already proved her proficiency as a servant.

Jeanette's mother did not attend the ceremony. Pat tried to persuade her but she was adamant. 'Ain't no way I settin' foot in Braxton's house,' she declared emphatically. 'Not after what he done to your pa.'

Jeanette herself had been stunned by the message Pat had brought her. 'Marlon wants to *marry* me!' She had laughed in his face. 'Was he drunk when he said that?'

Yet as Pat outlined his scheme and explained the advantages, she had readily accepted the idea. She was soon imagining herself as his bride, living in the mansion as one of the family, not as a servant. She admitted to a certain fondness for Marlon and believed she'd be able to reform him.

Marlon himself raised no objections. On the morning of the marriage, he was groggy with a hangover and went through the ceremony in a daze, supported by Arnie Goodpaster on one side and his bride on the other. He, too, could see the advantages of the marriage even though he couldn't recall actually seducing Jeanette as his father claimed he'd done.

Braxton attended the ceremony and it was clear from his agitated manner that he would rather be elsewhere. He was on tenterhooks, frowning heavily at Jeanette and avoiding having to look at Pat. He seemed worried that Jeanette might implicate him to the pastor.

Deborah watched the proceedings with an air of detachment. She was dressed in the latest fashion, her face painted and rouged and her hair brushed until it shone. Mrs Walsh attended her. Her expression gave no clue of what she was thinking. Pat searched her face for some acknowledgement of his presence in the parlour, but she only stared right through him.

He was dressed, as he had dreamed, in clothes that made him look like a dandy. Although the stock was starched and cut into his throat, the coat was tight across his shoulders and the stockings made his feet hot, he carried himself proudly. Like Deborah, he had brushed his hair for a long time, but with less success. He looked impressive, he was sure, even though he was uncomfortable in the formal clothes.

He carried Braxton's pistol in his belt, something the servants observed and appreciated; it *was* a shotgun marriage.

Despite Braxton's arrangements for the wedding and his deeding of Five Acre Field to Pat in the office of his banker, Pat did not trust him. He carried the pistol in plain view to remind the planter of his obligations. As the ceremony was concluded and Marlon was urged by Arnie Goodpaster to kiss the bride, Pat relaxed.

Jeanette looked radiant, obviously determined to make the most of becoming the wife to the heir of Braxton Plantation. She smiled indulgently at Marlon's demand for a drink instead of a kiss, but declined to join him when he expansively offered her a whiskey too. Mrs Braxton was crying so she comforted her.

Pat tried to edge around his sister to speak to Deborah. Arnie blocked his way. 'Mr Braxton wants to see you.' He indicated with a nod of his head that he should go through to the piazza.

Pat studied his face for signs of trouble. Arnie's smile was bland, reminding him that, unless Cletus Braxton himself had revealed the terms of their deal, no one else knew the real reason for the marriage between Marlon and his sister. Nevertheless, he was alert for the unexpected as he stepped on to the piazza.

Braxton was alone. He stood with his back to him, his hands clasped across his chest, staring out at the garden. He obviously heard Pat's footfall on the tiles of the piazza, but he refused to turn around.

Pat coughed, and still Braxton did nothing.

'What do you want?' he demanded, feeling foolish at being made to wait like a servant about to be disciplined. He glanced around the piazza, wondering if there was someone in the garden waiting to attack him. Yet Braxton had dismissed the gang of thugs exactly as he'd promised.

'My gun!' Braxton's voice was mean with anger. 'Put it on the table and get out. I never want to see you in my house or on my lands again. I would be happy never to set eyes on you for the rest of my life.'

'Is that so?' He was still wondering if the planter was preparing a trap for him. He decided to play a game of his own to make Braxton less sure of himself. He kicked the table so it skittered noisily across the tiles. He sat silently in a chair where he could watch all sides of the piazza for safety's sake.

Braxton unclasped his hands and puffed out his chest, uncertain what to do. 'Are you still there . . .?' The silence made him anxious so he spun around to see what was happening.

Pat held the pistol firmly in his hand, resting it on his knee so it was pointing at Braxton. He relished the power it gave him.

'Look here, Romain . . .' Braxton edged sideways, shielding himself behind a pillar. 'I've done all you asked of me. Leave my gun and get out.'

He stood up and put the gun in his belt, noticing the tension leave Braxton's face. 'I shall keep this, Cletus, in case you are tempted to renege on our deal.' He patted the handle.

Braxton sighed and the anger drained out of him. He sat down heavily on a chair and covered his eyes, waiting a minute before he looked up.

'I'm still here,' Pat said to taunt him. 'I'll go soon enough, after I drink the health of the happy couple. You can be sure I don't want to spend a moment longer in your house than is necessary.'

Braxton gestured at him to go away, muttering under his breath.

'Say it to my face, Cletus. Look me in the eyes like a man instead of the lecherous bully you are.'

'I'm warning you!' Braxton pointed at him accusingly, and he saw the hatred in his eyes.

'You've provoked me enough. Keep away from the mansion, from me and my daughter. If I hear you've attempted to speak to Deborah, it will be the end of your smart ass ways for ever.'

'I'll remember.' He chuckled although he couldn't shake off the apprehension stirred in him by Braxton's evil glare. He swung around and strode to the door into the parlour, feeling the planter's eyes burning into his back. He realized then that even with his sister safe, one careless move and Cletus Braxton would exact a painful and humiliating vengeance on him.

'Where have you been?' Jeanette's question when he entered the parlour helped him steady his nerves.

'Talking with your father-in-law.' He smiled to reassure her. 'Do you feel all right?'

'Of course.' She glanced at the other side of the room where Marlon was talking excitedly to Arnie Goodpaster. 'He's rather sweet really. Thank you.' She rose on tiptoe and kissed him on his cheek.

He felt someone watching him and turned and saw Deborah. He winked at her but she gave him a withering look before lowering her long, black lashes and moving away. His spirits soared.

'Marlon,' he called, striding across the room and extending his hand. 'Let me congratulate you. Take care of my sister.' His voice was raised so all he said could be heard by Deborah.

Marlon's hand was limp in his own and he released it hastily but he took the glass of whiskey Marlon offered him.

'I wouldn't mind being married myself one day,' he said, glancing at Deborah. She was staring fixedly in the opposite direction. 'I need a strong woman with a mind of her own. Someone who's ambitious.'

'You have some big ideas, son.' Arnie sneered at him over his whiskey.

'Why not? Who'd have thought a few weeks ago that you and I would be standing in this parlour drinking the health of Marlon and my sister?'

Marlon giggled. 'I like you, Pat.' He gazed up at him through bleary eyes. 'You're a sport.' He swayed, losing his balance until Pat steadied him. 'Lesh have another drink.'

'Later.' Pat moved away, intercepting Deborah as she was about to leave the room. Mrs Walsh was in front of her, escorting Mrs Braxton, and couldn't turn back. He placed his hand on the doorjamb and leaned across the doorway, blocking her exit.

'You're not *Miss* Deborah to me any more,' he said, grinning expansively to show his friendliness. 'We're related by marriage now, Deborah. Just like brother and sister.'

'Really?' She studied his face unhurriedly, feature by feature.

His gaze lowered pointedly to her breasts, his lips moistening at the view of her exquisitely curved bosom. The deep red velvet of her dress heightened the translucence of her neck and face. His gaze arched slowly back and forth.

She leaned forward, her voice sizzling with disgust against his ear. 'I have a drunkard for a brother, a conniving chamber maid for a sister-in-law and you, a goatish, moronic, blackmailing tobacco-grubber as a relative! I hate you.' She pushed his arm out of her way and swept through the doorway.

'Deborah!' He ran to the foot of the stairs and called after her. 'If you forget your ideas of your own importance then you could live a little too.'

He quaked inside at his rudeness, blaming his anger on what she'd said about Jeanette. He slunk out of the mansion by the back way, embarrassed by Marlon's drunken shouts and his sister's happy laughter.

Angrily he tore off his cravat and flung it away. It caught in a magnolia bush and hung there like a demented banner. He pulled off his coat and hooked it over his shoulder with his thumb. He plodded in despair from the mansion garden down the trail to his home.

'Why do you sleep with that gun beside the pallet?' His mother stood over him with the steaming morning mug of coffee in her hand.

He shook the sleep from his eyes. 'It's Braxton's,' he said lazily. 'I'm saving it for him.'

'I hope he don't send a gang to collect it.'

'We're all right, Ma.' He took the coffee from her. 'Aren't you happy Jeanette's married Marlon? No one can push her around again.'

'That's what you say.'

He shrugged his shoulders as she left him to dress. It was impossible to know what would make her happy. He had tried to explain to his father that Five Acre Field was theirs again. The old man showed a flicker of interest until his mother poured scorn on the idea and told him to clear out of her way and fix up the house.

Even when he did that, rebuilding one side with new timber and putting a solid support under the porch and replacing the rotten railings with new ones, she had demanded to know how they could afford it.

'I mortgaged next year's tobacco crop,' he told her. 'We've plenty of money. Whatever the field yields is ours to sell. It ain't Braxton's.'

Her reaction had been a gloomy downturn of her mouth and an exaggerated glance upward in appeal to the heavens to protect her from her son's extravagance.

He dressed slowly that morning, aware of the changes in the household since Jeanette's marriage. His mother lived in constant dread that a calamity would befall them. She regarded him reproachfully when he stayed in the house, and waited anxiously for his return when he went out.

Summer had given way to Fall and a change in the weather. It was the time for rain when the air-cured tobacco was taken down, bulked in piles, covered, and left for a week or two. The process humidified the leaf and made it pliable. Pat found it strange not to be involved as he had been for the previous five years.

He stepped out into the small parlour to face his mother. 'You stayin' home 'gain today?' she demanded.

'No, Ma.' He shook his head, handing her the empty coffee mug. 'I'm going to help Sarah's papa at the still.'

'Jed Allason managed well enough before you had time on your hands.' She sniffed.

'What would you like me to do instead, Ma?' There was a note of desperation in his voice. 'The garden's dug, the field's cleaned, the house is repaired . . .'

'What happened to your plan to own your own plantation? Is this it?' She gestured out of the door at the Five Acre Field.

He tugged his ear. 'I'm thinking about that.'

'You should go away from here, Pat. Before the worst happens.'

'Why are you scared, Ma? Cletus Braxton don't have time to even think of me. Jeanette said he's going to live in Washington.' He watched his mother's wrinkled face lighten at the news.

'Then I hope he takes Miss Deborah with him,' she snapped. 'She'll meet a good man there and be an asset to her father.'

He felt oddly insulted by her remark. 'Why should you want that?'

'Because if she ain't here you'll be yourself again and won't believe you have a chance with her.'

'You don't think I have? I bet I saw her smile at me when she rode past in the carriage last week with Mrs Walsh.'

His mother seized the broom and smacked it across his backside. 'When will you grow up?' She ushered him to the door. 'Since you're going to help Jed Allason, make sure he puts aside a couple of bottles for your pa.'

If there had been a way to include Deborah in the deal he made with Braxton, Pat would have done so. Her persistent refusal to treat him like the charming, well-intentioned young man he was really, baffled him. He glanced over the fields to the mansion before he made his way towards the river.

Jeanette had told him Deborah behaved the same way with everyone although she could be pleasant in company. With Jeanette she was coldly polite and never made any mention of Pat. Her one joy was riding which her father forbade her to do. She defied him on occasions when he was away and she could escape without Mrs Walsh knowing.

He wanted to see her again. He believed five minutes alone with her would be enough to convince her he was not as bad as she thought. He walked into the trees to the still racking his brains, trying to think of a way to neutralize her contempt for him so he could prove his sincerity.

'You're brooding again,' said Sarah, seeing his frown of concentration when he reached the cabin. 'Papa ain't coming today.' She put her hand on his arm and led him out of the sun's glare to the river bank.

He sat down at her side, letting his frustration burst out in a great sigh. The river was murky, brown with mud washed into it by the rains draining off the tobacco fields. He watched it dolefully.

'Can I help?' said Sarah, running her fingers up his legs.

He pushed her hand away. 'No, you can't. Do what you like and I'll still feel the same about her. I remember telling Anne Carter not to waste her time when she thought she was in love with me. I know I'm not in love with Deborah. I just want her. Sometime she'll be mine, you'll see.'

'Then stop moping and fretting and be useful again.'

'Ma said something like that too.' He pulled away as Sarah's fingers reached for him again. 'I'm going for a walk,' he said, standing up suddenly. 'You're right. I'm not going to waste my time here.'

'But, Pat, I thought we could –'

'I'm sure you did!' He ignored her hurt expression and hurried away.

Mary was coming down the trail towards him. She smiled coyly. 'I've brought pancakes for breakfast.'

'I don't want it!' He brushed her aside and strode along the path, feeling wretched. He was behaving towards Mary and Sarah in the same manner Deborah behaved towards him.

It was too late to return and apologize. He would make it up to them when he had burned out his anger in a long walk. The day was overcast and cool, ideal for vigorous exercise. If he had a horse of his own he could have ridden to Richmond and back. Anything to use up his energy, and calm him down so he didn't feel so ill at ease with the world.

He walked for miles that morning. Afterwards, he couldn't remember where he'd actually been to. Neither hunger nor thirst slowed him down. He greeted people he met on the trails with an uncharacteristic curtness, overtaking them and forgetting them instantly as he drew away from them to walk by himself. His eyes were black and dazzling with fury, deterring anyone who tried to detain him with a kind word or greeting.

He was preoccupied with his despair. Options and ideas twisted through his mind, leaving his brain reeling with ill-defined problems. After hours of aimless walking, he realized it was pointless to try to resolve a nebulous frustration he couldn't identify. He turned and began the long walk back to Braxton County, knowing from the setting sun which trails to take.

It seemed hours before he reached the familiar surroundings of the tobacco fields; they were deserted and overgrown with weeds now the crop was finished. The track ahead of him was straight for a mile before it divided into the drive to the Braxton mansion and the trail to the river and his home.

It was nearly nightfall. He wondered if Mary and Sarah would be at the still. They were good, simple girls. He liked them both in different ways. It was a pity he could not marry them both, and the Sprowle twins as well.

Of the four, he had decided to choose one . . . Sarah. He would marry Sarah and settle down. With the produce from Five Acre Field and her father's still, there would be enough money to keep her family and his own comfortably. That surely would please his mother.

The image at the end of the trail, with its cloud of dust swirling behind it, was someone riding at great speed. It grew rapidly from an indistinct blur to a rider and horse galloping towards him. He wondered curiously who was coming and why the rider was in such a hurry.

An inkling that it had something to do with him sprung to his troubled mind. He tried to dismiss the idea as too fanciful but failed. Intuitively, he knew the rider sought him. Only Cletus Braxton had horses so fleet. Maybe his sister had been taken ill and someone was riding from the mansion to call him?

He stopped and stared, uncannily aware that something momentous was about to happen. He stared again, finally recognizing what he had suspected all the time: the rider rushing towards him was Deborah.

From her stance he realized with horror that something was wrong.

Instead of holding the reins with her customary smirk of dare-devil excitement, fear was etched into her face. She had lost control of the horse and lay across its back, clinging uncomfortably to its neck. She was seconds away from being thrown from the speeding animal and dumped under its hooves to the ground.

He dived for the horse's head, his fingers catching at the bridle. The horse faltered but did not stop, dragging him off his feet as he fought to bring it to a halt. He hung on, the scraping of his boots against the ground drowning the sound of Deborah's low moan of panic.

Unable to shake him off and hampered by his extra weight, the enraged horse gradually slowed. Pat forced his feet into the hard mud of the trail and brought it to a standstill. He clutched the reins and turned to look up at Deborah.

She slipped down from the back of the horse into his arms, placing her head gratefully against his heaving chest. He panted, holding her lightly, guiding her shaking legs to the ground.

She fell against him, her eyes glazed with relief. Slowly, he laid her down at the side of the track.

CHAPTER TEN

'Are . . . are you all right?'

The feel of her body, hot and quivering in his arms, made his flesh stiffen. His hands encircled her, one hand in the small of her back, the other gently caressing her shoulders. Her breasts were crushed against the hardness of his chest, her thighs clashing against his. Her breath tingled his cheek in long, surrendering moans. Her eyes were closed and she shuddered.

He whispered softly into her hair, 'Deborah, what's wrong?'

She clung to him when he tried to move away. His loins were rigid, throbbing with the ache of desire her closeness inspired. He wriggled so she couldn't feel the pressure and be frightened by his need.

Her craving for comfort and her submission to his embrace was a reaction to the trauma of her ride. She was dazed, unaware of what she was doing. He could feel the beat of her heart against his chest, transmitted through the taut flesh of her bosom.

'You're safe, Deborah,' he said softly to reassure her, rising to his feet. 'Lie still, relax, take deep breaths.'

When her fingers reached out and touched the muddied leather of his boots, he knelt again at her side and gripped her shoulder. 'I'm not going.'

He felt a great responsibility for Deborah. The demand of his body meant nothing compared with her safety. She was more shocked than she knew, she was acting like a woman in a trance. He drew away from her gradually so he could walk over to the horse. It was snorting from its crazed gallop but seemed calmed from whatever had disturbed it. He secured its reins to a tree.

Glancing back, he saw Deborah sit up slowly. She was watching him with listless grey eyes, devoid of emotion. Her face was tense with exhaustion.

'Your horse must have bolted,' he said, not sure if she was fully aware of what had happened. 'You nearly fell. Lucky I was here and stopped it.'

Her eyes flickered, filling with the sour thoughts that flooded her mind as her face formed its familiar aloofness. But it was too late to deceive him. He had felt desire throbbing in her limbs when he held her.

'What do you mean?' she said primly. She tried to stand but her legs were weak and trembly.

He made no effort to help her. 'Rest awhile. It's a long walk home to the mansion.'

'I could have stopped him.' She tightened her lips, seemed to find the distance he kept from her was acceptable, and added cautiously, 'Father will be furious if he knows. He always warned me I would take a fall . . .'

He shrugged his shoulders, smiling to put her at ease. 'I'm not the one to tell him.' He patted the horse's neck, wishing he could trace his fingers down her neck instead.

The horse's saddle was askew so he tried to straighten it until the horse became agitated at his touch and he inspected the saddle carefully. A strap had been caught up underneath it, the pin from its buckle digging into the animal's flesh.

'That's what caused him to bolt,' he said, showing her. 'As you rode, the pin pricked him, digging in deeper all the time. Your groom didn't saddle him properly.'

She pursed her lips, her eyes studying him speculatively. 'I saddled him myself.' The defiance in her voice died. 'I was in a hurry . . .'

'Mrs Walsh?' he asked with an understanding smile. 'You wanted to escape before she could stop you?' He walked over and held out his hand to help her to her feet.

She hesitated, lowering her eyes until her gaze rested on his thighs. She shivered.

'I'm not as bad as I'm painted,' he said. 'Let me help you stand up.' He bent down and grasped her hand before she could withdraw it. She hesitated for a moment and then a cramp seized her leg and she had to rely on his arm for support. He didn't flinch, letting her steady herself in her own time.

She held on to him loosely while she stamped her feet to

restore her circulation. She released him and smoothed the skirt of her pleated riding habit down over her thighs. Removing her bonnet, she tossed her head, sending her ringlets spinning like a shimmering flame. She patted her hair hastily into place and retied the bonnet.

'I'm battered and bruised all over,' she said self-consciously.

'You'll ache more in the morning.' He wanted her to relax and feel at ease with him. Leading the horse a few steps away from her, he looked back rapidly. There was a pensive glint in her eyes until her expression hardened when she saw he was watching her.

'The horse is too sore to ride. Are you able to walk?'

'Of course I am!' She seemed to relent. 'I wasn't aware you could handle horses.'

He flashed another grin at her. 'A country boy learns things. I have many talents.'

'I suppose you do . . .' In the silence that followed she appraised him.

He was aware of her eyes roaming intimately over his body. He arched his eyebrows and turned to her with a comforting laugh. 'You must have thought me a rough, ill-mannered lout before this. I don't blame you.'

'I still do.' Her grey eyes resumed their coldness. 'My father is due home tonight. I must return to the mansion immediately, before he comes.' She strode off along the path not waiting to see if he would follow.

He watched for a moment, enchanted by the spring in her step and by the flow of her long legs under her skirt as it swirled around her ankles.

'Perhaps I need the benefit of a lady's friendship,' he said when he caught up with her. 'It could help me be less of a lout.'

'Mr Romain,' she said archly, showing she had recovered her poise and peevishness. 'I do not wish to speak about you. You may lead my horse. Please do not feel this in any way changes the relationship between us.'

'I'm sure it doesn't,' he agreed affably, his heart dancing in delight at her attempt to re-establish her superiority. It meant he had a greater effect on her than she cared to admit.

'I do wish you would desist from mocking me. I am serious.' Her eyes sparked with fire.

'So am I.' He looked at her, his own eyes mellow and wide with innocence. 'Deborah,' he said decisively, 'you are the most beautiful woman I have ever been privileged to meet. Especially when you are angry.'

She recoiled, stung by the remark. She opened her mouth to rebuke him, sensed she was falling into a trap, and shut it firmly. She stared straight ahead, marching along in resolute silence, endeavouring to exclude him from her thoughts.

He was content to be striding one step behind her with the knowledge that her pliant, nervous body had been in his arms only minutes before. Given time, it would be again.

He was so engrossed in contemplating her, he didn't hear the sound of a carriage in the distance. She did, and turned abruptly, gripping his arm in total dismay.

'My father!' she said, blinking as though emerging from a dream. 'What shall I do?'

'Tell him the truth. He won't beat you.'

She looked at him reproachfully, and he felt he'd failed her. 'You don't know his temper. He's a violent man and hates to be disobeyed.' She realized she was clinging to his arm and instantly released him.

'Go,' she said, a cunning creeping into her eyes. She snatched the reins from his fingers. 'He won't have seen you yet.'

'I expect him to thank me for saving your life.'

'Hide!' She lengthened her stride, trying to get away from him.

He shook his head in bewilderment at her odd behaviour. 'If that's what you want,' he said. 'Shall I come to the mansion tonight?'

She ran on ahead without answering, leaving him standing alone by the side of the road. He cursed, annoyed with her and with himself for letting her leave him when they could have stayed together so she could explain everything to her father.

He wondered what was the reason for her display of fear. It wasn't like her. Glancing down the trail, he saw the carriage approaching rapidly. He wanted to do what she wanted, to please her. So he stepped off the road, disappearing into the gathering shadows where he couldn't be seen.

The coach passed his hiding place without stopping. Braxton was watching out of the window, his face a glowering mask of rage as he stared at Deborah running up the track in front of him, her horse following behind her.

Pat darted through the trees, keeping within the cover of the bushes so he wouldn't be seen. When the carriage overtook Deborah and stopped and her father jumped out, he was close enough to hear everything.

Braxton grabbed Deborah by her shoulder and pulled her to him. Pat was puzzled to see her bodice was ripped open and her breast exposed. Before he could think why, her father struck her a vicious blow across her cheek with the back of his hand.

'No!' she screamed, stumbling under the force of the blow. She raised her hands to her face and burst into loud sobs. 'He . . . he . . .' She shook, losing control and unable to speak.

Braxton's arm was raised for a second swipe at his daughter. Pat wished he had the pistol in his hand. He pushed through the undergrowth and prepared to leap out to restrain him.

'He . . . what?' Braxton demanded as his eyes fell on her pale, naked bosom and he realized she was trying to say something. 'Did someone do this?' His rage faltered. 'I told you not to ride alone. Cover yourself this instant. What happened? Who was it?' He shook her hard by her shoulder.

'Don't beat me,' she wailed, her tears vanishing now she had his attention. She raised her head, sniffing tremulously, and eased her breast under her corsage. Braxton clucked his tongue in exasperation.

'I'm sorry I disobeyed you.' Deborah pouted. 'I've learned my lesson now. I'll never do it again.'

Pat, listening in the undergrowth, waited for her to explain about the bolting horse and how he had saved her. Then he would push through the bushes and receive Braxton's approval, however grudgingly given.

'Tell me what happened!' Braxton demanded, ignoring Deborah's distress.

'He stopped the horse . . . dragged me from it . . . threw me to the ground . . .' The tears flowed from her eyes and she let out a heart-rending howl of shame. 'He tried . . . to rape me!'

Pat rose to his feet and took a step forward. Then the

implication of what she was saying struck him like a blow below his belt. He almost doubled up with the imagined pain. He sank down on his haunches, not daring to breathe.

'Who did?' Braxton seemed to know the answer to his question. 'The Romain boy?' His voice had an eagerness to it.

She nodded her head, ringlets bobbing freely on her proud shoulders and her face stained with convenient tears as she condemned him with her lie.

He watched, but scarcely saw, Braxton lead Deborah to the carriage. The horse was tied to it by the coachman and the carriage drove off at speed towards the mansion. He was under no illusion about what would happen next. His only thought was: *why?*

'To make you take the blame for her getting caught.'

He raised his head from his hands and gazed sheepishly at Sarah. He had told her and her sister, Mary, what had happened when he found them waiting at the side of the road for him to return. He sat with them wondering what to do.

Darkness enveloped the fields and the mansion was hidden from them. The two sisters had seen the carriage hurry past with Deborah sitting smugly by her father's side.

'Why accuse me of something I didn't do?'

Mary, who was sitting at his feet, rested her head on his knees, frowning into his eyes. 'I believe you,' she said. 'No one else will.'

'I do!' Sarah put her arms around his shoulders. 'I never trusted her. She's done it to save her own skin.'

'If that's right,' he said sadly, 'she can't know what she's begun. Braxton will lynch me. It's his chance for revenge.'

'What does he want revenge for?' Sarah hugged him. 'What have you done to him?'

'It doesn't matter.' He was too dejected to stop her hand rubbing across his chest.

'She can't *prove* you did anything to her.' Mary was indignant. 'It's her word against yours.'

'You know who her father will believe.' Sarah scoffed at her younger sister.

'We must *make* her tell the truth. How you were so brave.'

'No!' He patted Mary's hand gratefully. 'She wants it this

way. It's to protect her. Her father's evil, I know that. If I save her from his wrath, I don't mind taking the blame.'

'For something you didn't do?'

'You'll lose your life for her lie!' Sarah held his chin in her fingers to make him look at her. Her eyes glowed with outrage in the dark.

'I'll *change* my life, not lose it.' He relaxed his tense expression into a courageous smile to resassure them. 'Mary, will you help me?'

She looked at him fiercely, amazed that he should doubt her wish to do so. 'How?' she asked eagerly.

'Go to the house. See if Braxton's men are there. If it's safe for me to come, give a whistle.'

Her eyes sparkled. He blew her a kiss of encouragement and she dashed off into the darkness.

'She's a good girl.' He stood up, searching in the darkness for Sarah's hand and drawing her towards him. He held her while he pressed his lips to hers, caressing her mouth more than kissing it.

She clung to him when he tried to withdraw, wanting to savour every moment. Her hands rubbed up and down the broad, hard lines of his back and her body arched towards him.

'It's odd,' he said, wresting his mouth from hers. 'Tonight I was going to ask you to marry me.'

She gasped with disbelief.

'It's impossible now.' And in his heart he knew it wouldn't have been right, but he said nothing to her about that.

'What are you going to do?'

He began to walk with her across the field towards the light burning on the porch of his home. 'Whatever ma tells me.'

'Shall I wait for you?'

'You might die an old maid if you do, Sarah. I'll always remember you.' He fondled the curve of her buttocks in the dark and she squealed with delight. 'You and Mary will find husbands who'll treat you better than I could.'

'You always were special . . .'

He heard the whistle as they approached the house. Sarah stopped and wiped her eyes with the back of her hand. He kept on walking without looking back.

Jeanette was on the porch with his mother. They were both peering anxiously into the darkness. Jeanette had a cloak wrapped around her, hiding her size.

'Hello, sis,' he said softly as he reached the house. 'You've heard what's happened?'

'How could you, Pat! I came straight here to warn you. Mr Braxton's in a fury. You must go away at once.'

His heart lurched in dismay. 'You don't know how it happened. It's not true what she said.'

'Deborah's bodice was torn. I saw it myself.'

'She tore it herself.' He gripped the balustrade to calm his anger that neither she nor his mother doubted the story. Bitterly, he told them the truth.

Without a word, his mother left the porch and went inside the house. He waited in silence until she returned.

'Your clothes,' she said simply, handing him a bundle. 'You must sleep at Mort's tonight.'

'Ma . . .!'

'I know, son. It's for the best.'

'What about you? Braxton's men will come here looking for me. They could smash up the house when they don't find me.'

'Not with me here!' A voice growled from the darkness.

He stared at the end of the porch in amazement. His father was sitting there on an upturned whiskey barrel, chewing tobacco. Braxton's pistol was resting on his lap.

'Pa, you spoke!'

'Sure did, son. Got to guard Five Acre Field so they don't take it from us again. I'll grow tobacco there myself come Spring. Me and the boy can do that.' He patted the head of Tombo who sat on the floor at his side like a faithful puppy.

'I'll tell Mr Braxton you've gone away,' said Jeanette. 'He won't send his men here then.'

'Just tell him I've gone to Orange County.'

She looked at him quizzically, then remembered something. 'Marlon sent you this.' She passed him a leather purse.

'It's heavy, sis.' He gripped her hand, frowning his question, feeling that his words would dissolve into tears if he tried to speak.

'Marlon was worried about you. He said you must take the

money and buy passage on a ship. He told you there're opportunities in lands beyond Africa where America's started trading.'

'How does he know that?'

'He's not drinking so much. He must have heard about it from his friends.' Jeanette's eyes brimmed with love. 'He doesn't believe Deborah's story. He said he wants to help you.'

He kissed her on both cheeks then turned to hug his mother. On impulse, he pressed his lips against hers, holding her firmly in his hands while she squirmed with embarrassment at his kiss of farewell.

'Be a relief to get you out of the house,' she said, blowing her nose into her apron as he stepped off the porch.

'Good luck, son!' The defiant voice of his father echoed over Five Acre Field.

He glanced in the direction of the mansion, whispered 'Goodbye' to Deborah with a tenderness she would never know, and strode out into the night.

BOOK TWO
Mauritius, 1810–1813

CHAPTER ELEVEN

'The Isle of France?' said Pat to his companion, stepping from the skiff into the surf rolling up the beach. He walked through it to the shore, wetting his boots. 'I've never been more pleased to be on land, whatever it's called.'

He crossed the shingle and climbed up the side of a sandy, grass knoll, pausing there to flex his legs, expecting the ground to roll beneath his feet. When it didn't, he chuckled, his laugh sweeping back in the breeze to the man who was following him.

'Haven't got my landlegs yet,' he said, trying to quell the nausea that rose in his throat. 'So long since I walked on firm land. It's a relief to know it isn't going to dip under my feet and toss me on my backside to the other side of the deck.'

His companion slapped him on his shoulder. 'You adapted to the sea fast enough. You'll do so on land. In a few moments the queasy feeling will pass.' He paused, then added in a more serious tone. 'You've become a real sailor.'

He looked at the older man. Jem Puttock was the supercargo of the *Apollon*, the vessel he had sailed on from Baltimore. Jem was in charge of the commercial concern of the voyage, under its captain, James Lattimer.

He had secured a berth on the ship because of the money given to him by Marlon. In the eight months he had served as Jem's assistant, he had learned to be grateful for his praise. It was seldom given.

'I had to adapt!' He laughed to himself. 'It was either that or swim back to Baltimore. I've had enough of it now.'

'We'll only be anchored here a few hours.' Jem scanned the town beyond the beach. 'This is a French colony. American vessels aren't allowed by law.'

Pat was dismayed. 'We outsailed two ships of the British Royal Navy that are blockading this island so we could come here. We deserve a longer welcome than a few hours.'

'Aye.' Jem sounded worried. 'We might get that too. The Governor needs our cargo. I hope he'll trade instead of seizing it. We'll not tarry.'

'Is there much danger?' He was conscious of being dependent on Jem Puttock for his safety as well as his knowledge. The supercargo's friendship had helped him survive the months at sea when homesickness drove him to despair. Now he was eager to explore.

'Keep your pants on when you're wenching and your hand on your purse. You should be safe.'

Pat snickered, even the talk of women made him hard. Excitement rose in his breast as he followed the supercargo into the town.

The island's capital, Port Louis, struck him as being a grand place. It was dominated by the residence of the Governor, a French general, and had a parade ground and an avenue of palm trees between the house and the sea. The supercargo had to deal with government agents there through an interpreter. The procedure looked to Pat like it would take up all the time they would be on shore so he announced he was going to stroll around the town by himself.

Jem was disappointed. 'You should stay here with me so you can learn about these wily Frenchmen,' he whispered while they waited in an anteroom.

'It's the wily French women I find more appealing.'

From the supercargo's shrug, he realized Jem was offended. Yet he could see other members of the crew of the *Apollon* strolling the town. Many of them were accosting the dark haired, buxom women who gathered in groups to watch them.

He was sorry to upset Jem's feelings when the man had been such a help to him at sea. Now he was on dry land he could fare for himself, even if he didn't understand the language. As far as he was concerned, he didn't care if he never saw the *Apollon* again.

He left the government offices and strode across the parade ground, marvelling at the promise of this tropical paradise. Even though it was the island's winter, mid summer at home in Virginia, the sun was warm to his face. On either side of the parade ground were warehouses built of granite blocks with palms and shade trees and masses of gaily coloured bougainvillaea bushes growing beside them.

While the buildings were solid and impressive, the roads were worse than the cart tracks of Braxton County. They were rutted and mired with great holes strewn with rubbish, impossible for carriages to pass. The inhabitants trod their way gingerly along the tracks. He saw someone of obvious importance being transported by a curious contraption like a closet. It had a pole at each of its four corners by which it was held aloft by four burly negroes.

While he was staring at this odd sight, he felt a twitch at his coat tail. He spun around in time to see a dusky-skinned urchin trying to pick his pocket. The child laughed and skipped away, daring him to give chase.

'Better luck next time,' he called after him cheerfully, knowing what little money remained was hanging in the purse from a cord around his neck. In the bright sunshine and the cooling breeze, in a town where female inhabitants were in abundance and there was an air of excitement, he was too happy to be angry with the lad.

'Ah, so you are English?'

He looked around at the woman who had spoken. She wore a shawl over her shoulders and held a parasol in her hand, shielding her face from the sun. She was hatless, with dark hair that framed the magnolia white of her features. Her eyes, which were coffee-coloured, watched him from under dark, sweeping lashes.

'No, ma'am,' he said, wondering if he should bow in front of this elegantly dressed vision. 'I am from Virginia.'

'*Virginia?*' She uttered the word with astonishment, drawing out the syllables with a sexiness in her voice that set off an eruption of craving in his loins.

'*Mais oui*, then you are from that vessel in the bay, *L'Apollon.*' She raised her dainty chin in the direction of the harbour, unaware of the effect she was having on him.

He covertly studied her figure beneath her shawl. 'Yes . . . yes,' he stammered, tongue-tied as she swept a lingering glance over the length of his body, from his untidy locks to his worn, damp boots, and back again.

'You must be very careful with your money,' she said softly, so he had to draw closer to her to understand her French-accented English.

'We are a poor people here, neglected by France. The island is blockaded by the English, so it is hard to live.' She sighed. 'You *do* have money, is it not?'

'Yes.' He patted his chest, not thinking until later that it was a stupid thing to do.

'Then Port Louis is yours. Whatever you want . . .' Her suggestive smile left no doubt about her meaning.

'I . . . er . . .' He couldn't believe his luck. Closer to the woman, out of the sun's glare, he saw she was older than he at first thought, but surely not over thirty. He was not fussy.

'My name's Pat,' he said, to cover his unexpected shyness.

'Call me Michelle.' She held out her hand at chest level and he took it wonderingly. For the first time in his life, he kissed a woman's hand on introduction, squeezing the tips of her fingers to show his interest, and letting his lips linger on her knuckles.

She arched an eyebrow and crooned dreamily, 'You have a magic in your lips, M'sieur Pat. It makes my knees tremble.' She twirled the parasol. 'I feel weak, all over.'

'Perhaps you should lie down,' he said with a grin, pulling his coat around him so she did not see the effect her voice and her hint were having on him.

'I do know a *café*,' she murmured, 'where they have rooms to rest in . . .'

'Let's go!' He held out his arm to escort her and she took it with a throaty giggle. He noticed with surprise that the men from the ship whom he could see in the square were all accompanied by women. Most of them were light skinned, but not with the fairness and quality of his own companion.

'My home,' she said, answering a question he had not asked, 'is in the country. I am now staying at an hotel that is very strict on young ladies.' She simpered. 'I cannot take you there in case they think . . . you know?'

He gulped at the implication. 'I understand.'

'Do you?' She flashed a glance of curiosity at him. 'You do not seem like a seaman. They are usually more . . . how do you say . . . *vulgar*.'

'I'm not really a seaman.' He was aware of her powerful

aroma, a perfume of spice and an essence of lust. 'I'm the supercargo's assistant. I pay him for the privilege.'

'You pay . . .' She parted her lips in an alluring smile.

'I had to. I wanted to leave America.' The tugging in his loins was making it difficult to concentrate on what he was saying. 'I'd like to stay here.'

'That would be nice.' Her voice was husky which made up for its lack of conviction. 'We have some American settlers.'

'How many?'

She pouted, shrugging her shoulders in an air of dismissal since it was of no interest to her. 'Perhaps twenty. Mr Buchanan is the consul.' She giggled. 'Yours is the fifth American vessel here this year. Two of the others were prizes.'

'Who captured them?'

'French privateers, of course. They do not allow American vessels here but we need supplies. It is the British who are blockading us because the privateers attack their ships bound for India.'

'You know a lot about it.'

'We are watching for our future, m'sieur.' She squeezed his arm confidentially. 'The British have already captured Rodrigues, our neighbouring island. Soon they will take the Isle of France too.' Her eyes sparkled.

'Aren't you frightened?' He guided her around an enormous trough in the road, filled with water and giving off a stench that made his nausea return.

'I love the British,' she said throatily. 'My governess came from England.'

He glanced at her again, trying to assess what kind of woman she was. Her dress and manners impressed him and she exuded an air of sophistication. Yet she had a blatant sexual appeal, like a whore, and it was causing him agony.

'How much further to go?' he asked, ashamed that he couldn't control his impatience.

She collapsed her parasol and indicated a doorway with a tilt of her head. It was a wooden building, not like the granite warehouses of the waterfront. It reminded him of the outside of the slave huts of Braxton County with its wooden shuttered windows and wide open door. His enthusiasm wilted, giving way to apprehension as he followed her inside.

After the sunlight in the street, he could see nothing, only feel the heat given off by the presence of lots of people packed into the confines of a small room. He lost Michelle in the crowd and peered anxiously about him while his eyes adjusted to the gloom.

A hand grasped his wrist and pulled. It was Michelle and he followed her through the crowd to the other side of the room where he could see more clearly.

'What is this place?' he shouted above the din of people shouting, talking and laughing drunkenly. Someone played a fiddle and two men danced together, jostling him. 'I thought we were going somewhere . . . private.'

'We are.' Her smile was brief. A youth pushed between them carrying a jug of rum and four glasses which he took to a table. He was back in seconds, wiping his hands on his pants. He stood in front of Pat, waiting.

'Give him some money,' said the woman crisply. 'For the room.'

He swallowed the uneasy feeling that he was being led into a trap. He could walk out. The woman's hand caressed his waist and even through the material of his coat her touch excited him. *Too long at sea*, he thought with a sigh of resignation.

Regretting how obvious he looked, he pulled his purse from under his shirt and extracted a coin from it. It disappeared from his hand before he could see its value. The youth moved away.

'Come with me,' said the woman, leading him through a curtain of plaited straw into a corridor. There were cubicles on either side of it, the only light coming from a window open to the sea at the end of the passage.

The air was tainted with the smell of rotting fish and an odour of stale sweat and damp. He heard giggles and grunts from the cubicles as he followed Michelle the length of the corridor. To his dismay, she stopped in front of one of them, lifted the curtain at its entrance and peered in.

'This one's empty.'

His eyes grew accustomed to the gloom. He frowned and looked in. On the floor there was a pallet covered with a grimy blanket that seethed with a life of its own. There were cockroaches gathered around a stain in its centre.

Michelle shooed them away with her foot and they scurried under the pallet. She was about to sit down when he stepped over to her and managed to stop her.

'Is this . . . the best there is?'

Her smile mocked him. 'We are poor people. This is not what I am used to, either, M'sieur Pat.' She shrugged her shoulders, removing her shawl and handed it to him.

There was a nail in the wall of the cubicle and he draped the shawl carefully over it. Apart from the pallet there was no other furniture in the cramped space.

'Who comes here?' he asked, wondering how to avoid having to lie down on the mattress. The sound of guffaws, whispered conversation, and the exaggerated moans of females express-ing false delight reverberated around him from the other cubicles.

'The settlers,' she replied, sliding her hands under his coat. 'And sailors. Are you not going to undress?'

He needed time in that atmosphere. 'How many settlers are there in the island?' he asked conversationally.

A grimace of exasperation crossed her face as she changed from an elegant female to a woman impatient to conclude her business.

'About eight thousand,' she said with another shrug when she saw he was determined to talk. She unfastened her bodice. 'There are sixty thousand slaves too. There are so many more white men than women, a lady is very busy.'

He missed the hint because the sight of her breasts drew him like a magnet. He reached over as her bodice fell away and rubbed his hand over her bosom, pinching her dusky pink nipples.

She smiled at him archly and put her hands on the collar of his coat. He slipped from her grasp and removed the coat himself. He was about to let it fall to the floor when he remembered the cockroaches. He hung it on the nail, over her shawl.

She was waiting when he turned back to her. Her bosom was bare and she was watching him enquiringly. 'We lie down?'

He shook his head, taunted by the shapely beauty of her naked body. He gripped her waist, feeling the soft flesh in his hands like a piece of silk. He was ashamed of his roughness as he bent forward to kiss her lips.

She turned her head so his mouth brushed against her cheek. Her hand slipped between his thighs and her deft fingers found the hardening length of his penis. She squeezed and he shuddered involuntarily, pressing his mouth against the tendons of her neck, eating his way down to her breasts.

'M'sieur Pat,' she breathed into his ear, 'you have for me a cash money present, yes?'

'I hadn't thought of that . . .' His eyes bulged as she rubbed her fingers around his crotch.

'Give it to me now,' she said. 'And I give you the *everything*.' She withdrew her hand and pushed him away.

He was desperate for her to hold him again. The sight of her bosom swam before his eyes. 'Now I'm the one who feels weak,' he joked, shaking his head. 'It must be the heat.'

He pulled his purse from its hiding place against his chest and opened it. His fingers trembled and he fumbled to extract a coin. He looked at her leaning against the wall of the cubicle, her bright pink tongue protruding between the dark rose satin of her lips. He took out a second coin.

'Here,' he said, pressing the coins into her hand. 'It's a present, that's all.' He didn't want her to think he was paying her like she was a common whore. 'You're a nice lady.' His mouth dried as he lowered his head to kiss her lips.

She shifted out of his reach and tried to sit down on the pallet. He caught her by her arm and made her lean back against the wall instead. She was indifferent whether she did it standing up or lying down. She slipped her fingers in his belt but when she tugged, trying to remove his breeches, he remembered the supercargo's advice. He shook his head.

She stroked him expertly and he felt himself growing enormous in her grasp. He clutched her waist and drew her towards him, fondling her hips and thighs through the fabric of her skirt. She squeezed him until he was aching for release.

She let him go and wriggled away from him with a giggle, trying again to lie down on the pallet. When he refused to join her, she sighed at his fussiness and returned to the wall, leaning against it. She raised her skirt briskly. In the gloom he saw the curves of her robust hips and the dark hollow of her thighs. He pressed himself to her with a groan of wanting.

He was taller than she was and he had to bend his head to kiss her. In his haste, he missed her lips and his mouth closed on her nose. He raised a hand to the nape of her neck to position her head so he could kiss her properly.

His thighs banged against hers in a confusion of limbs. He was unhappy standing up but there was no other way. He withdrew from her, bent slightly at his knees, and tried her again, pushing upward, seeing her as she stood rigidly with her back against the wall.

It gradually became apparent to him that unless he lay down among the cockroaches on the pallet, he was not going to succeed.

Suddenly she snorted with exasperation, tired of his frantic efforts. 'Moment!' she grumbled, pulling away from the wall while he stood anxiously with his breeches around his knees. She turned and faced the wall, placing the palms of her hands flat against it to steady herself. She bent forward, shuffling backward with her feet. She reached around for her skirt and tossed it up over her hips.

The sight of the half-moons of her bare backside jolted him with desire. He edged forward to the beautiful caress of her hand guiding him closer. He poised and she opened herself with her fingers. He felt her on the tip of his being and drove in slowly.

With his hands, he held her breasts, feeling the smooth texture of her flesh against the calloused hardness of his palms. Her nipples were tight between his fingers and he teased them vigorously, causing her to sigh until she broke into a loud moan, thrusting backwards.

He slid his hand over her abdomen and up under her skirt, fingering her where she was impaled on him.

'*Mon dieu!*' she shrieked, abandoning her false grunts of pleasure for a shout of pure passion.

It was dark when she escorted him to the waterfront and left him. He stared out across the harbour wondering which of the bobbing lanterns swung from the mast of the *Apollon*. Her kiss was still wet on his cheek where she had pressed her body close to his in a lingering embrace of farewell. He shouted out to the *Apollon* for someone to meet him.

'Over here,' a voice said not far from his side. He walked over and was surprised to see a skiff hauled up on the beach above the surf.

'I've been waiting for you on Mr Puttock's instructions,' the boatman said.

'I suppose he's angry with me.' He gazed up at the sky and saw the stars diamonded against the blackness of the night.

'He will be if you don't hurry. We're sailing in an hour.'

'Sailing?' He was stunned. His thighs throbbed with the feel of the woman on them and he was in no mood to hurry. 'Why so soon?'

'Captain Lattimer believes the Frenchies might try to board and impound us in the dark. If you don't come now, you'll be left behind.'

He tugged at his ear. He didn't want to return to sea after such a short time on land. 'Tell Mr Puttock I'm sorry,' he said, surprising himself. 'I'm going to stay.' He turned from the boatman and hurried along the beach before he changed his mind.

He put his hand to his chest to reassure himself that his money was safe. He could live on that until he met one of the American settlers and got a job with him. He groped for the cord around his neck, seized with a sickening feeling of horror as he discovered it wasn't there. He felt inside his shirt, under his coat and all around his body. His purse had gone.

'Wait!' he shouted as he ran back along the beach. 'I'm coming!'

The skiff was beyond the range of his voice and his words were bounced back to him by the chill night breeze. He sank to his haunches on the beach, his anger changing rapidly to bitterness at his stupidity. The surf lapped the shore and the moon emerged from behind a cloud, outlining the island's jagged peaks and the tall palm trees surrounding the town.

'Well, I'll be damned,' he muttered. 'I'm marooned.'

CHAPTER TWELVE

He woke before sunrise, his body aching. At first he was confused by the sound of the sea without the pitch and rolling motion of being afloat. Only when he opened his eyes and saw the sky was still, did he realize that he was no longer on the *Apollon*. He stood up and walked to the sea's edge, dashing water on his face to revive him.

He was sticky under his clothes despite the chill of the dawn. He shook his clothes out to see if his purse was somehow concealed under his shirt or in his coat. He was not greatly put out at the loss of the money since the amount remaining of Marlon's largesse was small. His own gullibility annoyed him more.

He climbed from the shore on to the waterfront and surveyed the town. The sky was brightening as the sun rose beyond the range of broken mountains surrounding the town. The curious shape of the peaks, one flat like a table, one sticking up like a man's thumb, impressed on him the difference compared to the plains and rivers of Virginia.

He refused to feel homesick or downcast. Despite his inauspicious beginning, he sensed a cheerful, carefree atmosphere in the place and it appealed to him. He picked his way carefully along a street, aware of the vague shapes of people hurrying ahead of him. Some were carrying baskets on their heads, or loads slung on yokes from their shoulders.

He followed them to a street thronged with people milling around or squatting on the road with their baskets and heaps of garden produce in front of them. There was a low buzz of chatter, the dawn chorus of market vendors, as the grey-gold of daybreak gave way to morning.

The people in the street amazed him as much as the different kinds of produce they were selling. Every colour was to be seen in the women and men haggling with each other: there was the coal-black of the African and the tanned-leather features of the Indian; almond-eyed Orientals mingled with high-coloured half-breeds. There were even florid-faced Europeans sweating profusely as they pushed their way through the crowds.

No one took any notice of him so he found a corner where he could watch the hectic commerce of this native bazaar. He remembered being told about the British blockade reducing the availability of many goods. Even so, it was difficult for him to believe that the grass and roots on sale were for humans to eat. He recognized none of the fruits until the sight of pineapples reminded him of his own hunger and thirst.

'How much?' he asked, hunkering down in front of a buxom brown-skinned woman with her hair tied in a kerchief. She was seated before a pile of pineapples which she watched protectively. He pointed to one of them.

The woman's broad face turned to him blankly.

'How much?' he asked again, picking up one of them.

The reply was a torrent of a language he couldn't understand but which sounded abusive. The woman stretched over and snatched the pineapple from his hand, making it clear from her hostile gesture that she wanted him to leave her alone. He rose to his feet, puzzled at what he had done to cause her anger. Then he remembered he hadn't got any money anyway. Perhaps she knew.

He waited in the street for a while, fascinated by the scene and not aware of time passing. The crowd thinned as the produce was sold quickly. The pineapple lady did a brisk business and her heap soon disappeared, leaving none for him. His mouth was dry and his stomach churning. He walked despondently from the street, wondering how he could find something to eat.

A woman walked in front of him; she was tall and straight-backed and carried a basket on her head abrim with her purchases. Her hair, where plaits protruded from her madras-check headtie, was grey, and she moved with the controlled gait of age under the weight of her load.

He was about to overtake her when a bunch of bananas fell from her basket to the mud of the street at his feet. He grabbed it up from the ground, grateful that he had some kind of food at last. He glanced at the woman; she did not pause in her progress along the road and would be unlikely to miss a few bananas.

Suddenly he was filled with disgust at what he was about to do. *Have I sunk to stealing from the natives?* he thought scornfully. Holding the bananas out in his hand, he ran to catch up with the woman.

'Excuse me, ma'am,' he said when he reached her side. 'These fell from your basket.' He offered her the bananas, pointed to the basket and down to the ground.

She regarded him with astonishment. He tried to thrust them at her but she drew away in alarm, steadying the basket with her hands to prevent it toppling off her head. She did not falter in her stride.

'Dammit!' he said, embarrassed by the attention he was attracting as people turned to stare. 'These are *yours*.'

'*Merci*, m'sieur.' The woman still didn't stop but she looked at him with interest.

When he saw her glance, he grinned at her apologetically, curbing his impatience. 'You dropped them back there.' He waved down the street, still holding the bananas. The woman continued to walk, apparently expecting him to accompany her.

'Don't you want them?' he asked hopefully.

'But yes,' she said in careful English. Her smile was wise as she assessed him from the depths of her cautious, dark eyes. Her face, the colour of old tobacco, exuded a commanding air that made him wonder if she served a household of importance.

'I'm glad you speak English,' he said when the woman didn't say anything more. 'I think I frightened a lady selling pineapples because she didn't understand me.'

'Ah, yes.' The woman's smile broadened. 'I did see you.'

'You did?' He wiped the sweat off his brow, feeling foolish at the way he was behaving. The sun had crested the mountains and the day was bright; crows were circling above the market street, their loud cawing competing with the shouts of the vendors.

'Take your bananas,' he said, thrusting them at her again. 'I must be going.'

'Where? You are a stranger here, no? Where does a young man go at this hour? Your ship has sailed.'

'How do you know that?'

'I know many things, m'sieur.' She grinned at his surprise and added, 'A new face in town, especially one as *sympathique* as yours, is the subject of much gossip.'

'Is it?' He bit his lip, ashamed that he had drawn so much attention to himself.

'You look,' the woman said before he could leave her, 'like you are in need of coffee and a bath so you can begin the day like a man, not like a beggar . . .'

He was amazed by her insight until he realized how his bedraggled appearance must have made him look to her.

'My master's town house is at your disposal,' she said as though offering hospitality to strangers was nothing unusual. 'He favours the English and would welcome you but he is at present on his plantation at Flacq.'

'I'm not English.'

'That is not important.' She firmly dismissed any possible objection. 'You are a stranger in need.'

The street ended abruptly, the wooden houses on either side giving way to a level green plain almost the size of Five Acre Field. Beyond it, mountains formed a majestic backdrop. At the base of the rising hills surrounding the plain on its three sides, were houses more impressive than those in the market street leading to it. Some were of stone, others of wood painted white to resemble sturdier constructions. Gaily coloured flowers festooned their gardens, lending the plain an appearance of beauty and tranquillity.

'This is the Champ de Mars,' the old woman said proudly. 'In the afternoon, the belles of the town promenade here.' She chuckled. 'That is a sight to thrill you.'

He glanced at her again, disturbed that her knowledge of him was so uncannily accurate.

'People call me Ma Doudou,' she said as she led him up the path through the flower garden to the verandah of an imposing two storey house. 'You are welcome to the house of my master, Augustus Genave.'

She indicated that he should sit in one of the large hammock-like wooden chairs that faced out to the garden. A surly-looking youth emerged from the house and helped her lower the basket from her head to the floor. Finally she took the bananas from him, giving him an enigmatic smile before she followed the youth as he carried the basket into the house.

He sat down. The chair was upholstered with yarn made from coconut fibre, webbed over its frame to form a strong seat. Its pitch was deep and he sank into it, his legs supported by its raised front. The arms were long with an additional piece on each one that swung out, extending its length. It was a curious but comfortable chair.

From it, through the mass of flowering bushes and tropical foliage, he could see the green sward of the Champ de Mars plain. The air on the verandah was cool, with a gentle breeze wafted down from the mountains to its right. The town, now fully awake judging by the growing noise of crowds in its streets, was to the left, between the Champ de Mars and the sea.

He looked up at the sound of someone emerging from the house and gliding towards him. Instead of Ma Doudou, a young woman in the simple dress of a house servant eyed him curiously. She placed a bowl of coffee on a table at his side, together with bread rolls that had the tempting smell of being freshly baked, and a hand of bananas.

He picked them up. 'My bananas!' He grinned at the young woman. He was amused by her reaction since she did not seem the timid type. Her body was curvaceous and thrusting, with a face blessed with a smooth skin the colour of spun gold and dark eyes sparkling behind long lashes. She retreated slowly in to the house under his gaze.

As he sipped the coffee, his eyes strayed to the sea beyond the town. He knew then, with a flash of insight, that he had made the correct decision in staying on the island.

He was roused from his reverie, after he had eaten all the bread and the bananas, by the return of the young woman. She stood in the doorway of the house, beckoning him with her finger. Since she made no attempt to speak, neither did he. He concentrated instead on the undulation of her hips while she sashayed through the grandly furnished drawing room to a screen placed in the corner. She indicated with her eyes that he should step behind it.

He did so and saw a bath filled with water. A pail of water was on the floor beside it. Since it was obviously for him, he pulled off his coat gingerly, hanging it over the top of the screen. His shirt followed and he sat down on the chair to remove his boots. Then he realized the young woman had come behind the screen and was staring at his body.

'Is there something wrong?'

She smiled knowingly but made no attempt to leave. He removed his boots. When she still didn't leave, he stood up and peeled off his breeches, flinging them in her face. She caught them, grinning broadly as she gathered up the rest of his clothes and turned to leave.

'Hey! Where are you going with my clothes?'

She didn't answer. With another mysterious smile she was gone.

The water was cold, blissfully refreshing. He sank down into the bath, and soaked his tired limbs before scrubbing them vigorously with the lye soap. Although the bath was small for his large frame, he succeeded in soaping his body all over and in washing his hair. It wasn't as good as a bath in the Mattaponi but it cleansed him until he felt like a new man. He lay back, his eyes closed, letting the water soothe him.

A jet of cold water struck him in his face. He twisted in the bath with a shout. Wiping water from his eyes he saw the woman standing over him with the pail in her hand. There was a flicker of amusement in her soulful eyes as she emptied the rest of it over him.

'You should have warned me!' he said, standing up and splashing water over the edge of the bath to the polished floor. He pushed his hands in his eyes as he stepped towards her, pretending he couldn't see.

His attempt to hold her was blocked by a towel placed on his face and rubbed aggressively over his chest and down his abdomen. He remained still, feeling a heat rising in his loins as the woman's hand descended lower, towelling him dry.

She gripped his genitals roughly and squeezed, bringing tears to his eyes and causing his tumescence to fade.

'That's a cruel thing to do,' he cried, forcing her hand away. He was still tender from his lovemaking the previous day.

She broke into a wide, open smile, her eyes no longer sultry but flashing with mischief. 'Now you are dry,' she said in faultless English, 'you can get dressed.' She indicated the clothes that were draped over the screen, breeches, a shirt, a cravat and a coat.

'Stay awhile,' he said, reaching for her.

She laughed in his face, not unkindly but with a definite refusal. Her breath was sweet with an aroma of cloves. 'These garments belong to the master's son,' she said, handing him the breeches. 'He is your height.' Her eyelashes lowered. 'But not your build.'

'I am grateful.' He took the breeches and put them on slowly. He had a feeling he was out of his depth and it worried him. 'Why are you and the old lady doing this for me?'

She ignored the question. 'Ma Doudou is my mother. She likes you.'

'And I *like* you!' He fastened the breeches, searching her face with his eyes to see if she understood what he really meant. When she showed no response, he sighed, pulled on the shirt and completed dressing.

'How do I look?' He turned to face her when he had finished. His hair was wet and hung over his collar in damp curls. The breeches and shirt were a tight fit, but suited him.

The woman smiled strangely. 'Smarter than Lindsay. Now you must meet Mr Buchanan.'

'Your master?'

'The American consul. Troptard will take you there.' She left him without another word, disappearing into the depths of the house. He was puzzled by her behaviour, a combination of coquetry and intrigue.

The youth who had helped the old lady with the basket was waiting on the verandah. He was sullen and said nothing when Pat asked him about the woman and her mother. He gestured to him to follow and they walked out of the garden into the Champ de Mars. The youth stopped at the gate of a neighbouring house. He indicated that Pat should go through it and then he ambled back the way they had come. He pushed open the wicket gate and called out.

'Anyone at home?'

A voice answered gruffly from the depths of the verandah, 'Yes! Yes!'

He walked up the path through a garden laid out with tables and chairs, until he reached the front of the house. A man was sitting in one of the long chairs with his feet hooked over its extended arms. He lowered a ledger he was studying and waved at Pat to enter the verandah.

'Newcomer, eh?' The man extended his hand. 'William Buchanan, United States Commercial Agent at your service. Consul in all but name.'

'Pat Romain, off the *Apollon*.'

The man's handshake which began enthusiastically tapered to limpness when Pat mentioned his ship.

'Can't help!' the consul said immediately. 'Can't help!'

'I don't want your help.' He hid his dislike of the consul and assumed his most disarming smile. 'I'm a planter, from Virginia. I'd like to settle here.'

The consul coughed unhappily, torn between a desire to ignore him and curiosity. The latter won. 'Virginia? Did you ever see President Madison? He appointed me by letter when he was Secretary of State.'

'On my mother's side,' – Pat smiled – 'I am connected to his family.' He watched the consul's pompous face change from disdain to cordiality and decided his fudging of the truth was justifiable.

'Why didn't you say so at first?' The consul was alert now. He clapped his hands and ordered the old slave who shuffled to the door to bring burgundy and water. 'A guest,' he said, defining Pat's presence for himself as well as for the slave. 'No one told me a man of such eminence was aboard the *Apollon*.'

'The visit was so short –'

'The supercargo,' the consul interrupted him, 'took my warning too seriously. I told him there was a likelihood of the ship being seized. But I said I'd persuade General Decaen, the Governor, to turn a blind eye to his vessel's nationality. All he had to do was to sell his cargo direct to me, at a reduced rate of course. I'm a merchant. We have to trade with our own, not so? The fool took fright before I'd bought anything.'

'We heard American ships have been taken as prizes in these waters.' Pat wanted to keep the consul talking so he could formulate a plan for his future.

'They have. I can arrange things when it happens. We used to have two vessels a week put into the harbour. American vessels accounted for more than half the trade with the island. Then the French banned them, but the Governor knows we need their goods. The General can be amenable. Sometimes he trades, sometimes he impounds. The British are close, you see.'

'Do you think the British will invade?'

'Of course they will. Soon. The sooner the better. The French are demoralized without help from France, and the settlers are suffering. The island's been French for nearly a century, since 1715.'

'What will happen?'

'The settlers will welcome the British. Napoleon's caused them hardships.' Mr Buchanan picked up the decanter of burgundy offered to him by the slave and poured himself a generous measure. He added water from the clay pitcher then waved the slave over to Pat.

Pat mixed his drink the same way as the consul did, and tasted it appreciatively.

'Wine and water quenches the thirst and replaces the energy you lose in the heat.' Mr Buchanan smacked his lips and continued to speak, obviously enjoying having a fellow American to talk to.

'This island is suited for trade. Port Louis has a fine harbour even if vessels do need to be warped in. It's on the main trade routes, to the Cape and to India. It lies between the Orient and Africa. It's a fertile island.' He sipped his drink again.

'You're a planter you say? No better place to settle. Sugar, indigo, coffee, cloves, cotton, wheat, maize, millet, all grow splendidly here. You'll need some help of course, with the French authorities. I can help you, for a commission or a fee.' He paused, but Pat kept his eyes steady so the consul wouldn't know he had no money.

'Fruit and vegetables abound here,' Mr Buchanan added, as though to convince him. 'We've fish and game. It's nature's paradise, young man. I could go on extolling the virtues of the Island of *France*, which France doesn't appreciate, for ever.'

Pat took the consul's poor opinion of France as his cue. 'You evidently love the island, sir.'

'I married here, into an old merchant family. I'm well connected, you see. Creoles, good settler stock. A Creole is someone born here. Unfortunately,' he lowered his voice, 'some Frenchies satisfy their cravings, because of the shortage of European ladies, with other females. We call that leaving a portrait behind. Not I, sir.' He chuckled, drained his glass and filled it again from the decanter without offering Pat any more.

'What would you like from me first? Somewhere to live? An introduction to the Governor?'

'I'm staying at the house next door,' he began to explain his situation but Mr Buchanan interrupted him, without letting him go further.

'Old man Genave taken a shine to you?' His eagerness to help disappeared and he scowled. 'Fine Creole family.' He pinched his nose. 'Some portraits there though. What do you make of his son, Lindsay?'

'I haven't met him yet.' He shifted uneasily in his seat, aware that he was wearing Lindsay Genave's breeches.

'Nasty piece of work, that one. Keep clear of him if you value your honour. He won't like you at all.' Mr Buchanan studied him suspiciously.

'Do Americans own plantations here?' he asked to deflect the consul's scrutiny as well as gain information that could help him find a job.

'None of consequence.' Mr Buchanan had clearly lost interest in the conversation. 'As the guest of Augustus Genave you don't need me. He has the ear of General Decaen.' He rose to his feet, causing Pat to do the same.

'Without the approval of the General, and myself, young sir, you would have done better to stay on the *Apollon*.' The consul walked him to the edge of the verandah and nodded his head, dismissing him curtly.

He was apprehensive as he walked away from the house, puzzled by the consul's change in attitude towards him. He had hardly said anything for the consul to take offence. It was the mention of where he was staying that did it. Perhaps he should have told the truth, that it was Ma Doudou who had invited him to Mr Genave's house, not the planter himself.

His thoughts turned to Ma Doudou's daughter. Was she a

settler's portrait? The idea stimulated him and he shrugged off his doubts, walking jauntily around the perimeter of the Champ de Mars. He might find a way to paint a portrait too.

CHAPTER THIRTEEN

'What's your name?' he asked the woman, watching her hips swaying provocatively as she walked in front of him. She was showing him around the house.

'Claudette.'

There was no note of encouragement in her voice so he glanced around the parlour. Its floor was highly polished, reflecting the ponderous mahogany furniture in its glaze, giving the room a cool and sombre atmosphere. The ceiling was high with side vents for air to pass and its walls were thick, constructed of stone. The spaciousness of the large room was reduced to great effect with occasional tables, Queen Anne chairs with upholstery in Oriental fabrics, and lacquered screens.

He had never seen such opulence; Cletus Braxton's mansion was furnished like a slave hut compared with the town house. 'Mr Genave must be a very wealthy man,' he said with awe.

Claudette did not comment. She was opening the door of yet another room with the air of someone doing a duty for which she did not really care. He was intrigued by her attitude as each room revealed fresh wonders and she remained apparently unimpressed.

He saw Mr Genave's study with its great desk and elaborately carved chairs, and his bedroom with a four poster bed swathed in muslin to keep out the mosquitoes. There was a dining room with a refectory table to seat a dozen, a smoking room and a library with books in shelves lining the walls and a table on wheels containing crystal decanters filled with wines and various spirits.

'This is Mr Genave's second house,' said Claudette as though reciting a speech she had used often before. 'There is a small ladies parlour and guest chambers upstairs. His villa on the plantation is much bigger, of course.'

He blocked the doorway of the smoking room as Claudette turned to leave. 'Enough of Mr Genave, what about you?'

She hesitated, clearly expecting him to drop his arm and let her pass. He touched her chin, raising her head so he could see her eyes. She stared at him coolly, awaiting his next move with a display of indifference.

'Do I frighten you?'

She pulled away from his grasp and flashed her gleaming white teeth in a smile of scorn. 'No, of course not.'

He lowered his arm so she could pass. 'At least you looked at me then. You've avoided doing so all the time you've been showing me around this ostentatious house.'

She pouted, dismayed by his criticism. 'I didn't mean to cause you offence.'

'You haven't!' He grinned bashfully. 'Quite the opposite. You intrigue me. Why are you fierce with me one minute and coy the next. Are you teasing me?'

'I don't understand.'

He suspected she was deliberately taking refuge behind the language barrier. He glanced at her quizzically as she walked at his side along the corridor back to the drawing room. 'Yes, you do. I'll wager you have a full idea of what you're doing to me, here.' He touched his chest, indicating his heart.

Her gust of laughter mocked him.

'I mean it,' he said, frowning. 'You've captivated me.'

'You might ache for me *there*!' She bent suddenly and chucked her hand in his crotch. 'Not in your heart!' Her shrill laughter echoed in the corridor and she sped away leaving him doubled up in agony.

'Wait . . .' He drew several deep breaths until he could stand and the pain slowly subsided. He was alone in the corridor and leaned against its wall to think.

Far from being humiliated by Claudette's unexpected blow, he was enchanted by her. Apart from the air of mystery about her, she reminded him of the Allason girls. She was a sprightly filly who needed breaking in, and he would be the one to do it. He wondered how long it would be before Mr Genave visited his town house and his time as an uninvited guest would come to an end.

He strolled back to the drawing room and sat in one of the

stiff backed chairs hoping Claudette would come to see what he was doing. She didn't. There was no sound in the house. The only noise came from the Champ de Mars where officers were shouting commands in French and there was the heavy tramp of soldiers marching.

The activity drew him to the verandah. The plain was filled with men in a variety of uniforms, drilling in a desultory way despite the frantic shouts of their officers. There was an air of panic about the way they were being herded into columns in the heat of mid-morning. Men were fainting in the heat only to be left in the grass while the others marched around them.

The activity's purpose became apparent when one of the mobile closets – a palanquin – entered the plain from Market Street borne by four negroes clad in white breeches and military tunics, stained dark with sweat. The bearers deposited the palanquin close to the entrance to the Genave house, while the soliders were brought to attention by the perspiring officers.

A man in the uniform of a general stepped fussily from the palanquin. *Governor Decaen*, thought Pat. He had a good view of the governor since he was standing right outside the house. To his surprise, the general looked up at the verandah and seemed to acknowledge his presence with a nod of his head. Pat raised his hand casually in salute.

General Decaen had a worried look. He turned to face his troops, tapped his foot impatiently on the ground while he waited for silence, and then spoke in a high, fluting voice. Only the first rows of soldiers heard what he said. From the impassioned nature of his speech, and his gestures, Pat assumed he was urging the soldiers to fight bravely and defend French territory from aggression.

Claudette emerged from the side of the house carrying a tray covered with a cloth. She walked down the path, her back straight and proud, her hips rolling in a manner that suggested she knew his eyes were on her. She went up to the general with no sign of shyness and offered him the tray as he finished speaking.

General Decaen's smile of thanks was surprisingly intimate, his eyes holding Claudette's with a look of concern. She said something to him; he nodded, drank from the glass on the tray, wiped his lips with the cloth and returned the glass to her. He leaned forward and whispered in her ear. His hand, which Pat could see, touched the small of her back and slid as though by accident over her buttocks before he withdrew from her side. He turned and began walking through the ranks of his soldiers, inspecting them.

Pat stepped out into Claudette's path as she returned through the garden. The smile on her face faded when she saw him.

'What was that about?'

She pursed her lips and said nothing.

'I mean all those soldiers.'

She looked at him sternly and he got the impression he was not behaving the way he was supposed to. 'Stay inside the house,' she said quietly. 'No one must hear us speaking English.'

He did as she instructed, walking ahead of her through the verandah and into the drawing room. The shade in the room helped calm the excitement stirred by the heat, the marching soldiers and Claudette's proximity. He turned, longing to take her in his arms. Instead, she indicated that he should sit down.

'What luck you are dressed in Lindsay's clothes,' she said with a nervous smile. 'The General thinks you are French.'

'Is that what he told you?'

'He asked me if I have a new protector.'

He raised his eyebrow and lay back in his chair, stretching his legs out. 'You do!'

'The British are coming. The fleet has been sighted off the north coast. The soldiers are going to march there to defend the island from invasion. You must hide.'

'Why? I'm not English.'

'You are not French. That is what is important. They could shoot you as a spy.'

'Shoot me?' A knot of fear tightened in his stomach. 'I left Virginia because someone wanted to hang me. That was for something I hadn't done too.'

'You will be safe here,' she said briskly, ignoring what he said. 'They will never believe Mr Genave is capable of treachery in hosting a foreigner at a time like this. Ma Doudou will show you where to hide if any of the French come here.'

'What about Mr Genave? He might object to me being his uninvited guest.'

'He expected the invasion at the height of summer. It is late November now so he is right, as always. He will stay on his plantation at Flacq until it's over. Then he will make his own peace with the British.'

'You expect them to win?'

'But yes,' she said, her eyes wide. 'They have troops from Madras, Bombay, Bourbon, Ceylon and the Cape. Perhaps fifteen thousand men and a fleet of twenty ships of war, besides at least fifty Eastindiamen and transports.'

'Your intelligence seems better than the General's.'

'It is.' She shut her mouth firmly.

'Perhaps you are the spy, not I.' He chuckled. 'How many men do the French have?'

'Less than a third of the British forces.'

'Your General must be a very worried man.'

She smiled without speaking, her eyes sweeping over his outstretched legs and the bulge of his crotch in the tight breeches. 'He is brave.'

'If I can't go out in the town,' he said, 'what can we do?'

'We?' She rose from the chair opposite him. 'If you want to live, M'sieur Romain, you will do nothing, only what Ma Doudou tells you.'

'Where are you going?'

She paused as she was about to leave the room. 'Away from you,' she said pointedly. 'Before it's too late.'

Claudette, he could see, was like Ma Doudou. She had the old woman's commanding attitude as though he was bound to obey her. For the present, he would do so.

The surly Troptard served him lunch in the lonely splendour of the dining room. It was a stew of venison with the addition of burgundy and exotic spices that gave it a piquancy he enjoyed after the stale and weevily fare of shipboard life. He ate all Troptard placed on his plate and drank deeply of the excellent wine. If it weren't for the jarring sounds on the plain of the army preparing for battle, his contentment would have been complete.

'You have a lusty appetite,' Ma Doudou said when she entered the dining room as he finished the meal.

'Not for food alone.' He grinned, rising to his feet. 'I am indebted to you, madam, for your kindness. From what Claudette says, you are saving my life so I won't be shot as a spy.'

Ma Doudou hushed him to silence. 'You must sleep,' she said. 'In the master's chamber.'

'I couldn't –'

'Now! In case you need your strength later. There may be fighting in the streets. If the British attack this house, you must save it! Tell them you are American and that the house is yours. Mr Genave will reward you.' Her eyes defied him to protest.

He nodded, happy now he understood why she had brought him to the house. 'You are a wise old biddy, Ma Doudou. I'll try.'

'Mr Genave entrusted the safekeeping of the house to me. Providence sent you.' She smiled mysteriously, her grey plaits bobbing under her kerchief as she wagged her head. 'We must do what we have to do.'

'Where is Claudette?'

Her smile changed to an unhappy frown. 'She is not your concern. Please come with me.' She led him along the corridor to the master bedroom, pushing open the door for him to enter.

'Stay here,' she said. 'Sleep! I will call you if you are needed.' She closed the door firmly behind him.

He removed his boots then all his clothes because of the heat. He lay on top of the bed and pulled the muslin curtain around him. He did not intend to sleep.

He was puzzled how he was going to stop a conquering British army from ransacking the house. He could flee, of course. The shuttered window of the room opened onto the garden. He could escape through it and seek refuge with Mr Buchanan. Since the man was the American consul he should give him protection even if they had parted on less than cordial terms.

The delightful fragrance of mimosa drifted in from the garden. The room was shaded from the sun by the profusion of plants growing in the parterre. There was a subdued moaning sound as the breeze fluttered through the branches of a Madagascar fir tree. The murmur of a rivulet meandering behind the house added to the somnolence of the afternoon. He was asleep in seconds.

The touch that woke him was gentle. In the depths of the feather mattress, he felt safe, as though floating on a cloud, especially after the arduous months at sea and his night on the beach. He knew where he was and he lay in contentment, his eyes closed, while the woman's hands explored his body. Her touch was hesitant, expecting rejection. He moaned softly, feigning sleep while his loins stiffened under the gentle pressure of her fingers.

The soft caress of her lips tingled his cheek. He turned to her, his eyes still closed, and embraced her, the warm flesh of her body fusing with his own as she lay naked beside him, cradled in his arms. His hand lightly touched her hardening nipples and he marvelled at the fullness of her swelling bosom.

As he opened his eyes, she was looking into them. He blinked rapidly because she seemed to see into his soul. He kissed the soft tip of her nose, fluttering his fingers from her breasts to lodge between her thighs.

'Claudette,' he murmured, startled by the intensity of her response.

Tenderly he lowered his body over hers, hearing the passion of her gasps as he penetrated, gliding in on the moistness of her ecstacy. They throbbed and thrust in time, her strong limbs linked around his waist, her fingers clawing at his buttocks, as their desire exploded in a downpour of fiery sensations.

He lay with his head on her bosom, marvelling at its golden hue in the sunlight streaming through the cracks in the closed wooden shutters. The burnished copper buttons of her nipples were level with his eyes. He closed his lips over one and sucked on it until her fingers tore at the tendrils of hair at the nape of his neck.

'I adore you,' he whispered.

She said nothing, wriggling away from him. His head fell back into the embrace of the soft mattress and he became aware of her eyes lingering on him.

'Why are you sad?' he said, disturbed by the wistful expression that clouded her carefree features.

She shook her head, saying nothing as she moved from the bed, walking naked across the room. She passed in front of a ray of sunlight and it lit up pearls of moisture on her velvet skin. Her upturned breasts were proud, their nipples erect, her buttocks high and firm.

'You're like a wild animal,' he breathed with a pang of regret that their brief moment together was over.

She pulled her shift over her head and then flung open the shutter, letting the rays of the setting sun slant into the room. He raised his head from the mattress and gazed through the open window to the sea where the sun was poised over the horizon. The harbour was empty; all the vessels had put to sea.

'The British?' he asked lazily, content to remain in the chamber with her.

She waved northward without comment.

He remembered his duty. 'What about the French?'

'They have gone to intercept them.'

'Then we are safe?'

She shook her head, her eyes moist with sorrow. 'We will never be safe.'

'Why not?' He was puzzled by the doom in her voice. 'You can tell me,' he said encouragingly when she remained silent. He sat up in the bed and grabbed the muslin curtain, tugging it aside so he could see her face plainly. 'If something is wrong, I want to protect you. Claudette.'

'You are crazy,' she said flatly, stalking to the door of the chamber when he tried to hold her hand to detain her. 'Put on your clothes, *Lindsay's* clothes.' There was a hint of melancholy in her voice which he didn't understand.

'I've got my own clothes!' he retorted but it did nothing to lessen her despair.

'Ma Doudou burned them.' She left the chamber before he could answer.

He dressed slowly in the borrowed garments, realizing that his last link with his home in Virginia had gone. First Marlon's money was stolen and now his clothes had been taken from him too. They were only of sentimental value; his mother had washed that shirt countless times and laid it on the grassy bank of the Mattaponi to dry. In another man's clothes, in the house of a man he had never met, in a foreign land south of the equator, only half the size of Long Island, New York, he was without money and identity.

The feeling didn't disturb him until he wandered through the house and found it was empty. Claudette had disappeared and there was no one in the outside kitchen where he expected to find Ma Doudou. The house had been entrusted to him; it was a responsibility he didn't want.

Dusk was settling over the town with the swiftness that follows the tropical sunset. He walked the broad verandah, listening to the chatter of people promenading on the Champ de Mars. They were homeward bound before darkness was complete. He stepped out into the garden intending to take a closer look. Perhaps he could talk to someone who would tell him if the British were coming.

As he rounded a clump of bougainvillaea, a shape loomed out of the darkness and stood barring his path. It was Trop-tard. The youth nodded his head dourly, indicating that he should return to the verandah. For a moment he thought of pushing him aside so he would be free to roam the town.

'Claudette?' he demanded when Troptard didn't move. 'Where is she?'

'Claudette.' The youth nodded again, this time in agreement, gesturing back at the house.

With a sigh, Pat turned around and allowed himself to be walked back to the verandah. Troptard went inside the house, trusting him to stay, so he sat in a chair and watched the emerald sparkle of fireflies flitting in the branches of the flamboyant trees shading the house. When Troptard returned, he brought a lamp then moved around inside the house with a taper, lighting the candelabra. Soon the buiding was a blaze of light flickering gently when the breeze was roused.

Later Troptard beckoned him to the dining room where a dish of cold meat, bread and a bowl of fruit were set at the end of the long table, with a bottle of wine and a carafe of water. He was not hungry. His displeasure at being treated like a prisoner in the villa spoiled his appetite. Angrily he reached for the bottle of wine.

'Where the devil is Claudette?' he demanded of the sullen youth hovering behind him as he poured wine into his glass.

Troptard offered him the water jug and he waved it away. 'Claudette?'

Troptard looked at him blankly, placed the jug on the table and opened his palms, spreading them in front of him with a Gallic shrug of indifference.

He swallowed the wine. It was bitter and warming. His anger made him defiant. He poured himself another glass. 'What about Ma Doudou?' He might as well have been alone in the room for he got no response from Troptard. He reasoned to himself that she must be somewhere in the house unless Troptard had prepared the supper.

Although he was content to stay in the house, he hated being taken for granted by anyone, master or slave. He wanted to know what was happening. He turned on Troptard but the sight of the youth's impassive face made him too weary to argue, especially since Troptard showed no signs of understanding him.

He rose to his feet, the wine glass in his hand, and started to walk out of the dining room. He wanted the youth to try to stop him so he could punish him. He was in the mood to show that although he was destitute and a foreigner, he wanted to be treated with respect.

Troptard, perhaps intimidated by his warning scowl, moved out of his way. He reached for the door jamb to steady himself as the back of his knees felt strangely weak. His legs began to buckle underneath him. He grabbed frantically for support and found Troptard at his side. It occurred to him too late that it was the first time he had seen him smile.

He slid to the floor and Troptard made no effort to help him. His mind was muzzy and his vision blurred. He hit the floorboards with a thump. He struggled to stand but there was no response from his legs.

He was succumbing to an overwhelming weariness and there was nothing he could do about it. He tried to focus on the room as it spun in front of his eyes.

'The wine,' he moaned in despair. 'Drugged . . .'

He saw Troptard nodding happily in agreement, then he blacked out.

CHAPTER FOURTEEN

Pat swayed from side to side, the motion making him believe he was lying in his hammock aboard the *Apollon*. His head ached as he tried to remember his carousing of the night before and why he was at sea again. He listened for the creak of shipboard timbers and the rushing of the waves, only to find his dream disturbed by a discordant kind of song, a monotonous chanting of deep voices with a rhythm that matched the swaying of his body.

He opened his eyes in alarm. He was reclining on a soft mattress with a cushion for his head. Silk curtains hung at the sides of this narrow bed, their rose colour tinged with sunlight. He was fully clothed, even down to his boots. He experienced the strangest impression that he was somehow moving forward as well as being swung from side to side. Shadows drifted at speed across the sun-dappled curtains.

His bed had a roof; it was low with space for him to sit up. His head ached too much for him to try, so without moving his body, he cautiously opened a small gap in the curtain and peered out. His first sight was of trees, a forest that flanked the road and flashed past him in a blur. He closed the curtain, relieved that he was not at sea. The hills around Port Louis were burnt and dry, denuded of forestation, so he wasn't close to the island's capital.

His second glance, much longer now he seemed to be in no immediate danger, revealed the reason for the swaying. He was suspended in a palanquin, the type of conveyance he had seen on the day of his arrival in the island. Four bearers were trotting along the forest trail with the corner supports of the palanquin resting on their shoulders. Each carried a stick with which they poled themselves along as they sang a dirge that helped them maintain their steady pace. Each man wore only a blue cloth about his waist and a cotton handkerchief covering his head.

The palanquin lurched to a stop, flinging him against the pillow. His head ached too much for him to cry out and he remained motionless as the contraption was lowered to the ground. Although it was an opportunity to escape, he lay still, his senses alert, waiting to see what would happen.

An imperious voice demanded in French where they were going. His bearers shuffled uneasily, panting in the heat; no one spoke. The voice shouted again. He heard the sound of boots crunching on the gravel of the road and the clink of the weapon straps of an army officer as he approached the palanquin. The man's shadow fell over the curtain; Pat could smell his unwashed flesh, hot after a long march.

Although he had no idea of where he was going, or why, he was certain he must keep quiet. If the French officer discovered he could speak only English, he would assume he was connected with the British invasion and thus a spy. From the sounds of bolts being drawn on muskets, he was surrounded by soldiers. Escape was impossible.

The light as the curtain was drawn back sent a shaft of pain through his eyes. He closed them tightly, feigning sleep. He sensed the officer's suspicion, felt his hand descending to shake him awake.

'*Malade!*' A woman's voice screamed an awful warning, following it with a volley of French whose urgency, and the officer's startled reaction, left no doubt about its meaning to Pat. He was sick with a dreadful plague.

The Frenchman jumped away in alarm and the silk curtain fluttered back into place, filtering the sun's glare. Apart from his headache, Pat's main discomfort was a parching thirst. He listened with fascination, trying to understand what was being said. Despite the obvious danger, he was delighted to hear Claudette's voice as she berated the Frenchman for seeking to disturb him. Mention of Monsieur Genave and the plantation at Flacq brought the conversation to a decisive end.

There was a shout of command and the palanquin jerked into the air. Pat braced himself for a sudden fall to the ground. There was no further cry to halt. The bearers picked up their rhythm so he assumed he was safe, at least for a while. He peeped out of the curtain again, looking back. There was a second palanquin following his, with a retinue of eight men behind it, the spare bearers. Troptard was there too.

The sight of the youth made him angry. He rolled over in the palanquin, upsetting the bearers with his sudden movement. One of them stumbled. There was a shout and they all stopped, gazing back apprehensively at the second palanquin. No one took any notice of him. He swung his legs over the edge and struggled to stand up, causing the hammock to rock wildly.

'Wait!' called Claudette, alighting from her own palanquin with a grace acquired through experience. 'You'll fall out.'

Her authoritative tone annoyed him but since she was right he was obliged to remain until she instructed the bearers to lower the conveyance to the ground and she offered her hand to help him to his feet. He stamped the ground vigorously, rubbing his thighs to restore the circulation to them.

'I'm thirsty,' he said, searching her face with his eyes, demanding an explanation.

She turned to Troptard who was at her side with a bulbous glass jar encased in wickerwork. He unstoppered it and handed it to Pat who took it ungraciously and sniffed its contents.

Claudette smiled her understanding. 'It's water. Laudanum makes you dry.'

He held the neck of the jug up to his lips and poured the water in his mouth, drinking it down thirstily. It splashed over his lips and down his chin. The ache in his head eased.

As he lowered the jar, Troptard took it from his hand. He seized the youth's wrist, spinning him around and bending his arm up behind his back. The swiftness of the move surprised Troptard and he stayed unresisting in his grasp.

'Claudette, this boy drugged me. You *knew* . . .!' He gaped at her, wondering what he was doing in the middle of a forest in the company of sixteen men in blue petticoats, a surly youth and a woman whose voluptuous lips raised the heat in his loins whenever he looked at her.

'Shhh!' Claudette placed her finger on his mouth, her eyes melting his anger. 'It was the only way,' she said softly. 'Would you like to walk? We're through the French lines now.'

Her face in the early morning sunlight shone with a golden glow, showing her flawless high-coloured complexion and the sweet fullness of her winsome smile. He released Troptard and thrust him away in disgust. The bearers shifted warily, awaiting orders.

Claudette's hand slipped to his arm, a gentle touch to calm him but it sent a shivering of yearning spiralling through his limbs. 'Walking will clear your head,' she said persuasively.

'I want an explanation!' He strode along the path, out of the sun into the shade at the side, while she spoke to the bearers and they picked up the palanquin to follow them. He waited until she caught up with him.

'Ma Doudou asked me to stay in the house in case the British try to ransack it. Why have you drugged me and brought me here?'

'How else could I reach the British?' She tried to look apologetic. He saw only the allure of her eyes and the rise and fall of her bosom under the ends of the shawl draped around her shoulders.

'By saying you were sick I could pass the French patrols. Now we are clear of them, close to the British.'

He listened, wondering how he could assuage the desire throbbing in his guts at the sight of her. 'Come in my palanquin!'

Her eyes flickered with surprise. 'Don't you understand? I told Troptard to drug you so I could bring you to the British to speak for me.'

'Tell me about that in the palanquin.'

'The bearers can't carry us both.'

'Why should we go anywhere?' He caught her around her waist and pulled her to him. She struggled, heightening his longing for her. He swooped his head down and kissed the hollow of her throat, bruising her with the fierceness of his lips as she wriggled to free herself. The bearers paused behind them, watching impassively.

'Pat,' she moaned, fighting herself as well as him. 'I have important information . . . for the British.'

'I have something of importance for you.' He slid his hand under her shawl, the feel of her skin silky smooth to his touch. He gripped her shoulder, stopping her from twisting out of his grasp.

Suddenly he collapsed to the ground, his waist numb where

her knuckles had jabbed him below his ribs. He raised his head and through eyes swimming with tears, he saw her watching him sorrowfully.

'Stand up, Pat,' she said, offering her hand. 'There's no time for that, now.'

He brushed her hand aside and scrambled to his feet unaided. He turned away from her so she wouldn't see how effective her blow was. He sighed, wondering if he would ever learn that a woman always takes advantage of a man at his weakest moment.

'I'm sorry,' she whispered. 'Let's continue walking.'

He nodded, still breathless and unable to speak.

'It's the laudanum that made you like that,' she said soothingly. 'You're a gentleman really.'

'Am I?' He growled at her misunderstanding of his character. 'I'm hot flesh and blood. When you watch me that way . . .'

'I want you, Pat. I have a devil inside me too. But first we *must* find the British.'

'Why? I'm not helping you to spy.'

'I can tell them the French strength. General Decaen will surrender if the British accept his terms. The invasion could be over without the futility of a battle. I could save Port Louis from being destroyed.'

'First you want to save Genave's house, now it's the whole damn town.'

'The General gave me the idea. He thought you were French so I used you as my excuse for coming here. I told all the soldiers who stopped us on the road that you have the plague and I'm taking you home to Belrose to die.'

'What's Belrose?'

'Mr Genave's plantation.' She paused when she came to a fork in the road. 'It's to the east, at Flacq.' She pointed up the right hand fork, then led him over to the left. 'The British are along here, marching to Moulin-à-Poudre. There's water and cattle there. That's where General Decaen expects them to camp. They will sack Port Louis tomorrow unless we stop them. They don't know the General's willing to surrender without a fight.'

'Why should they believe you?'

The trace of a frown creased the smoothness of her brow

then vanished as she smiled at him confidently. 'You will convince them. You will say you're an emissary from the French.'

'It's a lie,' he said, weakening under her gaze, knowing he was going to do whatever she asked. 'What spell have you cast on me?'

Her wavy hair shimmered darkly in the sunlight as she tossed her head. He tried to understand her enigmatic expression but she turned quickly and beckoned the bearers.

'We must arrive with an air of authority and haste,' she said, holding the curtain up for him to enter the palanquin. 'They are more likely to believe me if I am with you than if I'm alone. If we are confident, then we shall succeed.'

They came upon the British at Moulin-à-Poudre as Claudette had predicted. Her knowledge seemed less remarkable when she showed Pat how every movement of the British forces could be seen from a signal post at the summit of Long Mountain. The French lookouts there reported to the forces camped below them.

They were escorted by perspiring British soldiers into the presence of Major-General Henry Warde, the officer in charge under the commander, General Abercrombie.

The activity was hectic and Pat watched keenly. Soldiers were slaughtering cattle they had rounded up and were lighting fires to prepare a meal while others were still arriving in a column that had marched from their landing at Cap Malheureux.

Pat was impressed with the efficiency of the British in setting up their camp, although in their tight worsted uniforms and regimental tall hats, they were badly dressed for the tropical heat. The forces were forming two lines on a gentle elevation, a forest stretching from them and extending with some intervals to the town itself, five miles distant.

If the French attack now, Pat realized with a shudder of apprehension, *they'll catch the British unprepared.*

General Warde listened to Claudette with growing astonishment at her information. 'Terms!' he exclaimed incredulously when Claudette told him General Decaen would be prepared to negotiate the island's surrender. 'The Governor will capitulate without a battle?'

Claudette pouted winsomely. 'Perhaps a small battle, yes? By the Pamplemousse River.'

'It's a trap!' General Warde chuckled and turned to his fellow officers. 'How like a Frenchman to send a Creole charmer to woo me into ambush.'

Pat and Claudette were standing under close escort in front of General Warde. It was mid-morning and the sun was at its fiercest. He felt the light touch of Claudette's hand on his arm and knew she wanted him to help her convince the British she spoke the truth.

'If the French wanted to ambush you,' he said with a cheeky grin, 'they could have lain in wait for your landing. Your troops must have been in poor shape then after wading ashore and being cooped up in cramped quarters aboard their vessels for weeks. None of you are used to this climate or terrain. Your men are dressed for a jaunt in a European November, not a hike up and down mountains in a tropical summer.'

'Logic, sir?' General Warde looked puzzled. 'From an American?' He scratched his head, muttering to the Colonel who stood by his side. 'Beauty and Reason combining to convince us the French are willing to capitulate. Maybe it's true.'

'It is true!' Claudette said haughtily. 'We wouldn't have risked our lives to come here with a lie. The French could shoot us for being spies, or you could. It's quite plain. You don't have to destroy Port Louis to take it.'

The General pondered for a moment. 'You will stay with us awhile, as our guests. Doubtless the French would like to know our strength and you have seen plenty to tell them if I let you return now.'

'They know your strength already.' Pat pointed up at the signal post on Long Mountain. 'That's why they are willing to treat for terms.'

General Warde waved him away irritably, giving him a feeling of pleasure at having riled him.

He was kept separately from Claudette and he worried about her safety. It was because of her foolhardy scheme that he was in this predicament; he had no heart for it. Whether the British believed them or not would depend on General

Dacaen. If the French forces refrained from attacking then Claudette would be proved right and they would be released. His hopes were shortlived.

From the bluff where he was sitting in the shade of a mahogany tree, he had a clear view of the trail disappearing into the woods below. At two o'clock there was a sound of a brief skirmish from the wood and about eighty hussar guards emerged through the trees. Pat recognized General Decaen in their midst.

General Warde rushed up to the bluff for his own view of the action. 'So this is how the French capitulate?' he said scornfully.

Pat remembered how the Governor had been urging his troops without success to defend the island. 'If General Decaen has to lead a reconnaisance party himself,' he said to prove his point, 'it's because his soldiers won't fight!'

General Warde called up companies of the 12th and 59th regiments and set off in pursuit of the French. There was chaos in the camp at the proximity of the French and when his guard left him to see what was happening, Pat rose quietly to his feet and ambled away. He would have liked to find Claudette but there was no time, so he hid himself in the trees and listened to the sound of gunfire as the British chased the French away.

He made his way to a small stream and drank from it as he was still feeling dehydrated from the laudanum. He hoped his disappearance would go unnoticed and the British would be too preoccupied to search for him. He climbed a tree and lodged himself comfortably in its branches. There were no snakes or vicious animals on the island for him to worry about. He was waiting for nightfall so he could return to the camp under the cover of darkness and try to rescue Claudette.

The snap of a twig set his hackles rising. Alert for danger, he leaned cautiously over the edge of his branch and peered through the leaves. A man was standing at the bank of the stream.

He appeared to be alone and was smartly dressed in civilian clothes. After looking carefully around him, the man seemed satisfied that he was by himself. He removed his coat and folded it neatly, placing it beneath the tree that Pat occupied.

The man was handsome, well built with a full head of dark, straight hair swept back from his brow. His side whiskers were cut short, one inch below his ear. Pat judged him to be in his thirties. He was unarmed so Pat felt confident he could beat him if he was discovered and had to fight his way free.

The man showed no nervousness, only a sense of relief at being alone. He raised his hands above his head and yawned, revealing his extreme weariness. He removed his vest and cravat and put them with his coat to make a tidy pile of clothes. It occurred to Pat then how elaborately dressed the man was for a simple walk in the woods.

His chest, when he removed his shirt and undergarment, was the white of a courtier, someone whose body rarely saw the sun. It was covered with a web of fine black hair. Pat was amused by the sight of a gentleman obviously more accustomed to city life disrobing in the wilds of a wood with the aplomb of being in his private chamber at home.

The man finally removed his belt, his boots, his breeches and silk shorts and stood naked by the stream. Pat poised above him, preparing to drop on his shoulders and knock him to the ground so he could escape. As he was about to plunge out of the tree the man did an odd thing. He knelt down, kissed the soil, and raised his head to the sky with his eyes closed and his hands clasped in front of him in prayer.

Pat was astounded. He shrank back into the foliage, letting the man enjoy his soliloquy. He prayed for a full five minutes which made him wonder what sins the man was confessing. Then he stepped into the stream and sat down, leaning his back against a boulder while the water gurgled around him.

Something about the man's stance, his air of self-assurance despite being naked in a strange land, convinced Pat he could be trusted. He shinned quietly down the trunk of the tree, slipped off his own clothes and stepped out of the undergrowth onto the river bank.

The man raised his head but showed no sign of surprise.

CHAPTER FIFTEEN

'Good afternoon,' the man said, gesturing at the stream with the air of someone inviting a visitor into his drawing room. 'How pleasant to have company. The water's very refreshing.' He spoke English with a burr, a lilt that was soft yet commanding. His eyes gleamed a welcome.

Pat stepped off the bank into the stream, splashing water over his body and hair, feeling he wanted to be clean before he approached the man. 'Are you English?' he demanded.

The man tilted his head to one side and eyed him curiously, causing Pat to wonder how the question had upset him.

'I was born in Scotland.' He scrutinized Pat closely. 'What's your regiment?'

The unexpected question made Pat laugh as he sat down in the river opposite the man. 'I'm nothing to do with the army. I'm from Virginia.'

The man was relieved and his frown of suspicion relaxed. 'What are you doing so far from home in this island?'

There was proprietorial tone in his voice that Pat ignored, assuming it was typical of British arrogance. 'I live here,' he said, deliberately lying to score a point off the man. He ducked his head under the water and when he emerged he saw the man had begun to sluice himself too.

There was silence between them in the midst of the gurgling stream and the whistling of birds swirling in the sky visible between the overhanging branches. Pat felt guilty about the unfair advantage his lie gave him over this courtly man so he asked amiably, 'What's your name?'

The man hesitated, wiping the water from his face. He smiled apologetically. 'Robert,' he said, with a twinkle in his eye. 'What's yours?'

'Pat.' He lay back, satisfied the man was no threat. He guessed he was travelling with the British forces in a private capacity.

'What do you do in Mauritius, Pat?'

'I'm a planter,' he answered immediately, hearing for the first time the British name for the Isle of France.

'How interesting. The French planters grow coffee, don't they? Sugar would be more suited to this island's conditions. It can withstand hurricane force winds.'

'I don't know much about sugar.'

'You should try to grow it. The soil here is similar to that of the Caribbean islands. Indeed, the whole island is remarkably like Dominica although it is twice its size. It has similar rugged mountain terrain, and these delightful woods and streams. Sugar cane is grown in abundance in Dominica, and that island is right in the hurricane zone. I do commend sugar to you.'

Robert realized he was speaking too much. 'Forgive me,' he said with a shy grin. 'I've studied it, you see, that's why I'm so enthusiastic.'

'Surely it's expensive to manufacture sugar. The cane needs processing.'

Robert watched him shrewdly then raised his hands, cupping water in them and letting it trickle through his fingers. 'The solution is here. Water power, water wheels, to turn the crushing stones.'

'What about labour to cut the cane?' He wanted to deflate the Britisher's evangelical enthusiasm.

'Slaves.' A shadow of doubt crossed Robert's face. 'How many are there here?'

Pat remembered what the whore had told him. 'Sixty thousand.'

'It's enough.'

'Haven't the British banned slave trading?' he asked, continuing to tease Robert. 'If the island becomes British, you'll have no opportunity to import new slaves. What happens when there's no one left to cut all that sugar cane?'

'Slaves breed.'

He blinked, baffled by the remark. 'I thought the British were against perpetuating slavery.'

'There are some circumstances,' Robert said, his eyes gleaming, 'such as building a new nation in these tropical conditions, when only a slave is suited to the toil of such a task.'

Pat plunged his head under the water again, disturbed by the Messianic glint in Robert's eyes. He had been drawn to him by his air of drive but now it threatened to involve him in a discussion of the man's ideals, he was more interested in his own plight. He stood up, letting the water drip from his body and shook his locks, sending spray from his hair showering over him.

Robert grimaced. 'I have a lot of ideas,' he said, taking the hint to change the subject. 'What about you? What are you doing here?' It was the third time he'd asked the same question.

'I was escorting a lady,' Pat said, hoping his trust in Robert wouldn't result in his recapture. 'We had a message for the British commander.'

'Ah, yes.' Robert smiled to himself. 'So I heard. I am relieved that Port Louis is to be saved.'

'You met Claudette! She told you that?' He wanted to shake Robert for not saying so before. 'Where is she?'

'I assume the young lady is returning in her palanquin whence she came.'

'She's not a prisoner in the camp any more?'

Robert frowned. 'Do you ask me to divulge military information?'

'No! Just tell me if Claudette is still there.' He gestured at the camp beyond the wood.

'Have you any idea how threatening you sound?' Robert stood up, stepping gingerly across the stones in the bed of the stream to its bank. Pat followed him closely, wondering if he was going to summon soldiers to arrest him.

'You should have listened to what I said. I *cannot* tell you if that enterprising young lady is in the camp.' He turned his back on Pat and bent down for his clothes. 'If you seek her,' he said, standing up and looking sly, 'you won't stay here.'

'Then she escaped too!' He pulled on his breeches hastily, ignoring Robert. 'I must go to Port Louis. I have the house to protect.'

'Indeed?' Robert was amused. 'The romance of youth . . . I believe I envy you.'

'Come with me!' he said impulsively, warming to the man. 'Claudette's told me of the way to pass to Port Louis without going through the French lines. You could stay in the house until the British come. There's only me there.'

'Oh dear, no.' Robert sighed, dabbing himself genteelly. 'There will be British forces billeted with the townsfolk but I doubt whether I will have the pleasure of accepting your invitation.'

'You lime-juicers are all the same, so pompous.' Pat slung his coat over his shoulder. He held out his hand, grateful for Robert's information, not realizing he might have offended the Britisher by his curt description of him as pompous.

'Alas, Pat,' Robert looked him straight in his eye as he gripped his hand firmly, 'there is protocol in life, whether you're an American adventurer or a British . . .' He searched for a word to describe himself, found nothing suitable and let the sentence die.

Pat pulled his hand free and dived into the trees to start the five mile trek back to Port Louis. It was not as easy as he expected and he was forced by darkness to spend that night in a wood, within sight of the French troops camped around the bridge over the River Seche.

With dawn, he crept close to the river, gauging where he could swim across. The French forces occupied the wooden bridge over it. From the distance came the sound of firing and it was soon clear that the British were rapidly gaining ground. He moved through the undergrowth until he found a place upstream where he could cross the river unobserved by the French sentries who might mistake him for a British soldier and try to shoot him.

He swam and waded, holding his boots in his hand, until he reached the other side. Curiosity made him wait to see what would happen. French soldiers were trying to pull up the planks of the bridge to impede the British advance. They managed to destroy half the bridge when they came under fire and were forced to retreat.

The British army's advance was only temporarily halted by the river. While the troops filed over what remained of the bridge, the artillery dragged their guns into the river and hauled them across, battling the rapid current to reach the other side.

Nearly four thousand men of the French forces assembled

to repel the invasion at the east of the mountain called Pieter Both. They did not stay long. Although the broken nature of the ground made the British advance appear ragged, their spirit was firm. They rushed into a charge despite the volley of grape fired at them. The French withdrew to their lines in great confusion. Pat followed them while a corps of British soldiers ascended the mount and, pulling down the French flag, hoisted the English one.

In the mêlée and chaos, aided by dusk and his bedraggled appearance, Pat passed unnoticed through the French lines. He reached Port Louis after nightfall. The streets were deserted and he made his way along them guided by the flickering lights shining through the cracks in the closed shutters of the houses, until he reached the Champ de Mars.

The silence of the plain after the shouted orders, the screams of the wounded, and the clash and panic of the skirmishing, caused him to pause with gratitude before entering the garden of the Genave house. He drank in the scent of the night flowers, letting the peaceful atmosphere soothe him.

The lower rises of the hills that surrounded the plain glittered where lights burned in houses. There was a serenity and an air of permanence about those hills, far removed from the warring armies. To Pat it mattered little which side won the island. His concern was for Claudette.

He approached the house stealthily. Lanterns hung on the verandah, casting their glow over the garden, reducing the shadows to hide in. He wanted to know who was in the house before he revealed himself. The verandah was deserted. He waited in the sparse shadows, his ears alert, listening for the sound of movement from those inside.

After a few minutes, the door from the drawing room opened. He held his breath, then sighed with relief, his anxiety vanishing. Claudette stood in the doorway, hesitant. She wore a gown of pink muslin trimmed with red, her hair combed and straightened, fanning over her shoulders of pale gold. The effect of seeing her illuminated by the lanterns' glow was stunning.

The dark face of Troptard appeared beside her, urging her out onto the verandah. Pat wanted to see what the youth would do. He harboured a distrust of him not far short of hatred and he would willingly thrash the fellow if he abused Claudette in any way.

Troptard walked boldly to the verandah rail, beckoning Claudette to follow him. To Pat's dismay he pointed his finger directly at where he was hiding.

Claudette blinked, brushing a fallen strand of hair away from her eyes. 'Pat,' she called timidly. 'Are you out there?' Her voice was low, showing she did not completely believe Troptard.

'Yes,' he replied softly. 'Is it safe?'

'Of course.' Claudette swept across the deck of the verandah with her arms outstretched to greet him. Troptard coughed and she hesitated, lowering her arms. She glanced anxiously into the darkness as he emerged.

'There's no one with me.' He leapt onto the verandah and strode over to her.

'Troptard saw you coming.' Claudette stepped aside before he could embrace her. 'The night has eyes. Come inside quickly.'

He followed her into the parlour. When Troptard closed the door and withdrew from the room, she let him hold her.

'Wait!' She giggled as his hand slipped under her corsage and he fondled her breasts. 'You are worse than –' She interrupted herself with a bubble of laughter. 'I've been waiting for you since morning.'

'How did you get here?' He drew her to a couch and made her sit down so he could watch her as she talked.

'With the palanquins. It was not difficult. We came last night. Troptard told me you had escaped.'

'How did he know?'

'He knows everything.'

'About us?'

'What is there to know about us?'

'This!' He succeeded in gripping her around her waist and placing one hand behind her shoulders, forcing her towards him. He was apprehensive lest she resist him so he kissed her tentatively. She responded with an open mouthed kiss that seemed to devour him, spinning him into a fury of action.

He plied the curves of her body with one hand, delving

under her skirt with the other. He felt her quiver in his grasp, alive to the sensations his insistent touch was stirring. He thrust himself on top of her, forcing her to lie the length of the couch. He was going to show her his ardour was too strong to be denied.

'Pat!' She hissed urgently in his ear, her warm breath tingling his cheek.

'No,' he said sharply. 'Don't speak.' His hand fumbled to raise her gown as his boots banged against the end of the couch.

She sighed, making him wonder if she really understood his overwhelming need for her. He had to possess her, on his terms, to tame the wildness that she unleashed in him. And he wanted her for himself alone.

'I love you,' he said between clenched teeth.

She shrunk from him, wriggling so she could slide out of his grasp. Her fingers found the sensitive spot under his arms and she tickled him there. He released her with a splutter of laughter and she stood up quickly.

'Pat,' she pleaded when he tried to hold her again. 'Not now.'

'Why not? We have the house to ourselves.' He saw the haunted look in her eyes and shook his head with dismay. 'Don't look at me like that! I would do anything for you.'

She extended her hand, drawing him to his feet when he took it. He was perplexed by her; she was totally in control of him and he couldn't understand why. Her eyes glowed with promise as she led him to the parlour door. His spirit soared with anticipation.

'Go to the master's chamber,' she said when they were in the corridor. He opened his mouth to protest. 'I'll come.' The husky assurance in her voice convinced him.

'I must close up the house,' she explained, begging him with her eyes to be patient.

'All right.' He bit his lip to cool his hot-blooded haste, eyeing her as she glided down the corridor with the svelte grace of a young gazelle.

He found the bedroom in a daze. He was excited after two nights of dreaming of her, yet he dreaded she might deceive him; she had the opportunity to do so. Perhaps he was crazy not to have taken her on the couch. His thoughts, coupled with his weariness after the day's march through the woods, exhausted him. He undressed carelessly, letting the garments fall to the floor. He left the candles burning and sat naked on the edge of the bed.

The creak of the door roused him. He glanced at it hopefully as it swung open. She was there. She had removed her gown and wore only a diaphanous rose pink robe that hinted at her nakedness beneath it. His throat tightened as she flitted across the room like a firefly, snuffing out candles until the only light that remained came from the candlestick in her hand.

She placed it on the table beside the bed and leaned over to extinguish it. He stopped her, his smile saying he wanted to see her. Her lips formed a moue of protest but she left the flame burning.

He reached up and pulled the bow that fastened her robe. The fine material fluttered open and she drew it off her shoulders so the robe shimmied to the floor, gathering around her ankles. Her naked body, robust and lithe with its pale gold hue and firm, shapely thighs, was offered willingly to him.

He held out his hands and she stepped closer. Placing his palms on her hips, he caressed her reverently. He looked up and saw her eyes watching him, love mixed with sadness smouldering in their depths.

He looked down again, his eyes level with her thighs. He leaned forward and his lips brushed the vibrance of her flesh, his tongue tasting its sweetness while his senses were assailed by the rich perfume of her eager, tantalizing body. He held her firmly, while his tongue explored. She writhed against him, pressing her fingers into the strong tendons of his neck, her breath coming in deep, soul drenching gasps.

When her panting soared to a shriek and she tremored as though she could take no more, he pulled her down onto the bed. Gently, he laid her out on the mattress and possessed her.

'Claudette,' he whispered when contentment calmed him. He held her in his arms in the great, comfortable bed, gazing up into the darkness trapped below its tester. The candle had long expired, leaving them in that intimate darkness that inspires confession.

'I've never felt this way before,' he whispered. 'I love you, Claudette.'

She tensed in his arms, disturbing his feeling of well being.

'What's wrong with me saying that?' he asked defensively. 'It's true.'

'Please, Pat, don't spoil it. Won't you go to sleep?'

'Are you staying?'

'I cannot. Even one moment with you is a risk.'

'Old man Genave won't turn up, will he?'

She was silent and he shook her, wanting her to laugh, yet even in the dark there was an aura of sadness about her. 'When this invasion is over and all is settled, I want to be with you every day, every night. I want you to be mine.'

'That's impossible.' Her hand touched his chin, her fingers resting lightly on his lips. He opened his mouth and kissed them.

'Do not make plans, I beg of you, Pat.' She withdrew her hand hastily. 'I must go.'

Before he had a chance to hold her, she slipped out of the bed. He lay his head on the pillows, amazed at his good fortune, and worshipping Claudette for being part of it.

The brilliance of sunshine like a splash of water in his face woke him from a long and dreamless sleep. Troptard was at the side of the bed, proffering coffee. He shook his head to clear it. Claudette was at the window, opening the shutters. He was filled with yearning when he gazed on her silhouette against the brightness of the morning.

'Drink your coffee,' she said brusquely as though the tenderness of the night before had been imagined. 'The invasion is over.'

He blinked. Troptard was waiting. He wanted him to leave the room so he could make love to her again. He took the coffee and tried to dismiss the youth with a wave of his hand and a stern frown.

'Troptard brought the news,' said Claudette brightly, sitting on the end of the bed and smiling at the youth to make him stay. He nodded smugly in response.

Pat realized she had no intention of being left alone with him so he sipped the coffee. Its strength and heat seared him awake. 'How did it happen?' he asked since she expected him to be interested. 'Was our journey to the British worthwhile?'

'I think it was.' Her eyes glinted mysteriously. 'Last night there was a false alarm. Some of the British marines undressed to their undergarments to keep cool. In the moonlight, the British sentries at the camp saw them in their white underwear and mistook them for the French infantry. They opened fire. When the French heard the shots, they thought the British attack was beginning, so they fled.' She giggled.

'General Decaen sent a British naval captain who'd been taken prisoner as a messenger to General Warde under a flag of truce. He took the draft treaty of capitulation with him.'

'So the French surrendered like you said they would.'

'Yes,' she said simply, offering no further explanation.

'What will happen next?' He handed the coffee bowl to Troptard. 'He could go now,' he said pointedly.

She ignored his ploy. 'When terms are arranged, the British forces will march into Port Louis. Their own governor will be sworn in and the island will be British.'

'Will you need me to keep them out of the house?'

She stood up, preparing to leave the room. 'They may billet some officers here. The British are honourable and will keep to the agreements. They're going to let us preserve our property, our way of life, our customs, laws and religion.'

'There's one custom I want to preserve.' He winked, holding out his arms for her.

She dodged behind Troptard, shaking her head severely, despite the glimmer of amusement in her eyes. 'Troptard will take you to see the British arrive.'

As he dressed, he cursed the ever-present Troptard under his breath. When he left the chamber there was no sign of Claudette and he was obliged to follow the youth out of the villa without seeing her. Market Street was in a hubbub with a mass of people jostling and chattering excitedly as everyone hurried to the waterfront. Although he tried, he was unable to shake off Troptard in the crowd.

At the harbour, the first ships of the blockading squadron were being warped in. The road leading to the Place des Armes parade ground in front of the Governor's house was packed with people as the Grenadiers of the British army marched into the town.

Troptard led him to a vantage point by the gates of Government House and he stood on the wall for a better view. Africans, Indians, Creoles and all races but French surged around him watching curiously as soldiers filed into the Government House courtyard.

A tall, handsome man walked with a group of officers, his civilian clothes in flamboyant contrast to their military uniforms. He was eyeing the crowd intently, not staring straight ahead pretending to ignore everything like the officers were.

'That's Robert!' Pat tugged at Troptard's shoulder with delight at seeing his friend from the stream. 'Call that man over here, Troptard. Let's take him to the house to meet Claudette.'

Troptard refused to move. He shook his head emphatically. 'No possible,' he said, enunciating his reply with care. 'That man is . . . the new British Governor.'

CHAPTER SIXTEEN

Pat raced up the path to the villa despite Troptard's attempt to restrain him. 'Where's Claudette?' he demanded as soon as he saw Ma Doudou waiting on the steps with her arms folded across her ample bosom.

She looked at him blankly, stirring in him an inkling of suspicion that something was wrong.

'What is it, Ma Doudou?' He cooled down his impatience for he respected the old lady. 'You look as though you don't know me.'

'Hush!' Ma Doudou's command and her warning eyes made him pause. He glanced around for Troptard and was relieved to see the youth had disappeared. For a moment, at least, he was without his shadow.

'You don't have to worry, Ma Doudou,' he said. 'That's why I want to see Claudette. The new governor, the British one, is a friend. I've asked him to make certain no one is billeted in the house. You'll be able to keep it safe for your master.'

Ma Doudou's face was a muddle of emotions, her jowls shaking while her lips tightened and an expression of reproach entered her eyes. 'I tell you *Hush*, Pat!' she said with a worried glance behind her. 'Claudette ain't here.' She hitched up her bosom and her eyes roved beyond him to the Champ de Mars.

'Take your news to the American consul.' Her smile showed she was relieved to have found a solution about what to do with him. 'Mr Buchanan would like to know you have influence with the new governor.'

'Now I've served your purpose,' he said bitterly, 'you want to get rid of me?'

'No.' Ma Doudou's hand touched his shoulder and she smiled benignly. Yet her face showed fear. 'Please go now. Troptard will come for you when you should return.'

When she withdrew her hand and tugged anxiously at her

kerchief, disturbing her coils of grey plaits, he recognized something was seriously amiss. 'I'll go when I've seen Claudette,' he said, pushing past her before she could stop him. 'She's in here, isn't she?'

Ma Doudou nodded meekly, abandoning her attempt to control events. Whatever happened now, her wise eyes seemed to say, was because it was supposed to happen.

Pat was alert enough to be cautioned by her fateful expression. He strode inside with his mouth tightened into a firm line, showing his determination to solve the mystery of the house.

There was no one in the parlour, its very emptiness mocked him. He was going to call out Claudette's name but an inner voice kept him quiet. Instead, he slowed his stride and approached the door leading to the corridor with uncharacteristic stealth. He opened it carefully, avoiding the squeak and peered up and down the length of the passage.

It was in darkness with all doors closed. Its high ceilings helped to keep the air cool while outside the sun was reaching its height. He sniffed cautiously, convinced he could smell Claudette's distinctive perfume. He had no doubt that she was somewhere in the house; it irked him that she was hiding instead of coming to hear his good news.

He wondered whether to try the kitchen quarters. He suspected Troptard was there and he preferred to avoid the youth. So he turned left along the corridor, not right. He opened the door of the dining room and peered in. A bowl of coffee was half-empty on the table and the chair in front of it was pushed back. Someone had left in a hurry.

He scratched his head, puzzled at who could have been there. He turned back into the corridor and opened his mouth to call Claudette. A sudden whimper, a low cry that ceased almost before he heard it, startled him.

It seemed to have come from Mr Genave's chamber, where he himself had slept the night before. He walked along the corridor, careful not to set the floorboards creaking underfoot. The house seemed to be holding its breath.

Quietly, he kneeled down in front of the door to the bedchamber. There was a key inside the lock so he couldn't see a thing. He put his ear to it and listened. The rise and fall of someone breathing excitedly, its pitch gradually approaching a crescendo, was unmistakable. He sat back on his haunches to think.

The sound was worryingly familiar. His own loins were stirred by it. He rose to his feet and gripped the door handle. The muffled cry of a woman's voice served to light a fire of rage in his heart. He pushed against the door; it wasn't locked and he hurtled unexpectedly into the room.

His first reaction of disbelief was followed rapidly by despair before the rage exploded. Claudette was lying on the bed, her skirts around her hips, her lithe legs locked around the waist of a man whose moon-white bottom rose and fell as he plunged into her.

The man's face was pressed into her bosom where her bodice was open and her tawny nipples exposed. The clash of his vile, pale body against her honey-coloured limbs didn't cease while Pat watched. She stared at him in horror, anguish mingled with ecstasy.

He rushed across the room and pulled at the man's shoulder. The man froze with shock, twisting his head to see who was interrupting him at such a crucial moment. Pat yanked him off, lent strength by his fury.

The man's penis, red and swollen with lust, pulsed at him mockingly. Pat smashed his fist into his jaw and watched him sprawl in a heap at his feet. He leaned down, grabbed him by his arm, pulled him up and hit him again. The man's breeches were bunched around his ankles and he toppled over as he tried to dodge away. Pat lunged at him, blinded by jealousy, his fists flying.

Someone leapt on his shoulders, distracting him. Hands clawed at his throat and he staggered backwards.

'Let go, Claudette!' he croaked when he realized it was her fingers digging into his larynx. She was choking him, her weight suspended from his neck. He didn't want to hurt her but unless he dislodged her from his back, she would throttle him.

He stepped backwards then bent forward sharply, pitching her over his shoulders. She landed with a thump against the man who was struggling to pull up his breeches. They fell back to the floor together.

Pat's fury faltered. He was reluctant to be angry with Claudette but her defence of the stranger confused him. He paused, letting her scramble to her feet.

'Get out!' she was screaming at him, her eyes blazing with an anger tinged with fear as she placed herself between him and the man on the floor.

Pat was baffled. He had assumed the stranger was one of the invading soldiers who was ravishing her. Yet she was protecting him and there had been a smile of bliss on her face when he burst into the room and discovered them.

He shook his head, trying to clear the doubt. 'Claudette –' he began but suddenly she flew at him, pushing him bodily towards the door.

'Go, please go!' she pleaded.

He gripped her flailing arms and held her off. She tried to kick his shins. The man rose to his feet behind her, his breeches in place. He smirked at her then he touched his cheek where Pat's fist had left a painful bruise and his eyes darkened with hatred.

Pat sized him up. He was about his age, or older, with a shock of red hair and a freckled complexion. He was broad-shouldered, tapering to slim hips that indicated a well exercised body, though one that was unused to toil. His hair was fashionably shaped, his nails well manicured. In less ruffled circumstances, he would appear foppish.

He was the kind of man Pat was bound to dislike by instinct, even if he had not caught him with Claudette. 'Who is he?' he demanded, still fending off her attempt to drive him from the room.

The man spoke and Claudette's eyes filled with anger. Pat let her go as he listened with astonishment to the conversation. It was in Creole.

'You're not English?' was all he could think to say in his dismay.

The man's glare of hatred intensified.

'This is Lindsay.' Claudette closed her bodice with a sigh. 'He is the son of Mr Genave.' She lowered her eyes, avoiding both of them.

Pat looked towards the open door. Troptard and Ma Doudou were lurking in the shadows. 'Damn!' he muttered to himself when he realized his mistake, and its implications. Yet Claudette was his .. he *loved* her.

'I don't care who he is, Claudette,' he said, feeling helpless. 'What he was doing —'

'Shut up, man!' Lindsay flung Claudette aside and she tripped, falling against the bed.

Pat went to help her but Lindsay stood in his way, his hands raised in a boxer's stance. 'What are you doing in my house?' he demanded.

The question brought Pat to a perplexed halt. Whatever he said was bound to cause trouble for Claudette and Ma Doudou. As he opened his mouth, a voice spoke from the corridor.

'The master has been billeted here by the British governor, Mr Farquhar.'

Pat turned and looked gratefully at Troptard who merely scowled back at him. 'I'm part of the advance forces of occupation,' he bluffed, hoping that Lindsay wouldn't recognize that he was wearing his own clothes.

'Are you English?' Lindsay's eyes glinted with renewed hatred.

He relied on Lindsay's geography being poor. 'I am from Virginia.'

'I hate the English!' Lindsay walked towards the door and Pat deemed it prudent to let him pass but Lindsay stopped in front of him. They faced each other, eye to eye.

'When I return, sir, you must be gone from this house. If we meet here again, I will kill you.'

Pat opened his mouth to speak but never had a chance. Lindsay's clenched fist smacked into his abdomen, knocking the breath out of him. He raised his fist to retaliate but Lindsay drove his knee into his crotch and smashed his forearm across his neck as he fell to the floor.

When the pain cleared, he heard the cackle of Lindsay's evil laughter echoing down the corridor. Troptard helped him to his feet and offered him a goblet of wine.

He shook himself free of Troptard's hand. 'No wine,' he gasped. 'I don't want more laudanum.'

'It's all right, Pat.' Ma Doudou's voice of reason was sweet to his ears. 'The wine is not drugged, it was ordered by Lindsay.'

'Lindsay!' He snatched the goblet off the tray, sniffed it and took a trial sip. It tasted as it should. He let Troptard pour water into the wine. 'You should have told me about him,' he said ruefully as he drank.

Ma Doudou patted his arm. 'I tried to warn you.'

'Oh yes.' He sighed bitterly. 'I always listen to old ladies, and young ones too. What made you do it, Claudette?' He walked over to where she sat on the bed and pulled her to her feet.

'Look at me. I trusted you. I thought you loved me.'

'Love?' Her lower lip trembled and she avoided his eyes as though she didn't know the meaning of the word.

'You must leave here, Pat.' Ma Doudou bustled over to them both, taking Claudette from his arms. 'Go before it's too late. I was wrong to involve you in our affairs.'

'No, you weren't.' Claudette recovered some of her composure. 'He helped when it was necessary.'

He was amazed as he realized how easily he'd been used. 'I risked my life for you, Claudette. Does that mean nothing? You've got Lindsay to protect you now.'

'It's not like that, Pat.'

'That's the way it seems. Now Lindsay's here I'm being pushed aside.' The memory of her blissful smile as she lay under Lindsay flashed into his mind. It strengthened his resolve instead of making him hate her. He would show her, and Lindsay, that he was a man to be reckoned with.

'I can't explain to you about Lindsay.' The sadness returned to Claudette's eyes, making him feel wretched.

'He is the son of our master.' Ma Doudou snapped her mouth shut, leaving the rest of her sentence unsaid.

'Is that why you had to make love with him?'

'I told you I cannot explain.'

Ma Doudou nodded her head in support of her daughter. 'Pat, a wise man doesn't fear the dark. He knows dawn will bring light.'

'That's too mysterious for me. I know what I saw.'

'Do you?' Claudette's voice was rapier-sharp and it caused him to pause.

'I don't want to think about it.'

'That's better.' She drifted past him to Troptard and had a

whispered conversation with the youth. She turned back and faced him. 'What happened at Government House?'

'It barely seems important now.' He gave vent to a heavy sigh that summed up the gloom he felt at her betrayal. 'That's why I hurried here to see you. The governor, Robert Farquhar, is a friend of mine. I made his acquaintance behind the British lines. We bathed in a stream together.'

'How does that help us?'

Ma Doudou hushed her into silence with a wave of her hand. Her brows were knit in concentration, plotting what devilment Pat could not tell. At least the old lady saw the importance of his information which seemed to escape Claudette.

He tugged at his ear, relishing what he was about to tell them. 'I talked to him outside Government House while the solders were preparing to occupy it. He plans to hold a Grand Ball for all the people of consequence in the island.'

He looked at Claudette triumphantly but she seemed unimpressed. 'He's invited me! What a wonderful opportunity to meet everyone. He wants to do all he can to see there's no animosity between the settlers and the British.'

'How will a dance achieve that?' Claudette asked cynically. 'The French know they've been conquered.'

'They haven't. That's the point of the ball, to show everyone that the British offer of friendship is genuine. I think it shows what a decent chap Robert Farquhar is.'

Ma Doudou's head was cocked to one side and she eyed him shrewdly. 'Is there anything more?'

'Yes. Claudette's going to be impressed.' He smiled at her, almost forgiving her for what had happened. 'Robert insists I take you, Claudette, as my partner. To Government House!'

The silence in the room was broken by Ma Doudou's swift intake of breath, like a snake hissing. Claudette looked appalled.

'Damn!' he said, punching his palm with his fist to drive away his dismay at their reaction. 'I thought you'd be pleased.'

Claudette shook her head sadly. 'I cannot go with you, Pat.'

'Because of Lindsay? You don't have to be scared of him. The Governor *wants* you there. He knows what you did to save the town being razed.'

'I cannot go,' she said again, dropping her eyelashes to hide her tears.

The tears convinced him she was sincere. 'Of course you can! If there's some problem with Lindsay, let me solve it. I'm not afraid of him.'

'You might not be, Pat, but we have to respect him. And protect him too.'

He failed to see what Ma Doudou was talking about. She waved him to silence.

'Claudette is my daughter. Has it ever occurred to you why she does not have my colour?'

'Sure.' He shrugged, wondering what difference that made. 'Her father's white, I suppose. She's a portrait.'

Claudette raised her head, her eyes still moist. 'Ma Doudou is a slave and so am I. That's why I can't go to the ball.'

'The new Governor knows that. It doesn't matter to him what you are.'

'It will to the other guests. You don't understand how we live here. We have to behave in a certain way so we can survive. We conform to our master's wishes and it is better if we accept them.'

'Is that why you were letting Lindsay bed you? You only *looked* as though you were enjoying it? To please him.' He waited hopefully for her reply.

She ignored the opportunity to set his heart at rest. 'Mr Genave is my owner, Pat. I can't go to Government House.'

'All right!' He was sorry she had let him down. 'So who's your father then if it's so important?'

In the silence that filled the room, Ma Doudou sucked noisily on her teeth. She reached a decision. 'Claudette's father,' she said, 'is Mr Genave.'

'Yes, Pat,' Claudette no longer tried to hide the tears in her eyes. 'Lindsay is my half-brother. He is the worst enemy you could have. You have discovered our secret. He will destroy you if you remain on the island.'

CHAPTER SEVENTEEN

Port Louis was transformed by the arrival of the British. The harbour lost its neglected air and became a forest of masts filled with vessels of all sorts and sizes from the line-of-battle ship to the canoe scooped out of a single piece of wood. The British flag waved triumphantly on all the batteries; British men-of-war rode where none ever rode before; Indiamen, transports, prizes, ships of all kinds displayed English colours over the French.

Pat was captivated by the air of excitement that pervaded the town. The close proximity of ships to the busy town added to its bustle. Crowds of people blocked the streets. Pale Britishers, flushed with victory, contrasted with the hale but disheartened Frenchmen. The streets were thronged with Chinese, Ceylonese, Bengalese, Moors, Arabs, Malagashes and Africans, with pedigree Creoles and proud *mulatres*.

A novelty that attracted the curiosity of the townsfolk was the Sepoys, the Indian soldiers who served with the British forces. They were a fine looking and awe inspiring body of men. General Decaen had proclaimed before the island was taken that whoever should capture a Sepoy should have him for a slave.

Port Louis, although bursting with activity, was perfectly secure. The shops were open all day and doing flourishing business. There was a gay display of jewellers, cutlers and milliners shops as well as merchants dealing in more practical goods; tavern houses were open on every street.

Since a declared object of the British had been the preservation of the town, the soldiers were encouraged to patronize it. Many had been confined for weeks in the cramped conditions of their ships at sea or isolated on the rugged island of Rodrigues. They filled the streets, shops and taverns, spending freely money they had accumulated for weeks without a chance to enjoy it.

The whores and those pale Creole ladies who, like fireflies, came out only after sunset, were entranced by the free-spending, heavy drinking invaders after years of deprivation wrought by the French. The town assumed an air of a European capital with its citizens, visitors and exotic inhabitants engaged in a grand pursuit of pleasure.

Pat played his part. Ma Doudou found him lodgings with an old man whose mixed ancestry was apparent from the yellowed parchment of his complexion and his rheumy, amber eyes. He was the uncle of numerous young women of the streets who called on him daily for advice and who kept him supplied with food, money and arrack, the island's coconut brandy.

With the British billeting their administrative officers on local families, Pat was fortunate to find accommodation. It was because none of the British wanted to live in a house as lowly and disreputable as the old man's two room cottage behind Market Street. Pat was pleased to make it his home, accepting Ma Doudou's decision without protest that he should move out of the townhouse to avoid antagonizing Lindsay.

That unpleasant young man, faced with a town full of despised British, retreated to his father's plantation of Belrose. There was a chance, however, that he would return without warning, so Pat was obliged to be wary in his dealings with Claudette. He wrestled with his conscience about her behaviour only briefly. The blind tolerance of infatuation was strong enough for him to forgive her.

He accepted her love for him was sparse compared with the generosity of his feeling for her. Constantly over the weeks of their relationship she warned him not to see in her the soulmate he sought. He agreed, although secretly he harboured a longing that she would change her mind. For the time being, he was content with whatever chances for pleasure he could indulge in with her.

Like him, Claudette had a passionate nature and, despite her misgivings, was soon partnering him in boisterous sessions of lovemaking, either in the old man's house when he was out or on the grass of the Champ de Mars in the moonlight. With Claudette as his mistress, he was able to resist enticement by the beautiful half-breed whores who visited the old man in his lodgings and seemed keen to know him better.

After the confusion and excitement of the capture of the island, life in town settled down to a new pace. Governor Farquhar issued proclamations directing the inhabitants to follow their usual occupations. Under the terms of the treaty of capitulation, the pledge of religious freedom and the full enjoyment of local laws and customs helped the indigenous population appreciate the benefits of the British occupation.

Port Louis resembled a vast European market rather than a captured city. Products from India, Bourbon (where Farquhar had himself been temporary governor), the Cape and England found a ready market, while those of the new colony were immediately dispatched to London. The immense sums of money put into circulation by the new government and troops was convincing evidence that life for the islanders under the British was an improvement.

It was said that there was only one wheeled carriage in the island at its capture. Pat didn't see it. Within days of the British arrival, Governor Farquhar's industry in rehabilitating the town was everywhere apparent. The streets, which were straight and laid out at right angles to each other and were impassable due to neglect, were repaired by army engineers. Footpaths were laid with basaltic kerbstones, the ruts in the roads levelled out and the potholes filled in.

During the weeks of the repairs to the town, Pat occasionally met Robert Farquhar when he was inspecting his men at work. The Governor took a walk after dawn every morning, accompanied by a small clique of army officers sweltering in their heavy uniforms in the heat. The Governor himself showed no sign of lassitude and his energy was unflagging. In the evenings he rode on the outskirts of the town, exercising his horse on the Champ de Mars or cantering along the roads that were already repaired.

One evening, as Pat strolled across the plain after visiting Claudette, he heard someone shout his name.

He had eaten well of Ma Doudou's cooking, and turned leisurely to see the Governor galloping up to him, ahead of his breathless retinue.

'Enjoying the good life, Pat?' Robert called, reining his horse to a halt.

His smile was genuinely friendly and it amused Pat that the clique of military men who were his courtiers could only scowl in greeting. He wondered if they approved of the Governor's informal methods for winning support for the British administration. His unconventional approach worked, for Robert Farquhar had become the most popular man in Mauritius.

Robert swung out of his saddle to stroll at his side, waving his escort on with a cheery grin. They seemed to know better than to protest although it was clear by their grieved expressions that they didn't like to leave the Governor alone with him.

'I can have no one securer than you to accompany me, Pat.' Robert laughed as his escorts rode away, taking his horse with them. 'I look back over the weeks to that day we met at the stream with pleasure. That was my last moment of respite.'

'You should have told me then you were going to be Governor,' Pat said to taunt him.

'You should have told me you were in league with Lindsay Genave.'

He gasped, a stab of anxiety pricking him at Robert's astonishing criticism. 'What do you mean?'

Robert chuckled. 'You have a bad reputation among my advisers, Pat. That's why they are reluctant to leave us alone together. Lindsay Genave is responsible for some agitation against British rule among the French and Creole settlers. You are his friend and therefore not to be trusted.'

'Friend!' His anger flared at the mistake. 'I've met Lindsay only once. He was in bed with his half-sister and promised to kill me next time we meet. Your intelligence is as unreliable as some of your advisers, Robert.' He used the Governor's first name casually, testing their relationship.

'You frequent his father's townhouse and are cared for by his slaves.' Robert nodded in the direction of the house. 'My advisers consider that's enough to assume you are Lindsay's friend and, being an American, perhaps sympathetic to his aims.'

He tried to understand where the conversation was leading. 'What do *you* think?' he asked crossly.

'A military man survives by being suspicious. My instinct is to trust people, to respect them. Plans are in hand for my ball, Pat. I'm asking the French and Creole settlers, including the Genave family. I want this to set the seal on conciliation.

'A grand ball and supper will introduce us to each other. There will also be hundreds of the fairer sex there.' He nudged him in his ribs. 'That should appeal to you.'

He grinned pleasantly to disguise his concern that Robert seemed to know a lot about him. 'Does the fairer sex,' he asked with mock innocence, 'include the tawnier maids of Mauritius?'

Robert gazed at him, his lips tightening with displeasure at the question. 'Only those who are free and legitimate will be present, Pat. It is my hope that the miscegenation favoured by the French in their colonization of Mauritius will have no place under my administration.'

'Spoken like a true governor!' he said sarcastically.

Robert patted him on his shoulder. 'All this must be exciting for you.' He indicated with a nod of his head that he meant life in Mauritius. 'You feel free here, you indulge yourself at your whim. You're a man of energy, Pat, with a healthy disdain for convention. You're just the type I need to set this island back on its feet.'

He was uncomfortable with Robert's arm around his shoulder as well as worried by what he said. 'I lied to you at the river. I'm not a planter. I have nothing here, no patron. I depend for my existence on the kindness of a slave and the love of her daughter.'

Robert chuckled as though the information was of no consequence. 'I knew I was right to trust you. When you've found your feet, you'll become the planter you aspire to be. You might even consider growing sugar, when you have no suspect friends and when you have your own land . . .'

The hint in his voice about having his own land intrigued Pat but before he could ask what he meant, Robert saluted casually. 'I must be on my way!' He increased his pace, striding into Market Street, leaving him alone at the edge of the plain.

Pat wondered why the Governor was appealing for his support and apparently offering him land if he gave it. *He's worried about Lindsay*, he thought as he strolled to his lodgings, *and he wants me to stop him.*

The threat of Lindsay Genave to Governor Farquhar's administration seemed remote in the weeks preceding the ball. It was a time of hectic activity. Dressmakers worked far into the night preparing copies of the latest European fashions for the English and French women who were to attend. Cooks, including Ma Doudou, were pressed into service to prepare food for the sumptuous supper that was to be served.

Some of Mr Genave's slaves arrived from Belrose in advance of their master's visit for the ball. Claudette supervised them in readying the house for his arrival. On the night before Mr Genave was due, she left Troptard in charge of the slaves in the house and made her way to Pat's lodgings. He heard her special knock and opened the door eagerly.

'You're late,' he said after embracing her.

'I can't stay long.' She told him about the arrival of the slaves while she settled down on the pallet, giving him a generous view of her legs under a profusion of petticoats.

The sight roused him instantly. He sat beside her on the mattress and clasped her around her shoulders with one hand while the other snaked under her skirts. She made a weak attempt to push him away.

'There's no time . . .'

He closed her mouth with a kiss, gently stroking the inside of her thigh. Her legs were spread apart and he discovered she was moist and throbbing, ready for him. He responded to her need with an ardent desire of his own. It was over in minutes, an animal lust that they satisfied in each other. He loved her for it.

'I must go.'

He didn't answer as she withdrew and stood up, smoothing down her skirt and petticoats.

'When Mr Genave is here I won't be able to see you.'

He bit his lip, suddenly jealous of the old man. 'Why not?' he asked suspiciously, wondering what it was she had to do for her master.

She laughed, and the sound reassured him. 'There'll be too much work in the house. You'd better not come there. I'll send Troptard with your meals.'

'Bring supper yourself, when the old man's asleep.'

'I'll try . . .' Her whisper set his loins tingling again. 'I'll need supper too.'

'I like that,' he said, rising to his feet and kissing her. 'Is Lindsay coming for the ball?'

She patted his waist affectionately. 'No. He's touring the plantations to see what support there is among the planters for action against the British.' She giggled. 'Most of the planters will be at the ball on Friday. Probably only Lindsay will keep away to show his disapproval.'

'I wish he'd keep away from you.'

She kissed him warmly on his lips and then suddenly he was alone with only the tantalizing scent of her body and perfume lingering in his room to remind him of her.

He smiled to himself. She was like the girls in the Mattaponi woods. It was fifteen months since he fled from Virginia. His thoughts immediately drifted to Deborah. He sighed. He was never likely to see her again yet he would always feel the challenge in his heart when he thought of her.

His nostalgia for Deborah surprised him. In Claudette he had what he craved from a woman: energetic and loving sex. It was enough. Or was it? As he lay down on the pallet, alone in the darkness, hearing the droning of mosquitoes and feeling the discomfort of the humid heat, he remembered the aloofness of Deborah's hard stare. The very coolness of her nature and the wrong impression she had of him was what kept him interested, even though she was ten thousand miles away.

Despite his satisfaction with Claudette's skilled lovemaking, he drifted to sleep with Deborah's name on his lips.

For three nights he did not see Claudette. Troptard brought his meals and explained in his surly manner that Mr Genave was in residence so Pat must keep out of sight. He also brought him a suit to wear to the ball. Pat assumed it was Lindsay's and donned the clothes with trepidation.

Troptard accompanied him through the crowds that thronged the streets on the night of the ball. The courtyard of Government House was packed with settlers and their wives, their slaves and the curious. The presence of so many slaves intrigued him.

'Claudette could have come too!'

Troptard shook his head. 'Slaves stay outside.'

The courtyard was a glittering display of finery. Women of all shades of complexion were bedecked in extravagantly expensive jewellery and wearing gaudy copies of the latest fashions. The men were resplendent in new suits and starched collars.

Many of the guests came by palanquin and each one was accompanied by four slaves as bearers together with others as flambeaux holders and escorts. It seemed that each guest had tried to outdo the other in the size and flamboyance of his slave entourage. Not even the oldest settlers could remember an occasion like it under the French.

'Where's Mr Genave?' Pat asked Troptard as he gazed around the colourful throng waiting for the ball to start.

Before Troptard could point him out, the doors of Government House were thrown open. The guests surged forward as the sound of an orchestra swelled out into the balmy night. The watching slaves clapped and jumped up and down with delight.

'Farquhar's won the slaves,' a man muttered beside him. He turned and saw it was Mr Buchanan. The consul apparently didn't recognize him.

'The Governor's a master in matters colonial,' he said pompously. 'Especially when his initiative, patriotism and humanity can be exercised.'

Pat was grateful that the push of the crowd carried him away from Mr Buchanan and up the steps to the house. The rooms of one wing had been opened up into each other to form a ballroom. The orchestra, augmented by British bandsmen in uniform, played a lively tune to set people in a party mood. Army officers mingled with the guests, introducing themselves with a forced charm which showed by its stiffness that they were acting under orders to be amiable.

Pat, knowing no one except Robert Farquhar, missed Claudette's company and even that of Troptard. He wandered from the ballroom to the other wing of the house where a long table stretched the length of the vast room. It groaned under an abundance of game, fowl, beef and fish.

Troops of stewards bearing trays of drinks filed through the ranks of the assembled guests. The ball seemed destined for success as the pitch of conversation grew louder, the music livelier and the mood gayer. The brighter it became, the more alone and dejected he felt.

Morosely, he studied what Robert Farquhar called 'the fairer sex.' The Creole belles displayed good figures and interesting features, with dresses that were colourful even if their complexions were pallid from their secluded existence. It was the custom for white ladies to avoid the sun. They stayed in the shadows of their homes all day until after sunset. If they had to go out in the day time, they went only in heavily veiled bonnets and long sleeved gowns, terrified of the sun darkening their skins.

They held no appeal for him, despite the encouraging glances and fluttering eyelashes that met his roving gaze. It seemed nothing would lift his dull mood.

The French and Creole settlers waltzed with a langour that was suited to the tropical heat. Afterwards, the British with a determined bonhomie engaged in an athletic English country dance which astonished the locals. The younger ones greeted the English antics with laughter while their elders smiled behind their fans.

Some of the French, entering into Mr Farquhar's call for conciliation, joined in the British capering, only to become speedily fatigued by the quick and agile motions which were so contrary to their slower movements when dancing.

'We've fireworks afterwards.' Governor Farquhar had crept up on him without him knowing, surprising Pat. He had a perspiring, long-nosed aide fussing in attendance.

Pat tried to smile. 'The ball is a great success, Robert,' he muttered politely.

'You aren't enjoying it?' Robert, ever sensitive, turned to the aide. 'Mr Rendye, please find a young English lady for my friend to partner in a dance.'

'I am afraid there are only six English ladies present, sir.' The aide tried to smooth away the worry lines from his sweating brow with his hand. 'Perhaps a Creole . . .?'

'No, thank you!' Pat was irritated by the aide's fawning. 'I doubt whether any of your guests would consider me worthy to partner them.'

'What nonsense, Pat!' Robert winked at him. 'There are some special guests of mine who are very keen to meet you. Follow me!'

Pat swallowed his ill humour, trailing after the Governor

and vowing to himself that this would be the last time he would allow himself to be patronized by the man. He resented Robert's facile charm and the way people responded eagerly to it. He sensed he was being manipulated by him and it stirred in him a perverse feeling to flout his authority.

The crowd parted as the Governor strode from room to room. Mr Rendye, his aide, scurried along at his side, searching the faces of the guests for the one the Governor was seeking. He paused before an old gentleman seated in a corner, surrounded by a bevy of admiring young ladies.

Robert Farquhar reached for Pat's elbow and urged him forward. 'Monsieur Genave,' he said with a flourish, 'may I present my good friend, Pat Romain, the young planter from Virginia about whom you have already heard so much.'

Pat bowed, surprised at meeting his unwitting benefactor at last. He saw the strength of character in his weather-worn face and in the hard glitter of his eyes. He liked the old man but as he waited for him to speak, he felt someone staring at him with an intensity that made him embarrassed. He glanced irritably at the young woman at his side, ready to discourage her keen interest in him with a scowl.

The sight of her struck him dumb. She was smiling at him in a way that was so familiar. His impulse was to seize her in his arms and shower her face with kisses of delight. He blinked, trying to understand what was happening.

'For ... forgive me ...' he stammered, aware of Mr Genave watching him curiously.

'But yes,' said the old man with a wry smile. 'Let me introduce you.' He nodded at the young woman, giving her permission to extend her hand. 'This is my only daughter, Giselle.'

The woman's pale features, heightened with a blush of rouge at her cheeks, were identical with Claudette's. Only her fair complexion and her hair, a sunburst of bright auburn with tresses that shone, were different.

He took her hand nervously in his and was instantly overwhelmed by the extraordinary sense of intimacy her touch stirred in him. He kissed her fingers in a daze, not wanting to release her from his grasp. Slowly, he raised his eyes to meet hers.

A feeling of panic seized him then. He thrust her hand away from him and turned on his heels, striding out of the room without daring to look back.

CHAPTER EIGHTEEN

Pat's mind floundered. He walked the seashore aimlessly following the rugged line of the cliffs until he was clear of the town. The noise of the sea battering the rocks drowned the throbbing in his brain as he grappled with the uncertainty his meeting with Giselle Genave had aroused. Every fibre of his body tingled with alarm.

His foolish act in walking away from her solved nothing. The image of her innocent pleasure suddenly dashed because of his churlishness troubled his heart. He stumbled wildly along the cliff path, his hair damp with spray from the sea, and his chest heaving with anguish. He was consumed with guilt. He had run from her yet he wanted to see her again, to apologize, to explain.

Explain. What? He stopped abruptly in his mad rush away from the town and turned to face the sea. Instinct told him there was no escape. He could plunge off the rocks and commit himself to the waves, trusting them for an answer. He shuddered at his own despair. No, it wasn't despair. It was a feeling that he was caught up, like a feather in the wind, in a current of events over which he had no control.

The shock of meeting Giselle, of seeing a pure, white version of her voluptuous half-sister, his own mistress Claudette, bewildered him. And that searching look in her eyes of smouldering azure as dark as the night, had reached into his thoughts. He was ashamed, appalled, by the lust of wanting that leapt in his loins at the touch of her finger on his. He had fled from her to save her from the very destruction that her pouting smile of tenderness seemed to crave.

He spun away from the sea with a curse on his lips. He smote his brow with his hand and dragged his fingers back through his damp, tousled locks. The action served to calm him. She was just a girl, after all. He had behaved abominably and must apologize to her, to her father and to Robert Farquhar.

It was unrealistic to assume that her polite expression of interest at being introduced to him meant anything stronger. But he knew those eyes. They were midnight instead of Claudette's dark sunset in colour, yet their message was plain. His knowledge of Claudette and the uncanny resemblance of the two women made him feel he knew Giselle already.

There were dozens of reasons to explain his vulnerability to her. Yet the more he tried to rationalize his feelings and his reason for his crazed striding out of Government House, the more he was aware there was little he could do about it. Since he had landed on the Mauritius shore, there was an inevitability governing his future. Meeting Ma Doudou, loving Claudette, and now . . . Giselle.

He looked up at the jagged peaks of the mountains encircling the town, outlined in the moonlight shining on them, and felt comforted. Fate was a moonbeam and he followed it, shrugging his shoulders as he turned and hurried back to the town.

He waited in the shadows of the Champ de Mars for Giselle and her father to return from the ball. Troptard held a flambeau aloft as they descended from the palanquins. Giselle took her father's arm to help him up the steps through the garden to the house. Pat followed, unseen in the darkness that closed in behind them. When he gained the safety of a bougainvillaea bush he crouched behind it to observe the old man and his daughter on the verandah.

With a silent chuckle at his foolishness, he remembered how he used to spy on Deborah and her father. The thought of Deborah stirred him again. He tried to analyse the difference in his feeling for Deborah and his reaction to Giselle. He had wanted to possess Deborah as an act of conquest. For Giselle, he wanted only to protect her even though the threat was from himself.

The gentle sound of French drifted softly to his ears. He stared through the darkness to where a lantern hung from the verandah roof, bathing Giselle and her father in its pale golden glow.

'We are English now, Giselle,' Mr Genave said firmly. 'Won't you speak English too?'

'Of course, papa.' Giselle's voice had the slightest trace of an accent that lent her words a touch of scintillation to Pat's ears.

'It was a wonderful evening,' she said enthusiastically. 'The British were so concerned to present themselves in an admirable light.'

'Yes, my dear.' The old man nodded kindly. 'Yet you didn't dance once. I thought you were bored.'

'Oh no, papa.' She suddenly looked sad, her expression tugging at Pat's conscience. 'I would have danced . . .' Her voice faded and she stared into the garden.

He shifted uncomfortably, reading her thoughts. He wanted to shout out and warn her. He was no good!

'That young American?' Mr Genave sounded sympathetic, his voice heavy with wisdom. 'I've heard a lot about him.'

'Have you?' Giselle turned eagerly to face her father. 'Tell me! Wasn't he extraordinary? He had a fire in his eyes, papa, that blazed. I wanted to run after him when he walked out. He was the only man there undaunted by it all.'

Mr Genave chuckled. 'The Governor wants me to invite him to Belrose. He is a planter, it seems. Mr Farquhar suggests he will help us grow sugar instead of coffee.'

Giselle gripped her father's hand. 'Will you, papa? Will you ask him to Belrose?'

'Of course, Giselle.' Mr Genave smiled as he allowed her to help him to his feet. 'I must do the Governor's bidding. Besides, we have need of a young man at Belrose. Lindsay is so seldom at home. He has no interest in the plantation, I fear.'

He waited while Giselle helped the old man off the verandah into the depths of the house. He watched Troptard douse all the lanterns except one which burned dimly in the corner, throwing shadows over the bushes surrounding the house. The shutters of the windows were closed and he had no idea where Giselle was sleeping. He felt wretched at the pang of desire that pricked him, and pushed it out of his mind.

Troptard opened the door of the house, glanced suspiciously into the garden and then, apparently satisfied, closed the house door behind him and settled down on the deck of the verandah in front of it. He lay on the boards, blocking the doorway with his body, and cradled his head in the crook of his arm as he went to sleep.

Using the stealth he had developed through his nights prowling the Mattaponi woods, Pat glided soundlessly around the side of the house. The moonlight showed him the outline of the kitchen cabin. He wondered if Claudette was there. His body yearned for release. He would take her, imagining as he did so that it was the sweet Giselle in his arms, not the practiced slave wench.

His arm was suddenly seized and twisted up behind his back. A shaft of light fell across his face as the door to the kitchen cabin burst open. He made no attempt to resist, guessing from the potent smell of his breath that it was Troptard who held him. His arm was hurting where Troptard gripped him, so he couldn't try to flee.

'Pat?' Ma Doudou clucked her tongue. 'What do you want?' She stood at the door of her kitchen with her hands on her hips. Her grey hair stood out in tufts from her head, the kerchief she usually wore to cover her plaits was draped around her shoulders. She seemed annoyed at his presence.

'Where's Claudette? I want her!'

'She's not here.'

The starkness of her reply distressed Pat. She was lying. He tried to twist free but Troptard's hold on him was like a vice. He wondered whether to struggle. He could buck backwards into his crotch and then swing his fist into Troptard's jaw.

'Release him!' Ma Doudou's curt command broke his plan.

'I suppose she's in bed with her father!' he said scathingly, rubbing his wrist where Troptard had held it. He felt helpless.

'She is a slave, Pat. Like me.'

'You're her mother. Don't you care?'

'Mr Genave is good to us. Claudette has to be good to him. A slave has no say in what she must do. We thank the Lord we have a kind master.'

'It disgusts me.'

'Why? Because you want Claudette for yourself alone. She is your wench, isn't that enough?'

'No!' He bit his lip, shaking his head defiantly. He was aware of Troptard's mocking eyes. 'I like Claudette.'

Trying to conceal his bitterness he added, 'I can't get used to her owner having first call on her body.'

'Pat . . .' Ma Doudou sounded sorrowful and touched his arm to draw him into the cabin. 'Won't you sit with me?' She indicated a chair in the corner of the cabin. A candle burned on a shelf. The embers of the fire in the kitchen hearth glowed dimly. Ma Doudou closed the door, shutting out Troptard despite his whimper of protest.

'I told him to go to sleep,' she said, waddling across the cabin to a cupboard. She took a flask from it and two goblets that obviously belonged in the house. Without asking if he wanted a drink, she poured an amber liquid from the flask into each goblet and handed him one.

He waited for her to drink before he ventured to sip. It was good cognac, like potent honey compared with the harsh whiskey of Jed Allason's still by the Mattaponi. He sipped thoughtfully, feeling a strength spread through his limbs, relaxing him.

'Why didn't you tell me about *her*?' he said, breaking the silence. 'It was like seeing Claudette's ghost.' He paused, then when Ma Doudou said nothing he added with a sigh, 'I think I'm falling in love with her.'

'Ah!' Ma Doudou beamed.

'Tell me! Tell me she's not like Claudette in anything more than appearance.'

'Hush!' Ma Doudou touched his knee to calm him. 'You'll wake the household. You'll wake Giselle.'

He crumpled under her gaze, feeling despair billowing over him. 'Help me, Ma Doudou.' He was amazed at himself for feeling so weak, and lonely.

'I don't know what to do. She fascinates me. I feel I know her, but I don't. Because she and Claudette look so much alike, I feel she's mine, yet she's not. I'm confused.'

'There's no need to be.' Ma Doudou poured more cognac into his goblet and he sipped it without noticing as he listened to her.

'Giselle was born in the same year as Claudette. Her mother died giving birth to her. She's especially precious to her father because of that. I was her wetnurse. She and Claudette grew up like sisters until Claudette was obliged by convention to take her place as a slave while Giselle became the mistress of Belrose. Mr Genave worships her, Pat, and she adores him.'

'Does she know . . .?' He gulped back the bile of disgust that rose in his throat. 'Does Giselle know about her father and Claudette. About Lindsay, her *brother*, and Claudette?'

'Of course not.' Ma Doudou was shocked. 'Giselle is an innocent, a beautiful and virginal young lady, devoted to her father and living under his jealous protection. Remember that, if nothing else.'

He squirmed with embarrassment at the warning in her voice.

'Belrose is a lonely, isolated plantation. The Genaves make their own rules. You must be careful if you go there.'

'You're an old schemer!' Pat laughed harshly. 'You and Claudette have used me before. What mischief are you planning now?'

'Nothing.'

'Nothing is right.' He stood up, almost banging his head on the low ceiling. 'I'm not fitting into your plans whatever they are. I ran away from Giselle tonight but I was running away from myself too. There is an ardour burning wild within me. I feel its heat.

'I will do something worthy of that woman, not tarnish her with my wanting. I'm keeping away from her, Ma Doudou. I'll go back to that brothel in the town, anything, to save her from myself. She will never be spoiled by me!'

The last image he had of Ma Doudou as he thrust open the door and stepped out into the night, was of the old lady's triumphant smile as she nodded her head with pleasure at his outburst. It made him feel again that he was caught in a current of fate that could drown him unless he was strong.

'No,' he said, turning his back on Robert Farquhar. 'I won't spy on the Genaves for you.'

'Pat, my dear chap, I'm not asking you to pry into their *private* business. Only into what the *nature* of their conversations is. The British position is still somewhat tenuous. Not all the French have accepted us yet.'

The Governor put his hand on his shoulder as he stood beside him. He was staring out of the window of the

Governor's office over the Place Des Armes parade ground to the harbour beyond.

Robert continued in his soft, beguiling brogue. 'I need to know what the French are saying in the bosom of their homes.'

'Then ask someone else!'

Governor Farquhar pursed his lips. 'You are fortunate to have been invited to Belrose Plantation,' he said, his voice tightening. 'You are a man without means here . . .'

'So what?' Pat ignored the outspoken threat in Robert's remark.

'Destitutes are a problem that have to be dealt with. I shall be allowing the French settlers who don't want to stay under British rule to return to France. What should I allow you to do? You're not a settler, you have nothing and no one. You came on an American ship. Would I have to put you aboard one, possibly against your will?' He squeezed Pat's shoulder as though suddenly remembering something.

'On the other hand . . . you have your experience as a planter! You could be of much use to a benefactor, even if he is French. Eventually you could qualify for a grant of land of your own.'

Pat jerked away, slipping out of his grasp. He sighed, staring at Robert reluctantly. 'What do you want me to do?'

'Go to Belrose, enjoy the old man's hospitality now he's invited you. Listen to everything. Report to me alone.'

'I don't speak French.' Pat felt a surge of hope. 'I won't understand what the family are saying among themselves.'

'Make Giselle your ally. She's a charming woman, quite taken by you, I hear. She'll willingly be your ears. Encourage her to tell you everything that is being said about my administration. Naturally, you won't say why, of course.'

'Giselle?' An odd emptiness yawned in the depths of his guts. 'You want me to use her. After I spurned her at your damned ball.'

'She will do as you say.'

'Maybe she will. But I won't deceive her. She's too innocent for me to take advantage of her.'

Robert Farquhar smiled knowingly but said no more.

Pat thought of the conversation as he rode along the trail

through the hills to Flacq. Troptard accompanied him, walking easily at the horse's side, unaffected by the heat and the distance of their journey. At times he was forced to dismount while Troptard led the horse across mountain streams and over patches where the trail was strewn with boulders and too treacherous for riding.

Troptard had come from Belrose to escort him. Ma Doudou and Claudette were already at the plantation. The town house had been closed up when Augustus Genave and Giselle returned to Belrose a few days after the Governor's ball.

'Do we have much further to go?' he asked Troptard, as he followed the youth leading the horse up a slope. He was feeling tired, in need of a drink, and short tempered. The thought of seeing Giselle filled him with trepidation. He hadn't spoken to her since the night of the ball and yet, because of his intimacy with Claudette, he felt close to her.

Troptard said nothing in answer to his question. They reached the top of the slope and the youth handed him the reins of the horse, gesturing with his head for him to mount.

Pat smirked. 'Aren't you worried I'll try to escape? What will your master do if you return without me?'

Troptard's eyes narrowed and Pat felt the impact of his scornful gaze.

'All right,' he said climbing onto the horse, 'I won't try to escape, so don't worry. I'll go when I'm ready. No one's going to keep me at Belrose against my will.' He dug in his heels to make the horse gallop so he could leave Troptard behind. Yet even the horse seemed to be under the youth's spell and continued to amble along, with Troptard strolling at his side.

The jungly forest surrounding the trail was thinning out. There were fewer branches overhead shading the path from the sun and the whole atmosphere seemed lighter. In the distance, beyond a great sweep of hills, was the sea.

They were facing east, the sun at its height overhead, and the distant sea was like a mirror reflecting the vivid blue of the sky. He sighed to himself, drawing contentment from the view, letting it quell his doubts about his meeting with Giselle.

'Yonder!'

Troptard's shout interrupted his reverie. He looked in the

direction the youth was pointing and saw the single turret and the red pantiled roof of the villa contrasting with the green of the trees that surrounded it. The uneven expanse of the fields around the house were thick with bushes. *Coffee*, he thought while his eye took in the rest of the scene. There was a river flowing close to the house, its course through the valley marked by the darker green of the trees that lined its banks.

He sniffed the air; the purity of the light breeze was cooling after the heat of the trail. Instinctively he looked at the soil. It was rich, reminding him of Five Acre Field and the Virginia plantation he had left. *Tobacco*, he thought immediately. *Tobacco, not coffee or sugar, is the crop for here.*

A scream shattered the heavy silence of the early afternoon. It hung over the vista, chilling him with a feeling of dread. He glanced anxiously at Troptard. The youth's shrug of indifference annoyed him. The scream echoed again, and again, punctuated by the awful sound of a whip cracking and the slap of leather against human flesh.

'By the devil!' He wheeled the horse's head from Troptard's fingers, 'What's going on?'

He dug his heels furiously into the flanks of the horse and the animal, freed from Troptard's restraining hand, responded. It galloped towards the noise while he crouched low over its neck to avoid the overhanging branches that threatened to sweep him off.

The screams continued unabated. The horse plunged through the undergrowth and brought him to a glade beside a clump of coffee bushes. A slave was lying on the ground, his loincloth in tatters around his waist, his thighs and buttocks streaked with blood. A white man stood over him, legs planted apart, the stock of a bullwhip gripped firmly in his hands.

The man barely raised his head as he approached. He continued to lash at the defenceless man at his feet, deaf to his shout of protest and the slave's frantic cries of agony.

'Damn you!' Pat shouted, reining the horse to a halt. 'Stop that at once.'

The man sniggered, increasing the speed with which he belaboured his hapless victim.

Pat leapt from the saddle and flung himself across the man's back. They fell to the ground together. Pat struggled to get hold of the whip. The man's face was in front of his, the passion in his eyes erupting to a bitter fury as he cast the whip aside and reached with both hands for Pat's throat.

'Lindsay!' he exclaimed in disgust when he recognized him. Then he was hit a blow on the back of his head and everything caved in as he fell limp in Lindsay's murderous grasp.

CHAPTER NINETEEN

A tear-smothered voice, little more than a whisper, murmured close to his ear yet it seemed to come from a long way off. Its lilting cadence was disturbed by concern and he let the French-accented English linger in his brain. He made no effort to understand it. He recognized the timbre, not the words, and kept his eyes closed, trying to recall what had happened.

He was lying down, a soft pillow under his head. He felt enormously comfortable, influenced by the concern of those standing around him. He listened without really hearing what they were saying as he became aware of his body. It ached. Most of all, his head throbbed with an agony that was like a bright sun shining in his eyes, even though he kept them closed.

A voice with an infinitely compassionate tone caressed his ears and then a cloth soaked in eau-de-Cologne, sweet scented and cool, was laid across his brow.

'He attacked me!' Lindsay's sullen voice made Pat flinch involuntarily. A hand stroked his shoulder to soothe him. He had no energy to protest so he lay still, trying to understand what was going on.

'He is our guest.' Mr Genave's voice quavered with indignation as well as age. There was no mistaking his authority despite its tremulousness.

'This American is here under our protection, Lindsay. We are to welcome him. You should have embraced him, not tried to throttle him to death.'

'Never!'

Augustus Genave squawked with fury. 'My God! What is wrong with you? He is not even English for you to hate him so much.'

'He is a trouble maker . . .' Lindsay's voice died, showing he realized he could not explain to his father the real reason for his hatred of Pat.

'That's for me to judge. You will leave him alone.'

'With pleasure!' Lindsay's voice oozed malice. 'Have you finished?' he demanded insolently.

'No.' There was a pause as Mr Genave sat down. Pat heard a tray clinking with glasses and guessed the old man was being offered a drink. He hoped for water himself but preferred to pretend he was still unconscious.

'Why were you striking that slave?'

At first Lindsay didn't answer. His reply, when it came, was spoken from a different part of the room. He had turned away from his father and was facing the window overlooking the plantation. 'He was disobedient,' he said sulkily.

'That is not sufficient reason to lacerate a slave to death. The American was right to stop you.'

'Shit!' Lindsay's voice erupted angrily. 'You've never bothered yourself with a slave's welfare before. What if I had killed the bugger, we'd soon get another.'

'Ah!' Mr Genave's exclamation was like a pronouncement. Pat sensed the tension in the room as the others waited for what the old man had to say. The hand stroking his shoulder quivered.

'You forget, son, we are no longer French. The British have banned the trade in slaves. Where can we buy more when one dies? Every African is valuable now. They must be cherished so they can give many years of work. We will not be able to replace the sick or elderly or maimed with ease in future.'

'Of course we will!' Lindsay strode across the room. Pat followed his progress by the vibrations of the couch as he passed close to where he was lying.

'Your precious Governor Farquhar cannot patrol every bay on the coast. When we need Africans, I can sail to Madagascar and smuggle some in at night. I can outwit the British any day.'

'I forbid you to do such a thing!' Shock showed in Mr Genave's shaky voice. 'We must obey the British commands if we are to take advantage of their presence here.'

'You're too old. You've gone soft in your head! I'll show you I can do it. Other settlers don't give up as easily as you.'

The slamming of the door as he left the room added to the impact of Lindsay's insults. The hand stroking Pat's shoulder was removed.

'Papa . . .' The dulcet tones of Giselle's voice contrasted soothingly with Lindsay's harshness. 'He didn't mean it.'

'But yes, he did.' Mr Genave sounded resigned. 'How is the American? Help me up from this chair. Let me see him.'

'He'll be all right.' It was Ma Doudou speaking in her no-nonsense fashion and Pat drew reassurance from her presence. 'Troptard done stun him, that's all. Lindsay stop the strangling when I arrived.'

Embarrassed at having Mr Genave, Giselle and Ma Doudou gazing down at him, Pat opened his eyes. His first glimpse, through a mist of pain, was of Giselle.

A ringlet of stray hair hung loose over her brow and she brushed it aside as she became aware of him watching her. Her eyes were soft with concern, her lips trembling.

He watched the joy spread through her features as she realized his eyes were open and he was trying to smile. Her happiness revived him.

'Sit up,' said Ma Doudou from the other side of the couch. She leaned over and her strong arms eased him into a sitting position. 'Drink this.'

He swallowed dutifully, keeping his eyes on Giselle. A blush stole through her pale features, lending her a radiance that filled him with both excitement and shame. He was thrilled by her proximity, yet ashamed at himself for his need of her. He drew up his knees so no one would see how his body was roused.

Mr Genave put out his hand. 'My son has given you a rude welcome, Pat. I hope you will stay and forget his discourtesy.'

Pat felt the old man's fingers, fragile skin and bone, in his hand and tried not to squeeze too hard. 'Thank you,' he murmured, then coughed, surprised at the weakness of his voice. He sipped more of the liquid Ma Doudou offered him. When he took his eyes off Giselle he could concentrate.

'I am sorry my arrival has caused so much confusion.'

'It is our pleasure, Pat. I hope you can forgive Lindsay. He is hot headed.'

'I am sore headed from the blow!' He rubbed his neck and Mr Genave laughed with relief at being able to dismiss the matter.

'Troptard is sometimes too diligent.'

'Troptard didn't mean to hurt you, Pat,' Ma Doudou said, springing to the youth's defence. 'Lindsay is the one you must blame.'

He said nothing, wondering why Ma Doudou was disagreeing with her master and encouraging him to hate Lindsay. He needed no persuasion to dislike that arrogant bully.

'You must be tired . . . after your journey.' Mr Genave smiled considerately. 'Ma Doudou will prepare some gumbo for you, soup that will restore your strength. My daughter will show you your quarters so you can rest.' He paused and looked from Pat to Giselle. 'I trust you won't run off as you did at Government House.'

'I am sorry.' He swung his legs over the side of the couch and stood up. Perhaps he rose too quickly for his head suddenly began to spin. He put out his hand to steady himself and found he was grasping Giselle's shoulder. He clung to her while the spasm passed.

'I'm all right . . .' He blinked, trying to withdraw his hand but finding Giselle was supporting him under his shoulders with her own hand. Her presence that at first had made him feel better, now made him weak. The concern in her eyes was too great to bear. He looked in desperation at Mr Genave and smiled apologetically.

'I understand.' The old man nodded, and strangely Pat felt that Mr Genave did indeed understand his quandary. 'So does Giselle. Go with her.'

Ma Doudou led the way, her sprightly waddle conveying her pleasure at Pat's acceptance into the household. She chattered happily but he was not listening. He was acutely aware of Giselle's arm around his back, her hand clasping him under his arm to give him support as he walked. It astonished him that there was such dependable strength in what appeared to be a dainty, ladylike frame.

'I can walk,' he said, trying to shake her hand off.

'Good.' She smiled, her eyes confidently scanning his face. 'I do not think I could carry you.' She maintained her hold on him though. It was practical, without a hint of deeper intention.

'I'm sorry . . .' He began to apologize for his behaviour at the ball. It was going to be hard to explain with her hand around his body. 'At the ball . . .'

'Say nothing,' she said lightly. 'It's happened before. People who've met Claudette and then see me, invariably doubt their own minds. We look so much alike, yet we're quite different. As you will see.'

'You don't mind?'

'It's rather amusing.'

'How are you different . . .?' His voice failed as her eyes widened with mock astonishment at his question.

'I'm not like Claudette at all!'

'You are in looks. A little.'

She nodded and it brought him a sense of peace, releasing him from his guilt. Ma Doudou was standing at the entrance to a room and he stopped by her and peered in. It was large; a bed in its centre was draped with a muslin curtain to keep out mosquitoes. A cooling breeze wafted in from a side window. There was a door open onto a gallery.

Giselle dropped her arm, releasing him, and he stepped through the room. He wanted time to distance himself from her, to be able to think.

When he walked out onto the gallery, its view made him smile with pleasure. Giselle, at his side, laughed happily at his expression. Coffee bushes stretched out before him, growing in the rise and dips of the land, and in pockets on the hillsides. Beyond were groves of uncleared tropical forest and more hills rolling down to the sea.

The gallery extended all around the villa, doors opening onto it from the bedrooms. It was an airy building of wood and granite blocks, built to withstand the weather and to take advantage of the breeze billowing over the hilltops. His room was situated over the front verandah with a view down a driveway that was well tended with flowering bushes and trees on either side. It lent the villa distinction.

'It's all so neat and tidy,' he said, recalling the dilapidated state of the Braxton mansion and its ill-kempt garden.

'That's my responsibility,' Giselle lowered her eyes modestly. She seemed to accept that he was no longer in need of her help and was assuming a shyness more becoming to her delicate beauty.

He was incredulous. 'You tell the slaves what to do?'

'Of course. Lindsay takes no part in running the plantation. Papa is too old. Someone has to see the work is done.'

Pat laughed and she blushed.

'Are you laughing at me?' Her cheeks coloured crimson.

He shook his head. The thought of an elegant young woman ordering tough Africans to work struck him as incongruous. 'You surprise me. I suppose I'm pleased.'

'Then I'm pleased.' She withdrew from his side and stepped back into the room, indicating that she was anything but pleased. 'We will leave you to rest now. Ma Doudou will bring you soup. Gumbo is made of ladies fingers,' she added with a smile of mischief, then passed quickly through the door before he could detain her and ask what she meant.

He flung himself on the bed with a groan. Nothing was working out the way he planned. He wanted to be aloof from Giselle. Instead, she was the one in command. He rolled over on the bed and gazed up at the ceiling through the muslin tester.

Ma Doudou had chattered about Lindsay's scheme to ship slaves from Madagascar. That gave him an idea. It was the kind of information Robert Farquhar wanted. Perhaps he could destroy Lindsay by exposing him to the Governor as a slave smuggler. He expected both Giselle and her father would be grateful.

He heard the door open and close again as someone entered the room. He assumed a slave was bringing his soup and continued to concentrate his thoughts on getting revenge. He expected Lindsay would keep out of his way. He would watch and listen carefully for any sign or hint that a smuggling trip was being planned. Then he would act.

The noise of a cup being placed on the table by the side of his bed distracted him. He turned to smile his thanks.

'Claudette!' He sat up quickly, setting his head throbbing with pain at his sudden movement. She noticed him wince.

'Don't be in a hurry, Pat.' She sat down on the bed beside him and put her hand on his brow. It was reassuring and he succumbed to the pressure of her fingers and lay his head back on the pillow.

'I don't have much time . . .' The huskiness of her voice

sent a tremor of anticipation through his body, tingling the nerve ends from his fingers to his toes. 'But I know the best cure for you.'

Her smile was broad and brazen as she leaned over him, her full lips open. Her touch shivered excitement through him and he abandoned himself to her embrace as his tongue was drawn deeply into her mouth. He surrendered, swamped by a mixture of pain and ecstacy.

Although he knew now there was no love involved, the hand that fondled him stirred a swift response. He recognized that his infatuation with her was not love as he had thought. It was lust, lent respectability by jealousy. His reaction to her now was purely physical. It was Giselle he loved.

'Your head still aches?' Claudette drew away from his lips. 'You are not yourself. Shall I go?'

He clutched her shoulder and pulled her back to him. 'No!' He sighed with wanting, shifting his body so he was lying on top of her. She smiled up at him from the depths of the soft feather pillow as he drew her skirt up to her hips. It was Giselle's smile he saw and it made him pause.

She thrust her body against the palm of his hand. His fingers closed over the plump moistness of her vagina. She moaned and he knew then the smile of wanting was uniquely hers, not Giselle's.

Pat had been asked by Robert Farquhar to use his influence to persuade Mr Genave to change from the high-risk coffee crop to growing sugar instead. Robert Farquhar reasoned that sugar could better withstand the vagaries of the tropical weather, particularly the hurricanes that swept across the island from time to time. He saw in sugar a crop that would bring an income for the island, and compete with the crop imported into England from the West Indies. In his conversations with Augustus Genave on the verandah at night, Pat advanced the Governor's views.

He had become accustomed to Mr Genave's moods and knew when the moment was right to introduce new topics to interest him. Mr Genave himself did nothing on the plantation, delegating his authority to a grizzled Frenchman who was his overseer, or to Ma Doudou as the housekeeper. In their different ways, Claudette and Giselle also helped in the smooth running of the plantation. In the evenings when he sat on the verandah watching the night roll in over the sea beyond the hills, Mr Genave discussed the day's activities and the programme for the next day with Giselle.

Pat sat with them puzzled by what role he was expected to play, since he was never asked to do anything and was treated as a pampered guest. The French overseer had shown him around the fields and, since he knew nothing about coffee, he had no idea if Mr Genave's plantation was successful or not. The slaves he saw were respectful and, judging by the orderly appearance of the fields and its trails, they did their tasks well.

He assumed from the neatness and industry of the plantation that Mr Genave was a wealthy man. His table lacked nothing and the twenty room villa was well furnished. He could see no reason for Mr Genave to change to sugar growing although he mentioned it when he judged the old man, made mellow by a superb supper and a snifter of cognac, was willing to listen.

'My dear friend,' Mr Genave said, having heard him out, 'sugar may be sweet for new settlers, but not for an old Creole like me. I was born here. I've grown coffee all my life, following the plan of my father before me. My slaves are accustomed to coffee. I have few of them and need no more. I am old. It is not for me to make a commitment for the future.'

His sadness emboldened Pat to raise the subject of Lindsay. 'Your son might be interested in growing sugar cane,' he said, as though ignorant of Lindsay's character.

Mr Genave shook his head wearily. 'Were he interested in the plantation, he wouldn't take kindly to an idea imposed on us by the British. Lindsay is a rebel. Until he is tamed by a woman of his own temperament, he will remain so, stubborn and foolhardy.'

'He's your son . . .' said Pat rather lamely, gesturing at the plantation to indicate what he really meant. He was wondering what would become of it.

'And Giselle is my daughter,' retorted Mr Genave. He turned to where she was sitting quietly in the shadows, listening to their conversation. Pat was constantly aware of Giselle's presence, of her eyes watching him in fascination. Deliberately he tried to ignore her but whenever he did so, Mr Genave just as deliberately involved her in their conversations.

'As you have surely seen, Pat, Giselle knows as much about Belrose as I do, possibly more.' He chuckled. 'Do you feel we should grow sugar instead of coffee?'

'Where will we get the slaves?' she asked bluntly, surprising Pat yet again by the boldness concealed beneath her gentle manner. 'Slaves have to be driven hard to cut cane so we'd need drivers too. More settlers.'

She smiled winsomely at Pat and he turned away, cursing Robert Farquhar in his mind for making him spy on two people he had grown fond of.

'You see, Pat, we are not able to agree with the Governor's idea.' Mr Genave shrugged eloquently, expecting the subject to be dropped.

'Lindsay would be a good slave driver,' Giselle said suddenly. 'He can get the extra slaves too.'

'Hush, my dear!' Mr Genave's face tightened with rage and his knuckles clenched around his brandy snifter. The effort of anger was too much for him and he had to take deep breaths to regain his composure. 'Help me . . .' he panted waving his arm at Pat.

He sprang to his feet and supported the old man when he rose in agitation from his chair. 'Shall I take you to your chamber?'

'No, stay here . . . with Giselle.'

The old man shuffled into the house and he was relieved to hear Ma Doudou and Claudette help him up the stairs to his room. He glanced over at Giselle, puzzled why she hadn't offered to help too.

'He loves Lindsay,' she said, frowning unhappily. 'It's all show. Don't take any notice of his rages. Do you know why you haven't seen Lindsay since you came here ten days ago?'

He pursed his lips, rubbing the back of his neck. He was troubled by the bitterness in Giselle's voice. 'I suppose he doesn't care very much for me being here.'

Her laughter mocked him. 'He's not afraid of you! Nor of

papa since he can get around him so easily. He's been taking orders for slaves. He's in Madagascar now. He's sent word that he is bringing in five hundred slaves from Tamatave next week.'

'That's impossible. He can't do that without being discovered.'

Giselle shrugged. 'Who will tell? Everyone wants slaves. He'll land them in passels after dark at various bays around the coast. He has his customers already. We're taking twenty here at Belrose.'

'But your father said he has no need for more slaves.'

'You believe that? No settler in Mauritius can resist the chance to buy new stock.'

He bit his finger, worried by Giselle's apparent connivance at Lindsay's scheme.

'I thought you'd be pleased,' she said hesitatingly. 'If we are to grow sugar here . . .'

'How can you do that when your father doesn't agree?'

'Belrose is a large plantation. Father doesn't ride over it any more. He relies on me and the overseer to inform him what's going on. We could grow whatever you like here.'

'What I like?' He felt hot under his collar.

'You're the planter, aren't you? That's why papa invited you here.'

She smiled at him with such a sweet allure, he was dumbfounded. Instead of waiting to hear the rest of what she had to say, he jumped from his seat, anxious to break the spell he felt she was weaving around him. He rushed off the verandah up to his room.

Slamming the door closed behind him, he threw himself onto his bed, beating the pillow with his fists. The feeling of drowning swamped him again. Giselle's attraction was fatal. She was teasing him with her innocence and guile. He wouldn't weaken.

One day he wanted to ask her to marry him. Until then she must be protected, against herself if necessary, since she could not know what he was really like. Why did she try to provoke him? He longed to devour her with kisses more passionate than any he shared with Claudette. But he wanted her for himself, and for ever.

He wanted her when he had something to offer, when he could go to her as a man, not as a worthless adventurer. Until then, he had to control his desires, taking his pleasure with Claudette, and dreaming of the day when Giselle would be his wife.

'This is your chance,' he told Robert Farquhar. 'What are you going to do?'

The Governor stood up sharply, indicating to Pat that the audience was over. 'I will decide. Go back to Belrose at once. Let me know if you hear anything more.'

He felt upset at being dismissed in such a cavalier manner. 'I've told you that Lindsay is shipping slaves into the island from Madagascar. That's illegal. I can prove he's doing it. There are new slaves at Belrose who can't speak Creole or French or English. They've been put to work under an armed guard to clear the forest to make new fields. For sugar. And there's another shipment due in two nights' time. You could arrest Lindsay Genave yourself.'

'I've told you, Pat. I will decide what should be done. In due course.'

When Robert put his hand on his arm, he knew he was anxious to get rid of him. *Why?* 'In due course?' he shouted in anger. 'You're not going to do anything, are you? You *want* Lindsay to bring in more slaves!'

Robert's hold on his elbow tightened. 'The British government had banned the slave trade, Pat.' He sounded pompous, not like the man he had met in the river so many months before. 'You are making a grave accusation.'

He pulled his arm free. 'Maybe the British government has banned the import of slaves, but you haven't! You want more of them here so that the settlers have plenty to grow sugar for you.' A new thought struck him and he gulped at the audacity of it.

'By the devil! You must be relieved that Lindsay is involved in the smuggling. He's a rebel and he thinks he's defying you, but he's not rousing the settlers against you. Oh no, he's doing exactly what you want, even if he doesn't know it. You're ignoring it deliberately.'

'Pat!' Robert Farquhar's voice was lowered. Now he was

pulling him away from the door instead of trying to get him to go. He was frowning, pleading with him to keep quiet.

'Diplomacy is a delicate, difficult art. I can trust you, Pat, can't I? What I do may seem odd to you because you don't know all the facts. Believe me, whatever I do is not for my *personal* gain, it's for Mauritius.

'I have to overlook what the settlers, yes, people like Lindsay Genave and the big plantation owners, are doing, so that Mauritius will prosper. The settlers have to be happy to be British, and their prosperity as planters will guarantee that they are content.'

'But what about those Africans being imported at the dead of night to labour under the planters' whips?' Pat could scarcely believe what he was hearing.

Governor Farquhar spread his hands as though it was no concern of his. 'Won't you stay for a brandy?'

He spun around and stormed out of the office, heedless of Robert's shout for him to wait. In his mind, he saw the image of a cut and bleeding slave at Lindsay Genave's feet. Somehow, he would stop Lindsay, even without the Governor's help.

CHAPTER TWENTY

Pat was naked. Claudette raised herself on her elbow, her dark, lustrous eyes sweeping the length of his body. He didn't stir but kept staring up at the branches of the tree shading them as they lay by a cave in a glade of the forest. Claudette had shown him the cave where, she said, runaway slaves used to hide in the days of Mr Genave's father. It was a shallow rift in the hillside with a spongy mat of grass in front of it, and the river gurgling over a stone-strewn watercourse twenty feet below.

He was listening to the flow of the water, to the birds chattering in the trees in the sunlight, to the sounds of the forest around him. From the distant fields where the slaves were hacking at the trees to clear the forest came the shouts of the overseer and the warning crack of a whip over their heads. It worried him and he hardly felt Claudette's hands stroking his chest. They had made love fervently and now he lay pensive, neither exhilarated nor satisfied, beside her.

She said something, almost striking his chest to make him respond. The curses of the French overseer drifting on the breeze from the far edge of the forest held his attention instead. He turned to her, blinking to clear his thoughts, wondering what she wanted. She was studying his face intimately, feature by feature; it made him uncomfortable.

'What did you say?'

'I knew you weren't listening.'

'I was thinking.' His tightening lips betrayed his annoyance.

He saw the hurt in the shadow that flitted across her eyes and immediately felt guilty. He caught her hand in his and caressed it, keeping it away from his loins. He raised himself to a sitting position, facing her as she sat beside him.

She was wearing a crumpled shift, raised to her hips, exposing the rich fullness of her coppery thighs. Her breasts were visible where the thin fabric of the shift stuck to her skin, her dark nipples erect and standing out like ripe coffee berries waiting to be plucked. Normally the sight of her, with her lips parted and her eyes smouldering with wanting, was enough to rouse him to renewed passion and they would make love again. Today he was too distracted.

He squeezed her hand tightly. 'We'd better be going.'

'Why? They won't miss us so soon after dinner. The old man is sleeping and Giselle's busy in the sewing room. Let's stay. I want to talk.'

'Talk?' He frowned.

'Yes. You're not in the mood for anything else.' She withdrew her hand and smoothed down the shift, covering her thighs. The gesture gave him a sense of relief since it released him from a second bout of lovemaking.

'I've been watching you, Pat. Something's wrong, isn't it?'

Her concern made him grin. He brushed his hair back with his hand. 'Why do you think that?'

'The way you made love.'

'I'm tired.' He hated criticism. 'Because of my visit to Port Louis.'

'You don't have a wench there?'

'What if I have?'

From the expression on her face she obviously realized she'd asked the wrong question. She smiled at him encouragingly. 'I might be jealous,' she said, making it seem like a joke. 'I missed you.'

'I was only away three days. I had to wait two days before Robert Farquhar would see me.'

She nodded as though waiting for him to continue. He sighed. Perhaps it would be better to talk about it, even to her. He explained briefly how the Governor was unlikely to stop the slave smuggling.

'Why do you involve yourself with such matters, Pat?'

The question surprised him. 'It's wrong! You should feel that more than I do.'

'I was born a slave so I know no other life.'

He was shocked by her fatalism. 'Those Africans that Lindsay buys in Madagascar weren't born into slavery. They've been robbed of their freedom because of him. He transports them here, to a strange land, against their will.'

'Why should it concern you?'

'I've told you!' He was exasperated by her refusal to understand. 'It's against the law.'

There was a disturbing hint of condescension in her smile. 'I think it's because of Lindsay,' she said softly. 'If he wasn't the one doing it, you wouldn't care about someone breaking the law. Slaves don't mean much to you really.'

He chewed on his lower lip until the pain hurt him. She was right, of course, but having his motive exposed to himself filled him with rage. He fought to keep his temper, restraining the impulse to deny what she said.

'You're right!' He slumped backwards with a sigh.

She seemed pleased by his confession and snuggled up beside him, manoeuvring to cradle his head on her lap. She stroked his temples, the touch of her fingers calming him and lending him some of her own strength.

'It is Lindsay,' he said. 'I want to stop him, but that's stopping the slave trade too.'

'Forget him, Pat.' Her fingers traced circles on his brow. 'He's not worthy of your hatred. You don't have to be *jealous* of him.'

He tensed. 'I'm not.'

She continued to caress his head, her fingers fondling the tendrils of hair at his neck. He gave himself to the feeling of relief surging through him.

'I was ... but not now.' He didn't explain that it was Giselle who filled his thoughts, not her. 'You've told me what you have to do because you're a slave. I accept that.'

'Then don't do anything about Lindsay. He's too powerful, Pat. All the planters want slaves. He has many friends. He'll kill you if you interfere in his schemes.'

'He won't.' He brushed her hand away and reached for his breeches. 'I'll find a way to trap him and to force the Governor to take action that will destroy him. That way I'll teach Robert Farquhar a lesson too.'

Claudette looked troubled, her lower lip trembling as she gazed up at him.

'Don't worry about me,' he said, misinterpreting the doubt in her eyes. 'I can look after myself.'

'I don't want to lose you, Pat. Not now . . .'

This time he did catch the hint of distress in her manner. He was tying his shirt and paused to look at her quizzically. For once her eyes were downcast. He wondered then how he had ever confused Claudette and Giselle in his mind. They shared a similarity in build, that was all. Claudette was wilful, sensuous and wanton. His beloved Giselle was shy and untouched, a dainty rose beside a thrusting sunflower.

'You won't lose me,' he lied, knowing she already had.

There was a rush of words in response and he stared at her, uncomprehending. His mouth gaped open and he tried to speak. She repeated what she had just said, more slowly, as though he was being deliberately dense.

'I'm going to have your child.'

'That's . . . that's impossible.' He couldn't think of anything else to say.

'It's true. Haven't you noticed.' She patted her hips. 'Ma Doudou has. She says it will be a boy.'

'But you can't . . .' He scratched his head but that didn't help him grasp the idea. A child? His? Would he have to marry her? No, she was a slave. The child would be a slave too, not his responsibility. So who would be its owner? Thoughts began to pour through his brain as he gazed, dumbfounded, at her.

'Am I . . . how do you . . . I mean, dammit, am I really the father? How do you know I am?'

'Oh, Pat!' Claudette's husky chuckle of disbelief eased the tension. 'What do you take me for?'

'Well . . .' He gulped. 'I know what you have to do with Lindsay, and even with his father, your father, and –'

'I'm my father's night nurse, nothing more,' she said, smothering her outrage. 'I'm not Lindsay's wench, either. He hasn't touched me since the time you burst in on us and that's more than nine months ago. I've only lain with you since then.' She gripped his arm firmly.

He shook his head, unable to bring himself to push her away. This wasn't the sort of situation he wanted when he was trying to give her up. 'A child?' he thought aloud, 'what will happen to it?'

'He'll be your son. He'll be free because the British will manumit him as you're his father.'

He was filled with a sudden surge of affection for her. He pulled her into his arms and hugged her close, patting her bottom playfully. Her belief that everything would be all right swayed him into agreeing with her.

'It will be nice to have a son,' he mused. 'I bet he'll be a handsome chap.'

Pat wondered how to tell Giselle. It was wiser to avoid mentioning the matter altogether, but he didn't want to deceive her. A slave giving birth to her master's child was a commonplace occurrence.

If the precedent was there, Pat's courage wasn't. He and Giselle had established a warm relationship, like brother and sister. He kept his true feelings for her hidden, and she treated him with equal deference.

They shared pleasures together, laughed at each other's witticisms, and discussed family and plantation affairs openly. She seemed an eminently sensible woman to Pat, and as aware as he was of the need to keep their relationship circumspect.

If he told her Claudette was carrying his child, she would be shocked. On the other hand, she would see him then as he really was. Curiously, he was no longer keen for her to know about the lustful side of his character. It had no place in their relationship.

He sat almost tongue-tied with her in the evenings on the verandah. He chose his words carefully in case he blurted out his worries about Claudette's child and about Lindsay's smuggling of slaves, which was continuing still.

Giselle's voice as they sat at opposite ends of the verandah interrupted his thoughts. He smiled at her and lowered his eyes back to the book he had been pretending to read.

'Don't think about Lindsay,' Giselle said, begging him with dark blue eyes that sought his.

Pat swallowed his surprise. 'How can you read my thoughts?'

'It's not difficult.'

He shook his head, pretending to be astonished so he could hide his dismay that he was so transparent to her.

'I saw how distracted you were when he was here today and you're thoughtful now. It's not hard to guess he's on your mind.'

He waited, enchanted by the sparkle in her eyes where the light from the lantern was reflected in the tilt of her head.

'You shouldn't let yourself be scared of him. You only have to stand up to him and he'll back down.'

'I'm not scared of him!'

'Good. Neither am I. I know him too well for that.'

He was shaken by her suggestion. Perhaps his lack of protest about Lindsay made her think he *was* scared of her brother. 'I've complained to the Governor about him,' he said softly, wondering if she'd regard it as a betrayal. 'About his slave smuggling.'

He was rewarded by a bright smile of approval. She rose from her seat and hurried over to his side, sitting down in a chair so close to him he could take the scent of her perfume with every breath. His loins stirred but he kept his thoughts on Lindsay.

'Tell me about it,' she said.

'I thought you'd hate me.'

'I could never do that.'

'Don't you disapprove? It's a kind of betrayal of your father's hospitality for me to report on Lindsay to the Governor.'

'What Lindsay is doing is wicked. I only let papa buy slaves from him so we can look after them properly. Some planters don't, you know.'

After he explained how he wanted to stop the slave smuggling, not to get even with Lindsay but because it was wrong, she touched him gently on his hand.

'I'll help you,' she said. 'What do you want me to do?'

His mouth was dry, his skin tingling at her touch. If she knew the pressure she put him under, she wouldn't dare to sit beside him and look so desirable, so willing.

'I need to catch him actually landing the slaves.' The words escaped in a rush as he tried to hide the effect her closeness was having on him. 'If I take a magistrate or some officials with me as witnesses, then the Governor will be forced to take action.'

'You won't be able to find anyone around here who'll testify against Lindsay. All the officials have bought slaves from him. That's one reason why he can trade in them so openly.'

'Then I'll have to arrest him myself and take him and the slaves to Port Louis.'

'You'll need a gun. I'll give you papa's.'

'I thought you'd try to discourage me.'

'I think you're very brave and I admire you for it.' She held his hand but he pulled it away with a bashful smile.

'Lindsay's receiving a group of slaves tonight. They're being put ashore on the beach in the bay. That's why he came to see papa today, because he wants to keep them here until he sells them.'

His heart thumped with excitement. 'What time? I could arrest him tonight!'

'At dawn, I suppose, as usual.' She stood up, still apparently innocent of the effect she had on him. 'I'll get the gun. Papa's sleeping already so it will be easy to take it from his room.'

He prepared for the expedition with care. Ma Doudou gave him a hip flask of Mr Genave's cognac to keep out the cold when he was keeping vigil. Fortunately the sky was clear of clouds so the moon would give sufficient light to see when the slaves were landed. He intended to surprise Lindsay when he was busy rounding up the slaves on the beach.

His intention was to arrest him, bind his hands behind his back and chain him to his slaves as part of his own coffle. He planned to force march him straight to Port Louis before Lindsay's cronies heard about his capture and tried to rescue him.

As he crouched, waiting in the shadow of the rocks that formed one side of the small bay, he heard the surf of the Indian Ocean pounding the beach. The waves were rough. It pleased him because it would add to the confusion and Lindsay would be too preoccupied to consider that he himself was about to be captured.

He took a swig of cognac from the flask and grasped the handle of the gun for reassurance. He did not expect Lindsay to surrender willingly. He would use the gun if necessary but only to frighten him. He needed Lindsay alive and uninjured so he could confess. As a Creole caught red handed smuggling slaves into the island, he would be an embarrassment to Robert Farquhar. That would be Pat's revenge for the Governor's cavalier treatment of him.

He slipped the flask back into the pocket of his coat, the night was mild, only the spray from the sea was cool. As he stared into the darkness, trying to distinguish movement in the moonlight blackness, he was certain he saw the outline of a shape where there was none before.

He withdrew under the overhang of the rocks, silently waiting. The shape loomed above him as it passed close to where he was hidden and then became a silhouette at the water's edge. On the cliff above the bay a lantern appeared, its flickering light serving as a beacon to the slave boat out at sea.

He had expected Lindsay to have accomplices. He would have liked help of his own but there was no one he could trust. Only Giselle, Ma Doudou and Claudette knew of his mission. He would have to rely on surprise, on a warning shot and lots of noise to terrify Lindsay's helpers into fleeing.

The lantern beacon remained lit so he guessed the captives were due. After half an hour, he heard a shout from out at sea and Lindsay's answering call from the beach. He pulled the gun from his waistband and peered ahead, ready to pounce as soon as the slaves were landed and Lindsay had them under his control.

There were shouts and screams, the commotion of people floundering as the waves washed them ashore. Dark shapes staggered from the sea and fell exhausted on the beach. They had been pushed out of the canoe that brought them close to the shore from the ship. Lindsay ran between them where they lay, forcing them to stand up while he clamped leg irons around their ankles and chained them together.

The Africans were dazed and only one of them was bold enough to escape. He crawled stealthily up the beach, unnoticed by Lindsay who was securing the rest. When he reached the edge of the beach, the African rose from his crouching position and ran into the trees.

'Troptard!' Lindsay shouted in annoyance. 'There're only five here. One must have run off into the bush.'

There was an answering shout in the forest, by the lantern, and Pat knew that Troptard was setting off in pursuit of the missing slave. With Troptard out of the way, his task would be easier.

He crept out of his hiding place, guided to Lindsay in the

gloaming by the moans of the Africans as he beat them to make them walk.

'Hey-up, you buggers!' he shouted, the whip strokes filling the terrified slaves with dread.

'Let me help,' Pat said softly, creeping up behind him and pressing the muzzle of the gun into his buttocks. 'Stand still and don't move or I'll blow your balls off.'

He smelt a fart of fear as Lindsay froze, his hands gripping the whipstock. 'Damn you,' he croaked, knowing Pat's voice.

'Damn *you*, Lindsay Genave!' Pat chuckled grimly. 'Drop that whip.' He nudged Lindsay with the pistol to make sure he obeyed. The whip fell into the sand. The slaves, chained to each other, made no attempt to run, bound by fear and being unaware of what was happening.

'Put your hands behind your back!' He removed the gun from Lindsay's buttocks and stepped back beyond his reach. 'No tricks. The Governor's men are behind me. It would give them target practice to shoot you while resisting arrest.'

Lindsay's hasty compliance pleased him. He suspected Lindsay was a coward and would do nothing so long as he didn't know he was bluffing. By the time he discovered he actually had no help, it would be too late. He reached in his pocket for the cord to tie Lindsay's wrists together.

'Give me the cord, Pat, I'll bind him.'

The woman's voice close to his ear nearly made him drop the gun in surprise. He suppressed his shock and glanced at her.

'What the hell are you doing here?'

'Look out!'

Her warning came too late. He felt the gun being snatched out of his hand as Lindsay took advantage of his moment of distraction. He tried to grab it back, flinging himself at Lindsay to prevent his escape.

Lindsay was smarter, sidestepping so Pat missed him and sprawled face down in the sand. Lindsay cocked the pistol and pointed it down at his head.

'I'm going to blow you to smithereens!'

His maniacal shout rang in Pat's ears. He tried to twist out of the way but his feet caught in the chain linking the slaves and he was trapped, unable to shield himself.

The slaves thrashed in fear and someone fell on top of him. The gun fired close to his ear.

The night erupted into a cacophony of startled forest animals and birds. There were screams of terror from the slaves and they dragged themselves away, falling over each other and shouting wildly. The commotion caused Lindsay to believe there were soldiers after him; he sprinted up the beach out of sight.

Pat eased himself slowly from under the weight of the woman lying across him. She had saved him. He reached out to help her to her feet, then drew his hands away in horror. They were wet with blood that spouted from a wound deep in her breast.

He leaned over her, cradling her head in his hands. Her mouth gaped open, her eyes staring wildly, frantically trying to focus through the pain. He lowered his head and kissed her gently on her lips. The fear in her eyes relaxed and they filled with peace at being safe in his arms.

'I love you,' he breathed as her eyes closed and she died, a smile of triumph on her lips.

CHAPTER TWENTY-ONE

'I'll hide you,' Giselle said with quiet firmness. It was dawn and she stood on the gallery outside her room, clad only in her linen nightdress of white with rose-coloured ribbons. Her hair was dishevelled, a red-gold aura of curls that spilled over her brow. Her eyes were grave with sleep after being roused by the sound of Pat tapping on her window.

She had listened without getting upset as he outlined how Claudette had died saving him from being shot by Lindsay. There was no trace of censure in her expression. 'You must tell Ma Doudou,' she said as he finished.

'I did.' He was impressed by her stolid reaction to the news. 'She's gone to bury Claudette.'

As his despair cleared and he absorbed the sight of Giselle standing close to him in her nightdress, the rise and fall of her breasts visible through the ruffles of her lace corsage, he was shocked by the force of his desire for her.

'I must go,' he said, unable to keep the tension from his voice. His hands were trembling. 'When Lindsay discovers there are no government troops chasing him, he'll try to find me. I bungled it.' He lowered his eyes, afraid to see what she thought of him.

'It wasn't your fault.' Giselle sounded sympathetic and he looked at her gratefully. She didn't notice because she retreated to her room without a word, leaving him on the gallery, pondering his position.

He would have to go to Port Louis, explain to Robert Farquhar what had happened, and seek the Governor's protection. Only then did it occur to him that he would probably never see Giselle again. He had lost Claudette and now he would lose Giselle because of his foolhardy scheme to impress her.

'Come on,' she hissed at him impatiently from the shadows of her room. 'We've no time to waste.'

He entered her chamber curiously, wondering what to expect. His eyes flew to her bed with its rumpled sheet and pillows showing the impression of where her head lay in sleep only minutes before. Giselle was by the door, a cloak around her shoulders fastened over her nightdress. He pursed his lips, longing to hold her, to draw comfort from her concern for him.

'I know a place,' she said with a determined toss of her head to show she had made her decision and was going to keep to it, whatever objections he may have. 'Come with me.'

'I can't stay at Belrose,' he protested as she opened the door to the main landing and walked out, expecting him to follow.

'Quiet!' she whispered, her eyes showing her exasperation at his lack of thought for her father asleep in the next room.

He followed her passively, frowning to himself at what she intended to do, and marvelling at her coolness in handling the news of Claudette's death. They went down the stairs together to the back door of the villa. It opened into the kitchen courtyard.

'Giselle,' he said softly. 'There's no need for you to do this. I'll make for Port Louis myself.'

'Lindsay will overtake you.' She pointed to a path through the shrubbery. 'We're going down there.'

'Into the forest?' He was appalled. 'You can't go there dressed like that. I'll go alone.'

'Pat!' She turned to face him, her eyes of azure in the dawn's early light sparkling with resolve. 'If you do as I say, everything will be all right.'

'But you –'

Her expression hardened so he bit back his protest and gestured to her to lead the way. It was ironic that the woman he assumed to be naive and gentle was the one in command of his fate. He trod carefully behind her along the forest path, straining his eyes to see that she was in no danger, ready to leap ahead and catch her if she missed her footing and fell. Instead, she showed a familiarity with the forest trail and a surefootedness that surpassed his own.

He longed to ask her where she was taking him, but her determined stance and the speed with which she hurried along the path deterred him. He wished that at least he had the pistol to protect them. He didn't share her confidence that the trail was without danger.

He tried to imagine what Lindsay was doing. It wouldn't take the murdering swine long to discover he had been hoodwinked. He would probably leave Troptard to round up the chained slaves and start to hunt Pat. His anger would be fuelled by the way Pat had tricked him and by his lust for revenge. Claudette's death probably meant nothing to him. That was the cross Pat would have to bear for the rest of his life. It brought the harsh reality of his plight into true perspective. Perhaps he was even endangering Giselle's safety by letting her hide him.

She was leading him through the forest along trails that were overgrown with grass and bushes that snagged at her cloak. There was a grey light above the trees and she seemed guided by instinct. Pat was impressed yet again by an unexpected side of her character.

She slowed down, watching the trees, listening. Then she paused, looked back to see if he was watching and stepped forward into the trees. She disappeared.

He searched the gloom of the undergrowth with his eyes, but saw no sign of her so he stepped into the trees too. They concealed a narrow path through overgrown grass and thick vegetation. It opened into a tiny glade. There was a small cabin there, made of unhewn logs and with a roof of ferns. It seemed to be part of the forest.

Giselle was at its door, opening it confidently. 'You'll be safe here,' she called as he approached.

'Whose cabin is it?' He gazed at the secret structure wondering who was going to emerge from inside it.

'Mine.' She sounded amused by his question. 'I used to play here with Claudette as a child. Papa and Lindsay never found us.'

'Who else knows about this?'

'No one, now Claudette's dead.'

He stepped through the door. There was a window which Giselle opened, letting in the light. Beneath the warbling of the birds of dawn, he heard the gentle gurgle of a stream. He was amazed to see it almost below the window. It added to the tranquil atmosphere of the cabin.

'Someone's been living here.' He pointed to the freshly

laundered sheet on the bed of burlap, and the recently swept hard mud floor.

Giselle smiled coyly. 'I cleaned it up. Repaired the roof, fixed the door . . .'

His throat dried at the whisper in her voice. 'Why did you do all this?' He sat on the edge of the bed, weary yet knowing he must control the heat throbbing through him.

She stood by the open window, unfastening her cloak. Her profile showed the determination in the tilt of her chin and the delicate lines of her temptingly curved mouth. She turned to face him with a frank and admiring look.

'For you. I dreamed of bringing you here.' Her eyelashes fluttered and she avoided his eyes as the glow from the rising sun highlighted her deeply colouring cheeks. She put her hand to her mouth but it was too late to stifle the meaning of what she'd said.

'No, Giselle.' He shook his head, feeling old and responsible, yet he was the same age as her. 'I'm no good for you. The trouble I've caused.'

She stepped towards the bed and he stood up to intercept her. Their bodies touched in the small confines of the cabin. She reached out and clutched at his hand when he tried to hold her away.

'Giselle!' He summoned the willpower to be sensible. 'You must leave here. I will rest and then I'll find my way to Port Louis. I'll ask Governor Farquhar to arrange passage for me on a ship back to America.'

'Why?' Her fingers laced in his own, her lips trembling, betraying the eagerness of her affection for him. She stared with longing into his eyes, her face rising to meet his, her lips apart and expectant.

He felt the tremor in her breast as she brushed tentatively against him. The closeness of her fragile body was enchanting and his self-control dissolved under her spell. He lowered his mouth gently to meet hers.

She quivered at the sweet tenderness of his kiss, responding to it with a burning desire that set fire to his own passion. It threatened to consume them both with the heat of wanting. He drew her to him as he sat down on the hard frame of the burlap bed.

'Pat,' she breathed in his ear, touching the lobe with her lips. 'You must show me the way so I can be good to you. I ache for you but I don't want you to be disappointed.'

He tensed as gusts of desire seemed to shake her. He gripped her slender waist with hands that were firm and masterful. 'Wait, Giselle,' he said with tenderness, holding her away from his body.

'When I look into your eyes, Giselle, I feel so ashamed.'

'Why, why?' She tried to press herself to him but he held her off, sorrow brimming in his eyes.

'I'm no good for you, Giselle. I want you, yes. But I must prove myself first so that I am *worthy* of you.'

'You are, Pat. There's no one like you in the whole of Mauritius.'

'You don't know me! I've been wicked.' He paused, wondering how to convince her. 'Claudette was my . . .' He didn't know how to explain when her innocent eyes were staring at him soulfully.

'Your bed wench?' She uttered the words for him, unabashed by their crudity. 'I know that. She told me.'

'It doesn't make you despise me?'

'Why should it? She was my friend.'

'She was going to have my child.'

'She's dead, Pat.'

'You don't mind?'

'I'm sorry she's dead. I didn't wish that for her.' She stroked his arm until he pulled it beyond her reach. She sighed. 'You think I'm a silly young girl.'

'I don't. You're a brave and beautiful young woman.' Despite his resolve, he touched her shoulder, worried by her forlorn features into thinking she was going to cry.

She pouted, blinking with bafflement. Her sudden loss of confidence exposed her bashfulness. The glimpse of her chaste, kind nature changed his sordid wanting of her into a finer, pure love. The glow warmed him and he drew her into his arms with a new affection.

She raised her eyes to his. There was a questioning gleam in them, a hesitant tremor on her lips lest he push her away again. His face spread in a slow, steady smile of happiness that was answered by the tension slipping from her body and she relaxed in his firm embrace. She seemed aware of the strength and warmth of his flesh and he responded to her trust with a surge of devotion and a feeling of courage.

Crushing her to him, he pressed his mouth to hers. She quivered at the hot tenderness of his kiss as their hands clasped each other. A dreamy intimacy involved them, without words, in a blissful sharing of hopes. They clung together, enjoying their new knowledge of each other, heedless of the chorus of birds in the forest around the cabin, singing with delight at the break of day.

He raised his mouth from hers, his restless spirit tamed. 'I . . . love . . . you . . .' he breathed and between each word he planted kisses on her brow, nose and throat. She returned his loving with a series of slow, shivery kisses that left him bursting with zeal.

'I've never known anyone like you,' he said truthfully.

She giggled. 'Am I doing it right?'

'You don't need lessons when you're in love.' They sat side by side on the wooden edge of the bedframe, their fingers entwined and their eyes engrossed with each other. He was overwhelmed at the excitement that pulsed through his body, filling him with joy instead of a lust to possess her. He marvelled that he was feeling this way about a woman.

She loosened her hands from his and reached up to touch his face. With both hands she traced her fingers over his forehead, following the curve of his thick, dark eyebrows, down the high cheekbone of his handsome face to the rugged cut of his jaw. Her fingers paused on his lips and he nibbled them playfully. She giggled and they fell into each other's arms with a happiness that defied the problems that faced him.

He lost touch of time, and reality, as they lay together. They kissed effortlessly, their hands exploring the intimacies of each other's bodies. He was content with Giselle beside him and made no move to take their love further. She, too, seemed willing to wait.

'I will come tonight,' she said, her breath against his ear, tingling him with happiness. He nodded, anxious not to disturb the warmth of that moment with words.

'I must go.' She smiled ruefully, indicating her nightdress and cloak and the daylight pouring into the cabin.

'What will you tell your father?'

'The truth.'

'About Lindsay, not us.'

She gazed at him thoughtfully. 'Papa could help you. At first it will be difficult for him to accept what Lindsay's done.' She stood in the centre of the small cabin, fastening her cloak. Her hair shimmied like spun gold in the shaft of sunlight streaming through the open window. Her eyes were deep with thought and happiness.

He knew he had never seen anyone so beautiful. Her complexion was white and illusive pink, her lips full and rounded over even teeth. Her lashes swept down across her proud cheekbones, adding a wonderful demureness to the volatility of her spirit.

'Be careful,' he said, jumping to his feet and scooping her into his arms for a farewell embrace.

'My goodness!' she said when he released her. 'What will you do about food? I can't –'

'Don't worry.' He stopped her in mid-sentence. 'I won't be hungry, knowing I have you. I'll sleep until this evening.' He gestured at the bed. 'That way the time will pass less slowly until you come back.'

'I'll have to wait until papa's gone to bed.'

'Shall I come to the villa to meet you?'

'No.' She frowned. 'Lindsay might be there. No one must know you are hidden in this cabin, not even Ma Doudou. Although she has a way of knowing everything.'

'I can't stay here for ever.'

'Lindsay's often said he wants to go to France. Perhaps he will now. He'll be ashamed at what's happened and papa won't forgive him. Not for a while.' She stood at the door, the misty rays of the sunrise filtering through the trees behind her. 'If he goes to France, you'll be safe.'

He sighed anxiously as she left him. The dense vegetation of the forest swallowed her up and the last glimpse he had was of her hand gesturing a kiss. He smiled to himself and withdrew into the cabin, amazed that a woman's love had finally claimed him. He lay on the taut, coarse canvas of the bed to recall how it had happened; within seconds he was asleep.

The sun was shining directly over the cabin when he woke. He listened contentedly to the forest noises and to the bubbling of the stream beyond his window. The euphoria of Giselle's presence lingered. He was proud he had controlled the demon of his desire. That night, in a careful display of affection, nothing hurried, nothing spoilt, she would be his. He rose lazily, enjoying being alone so he could prepare himself for her.

The noise of running water reminded him how hot and sticky he was. He opened the door of the cabin cautiously and peered out. The peace in the glade reassured him and he strode out into the sunlight. The stream was to his left and he scrambled down the bank to it.

In seconds he was naked, lowering his body into the cool water with a gasp of pleasure. He lay in its eddies letting the rushing of the gentle current wash him clean. Thoughts of Giselle filled his mind until gradually he became aware of a change in the atmosphere of the forest around him.

It was nearly indiscernible. There was no unusual noise yet the very air seemed to hold its breath for a few seconds as though there was an intruder approaching the glade. He kept his head poised above the water, listening, his eyes on the cabin.

A shadow flitted briefly across the doorway, then vanished. The hackles of Pat's neck prickled a warning and he sank back into the water, depending on the whirlpool of foam to conceal him from whoever was by the cabin door.

His lungs were bursting and he had to come up for air. He chanced a deep breath and was going to plunge again to hide below the water's surface when he heard voices.

'He's been here.' It was Lindsay, emerging from the cabin and kicking at the door in his rage. 'Where the devil's he gone now, Troptard? Look for his tracks!' Lindsay sank down to his haunches in the cabin doorway, showing how exhausted he was. His pistol dangled limply from his hand.

Pat was about to duck when he realized that Troptard was looking straight at him, unseen by Lindsay. The youth placed his finger briefly on his lips, indicating to Pat that he should not make a sound. It was puzzling and he wondered what to do. He felt along the bed of the stream for a stone, the only weapon to hand if Troptard told Lindsay where he was.

He edged slowly under the bank of the stream to hide, keeping his body low in the water, praying that Lindsay would not look up, nor Troptard betray him. He watched the youth bend down stealthily, and then rise up again with a small branch of wood in his hand.

Troptard glanced at him above Lindsay's drooping head and motioned to him that he should be ready to help. Slowly and with great deliberation, Troptard raised the branch like a cudgel above Lindsay's head, then smote it down with such force that it split into two.

Lindsay toppled forward and Troptard jumped on him like a cougar about to devour its prey. He drew a knife from his waist and without hesitating thrust it at Lindsay's neck.

Pat stood up in the stream and hurled his stone. It caught Troptard on his temple as he was about to slice the knife across Lindsay's throat. He was knocked off balance and fell backwards, the knife dropping to the earth. Pat rushed over and snatched up the pistol where it lay beside Lindsay's unconscious body, and pointed it at Troptard.

The youth leaped to his feet. 'Shoot him, master!'

Pat shook his head. 'There's been enough killing.'

'For Claudette!' said Troptard, his brow beetling with frustration at what he saw as his unnecessary display of mercy.

'Is that why you attacked him? For revenge?'

The youth nodded sullenly. 'I waited for you. I thought you'd help.'

Pat followed Troptard's glance to where his knife lay on the grass. 'So you want to kill me too?'

Troptard shrugged his shoulders. His indifference made Pat decide to trust him. He waved his pistol at the knife.

'Pick it up and cut some vines so we can tie Lindsay's hands. We'll take him to the villa.'

Troptard reached for the knife, nodding darkly.

CHAPTER TWENTY-TWO

Lindsay, when he recovered from his sore head and his lecture from his enraged father, agreed to leave for France. In a sense, thought Pat, Lindsay Genave was gaining more than he was losing. Passage would be provided by the British and he was to have a stipend from Mr Genave's agents in Paris. Had he stayed in Mauritius, the conflict between him and the establishment would inevitably have led to some retribution from Governor Farquhar.

Giselle negotiated the terms of the peace treaty, as Pat jokingly called it. He agreed not to give evidence against Lindsay, either of smuggling slaves or for killing Claudette. The killing of a slave was a crime but in the rural areas of the coastal plantations with government agents unable to travel easily because of the lack of roads, it was a crime seldom discovered. Claudette's death was recorded in the Belrose plantation slave ledger as an accident.

Augustus Genave himself travelled to Port Louis with Lindsay together with an escort of trusted slaves that included Ma Doudou. She was to care for him in the townhouse. Lindsay was subdued, chastened by his downfall, although the opportunity of going to France clearly delighted him.

Pat was relieved by his departure and remained at the plantation to begin his new life. His reward for keeping silent about Claudette's murder was a formal offer from Mr Genave to enter his employment as manager of Belrose. The French overseer, who was also keen to go to France where he was born, was pensioned off to accompany Lindsay.

Mr Genave was anxious about leaving Giselle in the villa while he went to Port Louis. She insisted that she must stay, explaining that Pat alone could not run the plantation since he was not fluent in Creole, the language with which planters communicated with their slaves, nor familiar with the work. Perhaps because he was worried so much by Lindsay, Mr

Genave lacked the will to deny Giselle what she wanted. So she was allowed to stay at Belrose with Pat.

As the palanquin containing Mr Genave began the descent to the bay where a coastal vessel was waiting to take him and Lindsay and their entourage to Port Louis, Pat realized what Giselle had achieved. They were being left alone in the villa by themselves.

He was jubilant as he looked across at her where she stood on the verandah watching her brother walk out of her life. When she felt his eyes on her she turned to him with a smile.

'I knew papa would agree to send him to France.'

'You were the one who made up his mind.'

'Aren't you pleased?' She reached up to him and straightened the collar of his buckskin shirt.

He was going to draw her closer when he caught sight of Troptard leaning with studied arrogance against the pillar at the end of the verandah. He was staring at them with a smirk on his face.

Pat let his arms fall to his side. 'You should have sent that one away too.'

'He will be your protector.' Giselle's smile melted his dismay. 'He'll help you deal with the slaves. They respect him and he knows their cunning ways.'

'I'm sure he does.' He gazed unhappily at Troptard. 'Can he be trusted?'

'You will learn that for yourself.'

Pat grinned at her challenge, deciding to start the youth's employment without delay. 'Troptard!' The youth's expression resumed its surliness.

'Come here,' he said sternly. 'Do you know I'm the manager here now?'

'Yes.'

'Have you ever been whipped?'

Troptard's eyes clouded over and he nodded dully without speaking.

'In Virginia, slaves are beaten with a paddle that leaves their backsides raw and bleeding. They can't sit down for days. I'll do that to you, Troptard, if you give me cause.'

A light of respect flickered in the depths of the youth's eyes. Pat guessed the animosity Troptard felt for him would never be banished, only set aside. It would help to keep him alert for Troptard's mischief.

'Your first task for me is to count how many slaves are working today, and how many are sick in their cabins. You can tell the drivers I will be coming to inspect them this afternoon. Any driver whose gang does not please me will be obliged to exchange places with one of his gang who will become the driver instead. Do you understand?'

Troptard touched his brow, his dour face broadening into a lazy smile as he realized the power Pat was giving him over the slaves. 'I tell you which drivers are no good,' he said grimly.

'I will listen to you, Troptard. Go now.' He dismissed him with a wave of his hand. When he turned back to Giselle, he caught an expression of surprise on her face.

'That's got him out of the way,' he said with a chuckle.

'You didn't have to do that. We know how many slaves there are.'

'Then please show me the figures in the ledgers so I can check what Troptard tells me.'

'Now?' There was a plaintive note in her voice.

He knew she wanted him to relax and idle away the morning with her but he had other ideas. 'Yes, Giselle. If I am to be the manager, I will do my work diligently.'

He relented when he saw her grimace of disappointment. 'There will be time for us at night, when the work is done. I want to see Belrose is a success. For you.' He kissed her briefly on her cheek, too quick for her to hold him. 'The ledgers,' he said, walking her to the door of the villa. 'You can explain them to me.'

A manager's task, Pat discovered, was similar to Arnie Goodpaster's work on Cletus Braxton's plantation. The field hands were supervised by him and he was assisted by slave overseers, or drivers, appointed from their ranks. At Belrose, the slaves performed a variety of tasks, according to their abilities and skills. They tilled the ground, kept the gardens clear of weeds, harvested the coffee crop, mended the tools, repaired the buildings. They were trained to work hard, used to the routine and seldom had to be disciplined. They were well fed and fit, and had been spared abuse by whip-happy French overseers so they were reasonably content.

He spent his first day in authority touring the plantation accompanied by Troptard. His reliance on the youth gave him an exaggerated sense of his own importance which bound him to Pat. By letting Troptard feel he was needed and trusted, he gained an ally. His experience with slaves in Virginia warned him how devious they were and he did not intend to let himself be lulled into complacency by Troptard's apparent willingness to be obliging.

The slaves lived close to their work, in a community of wooden cabins clustered near the river. These 'quarters' were visible from the upper gallery of the villa, and the slaves had learned they could be seen easily from it. Their huts, built or repaired by them with materials furnished by Augustus Genave, were arranged in rows. The occupants of each hut were permitted a garden around their crude wooden dwellings. There they grew gourds and vegetables and, Pat was intrigued to discover, tobacco.

It reminded him of Five Acre Field. The tobacco was inferior to the oronoco he used to grow for Cletus Braxton. It was thin and weedy, growing almost wild without proper care. Its leaves would have been considered unworthy of curing in Virginia. Seeing the plants stirred his nostalgia for his home. He wondered what had happened to Deborah. Had she changed? Did she miss him? He felt oddly uncomfortable at the thought of her. Would she be impressed with him now?

He sighed, switching his thoughts to Giselle. She was depending on him and he was determined not to fail her, or her father. He knew nothing about coffee and would have to learn from her and the old man about how it should be harvested. It seemed a futile crop to him; even sugar cane would be better.

As he followed Troptard around the plantation, and saw the land cleared by the new slaves for planting the ratoons that would grow into sugar cane, he wondered how tobacco would fare under his expertise.

His preoccupation with the plantation amazed Giselle. He spoke about nothing else during their supper together that night. Of course, he was conscious of the effort she had made to look especially attractive but it didn't occur to him to comment on it.

Her hair showed the sheen of careful and prolonged brushing, her pale cheeks had a colour that could only have come from a pot of rouge, and her dress revealed every curve of her bosom and hips. It was his anxiety not to be daunted by her seductive young body and wholesome good looks that drove him to prattle on about his plans for the plantation.

Giselle made Troptard push their chairs close together when they finished supper and went to sit on the verandah. Pat dismissed him as soon as he'd done it and told him to sleep in the slave quarters.

'You must see the slaves come to no harm,' he said to encourage him, aware that Troptard wanted to stay close to the villa so he could see what he and Giselle would do.

'He's a bright fellow,' he said when he finally left them alone. 'The slaves do what he tells them. I visited their cabins –'

'Isn't that enough plantation talk for tonight?' Giselle was watching him in dismay and he shut his mouth immediately.

There was a tug at his loins which he had been trying to resist all evening. The knowledge that she would soon be his was worth savouring.

'You've done nothing but talk about coffee and sugar and slaves since you came from the plantation.'

'Would you have me do anything else now I'm the manager?'

'Yes!' She pouted, not realizing he was teasing her. 'Papa's not here. I've been lonely all day.'

'You have the house slaves to keep you company.'

'Don't be silly.' She looked at him askance at what she thought was his crassness. 'I want you, not them.'

'Really?' He arched his eyebrow. 'Now you've had me made plantation manager, how will I find the time to be with you in the villa?'

'You said the nights were for us. I didn't expect you to take work so seriously.'

Her discontent drove straight to his heart and he smiled sympathetically. 'There's one part of the plantation I haven't had time to inspect yet,' he said, reaching out and running his finger down the alabaster smoothness of her bare arm.

'Where's that?' she said, her eyes narrowing with disappointment that he was going to start talking about slaves again.

'Your quarters.'

'Pat!' Her excited laughter rippled through the air and the furrow of tension vanished from her brow.

He pulled her to her feet, no longer caring if Troptard or any of the house slaves were lurking in the dark to spy on them. He embraced her fondly, his smile deepening as she shook with merriment, not nerves, in his grasp. They giggled like secretive children and walked off the verandah to the stairs with eyes only for each other.

At the door to her chamber, he paused, prising her from him. He looked boldly into her eyes. The yearning trust he saw there made him glance away, overwhelmed by anticipation.

'What's wrong?' she asked anxiously, clutching him in case he left her.

'The door is closed,' he said, hiding the impact of his own craving in flippancy.

She giggled again, fumbling to open it. A lamp burned inside, placed there on her instructions. Pat walked across the room to the doors onto the gallery and flung them open, letting the breeze gust in.

'Moths,' she said, pointing to the lamp to explain why she hadn't opened the doors herself. 'They're attracted to the light.'

He lifted the glass chimney of the lamp and blew out the flame, leaving the room with a silver gloaming of moonlight shining in through the door. 'Come here,' he commanded, his voice deepened by the frenzy of his feelings. When she stood beside him on the gallery, strangely mute now the nervous laughter had given way to apprehension, he leaned down and kissed her.

He kept his hands from her at first so his lips could convince her of his passion. His tongue explored the recesses of her mouth, chasing away any lingering doubt there may have been in her mind.

She responded by offering herself to him freely, pressing her body to his with a fierceness of unchecked passion. She sought his hands, drawing them to her, forcing him to hold her.

He didn't want her to do anything she would regret.

223

Tentatively he unlaced the ribbon at the front of her bodice. She sighed when the tight corsage opened. The moonlight shone on the ivory globes of her breasts, her nipples erect, straining to meet him as he lowered his lips. His tongue teased their dusky pinkness and she moaned softly, her fingers clasping at the long, tousled locks of his hair.

Deftly, he slid her dress off her shoulders, following its progress with his mouth, kissing her bosom and sparking off tremors of pleasure that made her shiver. She tried to place her fingers under his shirt but his head lowered beyond her reach. He loosened her skirt and her underslip and drew the garments over her hips so they slid down her thighs to the floor.

He stood back from her to see her better, like an artist admiring a canvas he had finished painting. Bathed in the soft glow of moonlight, the shapely curves of her nakedness taunted him.

He smiled with understanding at her shyness. When she realized he was not mocking her, she let her hands fall to her sides. She was emboldened by his gaze of admiration and leaned against the doorjamb, beckoning him to come to her.

He waited, it seemed longer than a minute to them both, before stepping to her side. He put his hands out to touch her but she held him off.

'Let me undress you too.'

The huskiness in her voice set him soaring with need. He nodded, feeling at peace with her. Her fingers proved unaccustomed to the fastening of his shirt and she was having trouble taking it off him. He bent forward and let her pull the garment over his head. He stood up straight and waited while she gazed at his chest.

'You've hair on your body,' she said simply. She rubbed her cheek against his chest. 'It's like fur.'

'Don't do that!' He tried to hold her off.

'Does it hurt?'

'It tickles.' They laughed together, buoyed by their happiness in their intimate discovery of each other's bodies.

Her hands tugged at his waistband and succeeded in loosening the strap. She opened his breeches slowly, rolling them down his thighs. He held up first one leg, then the other, as she eased the breeches off them.

They stood facing each other, their nakedness dappled by the shadows from the trees overhanging the gallery.

She stroked him curiously and he winced. 'It's beautiful,' she said, closing her fingers around his hardening penis.

'You're beautiful.' He pulled her towards him, his hands beginning an exploration of her flesh as her fingers roamed over his own body.

For minutes they touched each other, glorying in their discovery. While his practised fingers roused her, her own hands instinctively found the places that sent pleasure coursing through his limbs.

He thrilled at her gasp when he held her close to him, her full, young breasts rubbing against the hardness of his chest. He fitted naturally into the crevices of her body, binding her to him with his firm embrace. They kissed again, long and passionately, their desire for each other filling them with a shared devotion they both swore to cherish.

His words of love spilled out without restraint and she matched each murmur of endearment with one of her own. He edged her gradually across the gallery floor to the balustrade. She leaned her back against it, her deep golden tresses hanging down as her head tilted back and he buried kisses on her throat.

His ardour was too strong to control for ever and he poised, pulsing against her thighs. She parted her legs, her hips supported against the ornamental parapet that was all that prevented her from plunging over the edge of the gallery to the courtyard below.

He gripped her shoulders firmly, steadying her against him as he thrust upwards. She leaned away from him, straining against his body and then suddenly she collapsed, seeming to melt in his arms, her head lolling forward to his chest. She was pinioned by him against the balustrade, pierced by his hard flesh and flowing with love that trickled like honey over his limbs.

He entered her tenderly, swelling on the hot tide of passion that surged through them both. By her quivering limbs and hands that tore into his shoulders, he knew each bursting of sensation blossoming deep within her. The brutal fury of possession was matched by the sweetness of surrender until, at a perfect tempo, they were no longer separate beings but one, flowing with a love that united them.

She toppled backwards over the balustrade with a joyful cry of fulfilment as he caught her, steadying her with his hands while her legs were entwined around his waist. They sank to the floor of the gallery, bound together at the peak of their ecstasy.

He lay breathless with her until minutes later her hands traced passionate patterns of love at the base of his spine and he was roused again. This time their loving had the languor of forever.

Later, when the moon had disappeared, he carried her in his arms to her bed. He laid her on it tenderly and slipped under the sheet beside her. She nestled her head in the crook of his neck and they fell asleep clasped in each other's arms, breathing love.

For two days they stayed in Giselle's chamber, reluctant to quit the happiness and security they had found with each other. The house slaves tiptoed in and out of the room with trays of food and drink, while Troptard supervised the plantation.

On the third and fourth days, they mooned about the house, idling in darkened corners, talking softly, giggling secretly. On the fifth and sixth days, they strolled hand in hand through the gardens, listening to the birds and marvelling at the exquisite beauty of the blossoms and colours of the flowering shrubs and verdant trees.

On the seventh day, after they rose at midday from her bed and were sitting on the verandah drinking coffee from each other's cups, their idyll was disturbed by a shout from Troptard.

Pat turned away from Giselle to watch him running up the path from the coast. He tried to stifle the foreboding that leaped in his chest. Giselle's hand reached for him and he held it tightly, waiting for the youth to reach them on the verandah.

Troptard stopped at the verandah's edge, supporting himself against a pillar as he gulped to recover his breath. Pat was reluctant to ask him what was wrong.

'What is it, Troptard?' said Giselle, releasing Pat's hand and rising from her seat.

'Mr Genave,' panted the youth, his face heavy with doom.

A knife blade of alarm gouged Pat's stomach. 'Lindsay?' he demanded, striding to Giselle's side.

'He means Papa.' Giselle straightened as though ready for a blow. 'What's happened to him?'

'He's coming in the palanquin.' Troptard pointed down the hill. 'He's very sick. Ma Doudou says he near dying.'

Pat's light heart grew heavy as he saw Giselle turn pale, the happiness of the previous seven days draining from her cheeks. He reached out to comfort her but she brushed his hands aside and ran down the path to meet the palanquin bearing her father back to Belrose.

CHAPTER TWENTY-THREE

They spoke in hushed voices. Augustus Genave had been carried up to his bedroom in the arms of a single slave. Ma Doudou fussed, keeping Pat and Giselle out of the room while she removed the old man's garments and made him comfortable in his bed. He was breathing lightly, his eyes open but lifeless, his unshaven cheeks sunken and grey with stubble, his skin the transluscence of death.

'He looks so weak,' said Giselle when Ma Doudou eventually allowed her to see her father. Pat had stood at the doorway, then followed her down the stairs to the drawing room where she sat, her fists clenched in her lap.

'I spoke to him. His eyes are open but he couldn't see me.'

'Send for a doctor.' Pat was feeling neglected now he was no more the centre of attraction for Giselle. 'That old biddy could do him more harm than good.'

'Oh, no.' Giselle's glance expressed her surprise at his lack of understanding. 'Ma Doudou is the best doctor there is for him. She knows about herbs and potions. Papa's always trusted her. She was the midwife when I was born.'

'Your mother *died*.' He spoke without malice, only after the words were out and he saw her blink did he realize how cruel he must have sounded. 'I'm sorry,' he mumbled. 'What happened to your father anyway?'

'Ma Doudou said it was after he had seen Lindsay's ship sail.'

'He's definitely left the island?'

'Yes, he has.' She sounded sad. 'Papa was on the quay and just keeled over. They took him to the house and Governor Farquhar sent his personal physician.'

'I suppose Ma Doudou chased him away.'

'They couldn't do anything. Oh, Pat,' she covered her eyes with her hands, not looking at him. 'I don't want him to die.'

'It might be better, if he's suffering.'

'Don't you see?' She looked at him sharply. 'He'll think it's my fault. He loved Lindsay. It must have broken his heart to see him leave. Because of my suggestion.'

'It would have been worse if the Governor had to hang Lindsay.'

'That would never have happened if . . .' Her voice trailed off and she stared at the empty fireplace in dismay.

'If I'd never come to Belrose? Is that what you were going to say?' He rose from the chair and strode over the window, fighting back his own despair.

'Pat!' Her cry penetrated the cloud of remorse that hovered over him. 'I wasn't going to say anything like that.'

'You were thinking it!'

'I wasn't. If you could read my thoughts you wouldn't be so harsh towards me.'

He strode back to her side and lay his hand on her shoulder. She was shaking, trying to keep back her sobs. 'I don't mean to sound insensitive,' he said gruffly. 'If anyone's to blame for what happened, it must be me. I wanted to stop Lindsay smuggling slaves.'

'It began long before you came.' She gazed up at him with eyes filled with tears, the mute appeal for his affection touching his soul.

He strengthened his grip on her but before he could speak to tell her he understood, she blurted out between her sobs: 'Lindsay forced me to be his . . . lover!'

He released her and took a step backwards, reeling from the impact of her words. 'That's ridiculous! You were a virgin when . . .'

'Did you think so? Ma Doudou told me you would.'

'There was blood on my thighs, and on the sheet the next morning.'

'Pig's blood from a bladder I'd hidden under the bed. I smeared it on you when you were sleeping.'

He shook his head, trying to grasp the truth.

'I was frantic trying to find how to make papa send Lindsay away without me having to tell him what he was doing to me. You provided the chance, and saved me.'

'You . . . you didn't feel anything for him?'

'Yes, I did.'

He felt his world collapsing. The love that had made him a man had made a blind fool of him too. 'What did you feel?' he demanded, just so he could hear her say she loved Lindsay and had only used him for her own ends.

'Hatred, of course. I could have *killed* him. But that would have killed papa.'

'You didn't *love* him?'

'How could I after what he did to me? You restored my faith. I never thought I would fall in love. Because of you, I have.' She tilted back her head, her eyes gleaming mistily.

He was bemused but put aside his questions to comfort her. He took her face in his hands and brushed a kiss first on one eye, then on the other. His lips hovered over her dainty nose and descended on her lips. He was surprised by the passion with which she responded to him until he realized she was driven by her need for reassurance.

'Thank you for telling me,' he said. 'I respect you for that.'

'I dreaded that you'd discover and spurn me.'

'It was Lindsay's fault, not yours.'

'Do you still love me?'

'Of course I do,' he said hastily, wanting time to understand what he really felt. 'I ought to go to the fields.'

'No, stay with me.' Her hand trailed along his arm. 'In case papa worsens.'

'You won't have a doctor?'

'Papa would prefer Ma Doudou to treat him.' She rose to her feet. 'I think I'll look at him again.'

He nodded, holding open the door for her. 'I'll be on the verandah. Call me if you need me.'

'Thank you, Pat.' Her smile was wistful. 'For everything.'

Augustus Genave hovered close to death for three days. Giselle sat with him for most of that time, leaving his side only when Ma Doudou sat with him instead. Pat mooched about the house until he tired of the inactivity and joined Troptard on the plantation. He returned at night and listened to Giselle's report on her father's deterioration. Although he had no confidence in the herb teas and poultices Ma Doudou was giving the old man, he kept his doubts to himself so he wouldn't upset Giselle.

He discovered when he thought of Giselle during his long

walks through the acres of coffee bushes, that his feelings for her had undergone a change. He still loved her and, if anything, wanted to possess and protect her more than ever before. Yet the lie she had confessed to was like a termite gnawing at the foundations of that love.

What Lindsay had done meant nothing to him now. It was Giselle's deception that worried him. She had fooled him once, she could fool him again.

He had been driven from Virginia because of a woman's deceit. It was Deborah Braxton's lie about him trying to rape her that had set him free. And then Giselle realistically pretending virginal behaviour was the lure that trapped him. He didn't mind. He was a plantation manager now and it was satisfying to be working. He wanted Giselle with the same intensity, regardless of whether she was duping him or not.

He was asleep in his room on the fourth night when the soft creak of the gallery door opening woke him up. He reached for the pistol under his pillow. There was no moon and the room was in darkness. He peered anxiously towards the door to make out who was there.

'Are you awake?' a voice whispered. 'I can't see.'

'Giselle!'

'Keep your voice down. He'll hear you.'

'Who will?' He scrambled out of bed, groping in the dark until he found her. She fell wearily against his chest, hesitating for a moment when she touched his naked body. He held her firmly, crushing the frills of her bodice against him. 'Who will hear us?' he repeated.

'Papa. He's regained consciousness. He can hear and he can see.'

'I'll be damned! The old crow's medicine worked.'

'I knew it would. He can't talk yet and I don't know if he can walk. He sipped some cowheel broth tonight. Pat, he isn't going to die.' Her tears were hot on his skin, trickling down the broad mat of hair across his chest. He steered her towards the bed.

'I should go to him. I just wanted to tell you the good news.'

He silenced her protest with a kiss. She ran her hands down his sides to his waist, and he tried not to flinch at the tickling of her fingers. She reached around his waist and grasped the tight, muscular sphere of his buttocks in her hands. He bit her ear and she yelped with pleasure.

Raising her skirt to her hips, he lay her down on the bed. He mounted her with a certain anger intending, by taking her, to restore his confidence in himself.

The temper of his brutal act of possession heightened when her legs locked around his waist and she writhed beneath him with her own heat of love. It soared to an awesome, shuddering ecstasy they shared in harmony. His doubts were dispelled forever by the warmth and fury of her passion.

Augustus Genave did not die. Within four weeks of his return to Belrose, he was sitting on the verandah. His frail, skeleton-like body took on flesh under Ma Doudou's ministrations. He couldn't talk or walk. Pat, Troptard or some of the house slaves carried him down to the verandah every afternoon, and put him back to bed at nightfall.

Colour returned to his cheeks and his eyes showed a lively interest in what was going on. He understood all Giselle told him, trying to reply but unable to control the muscles of his mouth or to marshal the thoughts in his head to say anything coherent.

Pat worked on the plantation each day, learning about coffee and formulating plans of his own. He helped Giselle care for the old man, watching his eyes carefully to see if he understood that he and his daughter were lovers. If Augustus Genave knew, he gave no sign. Occasionally, his faded blue eyes turned to the sea and he gazed out to the horizon, his thoughts obviously on his lost son, Lindsay.

Giselle ran the business side of the plantation, acting as bookkeeper and storekeeper. The hours she spent caring for her father and in doing the plantation ledgers, in correspondence, and in supervising the smooth running of the household, left her little time to be with Pat. He was content. He liked his work. Two or three times a week, Giselle came silently to his bedroom. He never went to hers.

His first season with coffee was a disaster. It wasn't his fault. The slaves knew what to do. As with growing tobacco, there was a routine and the field hands were familiar with it after years spent on the plantation. His presence made no difference, to them or to the crop. He was the token white master who, by patrolling the plantation, reminded them of their status.

It was nature that spoiled the crop; a blight which spread throughout the coffee bushes, withering the berries. There was no harvest that year.

Giselle explained the situation to her father. The old man nodded to show he understood but could offer no comment. To Pat he looked fitter now than before his 'stroke'. Although his lower body was wasted and a houseboy was permanently occupied in looking after him, his eyes were alert and his features rosy.

'What will we do now?' Pat was sitting on the verandah with Giselle and her father, discussing the effects of the blight.

'Can none of the coffee be saved?' Giselle asked the question as a formality for her father's benefit, since she was aware of the answer.

'Troptard says the bushes will shrivel and die. Those that don't will yield coffee too bitter to drink.'

Giselle sighed. 'We were relying on this crop to pay the debts.'

'Debts?' The word shocked him.

Giselle's beauty had matured over the months. She carried herself confidently, aware of his appreciative glances, her looks showing how she thrived on his loving. The frown that etched her brow didn't suit her. If her father wasn't there, he would have crossed the verandah and taken her in his arms, smoothing the frown away with a kiss.

'What debts?' he asked in utter disbelief.

She tried to dismiss his concern with a wave, but her lips tightened and he knew she was worried. 'Nothing important,' she said. 'It doesn't really concern you.'

'You could still tell me.'

She hesitated, glancing at her father who sat staring out into the garden, apparently lost in reverie. She turned back to him and shrugged, the elegance of her beauty threatened by what she was about to say. 'It's Lindsay.'

'Damn!' He leapt to his feet and walked over to the nearest pillar and slapped it angrily. 'I should have finished him off when I had the chance!'

'Sit down, Pat. You'll excite papa. It's bad enough as it is.'

'What is?' He returned to his chair and sat on its arm, inclining his head to hear what she said.

'In the past, papa shipped coffee to France where his agent sold it and sent us stores in return. In good years, the agent kept the balance of the proceeds to cover the lean years and any extras we needed. We ordered everything through him and charged it to our account.

'Over the years, papa built up a considerable amount and some of it was transferred here. He used it to extend his influence with General Decaen, the French Governor, and to care properly for his slaves. He was always generous.' She paused and a tear glimmered in her eye.

Pat saw it but did nothing, waiting for the worst of her news. 'Tell me,' he said in a rasping tone that showed his impatience. He was still annoyed with himself for not dealing with Lindsay.

Giselle swept back a strand of hair that drifted across her brow. It was a brave gesture but it didn't hide her despair from him.

'Papa used to keep the accounts.' She looked at her father sadly. 'After his stroke I discovered all the money he used to have has been spent. Everything is bought on credit, the slaves' clothes, our food, everything, to be paid for out of the crop profits. Last year's crop wasn't very good so we have last year's debts to pay too.'

'What about the account in France?'

'I wrote to the agent to find out. Lindsay has already been there. Pat . . .' she paused, her lower lip trembling. 'Lindsay forged the stipend letter papa gave him so that it authorized him to take all the money and close the account. We have no funds in France either.'

'Nothing?' He looked from the verandah into the villa with its fine furniture and retinue of smartly clad slaves. Everything about the Genaves and the Belrose plantation suggested wealth. 'Doesn't your father own property in France, investments?'

'I know of none.' The corners of her mouth drooped. 'I was depending on the coffee crop to pay off the debts. We can't even pay your salary as manager.'

He shook his head to indicate that that wasn't important. He was thinking. 'Have you explained this to him?' He nodded at Mr Genave who was watching them both with a quizzical grin.

'Yes.' She looked at him hopefully.

'Perhaps he has holdings you don't know about? Some property here he could sell?'

'There's only Belrose and the slaves, and the townhouse. That's mortgaged and so are some of the slaves.'

He shifted from the arm of the chair to sit in it properly, tugging at his ear with his hand. He still couldn't believe it. Augustus Genave owned the plantation, slaves, the villa, the townhouse and led the luxurious life of a gentleman, yet he was worse off than Pat's own father in Virginia. It was all a pretence. He began to wonder about the other planters in the island. Were they in similar financial straits?

'I'll understand, Pat, if you want to leave.'

Her words dismayed him. 'Never!' He grit his teeth. 'I can't leave you, Giselle, you know that. We'll find a way.' He thought of the fields created from the forest by the Madagascar slaves, and of the ratoons which were growing there into fine looking sugar cane.

'Governor Farquhar has faith in sugar,' he said, trying to sound bright.

'Do you?'

'We can try.' He looked in amazement at the old man. He was nodding his head vigorously, his lips moving awkwardly as he tried to speak.

'That's what your papa wants,' he said, rising from the chair and moving to the edge of the verandah. He stared out at the hills that rolled down to the sea, and silently prayed that the sugar cane would yield a good crop and bring in the funds to carry them over to the next year.

Pat's prayers were rewarded. He worked hard during the months that followed, showing the slaves how to cut cane and bundle it. Since there was no money to build a mill and boiling house, the canes were transferred by a team of bullock carts to a neighbouring plantation for grinding. The juice was boiled in copper vats and became the crystals of sugar to be shipped to England. Payment was to be made in England according to the market price when it was sold.

The process took several months but the expectation of money coming in encouraged him. He supervised the hoeing of the fields and the rattoon planting for a second crop. He fitted into the routine willingly, spending as much time as he could with Giselle and her father, liking the atmosphere of feeling at ease with them.

Economies were made in the food they ate, in the provisions given to the slaves. Occasionally, he went to Port Louis. He discovered that other planters were feeling the pinch, all of them depending on sugar to help them survive.

Augustus Genave never saw the results of his first sugar crop. He died peacefully in his sleep and was buried as he wished, in the garden at Belrose. Giselle was saddened by his death although pleased his suffering had ended. Pat did his best to console her, thinking to himself that now she would inherit the plantation and could put it on a securer footing.

The news about the sugar cane price came in a letter addressed to Mr Genave ten days after he died. Giselle had spent the time after his death going through his papers. She had been strangely quiet, her eyes showing the strain of sleepless nights. Although she endeavoured to hide her distress from Pat, dressing and brushing her hair with care every day, he sensed her mood. He assumed she was grieving and respected her need for privacy. He was polite and comforting and got on with his work. He was waiting.

She came to him on the tenth night after her father's death. The lantern was burning in his room. He had just undressed and was lying on top of his bed, thinking of her. When he heard the creak of his door opening, he was pleased. He turned on his side, covering himself with his pillow so she didn't see he was roused because he wanted her.

'I hope I'm not disturbing you, Pat.' She closed the door quietly although there was no one in the villa to hear. 'I've got to speak to you, that's all.'

'Come here.' He patted the bed beside him. 'Sit down.' She was still wearing the dress she had worn at supper. That was odd because she usually changed to her nightdress when she came to his room. 'I hoped you'd come.'

'Did you?' She sat on the bed automatically, her tongue licking her lips showing her nervousness. When he put his arm around her waist to make her lie down beside him, she resisted.

'What's wrong, Giselle?' He noticed only then the apprehension in her eyes. 'We don't have to be secretive now the old man's gone.'

'You'll have to go too,' she said, putting her palms to her temples to squeeze out the problems that troubled her.

He sat up, his desire forgotten. 'What the devil do you mean?'

'I can't afford to pay you, Pat. The sugar failed.'

'Failed? We sent the sugar to England. It would earn enough to pay off your debts.'

'It didn't. The agent's written to say it was poor quality compared with West Indies sugar. And that sold cheaper than ours because there is duty levied on all sugar from Mauritius. It was sold at a loss. I even owe the shipping company for taking it to England.'

He lay back on the bed, cradling the pillow in his arms, oblivious of his nakedness. Giselle glanced at him, a look of longing deep in her melancholy eyes. He saw it and reached out his arm to draw her down beside him. He kissed her but she kept her mouth closed and struggled to pull away.

'It's no good, Pat. I don't know what to do.'

'You've got Belrose. Didn't your father leave it to you? You could sell some of its acres to raise cash.'

'He left it to both of us.'

His heart glowed and he opened his mouth to speak. The tears in her eyes made him keep quiet. She was watching him with a regret that made him feel uncomfortable instead of happy.

'Both of us,' she repeated flatly. 'To me and Lindsay.'

'Lindsay!' He clenched his fists as the anger surged through him.

'He won't come back,' she said, 'and I can't sell anything without his consent. The coffee's blighted, the sugar's useless. I've no hope.'

'Yes, you have.' He seized her. 'You've got me. Marry me! Let me take care of you.'

She shook her head sadly. 'I can't. Oh, I've thought about

it. I used to dream that you would ask me. Of course, there was papa to care for so I couldn't leave him. Now I can't marry you, Pat, because I've nothing to offer.'

'You have! If Lindsay won't come back, we can run the plantation together. I'll make it pay, somehow.' He stroked her cheek, wiping away the single tear that glistened on it in the lantern's light.

'Don't tease me, Pat.' She pulled away and stood up before he could stop her. He jumped out of bed and dived for the door, standing in front of it, blocking her exit.

'I'm not leaving Belrose,' he said.

'And I'm not marrying you.'

'All right.' He shrugged his shoulders, his face broadening into the kind of boyish grin she used to find irresistible. 'Let's make a deal.'

She shook her head but her eyes showed her interest. 'I love you, Pat. I always will. It's no use, though.'

'The deal is this. Let me stay. Let me run the plantation my way. Give me a year. You can get credit for another year's expenses, can't you?'

She pursed her lips doubtfully.

'You'll have to anyway, since you've got to live and Lindsay's not coming back to run Belrose, is he?'

She nodded in agreement.

'In a year I can make a success of this plantation. I promise. Will you marry me then, when I've done it?'

'Pat, I don't know. I can't think properly. I want to, yes, I want *you*. You look so wonderful standing there, so determined, and you've got no clothes on . . .'

He caught her as she tried to pass him and lifted her off the floor into his arms. He opened the door and walked boldly across the landing with her, not bothering about the scandalized eyes of Ma Doudou staring at his naked body from the bottom of the stairs.

Kicking open the door to her chamber, he carried her over to the bed. He placed her on it and tried to move away but her hands around his neck refused to release him. With a grin of triumph, he snuggled down beside her.

He smothered her face with kisses and gently unlaced her gown.

An hour later, when she was sleeping peacefully, a smile of fulfilment lingering on her lips, he crept from her chamber to his own. He sat at the table, the lantern burning brightly beside him, and began to compose the letter he had planned for a long time to send to his brother, Mort, at the hardware store in Braxton County, Virginia.

BOOK THREE
Belrose, 1813–1816

CHAPTER TWENTY-FOUR

The activities of newcomers in any community are always regarded with suspicion or amusement. In Mauritius, the French settlers viewed the British with suspicion, waiting only for them to leave when the island became French again. The majority of the free inhabitants, though, were Creoles who were born on the island of French parents. Their attitude to the British was more one of amusement at their activities rather than loathing or suspicion.

Governor Farquhar's odd ideas were given a chance by them – and found not to be so odd. Roads were constructed along which it was possible to ride in wheeled carriages from one side of the island to the other. The town of Port Louis was smartened up. Oil lamps shone in the streets at night and the streets themselves were repaired.

A social 'season' was established, commencing at the beginning of June and continuing until October. During this time the weather was cooler and balls and dinners followed each other in rapid succession. Horse racing was started in the Champ de Mars.

Governor Farquhar handled the civil administration and he was joined in January 1813 by Major General Sir Alexander Campbell who took charge of the military garrison. The General's scornful comment on arrival was that Mauritians were so docile they could be governed by four men and a corporal. He brought with him a pack of hunting hounds with which he intended to hunt deer. These were viewed with suspicion by the slaves and with amusement by the settlers as yet another example of English eccentricity.

To Governor Farquhar's dismay and the islanders' peril, General Campbell's hunting hounds developed rabies which spread rapidly throughout the island. People were soon dying agonizing deaths when their own dogs turned rabid and attacked them. Mr Farquhar was obliged to order that every dog on the island be destroyed to stamp out the epidemic.

The same year, another of Mr Farquhar's edicts caused even more concern among the settlers as they realized that, having been denied their dogs, they were now officially prevented from buying newly imported slaves. In January, Farquhar promulgated the Act of Parliament passed in Britain six years earlier that abolished the slave trade in all British colonies.

Pat drew satisfaction from the news when he heard it while on a visit to the capital. He disagreed with the planters who claimed that without new slaves they would not be able to run their plantations. He had no patience with those who refused to labour in their fields themselves.

At Belrose, he worked alongside the field hands, setting the pace for them to clear vast tracts of land. The coffee bushes were dug up and burnt. The flat land, planted with sugar cane, was cleared before the shoots took hold and ruined the soil.

Word spread throughout Flacq and then to other districts in the island that the American at Belrose was destroying his plantation. The settlers laughed scornfully among themselves at his behaviour. Giselle's neighbours warned her she was wrong to abandon coffee growing which had brought her father his fortune, or to give up sugar which would earn high revenues once the English import duties were lowered to the same as applied to sugar sent to England from the West Indies.

If Giselle had any doubts about Pat's strategy, she did not divulge them. He had told her his plans and she was willing to let him try. As fields were cleaned and the groups of slaves, with Pat and Troptard working alongside them, hoed the soil into neat rows, the reaction of the more perspicacious planters changed from amusement to suspicion. They sent their slaves to quiz the Belrose hands on what the American was going to grow.

Since Pat had not told them, they didn't know. He set up a nursery of plants close to the villa in a fenced plot which he tended himself. He was observed taking a keen interest in the field hands' own gardens and in the condition of the plants they grew around their cabins. His eccentricity was confirmed in the minds of the neighbouring planters when he sent his slaves to carry sand from the beach and to collect up dung from cattle, donkeys and even from goats.

The construction of a long wooden barn on a rise behind the Belrose villa changed the neighbours' reaction from amusement back to suspicion. No one could imagine what was the purpose of the oddly shaped barn since it had no sides and its interior was open to the elements. It contained only beams with hooks hanging from them, running at the height of a man's head from one end of the barn to the other. When it was discovered that Giselle had borrowed money to pay for her American's folly, the neighbourhood concern increased.

Giselle was regarded by the neighbours as a fallen woman and a disgrace to her dead father's memory because she allowed Pat to the live in the villa. After her father's death, for propriety's sake she should have sent him away or married him. That she did neither and actually connived in his schemes was a scandal the neighbourhood thrived on.

Pat's own position was invidious, as he was the first to admit. Not only was he upsetting local tradition, he was an American in a British colony. Great Britain and America had been at war since August the year before. This worried Pat since his communications with Virginia were interrupted.

He refused to let Giselle see he had any misgivings about his ideas. Their life together entered a routine. He did live under the same roof, but moved from the upper floor to the lower one where he slept in Mr Genave's old smoking parlour by the back entrance to the villa. He told Giselle it was to facilitate his pre-dawn start when he rose and made his way to the quarters to rouse the hands for the day's work. Another reason for moving was to protect Giselle from gossip.

He longed for them to be able to live openly as man and wife, to confound the wagging tongues of the neighbours. But since he had sworn to make a success of Belrose, he intended to abide by his promise. It was Giselle who weakened first.

'We *could* get married, Pat,' she said, reopening a conversation they often had. They were sitting at the supper table, supper being the only time they spent together with him working on the plantation from dawn to after dark.

'Does it worry you?' He gazed at her anxiously, searching her face for a clue about her real feelings.

'No.' Her eyes gleamed. 'People can say what they like. It worries you though, doesn't it?'

He was touched by her concern. 'You were right to refuse me last year. If we were married, could I work so hard? What would you say if your husband didn't come to bed until midnight and left at four the next morning?'

'At least you'd be with me for four hours!' Her lips curved in a rueful grin. 'That's more than now.'

'It's enough,' he said, not believing his own lie. 'Give me six months and we'll make enough money to start afresh.'

'Money! Is that all you think of?'

Her outburst surprised him. 'Of course it isn't. There's the plantation, there's you.' He laughed, treating it as a joke, appreciating the stress she was under. 'I made a vow, Giselle, to restore Belrose to greatness before we marry. I'm going to do that. Then I'll be worthy of you. You'll be the reward.'

She put her hand out across the table and he squeezed it tenderly, but he had to turn away from the look in her eye. 'I'm starting out for Port Louis before dawn,' he said gently, hating himself because he had become more devoted to his work than to her. 'Mr Buchanan, the American consul, has sent word he has some cargo for me. I think Mort's sent the seeds at last.'

'Why didn't you tell me before?' She rose rapidly from her chair and leaned over him. She kissed his cheek, rubbing her hands across his chest. 'I'm so proud of you, Pat.'

He didn't answer, trying to control the surge in his feelings set off by her touch.

'If only you'd been here years ago. The plantation's never looked so good. You manage the field hands as though you're one of them. Not even the drivers carry whips anymore. Everyone works hard and they all smile like they're enjoying it. They don't seem to get sick so often. Troptard's changed too, he actually helps me without being asked.'

She kissed the top of his head, burying her face in his unruly locks. He smelt of the earth, of toil, of a manliness.

'Ain't you finish supper yet?' Ma Doudou bustled in from the kitchen together with a serving girl carrying a tray. 'Needs to finish my work, I does, 'cause we startin' early in the mornin'.'

Ma Doudou's obvious disapproval forced Giselle to release him. He gazed up at her with an apologetic smile. 'Ma Doudou's right,' he murmured. 'When the first crop's harvested, then we can relax.'

'When will that be?'

Her impatience hurt him. 'In Virginia, tobacco takes six months. I think I can do it in less here.' He smiled to calm her.

'Six months!' Giselle's mouth dropped. With a glare of despair at Ma Doudou, she walked swiftly from the dining room, leaving him watching her go with a feeling of guilt.

'Tobacco seed?' William Buchanan handed Pat the consignment papers with a snort that was intended to convey his contempt for him and his absurd idea. 'Ten sacks of it?'

He was too excited to notice the scorn in the consul's voice. 'Thank you, sir,' he said, eager to leave his office and collect the sacks where they were waiting on the quay.

'Don't know why you can't grow sugar at Belrose like the Governor wants. Difficult days for us, Romain.' Mr Buchanan assumed a patronizing air. 'We Americans are here on sufferance. You've already had a foolish disagreement with the Governor about slave trading.'

'I was right!' He was stunned by the consul's warning. 'The law banning the slave trade should have been promulgated here long before this year.'

'The Governor sits on a nest of rattlesnakes, Romain. French serpents and Creole cobras and British vipers too. By adapting the orders of his Tory master, Lord Liverpool, to local conditions, he doesn't stir up that nest of snakes. You have no right to do so, either.'

Although he felt like contradicting the pompous old man, Pat was anxious to collect the tobacco seed that Mort had sent from Virginia. 'Yes, sir,' he said meekly, edging towards the door.

'We are guests here, Romain. Allowed to stay at Mr Farquhar's pleasure. Our countries are at war. You would do well to remember that.'

'Yes, sir.'

Mr Buchanan sighed, apparently piqued by Pat's refusal to discuss his plans with him. 'You won't be able to rely on my protection much longer.'

'Sir?' He paused, raising his eyebrow. He had no idea that he had ever enjoyed the consul's protection.

'I'm being retired, Romain. There is to be a new consul sent out from America by President Madison. He won't take kindly to American troublemakers here, I can assure you.'

Pat nodded his thanks again, waved the papers at Mr Buchanan and managed to get out of the consul's office before he started lecturing him. He hurried down to the quay where Troptard was waiting. It took an hour to find the official to release the cargo. In another hour, Troptard had hired a small coastal vessel and the sacks of seed were loaded onto it.

He set sail for the east coast with a light heart, pleased that after his months of preparation, he could start the Belrose Tobacco Plantation.

He had experimented with seedlings grown from slave tobacco, nurturing them in his nursery near the villa where they were shielded from the gaze of curious visitors by the picket fence. The fence, built from local wood, took root in the fertile soil and grew long, leafy branches. But the slave tobacco, despite his efforts to prune and grow it properly, was thin, lacking the body of the Virginia variety.

In anticipation of Mort sending the seeds, he had prepared an area of ground to sow them. The cow, donkey and goat dung was hoed into this plot by the slaves as manure. Seed beds were made in it and tended daily to eliminate weeds. When he judged the beds were well watered and had made allowances for the reversed seasons in Mauritius, he sowed the seeds from five of the sacks. In Virginia, it would be done in April; in Mauritius, he chose October.

Because of their small size, he could not sow the seed directly into the fields. Ten thousand seeds could be accommodated in a teaspoon. It was a risk using the five bags for his trial but he was impatient to succeed for Giselle's sake. He prepared sufficient land to take the hundreds of thousands of seedlings as soon as they were strong enough to be transplanted.

After the powdered seeds were sown, they were covered with a thin layer of sand. In Virginia, he would have covered them with ash from the timber burnt to clear the land. Sand, he hoped, would be more suited to the Mauritius climate since it would preserve moisture.

The seed beds were covered with palm leaves and watered twice a day until the seedlings appeared. The profound joy with which he gazed on the first slender shoots must have matched that of Columbus sighting the new world. He tried to communicate his enthusiasm to Giselle as he showed her around the nursery.

'We've got millions of seedlings,' he said. 'It's going to work.'

'I pray every night that it does.'

'You'll be able to pay off all the debts.'

'And we'll be married.'

'Yes, yes, of course.' He danced to the end of the row of seedlings where Troptard was supervising a gang of men who were raising the palm leaf covering over them.

'What are they doing?' Giselle asked when she caught up with him.

'Erecting a roof over the young plants to give them a chance to grow. We'll be hanging nets on both sides so the birds can't get in. During the night, we take the cover off.'

'Is that why you weren't in your room last night?'

He looked at her sorrowfully, recognizing why she must have been looking for him. 'The first two weeks are the most difficult,' he said, smiling. 'For the plants. They have to be strong enough so they can be put out in rows in the fields.'

'How will you do that? There're so many of them.'

'I'll do it myself. The men will help. We wait for a good shower of rain to moisten the soil, hoe in the manure, and then plant each seedling individually. It's back breaking work. If the moon is clear, we'll try to work at night too.'

'I'll miss you.'

'Tobacco's like that. It needs constant care but the results are rewarding.' He wanted to cheer her up. 'I'm making some contacts so the crop can be exported to England. If it's as good as the tobacco grown in Virginia, it will fetch a high price.'

'Do you have to watch over the plants all day? You can't make them grow faster.'

'I can make them grow better. The only attention they'll need in the first month is weeding. And picking off the caterpillars which are their greatest enemy. The men will like doing that.'

He wondered if she noticed he was no longer referring to the Africans as slaves. They were men like himself and he had resolved to reward them with a cash bonus from the profit on the first crop. He expected her to object to his scheme but by the time they were married he was sure he could win her support for his easing of the slaves' lot.

He tried to explain to Giselle that during the next six months he was going to have very little time spare to spend with her. After the first month of planting he would have to prune the off-shoots from the seedlings. He could train some of the hands to do that but most of the topping task would be his own responsibility. The nails of his forefinger and thumb would grow hard and sharp again, just as they were when he worked for Cletus Braxton.

'Three months,' he told Giselle as he walked her back to the mansion. 'That's the normal time for a plant to be ripe for cutting. The second crop, from the same plant, ripens much quicker.'

'A second crop?' The disappointment showed in her voice. 'Does it go on for ever?'

'Not for ever.' He patted her arm, wanting her to return to the villa so he could get back to the nursery to help Troptard. 'You'll be busy too. In the house –'

'Pat?' Her voice was timid as she interrupted him. 'Ma Doudou says we should be married. It's a disgrace for her that we're not. She says we're not setting a Christian example to the slaves.'

'By the devil!' Her remark riled him. 'Do we have to do what *she* says?'

'She's always right, Pat. You know she has powers.'

'Then I must watch she doesn't put a herb potion in my coffee to bewitch me.' He held his hand around her waist and kissed her. 'When my job is done, Giselle, you will be Mrs Romain. Not before.' An idea occurred to him and he uttered it like a pledge. 'We'll ask the American consul to be our witness. Tell that to Ma Doudou. That will give her status with the slaves. She can have a new bonnet too!'

Despite Giselle's misgivings, the months of waiting for the tobacco to be ready for cutting passed quickly. She was caught up in entertaining the planters and their wives who called to see the tobacco for themselves. Even more disturbing for the neighbours was Pat's treatment of his slaves as equals by actually working in the fields beside them. They expressed their disapproval behind Giselle's back.

The cannier planters bribed the Belrose slaves to steal some tobacco seed so they could try to grow it themselves. They were protecting themselves in case Pat was right and had found a new profit-making crop. When Troptard told him of the bribes (for the slaves kept nothing from Troptard) Pat gave him seeds from the local plants and the bribed slaves pretended they had stolen them.

The cutting began on a warm day with the cut plants being left in the sun. They were gathered up at nightfall and hung on the beams in the drying barn. The visits of the neighbouring planters continued unabated. Giselle entertained them politely, knowing the real reason for the visits was to see how the tobacco was being cured.

Only Pat knew the leafy colour he was waiting for. He kept that secret from Troptard, just as he kept to himself the knowledge of when was the best moment for cutting. When he was satisfied the leaves had dried to the right degree, they were bulked in piles, covered and left to sweat for a week with heavy stones placed on top of them.

Next they were bound together in small bundles in the manner he had learned in Braxton County. When they were moist and pliable they were packed into wooden casks made by the Belrose coopers. Pat showed the men how to stand barefoot inside each cask, laying out the bundles in smooth layers and stamping them down until each hogshead was full.

Each one was so tightly packed not another bundle of leaves could be added. The head of the cask was inserted and secured with hoops. Finally, his first crop of Belrose tobacco was ready for shipment and, much to the consternation of his neighbours, none of them knew how to emulate him.

The hogsheads were rolled on their sides to the beach, two large hoops fixed to them to absorb the shocks. Pat sailed to

Port Louis with the hogsheads while Giselle went by land, accompanied by Ma Doudou.

After a lengthy correspondence, Giselle had secured an agent for the tobacco in London and a ship was found to take the hogsheads to England. Governor Farquhar gave the venture his reluctant blessing as an experiment only, since he was adamant that the colony's agricultural future lay with the cultivation of sugar.

To celebrate achieving his ambition, Pat took Giselle to meet Mr Buchanan. He led her proudly up the path to the consul's house, relying on her beauty to calm Mr Buchanan's wrath at his arrival without an appointment. His strategy worked. Mr Buchanan invited them to sit on the verandah as Pat explained his mission.

'We'd like you, as consul, to witness our wedding. Since I'm an American –'

'Not me!' Mr Buchanan beamed expansively at Giselle, ignoring Pat. 'My successor arrived yesterday with letters of credential from President Madison.'

'Well, perhaps you'd do us the honour of asking him on our behalf?' Giselle smiled winsomely but her eyes told Pat she didn't think much of Mr Buchanan.

'Why not do it yourself?' Mr Buchanan waved his hands as though dismissing the matter. 'He is accompanied by his widowed daughter. You can invite them both. They're at Government House in private audience with Governor Farquhar now.' He scowled. 'Damn political appointment for a lackey of President Madison's!' He spat in the direction of the spittoon and missed.

'What's his name?' Giselle tried not to lose her temper at the consul's boorish behaviour. 'I will write to him myself.'

'His name?' Mr Buchanan looked at her suspiciously and then realized what she'd asked. 'Oh, his name is . . . Cletus Buxton, or some such. He's accompanied by his daughter. Her name is Deborah.'

CHAPTER TWENTY-FIVE

The moaning of the fir trees in Mr Buchanan's garden when the breeze from the Champ de Mars hills rattled through its leaves, filled the sudden silence on the verandah. Pat could feel the blood draining from his face and he clutched the arm of his chair until his knuckles showed white through his sunburned skin. He looked at Mr Buchanan and at Giselle without seeing them.

Dimly he heard Giselle taking their leave of the consul. When she tapped him on his elbow he rose from his chair and followed her out without speaking. The sun, beyond the shade of the trees in the consul's garden, was blinding. He blinked and stared at Giselle.

'Don't look at me like that, Pat,' she said, rebuking him. 'It's not my fault Mr Buchanan can't be our witness. I don't like him anyway. I hope the new consul is better mannered. Do you think I should ask him and his daughter for tea?' She linked her arm under his elbow, expecting him to escort her.

'No.' He shook his head, barely hearing, hanging back and resisting her attempt to have her walk with him.

'No, what?' Giselle's eyes widened. 'You're in a funny mood. I suppose Belrose is too far to expect Mr Braxton and his daughter to travel all the way there. They'd have to stay the night and that's more expense for us. I wonder what his daughter's like? I must ask Ma Doudou to find out.' She twirled her parasol. 'Come on, Pat, we can't stand here all the afternoon.'

He let her prattle on as he followed her back to the Genave townhouse, a few yards along the Champ de Mars path. A racetrack had been marked out on the plain and in the season it was filled with people who came to watch the races. Now it was quiet with a few couples strolling its perimeter. Later, as the sun went down, the town belles would emerge from their homes to promenade with their friends and to giggle at the off duty soldiers from the garrison.

It was an idyllic existence. He enjoyed being in Mauritius. He had his job as plantation manager, he had produced a spectacular tobacco crop, and he was as good as engaged to a very beautiful and practical young woman who loved him.

Ironically, it was no surprise to him that Cletus Braxton and Deborah had arrived in Mauritius. He dreaded that something disastrous would happen now he was on the verge of attaining all he ever wanted: a plantation, a wife and wealth. Cletus Braxton, he surmised, had probably become an embarrassment to President Madison and so, as a 'reward' for his services, a posting to Mauritius must have been an ideal way to get rid of him.

Pat wondered what Deborah looked like. Three years had passed since he'd last seen her. He remembered her tall, long-limbed body with its firm breasts and well-rounded hips. Her eyes had been hard because she was suspicious of him. Perhaps now she had mellowed, allowing the passion he knew lurked within her to shine out. He wanted to see her.

'We could ask them to tea here,' said Giselle, interrupting his thoughts as they reached the townhouse. 'We don't have to return to Belrose yet. We could stay as long as it suits them ... to arrange a convenient afternoon.'

'No!' He shook his head emphatically. He wanted to see Deborah alone. He slung himself into a verandah chair without looking at Giselle, knowing she would be pouting at him in surprise because he disagreed with her.

'Why not? He's your consul.'

'We must get back to Belrose,' he said lamely. 'I don't want to be caught up in the social season, do you?'

'It would be fun.'

'You stay. I'll go back to Belrose.'

'I wouldn't stay without you.' She paused. 'Pat, what is there to do at Belrose now? If we stayed, I could get material for my wedding dress. It will be so much easier to arrange now we're both here.'

'You can do that another time.' He was only half-concentrating on what he was saying and Giselle noticed.

'Another time? When, Pat, when? That's why we came to Port Louis, to make the arrangements.'

'We came to ship the tobacco.'

'Well, that's done. You've proved what you wanted. Belrose is a success, thanks to you.' She stood behind him, stroking the locks of his hair where they hung over his collar. 'We had a promise . . .'

'Oh yes.' He jerked away so her hand fell against the back of the chair. He swallowed, moderating his outburst. 'We still have to wait. The tobacco might not sell for enough money to pay off the debts. That's what I vowed to do before we can marry.'

'It could be months before we hear from London.'

'Don't worry, Giselle.' He stood up, guilt at his mood troubling him. He held his arms open and smiled brightly at her. When she came to him, he closed his hands around her waist and hugged her.

'Let's go back to Belrose. I've a lot to do on the plantation. We've got each other and we've waited so long. A few months more won't make any difference.' He kissed her.

'And you know,' he said, looking wise, 'it really would be better to pay off the debts first. Then we can start married life without a single care.'

'I suppose you're right.' She kissed him trustingly until he withdrew from the embrace.

'I'm going for a walk.'

She reached for her bonnet lying on the chair where she had placed it when they arrived from Mr Buchanan's house. 'I'll come with you.'

'That's all right,' he said, meaning it wasn't. 'I've got to go to the quay.' He was lying. 'I'll walk quicker by myself. And I'll be back sooner.'

'Very well.' The downturn of her lower lip showed him she wasn't convinced.

He waved at her with a false heartiness and dashed out into the Champ de Mars, relieved at being out of her way for a few moments. In case she was watching him, he set out in the direction of the waterfront but this was also the way past Mr Buchanan's house. The shadows were lengthening as the sun dipped to the horizon. He joined the throng of people walking around the plain, hoping he would not be noticed as he passed Mr Buchanan's.

If Mr Braxton and Deborah were visiting the Governor, they would be expected to return along the road that linked Government House with the Champ de Mars, a distance of a little over half a mile. He assumed they were carried there by palanquin, or even in a coach since the road was passable by wheeled vehicles.

His thoughts ranged over his youth in Braxton County and his early desire for Deborah. He remembered how he vowed to have her even though he was only a labourer in her father's fields. When a coach rumbled past, he watched it curiously before realizing it was the object of his waiting. He caught a glimpse of Cletus Braxton's jowly features and of Deborah's bonnet as she sat primly at his side.

He lowered his head in case they saw him. For a moment he panicked. Could Mr Braxton do anything against him in Mauritius? Did the man still believe he'd tried to rape his daughter? Slinking through the hastening gloom of the twilight and keeping out of sight of the carriage's occupants, he followed them to the Champ de Mars. He positioned himself under a tree close to Mr Buchanan's house and pretended he was waiting for someone, his head lowered but his eyes raised so he could watch.

Cletus Braxton eased himself out of the carriage. He had grown fatter and was panting in the heat of having to wear full dress kit for his Government House visit. He walked fussily up the path without waiting for Deborah. No one helped her descend.

Pat held his breath, hoping he would see her face beneath her full bonnet with its side flaps. He suspected she felt annoyed at being left alone to follow her father up the steps. He wondered why Mr Braxton was deliberately discourteous towards her.

He imagined he glimpsed a wisp of her glowing auburn ringlets from a corner of her bonnet. But it was her figure that caught his attention. In three years she had become even more shapely; her waist was slender, spreading to full hips. The strictures of her high necked gown accentuated the curves of her ample bosom and she walked the steps to Mr Buchanan's house with a graceful dignity.

He stared at her openly until she was hidden by a profusion of hibiscus bushes. There was a familiar tug at his loins and he knew then that nothing had changed: he had to possess her.

He regretted telling Giselle he wanted to return to Belrose. If he changed his mind and they stayed, would he be able to approach Deborah? He reasoned it would be best to take Giselle back to the plantation and then find some excuse to come back to town by himself. Only without Giselle could he hope to make contact with Deborah. For a brief moment he considered whether he should tell Giselle that he had known the new consul in Virginia. He thrust the idea from him as soon as it entered his mind.

Ma Doudou, as usual, was a valuable source of information. Pat listened surreptitiously while Giselle quizzed her later that evening. To disguise his interest, he pretended to be dozing in the flickering light on the verandah as Ma Doudou sat opposite Giselle and answered her questions.

'She's a widow,' Ma Doudou said with a gurgle of relish. 'Married two years before her husband was killed. In a slave uprising, I hear.'

'How horrible.' Giselle clucked sympathetically. 'Is she still in mourning?'

'She certainly ain't.' Ma Doudou was enjoying her story. 'I seen her with my own eyes. She ain't much older'n you. She was wearing a dress as bright as the morning sun. Don't know what the Governor made of it but the sentries at Government House were jostling each other for a better view.'

Giselle considered Ma Doudou's outrage with a hint of amusement. 'I suppose because she's a newcomer she wanted to make an impression. I'm sure her dress must be the latest fashion where she comes from.'

'It was as red as them hibiscus, and her hair a few shades darker. Cut short, it was, like a boy's.'

'Cut short?' Pat's surprise made him sit up with a jolt, forgetting his pretence of being asleep.

Giselle looked at him curiously. 'Ma Doudou's describing the new consul's daughter.'

'I . . . heard,' he said, feigning a yawn to cover his embarrassment. 'Are you sure her hair is cut short? It sounds odd.'

'Oh yes.' Ma Doudou rolled her eyes and nodded, setting

the folds of flesh wobbling under her chin. She tugged at a plait. 'She has the body of a woman all right, even if her hair's short like a man's. She had every officer panting to be introduced to her. She won't want for suitors here.'

He hoped Ma Doudou's words weren't prophetic. There were so many bachelor officers among the British garrison and on Mr Farquhar's staff, she was sure to be inundated with admirers.

'Why's she here?' he asked tetchily, earning another glance of curiosity from Giselle.

'From what Ma Doudou says it seems she's in search of another husband.'

'That's as maybe,' Ma Doudou smacked her lips, savouring a tidbit of information. 'Mr Buchanan's cook tells me she is going to be her father's hostess. The new consul's a widower so he tell people he brought his daughter to help him in his official duties. He didn't bring no maid.' She sniffed her disapproval.

'You know a lot about it.' Pat wondered whether his own arrival had been reported as extensively on the slaves' network of gossip.

'It's my opinion,' said Ma Doudou, implacable now she had been invited to comment on the Braxtons, 'that something ain't right.'

'Good heavens!' Giselle raised her eyebrows in alarm. 'Whatever do you mean?'

'It ain't natural. A woman like her without a husband. She could have plenty where she comes from. Something's odd.'

'Perhaps the man she loved has gone away?' Pat suggested wistfully.

'She's two years a widow, Pat. She must be so unhappy and lonely. Why don't we invite her and her father to visit?'

'She'll have more invitations than she can cope with.' Pat slumped in his chair, pondering. Perhaps Deborah knew he was in Mauritius and had accompanied her father so she could meet him again. It was an engaging fantasy.

'I have to go back to Belrose tomorrow,' he said defiantly. 'You stay if you like.'

'Not without you.'

Her reply was what he expected. They left for Belrose the

next day and he tried to ignore the tension developing between them. It was easy for him to lose himself in the plantation work. New seed beds had to be made and he wanted to experiment with year round planting since the temperatures at Flacq were not as extreme as Virginia.

He worked hard, hoping to put the thought of Deborah out of his mind, yet every day that passed without confronting her made him worse. He was short tempered with Giselle and had to blame his irascibility on the slaves lest she suspect him of growing cool towards her. He listened miserably to her bright chatter of what they would do when the tobacco was sold and they would have enough money to get married. When she began to talk about starting a family, he knew that the time had come for action.

He announced unexpectedly the next evening that he was leaving for Port Louis at dawn. Thus she had no chance to get ready to accompany him. 'I'll only be gone for one night,' he assured her, patting her shoulder so she didn't feel neglected.

'I want to check some stores. I'll go'n see the new consul while I'm there,' he added, hoping that would cheer her up. 'I'll tell him how we want him to be the witness at our wedding.'

It was the last thing he wanted really and her gushing smile of happiness tore at his conscience. That night he made love to her with a ferocity that left her breathlessly unaware of the real reason for his torrid passion. He hoped she attributed it to his desire for her to be his wife. Yet it was the thought of being with Deborah that really inspired him.

He lay in wait for her, lurking behind the hedge of bougainvillaea that surrounded the Genave townhouse. By standing on a bench as though he was inspecting the hedge, he could see the entrance to the consul's residence. Cletus Braxton was renting it from Mr Buchanan who had retired to his Creole wife's property in the country.

Pat was waiting for a chance to see Deborah without her father so he could talk to her. Since she had not made contact with him he had dismissed the notion that she might have come to Mauritius specifically to meet him. He was certain, however, that she would not be as frigid towards him as when they were both young and callow in Braxton County.

With the sun slipping down to the sea, promenaders began to circulate around the plain. He watched eagerly. He expected Deborah to take the opportunity to escape from her father. After a while three people, two men in army officer tunics and a woman, emerged from the consul's house.

Even at that distance, he recognized Deborah. She bore herself proudly, swirling her parasol and striding out at a brisk pace, while the officers hurried to keep up with her. They were providing a flow of chatter and small talk which he overheard as they passed close to where he waited behind the hedge.

'Do come with us,' one of the officers said in a boyish voice.

'You've never been on a picnic like it,' added the other in an excited tone. 'We climb up the side of the Pouce mountain –'

'That's the one over there,' his colleague interrupted, pointing at the hills and not in the least perturbed that Deborah was ignoring him.

'And we get some of the natives to roast a pig.'

'A pig!'

Deborah's exclamation of disgust sent a tremor through Pat. She hasn't changed, he thought happily, feeling sorry for the two army officers who certainly wouldn't be able to make an impression on her.

He slipped out of the garden to follow a few paces behind Deborah and was astonished to see he was not the only man promenading in her wake. There were two bachelor planters, a merchant, a clerk from Government House and a prominent middle-aged but unmarried jeweller.

He knew them all and he was forced to pretend he had joined them by accident and his object in being on the Champ de Mars was simply to take the air. With such an entourage, he saw speaking to Deborah would be impossible. He turned back to the garden, dejected as he wondered how to make contact with her. A letter, perhaps, suggesting an assignation?

He considered. Surely she was not still obliged to do what her father wanted. She had been married and widowed so she had tasted independence. Giving it up would be hard for such a headstrong young woman.

That night he slept fitfully as he reviewed possible tactics, wishing he had Ma Doudou or even Troptard to advise him. He was pleased when dawn was near and he could get up. He was too distracted to think as he dressed only in breeches and a shirt, pulling on his boots absentmindedly.

He left the house to walk around the plain in the privacy of the pre-dawn darkness so he could think what to do. His circuit took him past the consul's house and he gazed up at it, seeing the sky spreading with orange where the sun had begun to rise beyond the hills in the east. There were no lights in the house and with the dawning behind it he could see only the silhouette of the building.

He moved close to the house, watching it pensively, wondering which room was Deborah's. To his dismay, he realized he had been seen. There was the movement of someone walking across the verandah to lean over its rail.

'Go away!' a voice said angrily.

'Deborah!' Without thinking, he leaped over the wicket gate and strode up the path through the garden to where she stood at the verandah's corner.

'Go away . . .!' A note of panic entered her voice. 'I'll call the guard.'

'Don't you know me?' Pat's voice croaked as he struggled to speak before she cried out for help. 'It's me. Don't you remember me? I'm the one who saved your life when your horse bolted.'

'Don't be silly!'

Evidently her curiosity had got the better of her for she didn't call for help, even if she hadn't recognized him from his voice. He slowed his pace as he drew closer so as not to alarm her.

'I've never been riding here,' she announced firmly. 'If you come a step nearer I shall report you to General Campbell. He's a friend of mine.'

'I'm not a soldier, Deborah. Don't you remember . . .?' He stepped up to the verandah rail hoping she could see him in the early shafts of light that filtered through the garden trees.

'Remember? Why should I? I've never seen you before.'

'Yes, you have. *In Braxton County*.' He was rewarded by hearing her gasp. She pulled her night gown closer as he moved to the verandah step where she would see him plainly.

'You!'

'You didn't know I was here?' He ignored the lack of welcome in her voice. Ma Doudou was right. She had cropped off her ringlets. In the morning's milky light the short hair added to her allure. Her face was pale, without paint or powder because of the early hour, and her eyes were wide with surprise. He wanted to step forward and embrace her.

'Keep away,' she said as though reading his thoughts.

'I'm a planter now, Deborah. In a few months I shall be rich when my tobacco is sold in England.'

'Indeed?' She sniffed.

'Do you remember the last time we met? You told your father I tried to rape you.'

'You did!'

It was his turn to say 'Indeed?' There was silence as they stared defiantly at each other. He broke it first.

'Why are you out here at this hour?'

Suddenly she sighed, her proud shoulders slumping forward. She shook her head, discouraging his approach, even though he sensed her need for him.

'I'm lonely, Pat,' she said, using his name as though it was often in her thoughts. She sat down on a chair and he drew closer to hear what she was saying. She lowered her voice to an undertone.

'Every day there are people pursuing me, like I'm a prize they're all competing for. Father says it's good for America, and I have to put up with it. I have no friends. When I can't sleep I sit here and think of how it might have been.'

'How what might have been?' He caught his breath and almost added: *You mean us?* but she continued to speak.

'Marriage. My husband was . . . er . . . killed.'

'By a slave?'

'Yes . . .' She looked at him sharply, as though anxious to hide something from him. She spoke hurriedly. 'I thought he was wealthy but he left me impoverished. That's why I had to come here with my father.'

'Well, I'm here too! We're almost family. I'll cheer you up.'

She shook her head as an impulse reaction to any offer. He saw then how the years had emphasized the hardness in her eyes and toughened her beauty. It didn't change how he felt for her.

She was watching him again, a speculative gleam in her eye. 'Are you really going to be rich?'

CHAPTER TWENTY-SIX

Pat returned to Belrose in high spirits. Deborah had agreed to see him again. He was to send her a note when he was in Port Louis and they would meet at dawn on her verandah. He attributed her changed attitude towards him to the experience of losing her husband and to the humiliation of being a poor widow when she expected a life of luxury. She had expressed great interest in his tobacco plantation and in his prospects.

He did not mention that his wealth was linked with his marriage to Giselle. Without marriage he was merely a manager without even a share of the tobacco revenue. The possibility of a relationship with Deborah outweighed the need to be strictly truthful. Time would take care of the problems. He wondered if he would be able to have both of them, Giselle as his wife and Deborah as his mistress, in the manner of the French planters.

He loved them both, although in quite different ways. Deborah represented the unobtainable, the challenge he had set himself as a youth and still hoped to win. Giselle, on the other hand, was his already. They shared hardships joyfully together and, when she was his wife, he would share the rewards.

His march across the hills from Port Louis to Flacq gave him ample time to consider his future. By the time he had reached the boundaries of Belrose, he had resolved to be as loving to Giselle as he could, while taking every opportunity to win Deborah.

In the distance he saw the single peaked tower of the Belrose villa, and the tiled roof with its two dormer windows. As he drew closer he could see the broad wooden gallery that encircled the upper floor and provided a roof to the verandah below.

The villa was large; the windows and doors on all floors wide open to catch whatever breeze drifted down from the hills. He saw the curtains dancing where the wind played with them and imagined he could see Giselle watching for him from the window of the tower. Word would have been passed by the slaves that he was on his way. Ma Doudou would have been told and she would have alerted Giselle. He waved at the villa, not seeing her, but knowing she would appreciate the gesture.

The curing barn drew his attention. The second crop was hung there and it would be ready for packing in two weeks. Then the production cycle would start again, with the fields being prepared and new seedlings grown for the next crop. There was so much to do. He glanced back at the house.

Now he was nearer he could see where tiles were loose in the roof, where a guttering was broken and needed replacing and where a post on the gallery looked rotten. A coat of paint was long overdue and the stone walls of the house were grey with the effects of the weather. The fretwork frieze of the gallery was damaged in patches and needed renewing.

It was easy to calculate that whatever money the tobacco brought in would have to be spent to repair the villa and to maintain the plantation, as well as to pay off the debts. It would take many seasons before Giselle could consider herself a woman of means. The thought made him pause a few yards from the house and its courtyard.

Giselle saw him and ran out of the villa in a swirl of yellow organza, rushing towards him with her arms open to welcome him back. How different her generous good nature was to Deborah's.

'My darling!' She threw herself into his arms. 'I'm so glad you're back.'

He held her off when she tried to kiss him. 'I'm sticky and dusty from the walk. You'll get that lovely dress dirty.'

'Do you like it? I wore it especially for you. I thought we would sit on the verandah and drink a little wine and talk until supper. I know you must be tired.'

He walked towards the villa, releasing his hand from hers and pulling off his coat. 'I must go to the fields,' he said gruffly. 'I'll come later.'

'You don't have to work today. Troptard's taken care of everything.'

'I feel if I don't see the plants myself, they might not grow. The men expect to see me.'

'You've been gone two nights,' she said, mildly critical. 'You said you'd only be away for one.'

'The person I wanted to see wasn't available.'

'Who was that? The consul?'

'Yes, that's right. I waited in the hope he'd see me. But he was out of town.'

'Did you see his daughter?'

The question took him by surprise. He thrust his coat at her and thought quickly, wondering if there was a way she could possibly know of the connection between him and Deborah. 'Yes,' he said with a grin. 'She was walking on the Champ de Mars with a retinue of British officers trailing after her like a pack of eager young puppies.'

'Is she beautiful?'

'I suppose they think so.' He shrugged. 'I must inspect the plantation now. See, Troptard is waiting for me. I'll come later.'

'Not too late,' she said. 'I miss you.'

When he was satisfied that all had gone well on the plantation during his brief absence, he returned to the villa and had a bath in his room. A house slave filled the tub and emptied a bucket of water over him when he had soaped himself thoroughly. He could hear Giselle singing as she arranged flowers in the dining room. He smiled to himself to think that he was the cause of her happiness, until he wondered what Deborah was doing.

He dressed in a clean shirt and breeches that were well worn but freshly laundered. It annoyed him that he had to dress in Lindsay's cast-off clothing. When the tobacco money arrived he would buy clothes tailored especially for him in the latest style. The knowledge that to be entitled to any of that tobacco revenue he would have to marry Giselle was vaguely disturbing. It was never so before. He cast aside the doubt and went to meet her.

This time he kissed her passionately on her lips. The bath had restored his vigour and he was looking forward to a night with her, even though his thoughts were on Deborah. She pressed a glass of wine in his hand. He raised it to his lips.

'A toast,' she said, holding her own glass and smiling at him over its rim with her eyes. 'To us.'

He was amused by her exuberance and said, 'To us,' just to please her. She was so good to him, he wondered why he still harboured a desire for Deborah. Yet the very thought of Deborah stirred him. He sat down lest Giselle see he was roused.

'Tell me all you did in Port Louis,' she said, showing she wanted to share his visit with him.

'Nothing much.' He shrugged. 'I've arranged warehouse space to store the tobacco.'

'In Port Louis? Why?'

'Because, my Giselle,' he smiled at her curiosity, 'sometimes we will have too much to store here. If we have hogsheads of Belrose tobacco in a warehouse in Port Louis it can be shipped whenever there is space in a vessel going to England. We can supply the agent regularly, not just seasonally as they do with sugar.'

'You are clever.'

He pretended modesty but he was pleased to bask in her admiration. Deborah never praised him.

'How do I look?' She was on her feet, prancing across the verandah, twirling as the yellow organza fluttered around her. Her hair fell in tresses over her shoulders, which were bare and flawlessly white. Her breasts were outlined enticingly by the skin-hugging fabric of her silk bodice.

'Beautiful!' He sipped his wine, pleased that she expected him to come to her room that night. On his next visit to Port Louis he would find some way to have Deborah. Until then . . .

'What?' he asked, raising his eyes, aware that she had said something he didn't hear.

'I asked if I looked, er, fatter.'

He gave her a cursory glance. 'No.' He knew if he said yes, she would be upset.

'Not here?' She patted her hips but he had lost interest in her game and merely shook his head.

'I thought,' she said coyly, 'that you might be able to see a difference.'

'Well, I can't. Is supper ready? I'm hungry.' He stood up

and walked towards the door of the dining room, missing Giselle's frown of dismay.

During the meal, the conversation took a similar note but he regarded it as part of her thoughtless chatter not requiring comment. Giselle said something about how he mustn't think she was eating too much.

'Some days I feel so extraordinary,' she said. 'I crave the most amazing things. That's why we're having papaya sauce on the chicken tonight. I just fancied it.'

He nodded.

'Then sometimes,' she said pointedly, 'I feel sick in the mornings . . .'

'What do you expect if you eat such concoctions at night?'

'That must be it.' She pushed her plate away, a shadow of disappointment flitting across her eyes.

'Of course it is.' He stood up, disinclined to take part in her small talk. 'I feel like going to bed early tonight,' he said, thinking it would please her. 'Tell Ma Doudou to clear away the wares now.' He strode back to the verandah without waiting for her nod of agreement.

His high spirits wilted and for some reason he could not understand Giselle's contrary mood. Her exuberance changed rapidly and within a few minutes she was carping at his paying more attention to the tobacco than to her.

'I'll come to your chamber tonight,' he whispered, deciding to leave her until she calmed down. He went towards his bedroom expecting her to go up to hers.

She didn't stir from her seat. Her eyes were dull with an odd frustration festering in them. He put it down to her mood. He supposed it was because he had not done anything about arranging their wedding. He wanted to delay that moment for a while.

'Don't bother to come tonight,' she shouted after him. 'I've got a headache!'

He turned, arching his eyebrow to mock her, yet she ignored him. 'All right!' He shrugged his shoulders to indicate that he didn't care. 'It's the wine.' He nodded his head in a goodnight gesture, puzzled why she wasn't watching him fondly the way she usually did.

I'm wise to your game, he thought when he was lying on his bed. Giselle was obviously planning to tease him, to keep him away from her until they were married. He didn't mind. Tobacco was a crop as demanding of attention as a woman. Besides, there was the possibility of making love to Deborah if he courted her properly.

The retching sound of Giselle vomiting in her room disturbed him the next morning when he returned to the villa from the fields to change his shirt. A shower of rain had drenched him and he needed to change his clothes, not intending to wake Giselle.

'What's wrong?' he asked, knocking on her door and then opening it slowly, wondering what sight would meet his eyes.

Giselle was sitting in a chair, her head bent over a basin held by Ma Doudou. Her hair was in disarray and her nightdress dishevelled. She waved him away with a moan.

'She's sick,' said Ma Doudou with a reproving frown.

'It's nothing.' Giselle tried to straighten up, her face wan. 'Something I ate last night, I suppose.'

'There ain't nothing wrong with my cooking!' Ma Doudou was offended.

'Perhaps you've got a chill.' It was a puzzle to him. 'Why don't you stay in bed today?'

'I'm all right, Pat.' She brushed her hair out of her eyes. 'Go back to the tobacco.'

He saw he wasn't wanted so he gave her a brief smile to encourage her and left the room. As he closed the door, he heard Ma Doudou say, 'You ain't tell him yet?' in a shocked voice, to which Giselle replied with determination: 'I'm not going to!'

It sounded like female talk to him so he thought he'd ask Giselle later what it was about. He became so absorbed in the plantation, and in fantasies of what he and Deborah could do together, he forgot all about that overheard snatch of conversation.

He sensed the rift in his relationship with Giselle over the weeks but dismissed it as part of her campaign to keep him under her influence. When she took to her bed for a few days and Ma Doudou said she must not be disturbed, he was worried but the tobacco topping was at a crucial stage and he had no time to see her anyway. She seemed paler and thinner when she recovered and went about her duties of house and book-keeping again. She told him she had had a bout of fever.

'That's why I didn't want you to see me,' she explained. 'If you caught it too, you wouldn't be able to work on the plantation.'

He attributed the note of irony in her voice to her illness. He was less at ease with Ma Doudou who had a constant glare of disapproval in her eyes whenever she looked at him. Her censure of him was more obvious when he asked her to do something. He guessed her reproach was because somehow she had learned of his dawn meeting with Deborah. What else had he done to incur her wrath?

Although he longed to go to Port Louis and see Deborah again, it was difficult for him to leave the tobacco. Troptard went there from time to time to collect supplies and the mail. He thought of sending a note to Deborah but refrained because of the danger of discovery by her father, or by Giselle.

The letter he and Giselle had been waiting for was brought to them by Troptard several months after the despatch of the first shipment of tobacco to England. Pat was in the nursery supervising the watering of the new seedlings when Giselle came running out of the house waving the packet at him.

'Carry on, men,' he said, leaving their side reluctantly to see what had disturbed her. He met her on the path that wound through the flower garden, and steered her over to a seat in the hibiscus arbour where leaves provided shade from the afternoon sun.

'I wish you wouldn't come out when I'm working on the plantation,' he said without considering why she was so excited. 'You upset the men's concentration.'

Her smile wavered for a moment and then she decided to treat his comment as a joke. 'It's a letter from London.' She thrust it at him. 'You open it.'

'Why can't you?'

'It will tell us how much the tobacco sold for.'

'I've been thinking about that.' He took the packet from her and twisted it nervously in his hands. He knew what was on her mind. 'There's so much to be done here. Look at the villa.' He pointed behind her. 'It needs repairing. I think we ought to wait awhile, to get the debts paid and everything fixed up, before getting married.'

'Open it!'

He looked down at the packet, trying to guess what news it contained. There was a red seal on it with spindly copperplate handwriting addressed to Pat Romain, Esquire, Manager, Belrose Plantation, Flacq, Isle of the Mauritius, West Indies.

'No wonder it took a long time to get here,' he said lightly, trying to smother his feeling of apprehension. If the crop was phenomenally successful, Giselle would expect immediate marriage. He didn't feel as enthusiastic as her now.

'What does it say?'

Slowly he unfolded the parchment that made up the packet. The lines of handwriting swam before his eyes as he tried to decipher it. Giving up, he turned to the pages containing the detailed accounts for the receipt and sale of the Belrose tobacco and all the expenses, taxes and commissions. The final figure showed a profit that was modest, less than he expected but satisfactory in proving that tobacco was a viable crop.

He held out the pages to her without speaking. She scanned them eagerly, reading through the letter, then let her hands fall to her lap, the papers still clutched in them.

'It's not enough . . .'

He shrugged, not letting her know it suited his plans. Yes, he wanted to marry her, but not yet. This would give him time to deal with Deborah.

'They want more tobacco,' Giselle said hopefully. 'The agent had to set the price low to attract buyers. Tobacco grown in Virginia is coming onto the market again now that the war between Britain and America has ended. The next shipment will sell better if buyers like the quality.'

'That means I'll have to go to Port Louis.' He sighed to pretend he was reluctant to do so. 'I can arrange a new shipment straight away.'

'While you're there,' she said with a radiant smile, 'you can arrange our marriage too. I've decided to give you my share of Belrose. I've written to a lawyer to prepare the papers to put half the plantation in your name. I'll sign the papers on our wedding day.' She looked at him expectantly.

He embraced her firmly, hoping by it to convince her that he really was as happy as she.

'If only we could buy out Lindsay,' she murmured when he drew away. 'Then you'd be content, wouldn't you, Pat?'

He nodded distractedly, unmoved by the mention of Lindsay because he was planning how he could make the most of his visit to Port Louis.

It began in a more promising manner than he dared hope. As soon as he arrived in the capital, he sent a boy with a note to let Deborah know he would meet her at dawn. He spent the day arranging the shipment of the tobacco hogsheads to London, and using the letter of credit from the London agents towards raising funds locally. He ordered a new suit for collection on his next visit. He would explain to Giselle that it was for their marriage. He hadn't decided when that would be. It would depend on Deborah.

She was waiting on the verandah when he arrived. He moved stealthily through the garden and was at the edge of the verandah before she saw him. She was sitting in a chair in the corner. The moon was a warm, shining pearl, hanging low over the sea, lending a magnolia glow to the tailend of night.

'I thought you were never coming!'

Deborah's stern greeting was not the friendly one he hoped for yet he forgave her because he knew her nature. 'I couldn't leave Belrose before because of the tobacco,' he said, expecting her to understand that much at least, 'I thought of you every day.'

She stared at him unsympathetically. 'You might have thought of me without friends in this god-forsaken town, and come sooner.'

'I had my work ...' He spread his hands to indicate his helplessness although he was intrigued to discover that she had missed him.

'Father has his whiskey. He brought barrels of it with him from Braxton County. I have nothing.'

'Don't you go out? The season –'

She shot him a withering look. 'The British are charming but no action. I wish they weren't so infuriatingly polite.'

His throat tightened at what seemed to be a hint. He smiled suggestively. 'Is there is anything I can do –'

She interrupted him as though she didn't understand. 'How was the tobacco sale? Did you make the money you expected?'

'It brought a high price.'

She noticed his hesitation. 'So,' she said cynically, 'you haven't made your fortune yet?'

'Half of Belrose will be mine soon.' He hadn't meant to tell her that but the sneering note in her voice made him desperate to impress her.

'What about the other half?'

'It belongs to Miss Genave's brother, Lindsay.'

'A brother? Tell me about him. Is he married?'

'I doubt it. He's no good. His father sent him to France. Giselle, that's Miss Genave, my employer, wrote to him after their father died, but he never replied. No one knows where he is.'

'Such a pity you can't get the whole plantation. Does it have a nice house?'

'Yes.' He shrugged, wondering why it was of interest to her. 'It's twice the size of Braxton.'

'How interesting.' Her eyes flashed in the moonlight.

Someone less infatuated than Pat would have interpreted her look as one of avarice. To Pat her eyes sparkled with desire. The gaze made him weak.

'Haven't you brought me a present?' she demanded suddenly.

He didn't know what to say. He had no money to buy presents. 'I'll bring it for you tonight.' He thought quickly. 'Something special. It won't be ready until later.'

She nodded without speaking, her cold, calculating eyes challenging him. He stepped onto the verandah and caught up her hand in his before she had a chance to withdraw it. He kissed it, clasping her fingers so she could not pull back. To his delight, she made no protest so he brushed his lips from her hand to her wrist.

'You are very beautiful ...' He turned the hand over. 'I've always adored you, Deborah.' He lowered his mouth to the inside of her wrist, pressing his lips against the sensitive

273

areas of her flesh until he was stopped by the lace cuffs of her nightdress.

'I've never thought of being a planter's wife,' she said with a slight sneer as she withdrew her arm. 'It might be agreeable to live in a grand villa with lots of servants and to ride in open country when I feel restless . . .'

'I will give you that chance!' Pat groaned, driven by his desire to make a promise he could not fulfill. He was grateful for the shelter of darkness that kept her eyes from seeing the agony he was in. 'Let me come tonight, Deborah. We could do such things together!'

Her expression of shock was tinged with amusement. 'I can only see you at dawn.'

'Where do you sleep? I'll come to your window.'

She drew back her shoulders and stared at him severely. 'I will wait for you here tomorrow,' she said. 'Do not forget my present.'

He returned to the Genave townhouse in a euphoria of anticipation. Deborah was proving to be a woman worthy of his attention. He liked a challenge. He guessed what she was up to, that's why he didn't tell her his future prosperity depended on him marrying Giselle. Now he *was* prepared to marry Giselle as soon as she wished because at dawn the next day the high and mighty Deborah Braxton would finally be his.

He froze in his reverie as a shape loomed out of the shadows surrounding the house. 'Who's there?' he called nervously, reaching about him in the dark for a stick to defend himself. He found nothing. A soft snigger of contempt from the darkness taunted him.

'Who's there?' he demanded again, peering closely at the verandah.

'Master.'

'Troptard?' Pat was incredulous at the youth's presence. He had left him at Belrose in charge of the slaves. 'Is it really you?.

'Yes . . .' Troptard's voice was heavy with menace.

'What's wrong?' Pat jumped up on the verandah beside Troptard and peered anxiously at his dour face.

'Miss Giselle send me to tell you not to come back to Belrose.'

'Not come back! Why not?' His heart thumped with guilt. 'What's happened?'

'It's Lindsay,' Troptard announced bitterly. 'He done return to Belrose soon after you left. He say he the one in charge of the plantation now, not you or Miss Giselle!'

CHAPTER TWENTY-SEVEN

'Coffee, master?'

Pat raised his head and sighed. He took the mug from Troptard without a word and sipped at its contents automatically. The harsh black liquid burned his throat, reviving him as it spread through his system. He became aware of Troptard standing over him. He felt threatened.

'What can I do?' The words burst out as he gave way to his exasperation. Troptard said nothing.

He sipped at the coffee again, more carefully this time. The irony of the situation did not escape him. Giselle's message was a licence to stay in Port Louis. He could spend all his time in pursuit of Deborah Braxton without feeling guilty that he should be at Belrose with her.

He knew he had a chance to share love with Deborah. Her scornful attitude was superficial. Once she was in his arms, she would be more than willing. He was certain if he could rip off the veil of contempt through which she greeted the world, he would find a woman of passion.

By staying in Port Louis he could escort her to all the balls and dinners of the season. What could be more natural? They were both Americans from Virginia. They were made for each other, if only she realized it. He wondered if her father would see it that way too.

'. . . Belrose.'

'What?' He stared in amazement at Troptard. 'Belrose?' He shook his head to clear it, wondering what the youth had been talking about.

If Troptard knew he was thinking about Deborah instead of the Belrose plantation, he would have been dismayed. He was loyal and respected Pat for the status he had given him over the plantation workers. Troptard enjoyed the challenge of growing tobacco, and the importance the success of the crop gave him in Flacq. He had as much to lose as Pat with Lindsay's arrival.

Pat wiped his hand over his brow and gazed blankly at Troptard.

'You stayin' here?' the youth demanded.

'I might.'

'Lindsay go'n come for you sometime.'

Pat's heart missed a beat. There was a glimmer of doubt in Troptard's eyes. It annoyed him. He pulled himself from the chair and walked over to the verandah rail, gripping it. The sun had risen and early risers were crossing the plain in the restrained heat of daybreak. From Market Street came the sound of vendors shouting and people haggling. It reminded him of Ma Doudou and his first morning in the capital.

'You think I'm scared of him!' Pat swung around, catching Troptard off guard. The youth stepped back as though he'd been slapped, a quiver of alarm on his lips.

'I'm not scared of Lindsay. He can come for me any time!'

'You stayin' here?' Troptard repeated the question, his voice dull with disappointment.

'Isn't that what Giselle wants? Yes, I'm staying here. I have important things to do.'

He was conscious of the reproach in Troptard's deep, soulful eyes. 'You can go back,' he said irritably. 'I don't want you hanging around here.'

Troptard's face brightened. 'You have a plan?'

'No, I don't. What do I want a plan for?'

'To deal with Lindsay.'

At last, sense penetrated his brain. He slapped the pillar with his hand. 'Ma Doudou put you up to this, didn't she?'

Troptard's face resumed its inscrutable frown. He stood with Pat's empty coffee mug in his hand, giving no sign of what he was thinking.

'Dammit, man! What do you expect me to do? Ride back to Belrose and challenge Lindsay to a duel? It's his plantation, well, half of it is. I've no rights there.'

Even as he spoke Pat knew he was incapable of justifying himself. There was the tobacco, there was Giselle. Both needed him. He sighed, casting a lingering look in the direction where Deborah lived.

'She said not to come back . . .' His voice tailed off. 'Come on, Troptard,' he said, relieved at having made his decision.

'Close up the house. If we set off at once we can reach Belrose by nightfall.'

The relief in Giselle's eyes when she saw him striding up the path to the villa convinced him his decision was right. Her smile was tinged with concern and it made him realize she had told him to stay away for his own sake, not for hers. Her glance said she needed him although she was unable to speak because Lindsay was standing beside her.

'The American returns!' Lindsay's voice was thick with sarcasm. 'I expected you to stay in Port Louis and spend the tobacco money you've withdrawn.'

Pat saw a flicker of responsibility in Giselle's eyes, and realized she must have told Lindsay everything. Perhaps he forced her to. He studied Lindsay, controlling his urge to curse him.

The man's figure showed signs of good living during his exile in France. There was the suggestion of a paunch under his waistcoat and his red hair was dull and greasy. His shoulders were still broad but he no longer carried himself arrogantly and his face was raddled and lined with debauchery. He was a man gone to seed. Only his eyes, the piercing yellow of a rattlesnake, remained the same: poisonous with hatred.

'I could kill you now,' Lindsay said with the confident air of a man above the law. The blood drained from Giselle's face.

Pat was made aware by Lindsay's stance of how vulnerable he was, standing without a weapon in the sun at the foot of the verandah steps. Giselle's distress tugged at his feelings but he could do nothing about it. On the long trek back to Belrose from Port Louis, he had considered what strategy to adopt. The only way open to him was to confront Lindsay, defy him, and to do whatever he could to protect Giselle.

In the back of his mind, he considered what Deborah would think. Would she be disappointed when he didn't turn up for their assignation? He had tried to see her but the steward would not let him beyond the gate. He had left a note saying he had to return urgently to Belrose and promising to contact her again as soon as possible. She would probably laugh cynically when she read it and forget him. He wouldn't forget her.

'Nothing to say?' Lindsay sniggered, swaggering to the edge of the verandah so Pat could see the two pistols protruding from the waistband of his breeches.

'I am manager of this plantation,' Pat said, his affable manner disguising his urge to leap at Lindsay and throw him to the ground. 'I have my work to do. That's why I've returned. The plantation income is safely lodged in Port Louis.' He nodded to Giselle indicating his report was to her, not to Lindsay.

'Manager?' Lindsay sneered. 'Is that what you call your paramour, Giselle?' He squeezed her cheek with his fingers then his hand dropped as she struck him a blow across his own cheek.

'Keep your hands off me!'

'Giselle!' He looked at her in astonishment, rubbing his cheek. 'Temper, temper! So he *is* your fancy man, is he not?'

'Don't do anything, Pat.' Giselle drew back her shoulders proudly. 'He is trying to goad you into striking him. Then he could shoot you.'

'Why should I want to do that?' Lindsay sat down, beckoning Pat with his hand to step onto the verandah.

Pat glanced at Giselle and when he saw her tilt her head to indicate that it was all right, he did so, standing where he could see her, aware that Lindsay was watching him malevolently.

'You've done a fine job here, Pat Romain. I've heard about the money tobacco can earn. It's pleasing to see my interest has been well taken care of in my enforced absence.'

'I did it for Giselle, not you!' Pat was determined not to be intimidated by Lindsay. He was certain he could beat him if it came to a straight fight. 'There are debts to pay before there will be any profit from tobacco. Only half of that profit will be yours.'

'How kind of you to be so concerned about our family affairs.' Lindsay's smile dripped evil. 'I am told this tobacco is unique. None of the neighbours have been able to grow it.'

'They don't have the seed and they don't know the technique.'

'A monopoly – and it's profitable?'

'In two more seasons it will have earned enough revenue to

pay off all the plantation debts, repair the house,' he gestured at the peeling paint of the verandah ceiling, 'and leave some over. In three seasons, with proper care and cultivation, tobacco could make you both very rich.' Pat sensed his value to Lindsay and used it as his trump card.

'So if I kill you, who else will grow tobacco for me? Troptard? Can he do it?' He glanced cynically at the youth and laughed. 'You will grow it because you're a proud American, Pat Romain, and want to prove you are better than the French settlers and Creole planters. You'll stay at Belrose because you love my sister and want to protect her.' Lindsay pinched his nose with his fingers, wheezing with pleasure at the nuances of the situation.

'Giselle, bring a drink for our plantation manager. I'm sure he deserves it for protecting you from fortune hunters.'

Pleading with her eyes that he would not lose his temper, Giselle hurried into the house.

'Yes,' said Lindsay, rocking backwards and forwards in his chair, his eyes shining brightly. 'You do accept my offer, is it not? You spoiled my business venture once, so now you'll make amends. My sister is my asset, your knowledge of tobacco growing is yours, since it keeps you alive. We will make an acceptable partnership.'

'I will stay on one condition.'

'Condition?' Lindsay's eyebrow rose with astonishment. 'You dictate to me?'

'You must promise not to interfere with what I do in the fields. Tobacco is a sensitive crop. It needs skill and understanding to grow. Without harmony and willing workers there will be no crop. You must not interfere with the slaves, nor whip them nor punish them nor have any contact with them at all. They work my way and they work well. They may be slaves in name but they are fellow men to me. Stay out of the fields and away from them.'

Lindsay scoffed. 'What time have I for slaves? You won't watch me grubbing around in the fields like a nigger. Run the plantation how you like, just produce the best tobacco and sell it for the highest price.' He paused, a smirk spreading across his blowzy features.

'Of course, you can no longer live in the villa. Such scandal,

I hear. Since you are so concerned about the welfare of the slaves, you shall live with them.'

Pat turned and stalked out of Lindsay's presence, knowing there was nothing more he could do.

The tension at Belrose affected the slaves as well as Pat and Giselle. Pat tried to encourage them. When their enthusiasm for the work waned, he worked harder himself as an example. Lindsay had been right. Pat was proud of his crop and its success would help Giselle. Although he no longer stayed in the villa, he saw her every day. She came to the fields to meet him. To his relief, according to her, she was not being ill-treated by Lindsay.

'He has his women in Port Louis,' she explained. 'He'll be spending most of his time there. We shall be together again soon.'

She was right. Lindsay was absent from the plantation often and Pat was able to spend a few hours in Giselle's chamber when he was away. Their love, now it was threatened by Lindsay and had to be kept secret, grew stronger.

Pat's thoughts, when he topped the tobacco plants in the hot sun, occasionally dwelt on Deborah. Despite knowing how fortunate he was in having Giselle's love, he often wondered what might have happened if Lindsay's arrival hadn't prevented him going to Deborah.

'Have you ever thought how strange fate is?' he asked Giselle when they lay side by side in her bed one sultry afternoon. Lindsay was in Port Louis. The tobacco was at the curing stage, the time when there was little to do except wait for it to dry and be ready for packing.

'If we had wed before Lindsay came, I'd be able to spend every night with you.'

'I'm glad we didn't.' Giselle looked worried. 'The less you and he see of each other, the safer you'll be. If you lived under the same roof as him, after three drinks you'd be at each other's throats. I hate it when you have to sleep in the slave quarters, but it's safer. For us both.'

'He doesn't molest you?' He hugged her naked body closer to him, squeezing her shoulders.

'I lock my doors at night. Ma Doudou would attack him

with her rolling pin if he tried. He's grown out of me, Pat.'

'Have you grown out of him?' He felt her tense in his arms. 'You're not still scared of him, are you?'

'Perhaps I am. I wonder what he's going to do next.'

'Swindle you out of your share of the plantation if he gets a chance, I should think.'

'If we were married, then it would be you he must swindle.'

'That's my fault.' He grimaced apologetically. 'I wanted to wait.'

'Why? Weren't you sure?' She snuggled up to him, putting her head on his chest.

'It's a big step.'

'You don't want to lose your freedom?'

He took a deep breath. 'What would you say if I was married to you and had a mistress too?'

She drew back in alarm, searching his eyes anxiously, then she relaxed. 'When we are married, you won't have the energy for a mistress.'

'Some men do.'

'Not you, Pat. When we're married, you'll be mine. Exclusively.'

'I like that,' he said, meaning it. He cuddled her as her hand slipped to his thighs and began to stroke him. A knock on the door disturbed them.

'Master!' they heard Troptard call as he rattled the handle of the locked door. 'Come quick!'

'What's wrong?' Pat answered lazily, reluctant to halt Giselle's caress.

'Lindsay comin' down the trail. He bringin' a palanquin with him.'

'Damn!' Pat sat up, kissed Giselle hurriedly on her cheek. 'I'll go out by the back way by the curing shed. He won't see me. Did you know he was coming back today?'

'No.' She bit her lip when he broke from her grasp. 'He only said he might bring a wench from Port Louis. Oh, Pat, I don't want his women here.'

'Don't worry.' He pulled on his breeches. 'If she's a town girl she won't want to stay here long.'

'I'll have to be nice to her.'

'You're nice to everyone, Giselle, without even trying.' He

kissed her once more and unlocked the bedroom door. Troptard was waiting and urged him out of the villa before Lindsay arrived.

Curiosity about who Lindsay was bringing to the villa made him linger in the flower garden, pretending to inspect the roses. He saw Giselle, now dressed, at the door of her chamber where it opened onto the gallery, peering down at the palanquin as it was borne up the path to the villa by four panting, muscular slaves. They lowered the palanquin from their shoulders with obvious relief and crept over to the shade of the bushes where they immediately lay down. Ma Doudou on the verandah, signalled one of the house slaves to carry water to them.

The woman's legs appeared first as Lindsay drew open the curtains of the palanquin and reached in to help her out. Pat was struck by the trimness of a pair of pretty ankles before the woman smoothed down her skirt and stood up. He expected Lindsay to have found himself a high class Creole whore. He raised his eyes to see her face.

'My God!' His exclamation caused Troptard to grip his arm in dismay to silence him. He shook him off. 'It's Deborah,' he whispered in awe.

Lindsay appeared not to have heard him as he escorted Deborah into the villa. Giselle, watching from the balcony above, tried to attract his attention to see what the fuss was about, but he ignored her.

'Find out what she's doing here!' he told Troptard, pushing him between his shoulder blades in the direction of the palanquin bearers. He waited nervously, one eye watching the verandah in case Deborah came out again, the other pretending to inspect the row of bushes.

'She's a friend of Lindsay's,' Troptard reported sullenly when he returned. 'He's spent the week taking her to balls in Port Louis. The bearers say she expects to stay here a week too.'

'A week?' His brain worked fast. Jealousy of Lindsay for securing the prize he saw as his rapidly evolved into pleasure at the opportunity this gave him for another attempt of his own. He intended to turn the situation to his advantage.

He left the garden and strolled boldly into the villa. Giselle, who was sitting in the drawing room opposite Deborah, beetled her brows with warning as he barged into the room. Linday's mouth was agape with outrage. He walked straight over to Deborah, seized her hand and kissed it extravagantly.

'How wonderful to see you, Deborah,' he gushed, turning to Giselle before Deborah could speak.

'This is the American consul's daughter, Giselle,' he said. 'It was going to be my surprise to introduce you, but now you've met her through Lindsay. I'm sure you don't know, Lindsay, that we're related through marriage. My sister was a servant in her father's house and married her drunkard brother.'

'Pat!' Giselle looked mortified until Pat winked at her to show he knew what he was doing.

'You two know each other?' Lindsay, at first dumbfounded, sounded as though he expected trickery.

'Is this Belrose?' said Deborah, feigning ignorance. 'You never said you owned *Belrose*.' She turned to Lindsay and fixed him with an accusing stare.

'He doesn't.' Giselle took her cue from Pat. 'My brother and I own it together.'

'Like I told you.' Pat smirked. 'When we met in Port Louis.'

Lindsay strode over and took Deborah's hand possessively in his. 'Why didn't you tell me about . . . this?.' He glared at Pat.

Deborah's eyes flashed with a familiar display of irritability and Pat knew he had succeeded in rattling both her and Lindsay. 'You should have told me you were bringing me here!' she said. 'I thought you had a plantation of your own, not one you share with your sister.'

'I'm not sharing for long. I'm going to buy her out!' Lindsay was angry. 'This will soon all be mine.'

Pat exchanged a glance with Giselle. Her expression showed she knew nothing about Lindsay's intention. He decided to goad him further.

'Would you like to see the tobacco, Deborah?' He extended his arm to her. 'You can tell me how it compares with tobacco at home.'

'She doesn't want to see it with you!' Lindsay's face swelled with fury.

284

Deborah's eyes sharpened. 'Yes, Pat, that's very kind of you.' She stood up and walked towards him so that Lindsay was forced to move out of her way.

'Deborah . . .' There was a note of desperation in Lindsay's voice.

'Yes?' she said archly.

His protest died under her hard glare of contempt. 'Very well,' he said. 'Please yourself.'

Pat shared another wink with Giselle as both realized Lindsay had met his match in Deborah. He led her out to the verandah, squeezing her hand close to his chest where it was linked in his arm. Deborah was flushed and she kept her eyes straight ahead. He guessed her pride had suffered and she was trying to work out how best to restore her prestige.

'I'll come too,' said Lindsay, joining Pat before he could say anything more to Deborah. 'You can explain your famous tobacco to me as well.'

Deborah pulled her hand out of Pat's arm and walked ahead, making it clear she was forgiving no one.

Pat's victory over Lindsay was short lived. After Deborah had seen the vast size of the Belrose plantation, she allowed Lindsay to curry favour with her again.

Pat was not surprised because he suspected she wanted Belrose and saw a better chance of getting it through Lindsay than through him. It added to the challenge. Now Deborah was actually at Belrose, Pat was sure there would be a way for him to steal a few moments alone with her. All he wanted was enough time to satisfy that searing need within him. It was a need he was convinced she knew too.

He sat in the arbour surrounded by the hibiscus blooms, red, yellow and pink, as the short dusk of the tropics settled the day and the fireflies began their jaunts through the leafy branches of the shade trees. He had learned that Deborah was to sleep in his old chamber on the upper floor. Doubtless, in the dead of night Lindsay would try to seduce her there.

Pat wondered whether to enlist Ma Doudou's help. If she put a sleeping powder in Lindsay's wine at night, he would fall unconscious. This would enable Pat to get to Deborah's chamber instead.

He heard his name being called softly, and he whistled in

reply. Moments later he heard the swish of a skirt on the path and Giselle entered the arbour. He held her tightly as he kissed her. She was giggling.

'Lindsay thinks you've duped him,' she said. 'He really believes you and Deborah have been lovers.'

'Did she tell him I tried to rape her?'

'Is it true?'

He grinned and made a space for her beside him on the bench. He told her about Deborah. He omitted nothing except his continued determination to possess her.

'Pat,' she said, sliding her hand under his shirt and rubbing it against the soft curls on his chest. 'I've had an idea . . .'

'Forget it. We daren't make love here. Deborah might see.'

'I don't mean that.' She giggled again and tweaked his nipple. 'A real idea.'

'What is it?' he said with misgiving.

'Lindsay's announced his intention of buying my share of the plantation. That's a lie. I know him. He's only waiting until there's money to steal and he'll take it and go. He probably thinks Deborah has money and that's why he's courting her.'

'He'll get his come-uppance.' He smiled happily at the thought of Lindsay being bested by Deborah.

Giselle interrupted his amusement. 'Why don't I buy out Lindsay's share? The plantation would be ours and we could be married then.'

'You haven't got the money!'

'Neither's Lindsay. I do have some jewellery I could sell . . . I could take another loan . . .'

He kissed her profoundly, letting his tongue probe deep in her mouth. He flowed with love for her, and hated himself for still being attracted to Deborah.

It could ruin everything.

CHAPTER TWENTY-EIGHT

Pat glanced wistfully at Belrose before striding after the palanquin carrying Giselle. He was filled with foreboding at what might happen while he was away from the plantation and it robbed him of any pleasure at going to Port Louis with Giselle.

'Come on, Pat!' Giselle's bright laughter at his moodiness did nothing to lighten his soul. He caught up with the palanquin and walked by its side down the path that led to the woods.

'I still think I should stay.'

'No, Pat.' Giselle was insistent. 'We must leave them alone together.'

'Why?' The idea of leaving Deborah alone at Belrose with Lindsay infuriated him. Lindsay was sure to make love to her and it would have been the perfect opportunity for him.

'I've explained all that.' Giselle eyed him quizzically. 'Let them fall in love. Lindsay will be willing to sell out then so he can go to America with her.'

'She won't have him,' he said, not caring if Giselle did suspect his feelings for Deborah. 'I know her. They'll row most of the time, and she'll sulk for the rest.'

'Then no harm will be done. We have to go to Port Louis at once. I've got the jewellery to sell and I can arrange everything with the lawyers for Lindsay's share to be transferred to me. And you've got another shipment of tobacco to send to London.'

'All right,' he said to please her, dropping back as the trail narrowed and the palanquin bearers trotted ahead. Giselle had got her own way but he couldn't help wondering if part of her scheme was to keep him away from Deborah.

By the time they reached Port Louis, he was exhausted. The palanquin bearers were the same ones who had brought Deborah from Port Louis. They were tough, athletic men who made light of their work and set a hectic pace along the trail. He had followed them at the same pace so as not to let Giselle out of his sight. Troptard and Ma Doudou had remained at Belrose so he alone was Giselle's protector.

'The least number of people who know I am carrying the jewellery, the better,' Giselle had explained.

The old gardener who looked after the townhouse in their absence was surprised to see them. He shuffled about opening the doors and shutters with a great display of contrariness while Pat relaxed in a chair on the verandah and Giselle found a bottle of burgundy and brought it to him with a clay pitcher of cool water.

'This will restore your strength,' she said, giving it to him to open.

He knew the meaning of that tone. He concentrated on pulling the cork from the bottle to control the rush of wanting her husky voice stirred within him. 'You lured me here on false pretences,' he joked as the cork came out with a satisfying sound.

She held two glasses for him to pour. 'It will be nice to be on our own. No Ma Doudou frowning at us all the time.'

'How are we going to eat?'

'I can cook.' She splashed water into his glass and then in her own, raising it to his. 'Let's drink to us.'

'When you look at me like that, Giselle, I'm powerless to resist you.' He made it sound lighthearted but he was serious. Her evening-blue eyes beneath her thick black lashes bewitched him.

'Good.' She pursed her lips in a suggestive half-smile.

The wine seeped through his weary limbs, changing the agony to a blissful laziness. He stretched his legs out, aware of her watching his thighs clad in the dusty gold fabric of his skin-tight breeches. He throbbed with a yearning, inspired by the sensual glint in her eyes.

They sat together without talking, sipping wine, idly watching the promenaders on the Champ de Mars. Gradually it grew dark. They remained on the verandah without lights because the gardener had given up playing houseboy and gone to sleep.

'We've finished the wine,' she said happily.

'And the water too.' They giggled and he put out his hand to hold hers. He felt the pressure of her fingers and wondered if she was as roused by his touch as he was by hers.

'It's so dark,' she said. 'I'll never find my way to bed.'

'Let me help you.'

That night they shared a harmony that seemed to be a gift from the stars. With the windows wide open to the night, they were part of the darkness. The moon glow came to their room later, and the stars in their diamanté vividness were visible from where they lay together, united in their love. Suddenly Deborah was no longer important to Pat. He hugged Giselle until she squealed at the tightness of his embrace.

'I love you,' he murmured with the emphasis on 'you'.

If she understood his doubt was resolved, she said nothing, only entwined her fingers in his locks and let her lips wander over his body, breathing in the musky fragrance of his manliness and showing that she loved him.

In the morning, he took her to the warehouse where the hogsheads of tobacco were stored while waiting to be shipped. Every month, a vessel transported the casks from Belrose to Port Louis. He had contracted with Mr Piggot, a merchant, to organize their forwarding to England. Together with Giselle, he inspected the accounts and was delighted to see that their income was rising.

'Mr Lindsay's been here,' Mr Piggot, a red-faced man with white side whiskers and a portly belly, told Pat. 'He's been wanting me to pay the credit in cash to him.'

'What did you do?'

'I told him I must hold the credit as a guarantee on expenses. The next vessel from England should bring mail. I'll know then what the current credit is for the Belrose tobacco with your London agents.'

'Don't give Lindsay any money!' Giselle's eyes held the merchant's. 'I'm buying out my brother's share in Belrose.'

'I'm relieved to hear it.' Mr Piggot's broad smile reassured them both. 'I don't like dealing with the likes of Mr Lindsay. No offence meant to you, ma'am. He has a bad reputation, that's all I'll say.'

Lindsay's reputation was the topic of discussion wherever they went. He had been boasting of his ownership of Belrose and the fortune his American overseer was going to make for him with the tobacco crop.

Pat and Giselle found her plan to buy him out was welcomed. Giselle sold her jewellery and a backer was found to finance the deal which was put into writing by a lawyer. Their negotiations took them three days, by which time Pat was getting anxious to return to Belrose.

'I don't like the thought of Lindsay alone on the plantation,' he told Giselle on the third night. 'He could do something drastic.'

'Not to the tobacco,' she said. 'He knows its value. He's waiting for you to harvest the next crop so he has more money to steal from us.'

'That's another five months.'

'He'll be gone before then.'

'How do you know he'll accept your offer?'

'We'll find a way,' she said with a smile, opening her arms for him to come back to her embrace.

'I want to go back to Belrose,' he said, biting his lip as something worried him. 'I'm not sure why.'

'Can't we stay a few more nights? I like it here, just the two of us.'

'It's the tobacco, Giselle . . . I should be there.'

'Very well.' She sighed, unable to hide her disappointment.

His plan to leave early the next morning had to be changed when a messenger came to the gate as they were preparing to set out for Belrose. Pat vaguely remembered the Englishman with his large nose and lock of hair that kept falling across his brow.

'Jonathan Rendye,' the man said, looking embarrassed at interrupting their departure. 'I'm aide to Governor Farquhar.'

'Can I get you some coffee, Mr Rendye?'

'No, thank you, Mrs, er, Miss Genave.' The man's face reddened and Pat realized he was embarrassed at finding the two of them alone together in the same house at that early hour when they weren't married. To the Englishman it would seem scandalous.

'Governor Farquhar,' Mr Rendye said, retreating to his message to hide his awkwardness, 'is walking on the Champ de Mars. He sent me to ask if you could join him.'

'Of course.' Pat jumped to his feet. 'Mr Rendye, stay here with my fiancée, would you, old chap.' He smiled at Giselle behind Rendye's back and bounded off the verandah to seek Mr Farquhar among the promenaders on the plain.

The Governor was walking with an escort of two officers from the garrison when Pat approached him. He dismissed them in mid-conversation when he saw Pat and beckoned him to stroll along beside him. The two officers followed a few steps behind and Pat was conscious of their constant scrutiny.

After greeting him cordially, Mr Farquhar came straight to the point. 'I have had worrying reports about you, Pat.'

'I've done nothing wrong.'

'You attract trouble, Pat, that's wrong. I'm told your tobacco crop is very successful.'

'Is that wrong?'

'The planters are jealous of your success. In Flacq they all want to grow tobacco too. You're undermining my plan and influence over them to grow sugar.'

'That's not my intention.'

'And there's Mr Braxton, the American consul.'

'I've never met him.'

'Is that true, Pat?'

He lowered his eyes guiltily under the Governor's gaze. 'I've never met him here.'

'In Virginia?'

'Yes. His son is married to my sister.'

'He doesn't like you, Pat. He has given me a worrying report on your conduct. He's warned me, unofficially of course, that you are quite a troublemaker.'

'Then unofficially,' said Pat angrily, 'I can tell you something about the American consul. He raped my sister and made her pregnant. She had to marry his son to give her child a father. I arranged it.'

Robert Farquhar was silent for a few moments. 'The consul is an influential man, Pat, with your President's support. Britain is anxious to repair the damage caused by the recent war. I am bound to listen to him.'

Pat was dismayed by the implication. 'Are you going to ban me from Mauritius?'

'It is in my power. You are not a landowner here, you have no ties. You kindle strife wherever you go. What am I to do?'

'If I were a landowner and had ties?'

'Then you are a settler. I can't deport you. But you're too restless to settle here, Pat. Take my advice, leave Mauritius before I'm obliged to send you away. I don't want any disruptive elements here, and I'm bound to oblige the American consul.'

Pat walked away from the Governor without a word. He was furious. He never set out to make trouble for anyone and now he was branded a 'disruptive element'. Giselle was waiting for him at the gate to the house, clearly bored with Mr Rendye's company.

He declined to tell her what was wrong when she asked and remained silent for most of the journey back to Belrose, letting resentment fester in his soul. Only the sight of the single tower of the Belrose villa and the cleared fields waiting for the tobacco seedlings to be planted relieved his angry mood. He approached the villa eagerly, wondering why Troptard had not come out to meet them.

'Where is everybody?' he wondered aloud as he helped Giselle from the palanquin.

Dusk was gathering. The doors and windows of the villa were wide open, curtains dashing against the furniture in the stiff breeze. 'Hellooo!' he called, striding onto the verandah, a sickening feeling hovering over his heart. Giselle followed him anxiously.

The villa was eerie without lights. He hurried through the downstairs rooms, his concern mounting as he thrust open the doors of each one and found it empty. When he reached the kitchen courtyard at the back of the house, the chickens pecking for rice on the flagstones scattered as he shouted for Ma Doudou.

'Damned odd!' he said, patting Giselle's shoulder in a futile effort to comfort her. 'Everyone's gone.'

'Deborah?' she asked fearfully. 'Lindsay? Do you think something's happened to them?'

'Wait.' He took her to the drawing room and made her sit in a chair. Then he ran up the broad flight of stairs and checked each of the bedrooms.

In Lindsay's there was blood on the sheets and curtains and the room was in disarray as though someone had ransacked it. Chairs were upturned and ornaments on the dresser were smashed. There was even a streak of blood on the ceiling.

He stepped out onto the balcony, trying to guess what had happened. There had been a fearsome struggle. Someone was cut and blood had spurted out over the room. He glanced around the balcony for anything unusual in the encroaching darkness. His attention was caught by a flicker of light behind the curing shed. He stared at it, listening carefully, horror mounting in his breast at what he heard.

He rushed down the stairs. Giselle was waiting for him. There was a girl about ten years old standing with her, weeping as Giselle tried to comfort her.

'It's Lindsay –'

'I know,' he said, not stopping to listen. 'By the tobacco shed.' He ran out of the villa, realizing too late that he should have looked for a weapon. His anger would have to suffice.

As he drew nearer the barn, he was puzzled by the silence. He expected to hear the noise of someone being beaten. He slowed down when he saw the slaves grouped in a mute semi-circle around one side of the barn.

The single lantern on the ground by the barn's open side threw a glow around their ankles, making their shadows ominous and threatening. They were watching something without emotion, their meek acceptance adding to Pat's apprehension of what he was going to see in the semi-circle's centre.

He crept forward stealthily. If the slaves were in control, his own life could be in danger. He regretted not having a pistol, or even a whip. The senseless brutalities of a slave uprising were awful. If one was happening here, he would be powerless to stop it.

He was given hope by the lack of excitement in the watching slaves. If a white man, or woman, was being slaughtered in front of them, he expected them to react with joy, not with the sullen silence that gripped them.

He stood unnoticed at the back of the semi-circle and peered through a gap in the crowd. Lindsay was in the middle, a brace of pistols in his hands, his eyes wild with rage. He seemed to sense that he was close to losing control of the slaves. There were too many for them to shoot if their tolerance snapped and they decided to attack him.

Deborah, her face twisted with a snarl of lust, was beside him, a knife in her hand. She was hacking at what looked like a stag's carcass hanging from a hook on a beam in the drying shed.

Pat blinked when he realized what she was doing. With a howl of fury, he pushed his way through the assembled slaves. His shout broke the spell. The slaves scattered into the darkness, screaming in panic as though a demon had been let loose among them.

Startled, Lindsay let fire with both pistols, one ball catching a woman in her back as she scrambled to get away. She fell to the ground with a shriek. Suddenly there was no one left to shoot at, only Pat hurtling across the now vacant space towards him. Lindsay stood his ground, detaching a whip from his waistband and unfurling it to defend himself.

Pat ignored him and lunged at Deborah. She gazed at him in a trance, the blade in her hand dripping blood. He smashed her wrist with his arm, knocking the knife out of her grasp.

'What are you doing?'

She stared at him without speaking. He stooped to pick up the knife then looked around. Giselle had reached the barn and some of the slaves were coming back, their eyes no longer showing fright at the whip in Lindsay's hand. Ma Doudou burst out of the shadows.

'Drop that, Lindsay!' he shouted as Lindsay raised the whip defiantly at the slaves surging towards him. 'Go back to the villa with Giselle. They'll kill you if you don't.'

Realizing the truth in what Pat said, Lindsay lowered the whip and slumped forward into Giselle's arms, fear flooding through him.

Pat breathed more easily. 'Hurry, Giselle. The men won't harm him if he's with you.'

He forgot about Deborah as he rushed over to the body hanging from one of the tobacco hooks. Ma Doudou was at his side, keening softly.

The body was Troptard's, suspended from a hook driven through his breeches. His head hung down, blood oozing from the cuts on his skin where Deborah had slashed at him with her knife. His breeches were in tatters, lacerated by the whip. His penis hung out through a rent in the fabric, blood dripping from a gash where Deborah had begun to castrate him.

Unable to speak at the shock of what had happened to his friend, Pat supported him in his arms while Ma Doudou took the knife and cut him free from the hook. He cradled Troptard's body in his arms, heedless of the blood smearing the new suit of clothes he had collected the previous day from the tailor in Port Louis.

'Let him stand,' said Ma Doudou.

'He's dead.'

'No, he ain't.' Ma Doudou caught Troptard's hands in hers and rubbed them vigorously as Pat placed him feet first on the ground.

Pat let him lean against him, wondering how he could possibly be alive when his flesh was a mess of pulp and blood. He watched Ma Doudou take a phial from the pocket of her apron and tip its contents into Troptard's mouth.

'Your potion won't help him,' he said sorrowfully. 'It's too late.'

''Course it will!' Ma Doudou slapped Troptard on both cheeks. 'You gonna walk home, Troptard,' she said sternly. 'I ain't carryin' you.'

'I'll take him.'

'No, Pat, let him walk. He's tough. If he walks, his wounds won't set wrong. I'll bathe his body in herbs and hot water and then he'll sleep. Tomorrow he'll be stiff but the cuts will heal. He'll live to get his revenge.'

'What happened?' he asked as Troptard swayed then succeeded in standing by himself.

'Lindsay took him to his chamber and whipped him.'

'Why?'

'Deborah lied. She said he tried to rape her. After Lindsay beat him in his room he forced all the slaves to come here and watch Deborah punish him.'

Pat shook his head in disbelief. Troptard opened his eyes, straining to see out of the puffiness and blood that blocked his sight. 'I didn't do anything, master,' he croaked.

'I know.' Pat tried to convey his trust in him with a smile. 'Take him home, Ma Doudou.' He turned away, sickened.

He gazed around the barn. Blood was spattered on the ground. The smell of sweat and urine from Troptard's fear mingled with the musty odour of the tobacco hanging up to dry. The lantern's glow threw grotesque shadows from the leaves to the roof.

Peace was returning as the night darkened and the slaves went back to their quarters. Pat had no fear of being alone. The slaves' grudge would be against Lindsay, not him. Troptard would recover.

He moved silently through the rows of hanging tobacco, touching a leaf here and there, holding one to his nose and sniffing it. He was trying to purify himself by its scent as much as inspect the tobacco to see if it had been spoilt by the commotion.

There were heaps of tobacco tied in bundles on the ground at the far end of the barn. The fringe of light from the lantern cast a vague glow over them and he walked towards them slowly, pausing to smell the leaves, judging even in the darkness when the tobacco would be ready for packing. He acted through habit, his mind in turmoil.

The sound of a woman sobbing halted him. It was coming from the end of the barn, by the bundles of tobacco piled on the ground. He hurried over, expecting to find a female from the quarters, frightened by the uproar and too scared to return to her cabin.

It was Deborah. She sat with her head down, her short auburn hair in spiky disarray. Her knees were drawn up to her chest, her hands linked around them. Her skirt had ridden up to her waist, revealing the private whiteness of her thighs, her shapely legs and her trim ankles. Her bosom heaved with deep sighs of sorrow, her shoulders shaking with anguish.

Her vulnerability touched him. He was seeing her for the first time stripped of all pretence and arrogance. What she had done had humbled her. She needed comforting as much as Troptard.

He knelt down beside her. 'Deborah . . .' He put his arm around her shoulders. 'It's all over now.'

She fell against him, showing no surprise at his presence. Her sobbing ceased and she raised tear-stained eyes to his.

Her bodice, he noticed incredulously, was open, the glorious swelling of her breasts overflowing the lace corsage.

With his free hands, he moved to smooth her skirt down to cover her bare thighs. She twisted, closing her legs over his hand, holding his fingers against the moistness of her flesh.

'He made me do it, Pat,' she whispered, her eyes brimming with lust. She wriggled closer to him, forcing him back against a heap of tobacco leaves. The scent of the crushed Virginia tobacco permeated the night air, a heady fragrance that sent his senses reeling.

Her hand groped the inside of his thigh. She fondled him with practised fingers.

He gasped, desire to have her leaping at her touch. Reason vanished as her lips touched his, urgently craving his kisses.

'You don't think badly of me, do you, Pat?' she breathed as she fed on his lips. 'It wasn't my fault . . . Lindsay made me do it.' Her fingers held him firmly.

Suddenly, he knew she was lying, as she always did. 'No!' The disgust in his voice filled the darkness of the barn. He pushed her away.

'You're shocked, Deborah.' He rose to his feet so her fingers dropped from him. 'I'll take you to the villa.'

His brusqueness belied the way he really felt. After so many years of wanting, he could satisfy his need and take her. No one would know . . . except him.

He strode out of the barn and sighed loudly with relief, leaving her. He knew that in the morning he could face Giselle, and Troptard, with a clear conscience.

CHAPTER TWENTY-NINE

Pat gazed over the fields from where he stood with Giselle on the verandah. All the way through the valley to the sea and right up to the crest of the hills, tobacco grew in straight, orderly rows. When he first came to Belrose it was a confusion of unclaimed forest, hapless coffee bushes and wasted land worked by frightened slaves. He had changed Belrose to a productive plantation attended by men and women who saw the results of their labour in cash.

Giselle shared his concern about the slaves. After Lindsay's attack on Troptard she had agreed that payment should be made to improve the lot of the workers. Troptard's advice was sought and his recommendations acted on. It had taken months to overcome the disruption caused by Lindsay and Deborah but with Troptard's help, after he recovered, the slaves settled down and the plantation was flourishing again.

Giselle stroked his arm, communicating with her touch her concern for the problem that faced them. She had just returned from Port Louis and her face showed her tiredness after the journey.

Pat looked away from the plantation he loved so much and became aware of how exhausted she was. 'Let's sit down,' he said, leading her inside the villa to the drawing room. 'Ma Doudou can bring us some wine.'

'Shouldn't you be helping the men?'

He studied her face intently, then decided there was no sarcasm in her remark. Yet so often in the past he had left her when she needed him because the tobacco seemed more important. 'We begin cutting tomorrow,' he said. 'I can take the rest of the day off.'

She smiled at him gratefully, untying her bonnet and placing it on the table close to her chair. Her face looked drained. He rang the silver bell, its tones echoing through the open door into the hall. A young girl with a cheeky smile bobbed into the room.

'Tell Ma Doudou to bring wine,' he said, 'and a jug of water.'

The girl giggled and sashayed out of the room. He turned back to Giselle and tried to be cheerful.

'The weather's been perfect,' he said. 'It's a fine crop. This will make your fortune.'

'Lindsay won't sell!'

Pat listened to the silence in the room as he digested her remark. Lindsay and Deborah had left Belrose the day after their thrashing of Troptard. It was too dangerous for them to stay. Even though the cuts and stripes on Troptard's skin healed under Ma Doudou's careful nursing, he was scarred and walked with a limp. He had vowed vengeance and an abiding hatred of Lindsay Genave was a permanent feature of his deep, brooding eyes.

Ma Doudou bustled into the drawing room with wine, beaming her delight. It was seldom he and Giselle relaxed together and she obviously approved. She fussed over them both, taking her time to place tables by their chairs and set out glasses. She handed Pat the bottle reverently, although she was unable to conceal her curiosity at the occasion.

'You can go, Ma Doudou,' he said, then regretted having dampened her eagerness. 'We start cutting tomorrow. What better excuse for a drink before the hard work begins?' He pulled the cork and winked at her.

She left the room, partially satisfied.

'Why won't he sell?' he asked after pouring the wine, adding water, and handing the glass to Giselle. 'Surely he's not thinking of coming back here? Troptard will kill him if he does.'

'Lindsay knows that.' She sighed. 'I offered him the townhouse in exchange. I said he could keep that and I'll keep the plantation. He laughed in my face.'

'It's Deborah.' Pat stared at his glass dolefully. 'She knows the value of tobacco, at least her father does. Is she living with Lindsay?'

'Oh no! Think of the scandal. Her father wouldn't allow that. He's very proud of his position. Deborah seems terribly respectable. She goes to Government House frequently and the word is that Mr Farquhar's quite taken with her. Lindsay lives in the house by himself.'

'If he won't sell,' said Pat thinking aloud, 'he must be plotting something.'

'I wish I knew what to do.'

Giselle's despair brought him to his feet; he moved swiftly across the room and knelt in front of her. He took her hands in his, squeezing her fingers. 'At least half of everything is still yours, Giselle. But how it hurts me to think my labours are enriching his pocket too.'

'He keeps a chest of money in the townhouse.' She seemed bemused. 'I haven't told you this before. I thought it would be all right. He stole it from me when he left.'

Pat sat back on his ankles and stared at her. 'How did he do that?'

'I let him take it. It's the money we raised from selling my jewellery. He asked for it as a deposit on the price of selling his share of Belrose to me. Now he says it's his. He won't give it back to me and he won't sell.'

'How does this affect us?' He stroked her arm, watching her tenderly.

She sighed. 'How can we be married until Lindsay's gone? We'd both be in thrall to him. While you're running the plantation, he's getting rich instead of you.'

'Do you inherit his share of Belrose if he dies?'

'Yes, under the terms of papa's will, I do.' She went rigid with shock. 'Pat, don't ever think such an evil thing!'

He smiled guilelessly. 'Nothing was further from my mind.'

'I know you.' She eyed him sternly. 'You're ambitious.'

'Drink up!' He rose to his feet and raised his glass. 'To the tobacco crop. May it make enough for us all.' He expected the change of subject to please her but her expression was still troubled.

'I met Governor Farquhar in town,' she said. 'Actually, he asked me to tea with him.

Pat's spirits sank. He had ignored the Governor's warning made the previous year. He anticipated then that he and Giselle would soon be married and he would become part owner of Belrose. If that had happened, the Governor would not be able to deport him.

'What did he want?' he asked warily.

'It was a social occasion. He asked about the plantation . . . and about you.'

'What did you tell him?'

'What a skilled, dedicated man you are and how the tobacco is growing so well.'

He groaned. 'Did he say anything about me?'

'He sent his regards. He seems to think you're very talented and that Mauritius is too small for you.'

'He wants me to leave!' Pat clasped his hands behind his back and strode restlessly up and down the room. Giselle's next words stopped him in his tracks.

'Perhaps you should.'

He blinked as he looked at her. Tiredness dulled her customary radiance but there was a musk-rose flush on her cheeks and her face had a sombre, compelling beauty. He was confused. He loved her and he believed she loved him.

'You want me to leave?' His words came out as a strangled whisper.

'It might be for the best.'

'But why?'

'Listen to me, Pat.' She waved him to his chair with a seriousness he was bound to respect.

'When the tobacco is ready to be shipped to England, you could go with it. I'll give you a letter of authorization to collect all the money it earns. Keep it. It's rightfully yours anyway because without you there'd be nothing. Wouldn't it be justice to cheat Lindsay out of his share?'

'Cheat Lindsay! I'll be losing you! I'd rather see Lindsay dead first.'

'Pat! The Governor said you have a wild streak, that you're a firebrand. I don't know what he's been told you did in Virginia, but he doesn't want you here. I begged him to let you stay until the tobacco's shipped.'

'Did he agree?'

'Yes.' She fluttered her eyelashes. 'This is your opportunity, Pat. You can keep the money. Make something of your life. If you stay here you'll always be in trouble. Anyway, you can't stay.'

'Can't I?' He slapped his fist angrily into the palm of his hand. 'It's nonsense. What will become of you?'

'I could join you. In England . . . or Virginia.'

'You'd let Lindsay have Belrose so you could be with me?'

'Yes.'

He rose from his chair and walked over to her. He took her chin in his fingers and placed a kiss firmly on her lips. Releasing her without a word, he strode out of the drawing room and onto the verandah.

The fields were the same, the tops of the tobacco plants waving gently in the breeze. The cheerful murmur of the men as they moved along the rows picking off grubs drifted over to him. He waved to Troptard limping up to the house, his head shaded by a broad-brimmed planter's hat.

If Giselle followed him to England, he thought, they could be married. They could settle in Virginia by the Mattaponi River and he could see his mother and father again. Giselle would be sister-in-law to Jeanette, and to Mort and to poor Tombo.

For a few seconds he was back in Virginia until the rustling of the tobacco leaves and Troptard's shout brought him back to the present. He gripped the verandah rail angrily. *I'll be damned*, he thought, *if I let Giselle give up Belrose!*

Pat read the letter again. It had arrived a week earlier but he had been too busy in the fields to find time to read it. He was unable to give his attention to Giselle either. At night, when the cutting and carrying and bunching and hanging of the tobacco was finished for a few hours, he was too exhausted to come to the villa to sleep. He would collapse on the baled tobacco in the barn, sleeping alongside the slaves.

After several weeks the tobacco had all been cut. Now the fields in all directions when he watched them from the verandah, were vast stretches of stubble. It was a desolate scene and reflected how he and Giselle felt.

Pat sensed Giselle's eyes on him as he read the letter the second time, trying to grasp its news. It was from his sister. Their mother, she wrote, had died, worn out by selfless toil. His father and Tombo worked Five Acre Field. Tombo had married Mary, the younger Allason girl, and she looked after him patiently in the old clapboard house by the Field. Marlon was running the Braxton plantation successfully, without upsetting the neighbours nor drinking too much.

'I do hope,' Jeanette concluded, 'that you will be kind to Deborah. She suffered a tragic accident which is why she had to leave here with her father. Her husband discovered her in the arms of one of his slaves. They were both naked.

'She told him the boy was raping her so her husband tried to shoot him. The boy killed him instead then ran away. He was never caught.

'Deborah was very strange afterwards. We hope she finds an understanding husband in Mauritius who will make her happy. She does seem to take after her father in many ways.'

He read the last paragraphs to Giselle and finished up with a chuckle. 'Deborah's the firebrand, not me.'

Giselle smiled at him thinly. She was sitting with her feet up, resting them on a stool. The flickering glow from the lantern highlighted her pallid features. He peered at her anxiously, trying to comprehend her mood. Normally she would have made some comment on the letter. Instead she stared out into the night without speaking. It was then he noticed the grey shadows of sleeplessness under her eyes.

'What's wrong, Giselle?'

She shook her head. 'Nothing.' She tried to sound surprised at his question but she lacked the energy for that. Her reply was flat and unconvincing.

Ma Doudou entered the verandah from inside the villa, carrying a tray. She glanced suspiciously at Pat and then took the cup of steaming liquid to Giselle. 'Drink this!' It was a command and Giselle took the cup obediently.

'What is that?' He wondered if something had happened to Giselle during his preoccupation with the tobacco harvest. 'Is she sick?'

'That be herb tea,' Ma Doudou said defiantly. 'She ain't sick. Leastwise, she does be sick but she ain't sick.'

Giselle frowned at her. 'You can go, Ma Doudou.'

The old lady pouted and turned away, tossing her head contemptuously at Pat. He leapt to his feet and stood in front of her, his arms spread wide so she couldn't pass into the villa.

'Tell me what's wrong with Giselle!'

'Don't say anything, Ma Doudou! There's nothing wrong with me, Pat.'

Ma Doudou's eyes narrowed and she looked from him to Giselle and back again. 'I bound to say it, miss. I ain't helpin' you no more, when you don't help yourself.'

'She's talkin' nonsense, Pat. It's nothing. I just get a little sick in the morning, that's all. It will pass.'

'Oh, aye.' Ma Doudou shook her head. 'You're stubborn like your father, and like your brother too. First one and now another.'

'First one what?' Pat tugged at his ear in exasperation.

'One baby, of course. Are you such a dolt you don't know that?'

'Baby! Is she going to have a baby?' His heart swelled with a sudden rush of joy.

'She don't want it,' Ma Doudou said bitterly. 'I help her 'bort the first one but I ain't doin' so no more. You marry her like you ought.'

He rushed to Giselle's side and put his arm around her shoulders, patting her back gently as she broke into sobs. She was trying to keep her face away from him.

'Giselle, I'm not cross. This is wonderful news.'

'I thought you'd hate me.'

'Why should I?'

'You might think I'm trying to force you to marry me.'

'But I *want* to marry you.'

'When the first baby was on its way, you didn't. You kept on putting it off.'

'I never knew you were pregnant!'

'You wouldn't listen when I tried to tell you.'

'I'm listening now.' He drew her to her feet and embraced her.

'No, I'm talking now. We're going to Port Louis as soon as the tobacco's cured and ready for shipment. We're going to be married. To hell with Lindsay. We're going to have our own family and live here together.'

'The Governor will send you away.'

'If we're married and I own Belrose, he can't.'

What to do about Lindsay competed in Pat's thoughts for

attention alongside his concern for the tobacco crop, and for Giselle's health. Now she had told Pat about the baby, her melancholy lifted and her vitality and optimism returned. Pat spent as much time as he could with her. He was concerned about her happiness and cheered her by discussing plans for their wedding. They decided this time they would not ask the American consul to be a witness.

'We should invite Robert Farquhar instead.'

'No, Pat. You've caused him enough trouble already. He could still find a way to deport you.'

'Not if I'm the owner of Belrose with you.'

'You can't be that until I've persuaded Lindsay to sell his share to me.'

Pat was silent. He didn't want Giselle to know how desperate he was becoming. If he didn't find a solution and Lindsay refused to sell, his marriage to Giselle would not save him. He would have to go from Mauritius, leaving Giselle and their child behind.

He tried to come to terms with his problems while they both made the voyage along the coast to Port Louis. There were so many hogsheads of tobacco ready for shipment, he chartered two vessels to take them all to the capital. Giselle travelled with him. She was filling out, her body showing the first signs of pregnancy. It excited him to look at her and to know that she was carrying his child. Ma Doudou accompanied them on the voyage to care for her, and Troptard went too.

Giselle had sent a letter to Lindsay telling him when they were coming with the tobacco and that they would need to stay in the townhouse for at least two weeks. She was not perturbed when he didn't reply.

On their arrival at the quay, Pat put Troptard in charge of the tobacco with instructions to see it was properly stored in Mr Piggot's warehouse. He was to sleep with it every night as watchman.

Mr Piggot, the merchant, was delighted with its quality. 'Quite the best you've grown,' he said, rubbing his pudgy hands together in anticipation of the riches it would bring him in commission. 'I've arranged for it to go on a vessel sailing for England next week.'

'The sooner the better.' Pat knew he couldn't count on receiving anything until the tobacco was safe in England and sold at auction.

'The price for Virginia tobacco is rising.' Mr Piggot bubbled with enthusiasm. 'You could retire on what this will earn.'

'We're getting married on it.' Pat hugged Giselle close to him.

'You too?'

'Why, I thought you were married already, Mr Piggot,' said Giselle politely.

'I don't mean me.' His eyes bulged 'I mean your brother, Lindsay. He got married last week. Surely you knew?'

'I didn't.' She tried to make light of her despair at the mention of Lindsay. 'He never tells me anything.'

'He married the American consul's daughter. Such a big affair. The Governor was there. I wondered at the time why you weren't. No doubt Lindsay is counting on his share of the proceeds from this crop to set him up.'

'No doubt.' Pat's firm tone rebuked Mr Piggot and he led Giselle away. His reaction to the news was suspicion. He no longer craved Deborah for himself and was astonished that he ever had done. He was worried only that the two of them must be plotting something and that their unexpected marriage was part of their scheme.

'I'm going to see Lindsay,' Giselle said, breaking into his thoughts.

'Why?'

'Why not? Half the townhouse is mine too. He knows we're coming to stay in it.'

'Perhaps that's why the wedding was so sudden. I bet it was Deborah's idea. She wants Lindsay under her control so she can take over Belrose.'

'How can she do that?'

'Simple. She and her father have been prejudicing Mr Farquhar against me. If I leave Mauritius, she expects you'll go with me. Then the plantation will be Lindsay's and that means hers.'

'What are we going to do?'

Giselle repeated her question when they reached the Champ

de Mars and found Ma Doudou waiting for them outside the house.

'Oh lawd, oh lawd!' she exclaimed when she saw them. Her face puckered with outrage. 'He done throw me out!'

Pat tried to calm her, leading her and Giselle into the shade of a tamanaca tree. From there he could see the long verandah of the townhouse. It was deserted.

Ma Doudou couldn't contain her indignation. 'Lindsay told me the house is his. I told him it ain't and that Mr Augustus done leave it to both his children together. He say he buyin' it from you, Miss Giselle, for he and his wife. I tell him he lyin'.'

'What did he do?'

'He turn blue vex. I tell him he ain't got no money to buy nothin'. Then he show me a chest full of coins. He say he payin' you with that.'

'That's my chest! My money. That's what he tricked me into giving him.'

'I was 'bout to tell him that too but Miss Deborah joined him. She tell him I'm a nosy baggage and to put me out the house.' She paused, her old eyes bright with resentment. 'I leave, miss, before I get cross and wallop him.'

Pat laughed. 'You did right. We'll stay at the hotel.'

'I want to speak to him.' Giselle's face showed her anger.

'No, Giselle, let him come to you. He needs your cooperation so he can have his share of the crop income. Deborah will send him to you soon enough.'

They slept at the hotel in separate bedrooms that night, Ma Doudou on a truckle bed in Giselle's chamber. The hotel was small and uncomfortable. It was a private house that had been converted on the arrival of the British five years previously to accommodate visitors who arrived by sea. Planters usually stayed in more inferior houses close to the market. In the morning, they strolled to the warehouse and found Troptard and Mr Piggot counting the hogsheads.

'Mr Lindsay and his wife were here,' Mr Piggot told them apologetically. 'He asked me to make an inventory of everything here that belongs to Belrose. He said I must ship the tobacco in his name since he is going to take over the plantation.'

'That's not true.'

Mr Piggot looked dubious. Then he caught sight of Troptard watching him menacingly. His pink face coloured and he edged closer to them both, 'Mr Pat, Miss Giselle, please don't take this personally. I'm just repeating what he said.'

'What is that?' Pat steadied himself for the worst, holding Giselle tightly to him.

'Well, he didn't actually say anything. His wife did.'

'Tell us!' Pat's voice was hard, giving no indication that a hammer was pounding in his head, splitting him with nervous agony as his dream for Giselle and himself collapsed.

'Miss Deborah told me that you are to be deported, Pat. Lindsay is to be given permission by the Governor to administer Belrose since you, Miss Giselle, are of unsound mind and incapable of running your affairs.'

Giselle gave a squawk of protest which made Mr Piggot step away quickly, gulping for breath after his long speech. Pat held on to her, willing her to be brave.

'Don't worry, Giselle,' he whispered into her ear. 'She's feeling faint,' he said to Mr Piggot. 'Is there somewhere she can sit down?'

Mr Piggot glanced warily up and down the waterfront behaving as though he was being asked to shelter a felon. 'Take her to the Place d'Armes,' he said. 'There're benches there.'

Pat glared at him, disgusted by the merchant's betrayal. Lindsay and Deborah had succeeded in turning everyone against them.

That afternoon they sat together in Giselle's bedroom, pondering what to do. They felt humiliated and by nightfall they were exhausted trying to find a way around their conflict with Lindsay.

It was clear that Deborah had inspired the Governor to act against them. Unless Pat could persuade Robert Farquhar otherwise, they could think of nothing he could do to fight his orders. They decided that, in the morning, they would go to Mr Farquhar, put their case to him and beg him for his help.

That evening, unknown to Pat and Giselle, Ma Doudou made

her way slowly along the streets of Port Louis, keeping to the shadows between the coconut oil lamps. She was known and respected by the slaves in the town and when she found the cabin she was looking for, tucked behind a large house in the Rue de l'Hopital, she knocked boldly on its door.

A woman who could have been her sister opened it and drew her inside the cabin's gloom. They embraced briefly, their paired bulk causing the other women in the cabin to shift around to make room for them both. Ma Doudou sat herself on a log that served as a bench and began a detailed narrative of recent events at Belrose. She was sure the combined minds of some of the most powerful obeah women in Mauritius could produce a solution.

In the tiny kitchen attached to the cabin, a girl fanned a wood fire, waiting for the water to boil in the cauldron that was hanging over it. She listened to the murmur of Ma Doudou's voice in awe. When the water boiled, she lifted the cauldron off the fire and put it aside until she was summoned to carry it into the cabin. She expected the coven of women would throw herbs into it and start chanting, entreating the mysteries of the night to do their bidding.

When the call came, her eagerness to oblige made her careless. She forgot to dampen the fire. A spark leaped from it, wafted by a sudden gust of air until it came to rest on the jute sack where the girl had been crouching.

While Ma Doudou and the women chanted and the girl stood entranced by the herbal aroma rising with the steam from the cauldron, the jute sack smouldered. Another breath of air from nowhere kindled the sacking into billowing flames that spread rapidly through the wooden kitchen.

The fire's brightness chased away the gloom in the cabin and Ma Doudou and her sisters of the night were astonished by the swift response to their incantations. They hurried from the cabin as the flames seized its walls, devouring the dry timber with relish.

In that part of the town all the buildings were of wood, and they were packed closely together. Ma Doudou hurried back to the hotel while the alarm was raised. She was content with her night's malfeasance.

The only way to stop the advance of the fire was to pull

down the neighbouring houses. The slaves couldn't do that without orders and their owners were too dazed by sleep and shock to think of it. The fire brigade was called out. Their equipment was primitive and although the men tried hard to prevent the fire spreading, it was advancing through the town on all sides, consuming everything of wood in its way.

Soon it was no longer a question of trying to stop the fire from spreading but of trying to rescue possessions from the houses in its path. Some of this was carried a safe distance to the Champ de Mars and to the waterfront where it was dumped without proper attention being paid to its condition.

A mattress stuffed with coconut fibre caught alight and smouldered unnoticed. The wind on the waterfront fanned it vigorously and it burst into flames, fueled by the other possessions piled on top of it. It was only minutes before a spark was carried by the breeze to the roof of Mr Piggot's warehouse. Separate fires started in the same way in the Rue Royale while another advanced towards Government House and a third tore down the Rue Desforges.

Pat found Ma Doudou beaming with a mysterious pride when he pounded on Giselle's door to wake her. He had seen the glow of the flames in the night sky over the town.

'Take her to safety,' he shouted. 'I'm going to the warehouse.'

Giselle put a cloak on over her nightdress. 'I'm coming with you.'

Together they ran through the streets to the waterfront. The fire already had a hold on the warehouse. The tobacco was so dry it needed only a spark to turn it into an inferno. It blazed beyond control, turning the night into day with its glare. Troptard, his face smeared with soot, limped wearily over to them.

Half the town seemed to be in flames. The streets right up to the Champ de Mars were alive with fire. 'The house,' exclaimed Giselle as she turned away from Troptard in shock. 'Lindsay and Deborah are there.'

'They'll be all right. It can't reach that far.' Even as he spoke, Pat sensed the danger.

With Troptard's help he led Giselle through the throng of panicking people pushing down the street towards the waterfront where they hoped to escape the flames. When they were halfway, the tide of people changed and they were flowing with those who were fleeing to the open space of the Champ de Mars for safety, instead of to the seafront.

Pat was worried about Giselle in her condition but since there was nowhere else to go, he did his best to protect her from the crush. Someone said Government House had caught fire. The soldiers were trying to save it.

There was space and air in the Champ de Mars and they could breathe better. Everywhere people jostled them, some moaning, some screaming, others shouting at each other to keep away from the few possessions they had managed to salvage. Still others stared in mute shock. Troptard guided them through the throng to the gate of the townhouse. Fire already had a hold on the roof.

'Look after Giselle,' Pat told Troptard. He was too bemused to grasp in full what had happened, first the tobacco crop destroyed and now the townhouse on fire. 'I'm going for Deborah.'

'Pat.' Giselle's warning was too late as he dashed up the path to the verandah away from her.

He tried the doors; they were locked and the shutters fastened. He pounded on the front door hoping Lindsay would hear and open it so he could help them save some of the house contents. Troptard whistled to him from the side of the verandah.

'Where's Giselle?' he asked as he ran over to him.

'Ma Doudou has her. This way.'

He followed Troptard to the side of the house where there was a door with a glass window that had not been shuttered. Troptard smashed it with a stone, knocked out the glass and climbed through.

Pat waited with growing impatience for him to open the door as smoke puffed out of the broken window making his eyes smart. The door burst open and Troptard staggered backwards. Pat caught him as he stumbled.

'What's that?'

Troptard was dragging a chest. 'Help me!' he cried and Pat, too dazed to question him, took the other handle and helped him carry the box out to the garden.

Ma Doudou's eyes gleamed in the light of the flames when she saw it. 'You does have your money back now, Miss Giselle,' she said, hugging Giselle to her.

'Look!'

Pat raised his eyes to where Giselle pointed. The door was opening on the verandah as flames descended from the ceiling, speeded by the valley breeze until they licked the transom. Lindsay and Deborah stood in the doorway arguing. Lindsay was tugging at Deborah's sleeve while she was trying to pull him back into the house.

'We've got the chest of money here!' yelled Pat, guessing what Deborah was arguing about. 'Run!'

His voice was buried by the sound of timbers collapsing. The roof of the verandah began to fall, a beam crashing down and showering sparks that even fell where he and Giselle stood watching. He shielded Giselle with his body.

When he looked again, Pat saw Lindsay leap from the blazing verandah into the bushes at the side of the house. His clothes were on fire.

The last glimpse he had of Deborah was of her frightened face slipping downwards into the fire that was burning the clothes off her body. Her flame-coloured hair suddenly flared alight like a flambeau as she disappeared in the white heat of the fire. He turned away, desperately saddened, trying to hide the sight of her death from his eyes.

Giselle took him into her arms and comforted him.

Under the cover of the darkness, Troptard left them both and limped away, using the shadows in the garden to conceal him. He drew his knife, holding it in readiness. Beneath the noise of the falling timbers, he heard Lindsay whimpering for help.

He found him rolling on the grass trying to extinguish the flames that licked at his clothes. His leg was raw and bleeding where a nail had torn his flesh when he jumped from the verandah.

Troptard waited only for Lindsay to raise his eyes and see him before he leapt onto him, drawing the knife smoothly across his neck, severing his jugular vein. Lindsay twisted once and then fell limp as his blood spurted out into the earth and his life drained away.

Pat saw him there and tried to keep Giselle away. It was too late. Her eyes were dry with shock and she said nothing. He held her as they followed Ma Doudou out into the open space of the Champ de Mars. Troptard came behind, dragging the chest.

'Let's go home,' Pat said. 'We can get married there.'

Giselle answered him with a brave, grateful smile. 'Yes,' she said. 'At once!'

Ma Doudou exchanged a dark look of triumph with Troptard as he limped off to find a vessel to take them back to Belrose.

FICTION

LORDS OF THE AIR	Graham Masterton	£3.99 ☐
THE PALACE	Paul Erdman	£3.50 ☐
KALEIDOSCOPE	Danielle Steel	£3.50 ☐
AMTRAK WARS VOL. 4	Patrick Tilley	£3.50 ☐
TO SAIL BEYOND THE SUNSET	Robert A. Heinlein	£3.50 ☐

FILM AND TV TIE-IN

WILLOW	Wayland Drew	£2.99 ☐
BUSTER	Colin Shindler	£2.99 ☐
COMING TOGETHER	Alexandra Hine	£2.99 ☐
RUN FOR YOUR LIFE	Stuart Collins	£2.99 ☐
BLACK FOREST CLINIC	Peter Heim	£2.99 ☐

NON-FICTION

DETOUR	Cheryl Crane	£3.99 ☐
MARLON BRANDO	David Shipman	£3.50 ☐
MONTY: THE MAN BEHIND THE LEGEND	Nigel Hamilton	£3.99 ☐
BURTON: MY BROTHER	Graham Jenkins	£3.50 ☐
BARE-FACED MESSIAH	Russell Miller	£3.99 ☐
THE COCHIN CONNECTION	Alison and Brian Milgate	£3.50 ☐

All Sphere books are available at your local bookshop or newsagent, or can be ordered direct from the publisher. Just tick the titles you want and fill in the form below.

Name _____

Address _____

_____

Write to Sphere Books, Cash Sales Department, P.O. Box 11, Falmouth, Cornwall TR10 9EN

Please enclose a cheque or postal order to the value of the cover price plus:

UK: 60p for the first book, 25p for the second book and 15p for each additional book ordered to a maximum charge of £1.90.

OVERSEAS & EIRE: £1.25 for the first book, 75p for the second book and 28p for each subsequent title ordered.

BFPO: 60p for the first book, 25p for the second book plus 15p per copy for the next 7 books, thereafter 9p per book.

Sphere Books reserve the right to show new retail prices on covers which may differ from those previously advertised in the text elsewhere, and to increase postal rates in accordance with the P.O.